Blurring to Gray

Book V of The Quietus of Fate

By Brian C. Kershner

ISBN: 1-942082-11-8
ISBN-13: 978-1-942082-11-8

Acknowledgements

Authors draw inspirations from all manner of places, and I have gotten many questions over the years as to where the names I come up with come from, or if there were people who were inspirations for certain characters, or where the ideas come from, etc. When I was young, I was a voracious reader, and I read mostly the fantasy genre (shocking I know). But I also was a child that adored movies and television, and consumed everything I could. From Star Wars, to Star Trek, to comic books, to the television show Quincy, to Real Genius. I was inspired by everything. Video games also were becoming huge when I was a kid, and I drew massive inspirations from those as well.

As I have continued to write and learn and experience, the inspirations for my characters and my storylines become increasingly varied. Human experience is filled with so many wonderful and terrible triumphs, failures, and compromises, that it is beholden, I believe, on authors to take as realistic as possible a view of the complex relationships, between characters and within their own psyches.

All of that said, I have a fascination with the dark middle chapters of long running series, and as you have seen in the previous book Dark Mirror, this part of the Quietus of Fate is no different. It is through our trepidations and challenges that we see true character emerge, and the crucible of the impossible often forges the unexpected. That is no truer than in the events that are about to unfold over the next two books in the series. So strap in, it may be a bumpy ride.

B.K.

Table of Contents

Celestial Water shall burn in Eternal Fire,
Torches will spread the fires of hate and intolerance,
An unkindness of Ravens rescue history with murderous ire,
And the Ram's horns shall answer only to divine guidance.

An Angel shall rise from the skin of a demon,
The truths of war will be exposed in the bloody fray,
All eyes will turn to the fate of the Chosen,
As the line between Light and Shadow blurs to gray.

The future is not yet written,
The past never truly dead,
The present favors the driven,
Time is how legends are bred.

-   Aralias Imstra
  Prophecies of the Coromor

Prologue

Of Family and Blood

Creator's Calendar Year 1205; Dark Mirror

Gideon Viruci and his daughter Taya rode side by side for a long time with no words passed between them. Taya's understanding had always been that Gideon's parents were dead and that was all there was to say about the situation. Truth be told, Gideon had never openly said anything about his mother or father, but then again, the way he acted, Taya had been sure that they were both dead. The only thing Taya knew for sure was that there were rumors that Gideon was related to some very powerful people on both sides of the war with Shau-ling, and that fact had always frightened her as she was growing up. Her father had always been surrounded by an air of mystery, and it had been clear to Taya for the majority of time on the run that the phasia's interest in a simple thief was more than it should have been. However, Taya was not a little girl any more, nor was she a spoiled little princess in a gilded tower. The war robbed her of her home when she was only five years old, so long ago that she barely remembered what the palace of Scalla looked like. A great many of her formative years were spent curled up next to her father in cold damp caves, bathing in ice cold rivers, and living off small animals, plants, and insects. She had had to shed her feminine naivety very early on, and couldn't think of a time when she would not be fighting. However, this type of life led to some unfortunate truths. It was too dangerous to know everything. The kind of raids that Gideon planned, the majority of which were conceived only in his head, had to be veiled in complete secrecy, even from Taya. Perhaps Gideon had always been that secretive, as it was as natural to him as breathing. There were times when Taya felt that her father kept her at arms-length, not just for her own good, or for the good of the war, but because he was not comfortable with her knowing what she probably should have. Now, with the revelation of a family that Taya didn't know existed, some of the secrets would be revealed. But Taya wasn't sure if this revelation would be more dangerous than not knowing. Regardless, Taya tired of the silence and began to speak.

"If my grandmother has been alive all this time," Taya said in as even a voice as she could manage, "then why haven't I ever seen her? Couldn't we have gone to her after Scalla fell?"

There were many things about her life that had always puzzled her, and one of which was why Gideon would never talk about her mother or the times after the fall of his kingdom. Her death still pained him, but not to the point of tears or sorrow. It was like an uncomfortable itch that he could never scratch.

"Dat's a little of a family secret yer askin' me to give out lass," Gideon replied, his accent particularly thick that morning, "and dere's a good answer if ye think ye are ready ta hear it."

Taya thought for a moment before answering. Gideon never gave a warning before speaking unless there was something so terrible that it would shock the person to the core. He had made a similar statement the day that Taya had asked what had happened to her mother, and Taya remembered crying on his shoulder as he told the tale of her murder at Draven's hands. It was a sorrow unlike any she would ever feel in her life, but as her heart hardened over the years she had become sure that she could face anything without breaking down. Her father's words now began to shake that well-honed belief.

"I want to know the truth."

Gideon took a deep breath and then began the tale that would change the way his daughter would look at life, and perhaps at him.

"Me father an' mother had always been kept a secret, an' dere be good reason fer it. See, me mother is a beautiful woman, an' she often used it fer da worst purposes. Well, one o' dese purposes landed her in bed wit' me father. Now, de whole mess ended up gettin' me mother inta deep trouble wit' her husband, and of course he was even more upset when he found out she was gonna have me. So, he killed her."

Taya didn't know whether to laugh or hit her father. At first she thought he was lying, but there was a seriousness in his voice and a familiar look in his eyes that said he was telling the truth. Before she had any chance to question him, he continued with his strange little tale. Though a cold and sobering understanding was starting to form in Taya's mind. She knew much about the enemy that they fought, knew about rebirth and the continuation of the war through generations. Could her father really be saying what reason said was impossible?

"However, dis would not be da end o' yer poor father. When mother was reborn, she was still pregnant wit' me, and so she hid from her husband an' had me in secret. Den' me foster-father Basille took me in an' taught me everyt'ing me know."

"So that means," Taya said reading through the lines of the story, "your mother was a member of the phasia."

There was no shock in the girl's voice, instead, it was a quiet acceptance. Gideon was a little surprised at his daughter's strength, but then again, she had been one of his best warriors for many years now, and her place in the war against the Shadow was all but confirmed. Gideon need only tell her the truth, and she would be a powerful adversary for any member of the phasia. He had only kept her power hidden this long for fear that their little band would be discovered and weeded out before they were large enough to take on all comers. If any of the phasia knew that there was a member of the third generation's *Erieal* in the midst of a petty rabble, they may begin to take the rabble a bit more seriously. That meant more battles and much more death. Brushing those thoughts aside, Gideon continued the tale with a half-hearted nod.

"But dat is only half da story lass. See me mother dinnae just pick any man ta be her conquest da night when me conception happened. Dere was a member o' her army dat intrigued her like no other man could. So, she had ta have him. Fortunately fer her, he wanted her too. Dat man, was none other dan Aerith Seth, and me mother is Bryn Aplee."

Finally there was a reaction from Taya, but not the one that Gideon had expected. She smiled and laughed.

"I knew there had to be something like that behind the origin of the infamous Gideon Viruci. And of course it would have to be two of the most notorious people in the history of the world who would have to be your parents. I'm sure the Creator was laughing when he made you father, and I wouldn't have it any other way."

Gideon smiled and then laughed.

"Den I suppose ye know dat me accent is fake?"

"Of course father," Taya responded with a smile and a flip of her long brown hair. "No one else notices when you slip, but as much time as I spend with you, I notice."

"Den do ye want me ta talk normal when we're in private?"

"Of course not," Taya replied. "It wouldn't be you if you didn't have your accent. Now, why are we going to see Bryn?"

"Yer grandmother has some information we need, and dat's all dat's gonna be said fer now. Trust me Taya," Gideon said as easily as he could, "when ye hear what yer old father's got on his mind, yer gonna be glad ye dinnae know."

Taya didn't ask any more questions after that, and Gideon had nothing to say either. Though she wondered what it was that her father had spinning around in that brain of his, she also had to temper her inquisitiveness with the knowledge that if Gideon was worried about it, by all means she should be as well. The long ride continued for two more days, and by nightfall of the third day they came to the edge of the kingdom known as Barer. Barer had always been known as the edge of the Frontier, a string of kingdoms on the outside edge of civilized life. Barer had also been the kingdom that for centuries had been ruled by the same king and queen, Grawn and Bryn Aplee. Because the kingdom was out on the fringe, little notice was paid to it, and only those loyal to the Aplee family remained in the kingdom. Barer was also the site of one of the greatest victories for the forces of the Light in the previous generation. Two phasia met there ends in that city, and as Gideon and Taya rode through the remains of the town they passed the broken remains of a fountain, the landmark of their victory. Taya nervously watched the horizon as she saw groups of Shadowwalkers circling, patrolling the skies over the palace of Barer. There were also quite a few roving bands of Jeresei patrolling the area. But strangely enough, every single one of the shadow-spawn were ignoring the pair on horseback. Within a matter of minutes they had made their way through the town to the gates of a large palace. This was a newer construct, one that had been built within the last few years. The old palace of Barer lay in ruins nearly half a day's ride away. It fell nearly the same time the town did during one of the many early raids staged by the phasia at the beginning of their rise to power in the third generation of the prophecies. Unfortunately, this town was one that was caught up in the War for Power, the eternal battle between the phasia. When Gideon and Taya finally stopped at the gates of the palace, they were met by the two immense guards, two members of the race known as Stone.

"Ye Stone can understand me, me know dat from experience. Now, tell Lady Bryn dat her son is here ta see her."

The Stone did not move for a moment, but then there was a very feminine and very familiar voice that called down from one of the palace towers.

"There must be something terribly important for you to come down here, Gideon," Ellis' voice called. "You are just lucky that Bryn has a soft place in her heart for you, otherwise the Shadowwalkers and Jeresei would have cut you down long before you crossed the border into Grawn's kingdom."

Gideon raised his eyes in the direction of the tower and spoke in a proud clear voice.

"I see you are still hanging on mother's coattails, Ellis," Gideon prodded. "You were never the one to take care of yourself."

Ellis seemed to ignore the comment as she ordered the guards to open the gates for their guests. As soon as the gates opened, Gideon spurred his horse and bolted through the open gate with Taya right on his heels. As soon as they had ridden through, the gates slammed shut behind them, and Gideon pulled his horse to a halt. Slowly he dismounted and waited for some instruction for what to do next. This instruction came in the form of the sight of his mother, clad in her typical revealing red dress, sauntering down the palace steps with an older man dressed in gray and a woman dressed in white in tow. Grawn did not look too happy to see Gideon, but then again, there was part of him that never did forgive Bryn for her affair with Aerith Seth. Ellis on the other hand did not have any particular look on her face at all. Her expression was always cold and emotionless, her features impossible to read.

"Hello, son," Bryn said coming closer to him and extending her arms toward him, "it has been too long since I saw you."

Gideon took two steps forward and entered her embrace. He had never been comfortable in her arms, but it was still soothing being that close to his mother. When he took a step back, she smiled down at him with those perfect green eyes flashing with pride.

"And who is this lovely young lady that rides with you? Oh, and Gideon, please spare me that horrible accent of yours, you know how much I hate it."

Gideon smiled, nodded, and then proceeded to speak in his natural clear voice. The sound shocked Taya at first, but then the shock went away and she began to soak in the melodic harmony of the sound.

"Mother, I would like to introduce you to your granddaughter, Taya Viruci."

Taya stepped forward and bowed slightly. Even though they were not officially in court, and Taya was out of practice, she still wanted to extend the Queen of Barer some common courtesy, whether they were related or not. Bryn was smiling when Taya straightened, and she seemed to look over her granddaughter as though she were examining every inch of her.

Then, Bryn stepped forward and hugged the shorter girl and gave her a small kiss on the forehead before stepping back.

"She is beautiful Gideon," Bryn said beaming, "but she looks more like her mother than she does like you."

"And that's a bad thing?" Ellis chided.

"Please, sister," Bryn remarked, "now is not the time for insults. Gideon did well with his first child, almost as well as I did with mine. But then again, perfection can only be achieved once. It's unfortunate that she has to travel in these rags rather than in a proper wardrobe."

Grawn balked at the comment, and Gideon could tell that he was barely restraining his urge to violence. However, at this point, Gideon could not tell whether Grawn was going to act against him or Bryn, as he hated them both equally. For the entire length of their relationship, Grawn and Bryn had been at each other's throats, both figuratively and literally. From the outside, their relationship made very little sense. Grawn would appear to those unenlightened as nothing more than an impotent cuckold to his wife's voracious appetites that she freely flaunted in his face. Everyone knew of the fiery arguments between the two and the unrestrained violence that Grawn would unleash on his wife, which had led to her demise on at least one occasion. But Bryn was not passive in the face of Grawn's rage, and as much as she incited it and fanned its flames, she retaliated in kind. But to those who understood the true nature of the pair, they would realize that as a pair of apex predators, an equal giving relationship was not possible. Bryn loved power and used her manipulative wiles to get everything she wanted, amassing influence and wealth through at times indecent means. Grawn would then use these seeming indiscretions to loose his fury, crushing armies, kingdoms, and taking whatever he wanted through clearly-justified force. Predators were nothing without prey, and if they could not find it outside the confines of their kingdom, then they would make prey of one another.

"So, what is the errand that you have come on, Gideon," Grawn asked in a straining voice, "it is good that you have brought your daughter with you, but you could have done that years ago. The risk you took now only means that there is something that you want. So say it now so that we can get back to more important things."

Bryn rounded on her husband immediately.

"There is nothing more important to me than my son, and now my granddaughter. I know that you do not like the fact that he is not your son too, but you have to look passed that now. Must you still hold a grudge after all these years my dear sweet and tolerant husband?"

"Bryn," Ellis commented feeding upon Bryn's sarcasm, "Grawn has been holding grudges since the day Shau-ling forged him from the Blaze. I don't think that the number of years has anything to do with it."

Gideon and Taya both smiled, and when Bryn looked back, her face did not have the same glow it did only a moment earlier.

"Grawn is right," she said slowly, "there must be some other reason for you to risk the trip to Barer. Surely you know that both Jeroch and Draven are waiting for a chance to pay you back from your little raids on their prison transports. You are slowly becoming a very powerful irritation to both of them."

Gideon smiled.

"Good," Gideon responded his pride showing through, "it's about time they began to take notice or me. We have been raiding them for the last few years, and yet they still treat us as if we are beneath them."

Ellis folded her arms.

"For that you should feel fortunate," Ellis responded. "Draven may not be my favorite member of the Brotherhood, but I must admit that he is one of our best. His attention to even the smallest detail coupled with his ruthlessness has made him very successful. It is no wonder he was able to take Trelon."

"Interesting you should mention that," Gideon countered, "you seem to be up on the current state of the war."

"It is always the best policy to know what is happening with one's enemies," Grawn replied.

"What do you know about the fall of Brea?" Taya asked, following her father's path.

"Nothing more than probably you do. Nightwing led the force that caused the evacuation of Brea. However, it was said that both Pike Rhuiden and Logan Ranthall were present at this battle," Bryn answered.

"It was Nightwing that intrigued me the most," Gideon continued, "that of course coupled with the mysterious disappearance of Gwydeon Sandar."

Bryn's face suddenly went cold as marble. She was hiding something, that much was obvious, but maybe there was more to it than Gideon had originally thought.

"Now, I have also heard from my spies that when Nightwing attacked Brea, his strategies were so sound that there was nothing the Order of the Sword could do to keep him and his forces out of the palace. Now I think that Nightwing is using Gwydeon against us, but I'm not quite sure how. I'm afraid to think of what might have happened, but I know in my heart that Nightwing and Gwydeon are one and the same now. The only problem I have with that is I don't think Gwydeon did this of his own free will. I think a member of the phasia was behind this transformation, and I want to know who it was, and how it happened."

Grawn stepped forward, slowly pulling up his sleeves. Taya, Bryn, and Ellis all stood by, the shock from Gideon's words holding them for the time being.

"You assume much, Gideon," Grawn said slowly, "coming here and demanding information about the actions of the Brotherhood. We could have killed you long before you ever got close to this palace, but it was because of your mother's love for you that we let you live. Now, even with all that kindness, you come into my palace and make demands of us. I think that you have overstayed your welcome, Gideon, and you should leave."

Gideon turned to face Grawn, and clutched his fist tightly. Inwardly he cursed himself for not taking the *Debuisa* out of the pack on his horse, but if this turned into a fight, his minute powers would not help him much against a full member of the phasia. The powers that he inherited from Aerith Seth had never shown a propensity for offensive damage, but if there was any possibility of surviving, Gideon would have to find some way to make those powers become offensive.

"I'm not going anywhere until I get my question answered," Gideon replied defiantly.

"Don't make me kill you in front of your mother, Gideon."

Gideon took a step back and then reset himself. He knew that Grawn's temper had always been one that you did not want to ignite, because once it was ignited, one of you would end up dead.

"You're just gonna have to kill me Grawn, because I'm not leaving until I have the answer that I'm looking for. Now, tell me what you know about Nightwing, or do something to shut me up."

There was a burst of wind that slammed into Gideon's chest sending him sprawling across the ground. The impact knocked the breath out of his lungs, and as Grawn slowly walked toward him, he was pulling black gloves out of his pockets and slowly began to slide them on. Gideon sat up slowly and wiped a trickle of blood from the corner of his mouth.

"Is that good enough to close that gaping mouth of yours Gideon, or do I have to cut off your tongue and feed it to you."

Gideon made it to his feet, and Grawn made a motion as if he were slapping Gideon, and a gust of wind blasted across Gideon's cheek, the force sending him to the ground again. The pain in his face was extreme, and as he moved his jaw around, he began to feel that his cheekbone might have been broken. There was another slapping motion from Grawn as Gideon sat up again, and Gideon's other cheek stung with the force of the wind. Blood now began to flow from Gideon's mouth, and his breathing began to become clogged by the bubbles of blood that were flowing down into his lungs.

"I could kill you at any time whelp," Grawn barked coldly. "Out of respect for my wife, I now give you the opportunity to save your pathetic hide. Get on your feet and take your bitch daughter out of my kingdom or else I will kill you where you stand. I can make the very air you breathe explode inside your lungs and send your insides splattering all over the ground while your daughter looks on. And then, I will do the same to her."

Gideon grimaced.

"Not a pretty picture, is it? Now, what will it be? Are you going to do as you are told, or should I have some buckets gathered up to clean up your remains?"

Gideon slowly got to his feet and stood defiant against his attacker. In his heart he knew that there was no chance he could ever defeat Grawn one on one, but there was more at stake here than just his life. If Gwydeon had indeed become Nightwing, then the forces of the Light might never be able to vanquish Shau-ling. Right now, that information was more important than the life of one mere thief.

"You're just gonna have to kill me, Grawn. I need that information before I can leave here. So, spare me your threats and just get it over with."

Grawn smiled and raised his left hand and pulled the glove tighter as he balled up his fist. Gideon's hand immediately went to his throat, and he began gasping for breath. Taya stood by watching, trying to figure out what she could do against a full member of the phasia. Suddenly, something inside of her snapped. The emotion of the moment must have empowered something deep inside of her, because she began to see the flows of air that were tangling around her father, cutting off his supply of air. With a single flick of her wrist, the flows of air wielded by Grawn were instantly reversed, and the elder phase fell to his knees, holding his own throat in pain. Each breath was labored and agonizing, and with each passing second, Grawn was slipping closer and closer to unconsciousness. Ellis and Bryn both noticed the change in the girl across the courtyard from them. Ellis started to raise her hand to act against the girl, but Bryn stopped her. By this time, Gideon had made it back to his feet, and with a single bound, he was on top of Grawn with two razor sharp daggers buried in his throat. With a quick outward motion of both daggers, Grawn had been completely eviscerated. Gideon staggered back to his feet and glared back at his mother. Bryn's eyes in the meantime were locked on Taya, who smiled with a self-satisfied pride.

"How did you do that?" Ellis asked, still shocked at what she just witnessed.

"Oh," Gideon said rubbing his chin and moving his jaw around to make sure that it was still in working order, "did I not mention that Taya is the Wind *Erieal* of the third generation of the prophecies? Sorry, it slipped my mind."

"I should kill you for that," Ellis said walking toward the girl. "I may not have liked Grawn, but he was a member of the phasia."

"Try anything and I'll kill you like I killed him," Taya said concentrating on the flows of air rushing in and out of Ellis' lungs.

Suddenly Ellis stopped in her tracks and fell to her knees. There was air getting into her lungs, but it was barely enough to keep her alive. She tried to concentrate on the power of the Blaze in order to strike against the young insolent girl, but the lack of air was making it too difficult. Her breath was getting more labored, but Taya was making sure that she had enough air to live.

"Now," Gideon said slowly dusting the dirt and sand off of his clothes, "if I were you, mother, I would tell us what we want to know about Nightwing, or I'll let Taya kill Ellis."

PROLOGUE

.

Chapter XXXII

Ascension

Creator's Calendar Year 1205; Dark Mirror

The lights in the Council chambers flickered as the tense moments passed between the three men. Pike stood his ground between the inner and outer circle of the Council and watched, his hands grinding on the haft of his axe *Fury*. The nervousness of the situation was beginning to invade his body and mind, betraying him. He should have been charging at Shau-ling and trying to bury the blade of *Fury* as deeply into the evil creature's heart as possible. Either that or he should have been trying to rip Nightwing's wings off. And yet something restrained every intention inside of Pike that screamed for violence. Of course he knew that any action would likely be futile and fatal, but that was not what restrained his hand. As Pike stood there watching his two companions, he knew that there was some sincerity in Shau-ling's words. Otherwise, Pike would already be dead, and Nightwing would be off to do more damage in the name of the Shadow. Pike knew he was not in the same world that he left over twenty years earlier, and that many things had changed. The fact that Shau-ling was standing in the same room having a conversation with him was one of the bigger telling factors of that. But there was more to it than that. The whole world had gone mad and everything seemed wrong. Here Shau-ling was well on his way to winning the war. The forces of the Light were on the run, and it would only be a matter of time, maybe not even a year before there was nowhere for the last pockets of resistance to hide. Even if

Gwydeon's plans to attack Sador would come to fruition and resulted in taking the city, how long could their depleted forces honestly hold two kingdoms? It was taxing enough just controlling one. So why would Shau-ling want to negotiate let alone offer a cessation of hostilities? None of it made sense.

Nightwing also looked at the situation in a detached way. Gwydeon Sandar's thoughts floated through the torrent of Blaze memories, searching for some meaning in his defection from the path of the Light. He had betrayed everyone and everything that he had ever believed in, and that was deeply trying on his heart. The love for his wife dominated his mind, and the images of her fighting against him to protect an old friend would not leave his tortured mind. But he had still done what was right. The killing was inevitable, a product of the war between the Light and the Shadow, but Gwydeon knew his army well. He had used the Stone as a distraction to hit the city where he knew it would cost the least amount of lives. Because people were scrambling to defend their posts from Stone that were not attacking, many lives were spared. Also, by making the deal with Pike, there was no need to take Sabrina through the force of Draven's army. Even working for Draven, Gwydeon could not be a cold-blooded killer. He would fulfill his portion of the bargain, but he would do it his way.

Shau-ling had the most interesting thoughts of all. He had come to a point of no return. If he opened his thoughts to the mortals that stood before him, there would be no going back. The war against the forces of the Light was an assumed fact, but the Light was not the power that it once was in the world. The phasia had crushed nearly every last vestige of that cult, and now only a few rag tag bands of resistance remained. However, if Shau-ling were to follow the path that he had in his mind, he would not only have to deal with the fanatical followers of the Light, but he would also have to battle his own children, the phasia. He knew that Pike had no reason to believe his words, but for the sake of the law of the Creator, he had to try. He could no longer abide the lies and the needless suffering. The world known to the Creator as the Dark Mirror was going to become a beacon in the heavens before it would burn itself to a cider.

"Pike Rhuiden," Shau-ling said, speaking in a much more human-like voice than Pike expected, "what I am about to tell you, you are forbidden by the will of Emries and the Creator to know. In order for me to tell you the tale, you must first forsake Emries and give away that which he gave you. You must renounce forever your place as a member of the People of the Dragon, and your mark as the Water *Erieal* of the second generation of the prophecies of the *Coromor*."

Pike thought hard for a moment before he spoke. This was a very large condition that Shau-ling was asking of him, but it was understandable. If even half of what Shau-ling had said to that point had been true, could it be possible that Emries had been leading them down the wrong path the whole time? But, if Shau-ling were lying, then when the parlay was at its end, Pike would have nothing but *Fury* and his own natural tenacity to depend upon for the rest of the war. After a moment of thought on that point, another strand of thought winged through Pike's mind. The chances were good that if Shau-ling did intend to trick Pike into giving up his powers, then the chances were also good that Pike would not leave the council chambers alive. It was then that Pike decided his own fate.

"I have no reason to trust you, Shau-ling," Pike said after a moment, "but I have no reason to trust Emries either. All that I have found while following the path set down for me by Emries is loss and pain. My wife died, my friends fell one by one, and I left the world I knew only to return to a time where nothing that I knew exists. And even if the forces of the Light overcome this hell that the phasia have created and are victorious, what world will be left to the survivors? In another few years, you'll just come back again and finish the job. But if you say that there is a way out of this without any more bloodshed, I owe it to those who have fallen, and I owe it to those still fighting to find out. So, I will accept your deal Shau-ling. I renounce Emries. I renounce the People of the Dragon. I renounce my place as one of the *Erieal* of the prophecies. Take from me whatever Emries gave."

Shau-ling nodded, and closed his eyes. In the next second, the small circles around the perimeter of the room began to light up one by one. After each of the circles were lit, the center circle began to glow green. Shau-ling motioned for Nightwing to move, and the huge metallic beast stepped between the lighted spaces and stood on the outer edge of the Council chambers as Shau-ling stepped into the center circle. A column of green light extended slowly from the floor around Shau-ling and then sped its climb until it extended to the top of the chamber. One by one, each of the smaller lighted circles began to duplicate this, with columns of lighter green, blue, red, white, black, and a thin mist began to rise around the room. After a moment, the entire room was lighted by the beams of energy, and when the last column had extended to the ceiling, Shau-ling stepped out of the center column and opened his eyes.

"Step into the Blaze, Pike Rhuiden, and take hold of the string of power that Emries gave you. There will come a moment when you will either give up the string or retain it. If you decide that you are not willing to give up the gift as you said you would, the Blaze not spare you this time, and will consume you. Do you understand?"

Pike nodded.

"Then, step into the Blaze."

Pike hesitated for a moment and then took his first step toward the light. He felt part of himself rebelling against the movement of his body, but in his heart, he knew he was doing what was right. Then, taking a deep breath, Pike took a step and entered the column of roiling green flame. Almost instantly Pike felt the sensation of power flood over him. The power sang in his ears and surged through his blood. In a matter of moments the feelings that raged through him changed from fear and uncertainty changed to that of joy. This feeling mounted until he was almost immersed in feeling. Then, he felt a knot in his chest. His heart was beating so fast that it threatened to burst from his chest. He could feel the power of the string of Water surge through him. It was fighting against the influence of the Blaze, practically begging him to fight back against the invading sensations. This was the moment that Shau-ling had told Pike about. He could feel the string slipping away from his mind, pulled out of him by the seductive flows of the Blaze. It would only take a few moments more, and it would be gone forever. But part of Pike's mind began to rebel. The string was still well within his grasp. He could reach out at the last second and keep the string. It was screaming at him to fight, to not give in. It wanted him to leap from the roaring fires and crush the enemies of the Light. It fed on his hate. He still had time to decide, but the time was growing short. Suddenly, the string was at the edge of disappearance. This was the moment of truth. Pike felt part of his mind reach out, want to hold on to the hate and the pain, but he restrained it. The inner conflict began to boil as he felt his control begin to slip. Then, just as the string slipped away, Pike's restraint snapped and his mind leapt out after the string, but it was too late. The powers of the *Erieal* were gone, and Pike was a normal man once again.

As he stepped out of the descending column of light, Pike felt his mind spin. Suddenly the world turned itself in all directions at once, and Pike fell to the ground as his balance left him. A moment later, he passed out. When Pike awoke, he found himself looking up at Nightwing. The sight shocked Pike back into reality, and he scrambled away from the metallic beast, forgetting himself for a moment. Nightwing stood by and did not react to Pike's fear, but instead waited until Pike regained his wits and then offered the hero his hand. Pike looked at the metallic clawed hand for a moment and then took it, pulling himself back to his feet. It was then that Pike noticed that the scar on his arm was gone. That was the scar that had marked him as a member of the *Erieal* of the second generation. Once he noticed its disappearance, he reached out into the blackness in his mind looking for the string of Water. When he found nothing in the blackness, his heart sank, and yet he was not as troubled by it as he was worried. His mind said that he had willingly given that part of himself up for something better, at least he hoped it was something better.

"You have done very well, Pike Rhuiden," Shau-ling said stepping forward, "there are some that have tried to duplicate the feat you just performed and all have failed. Emries has had some over the years who become disillusioned with the path he laid out for them. But, it is very difficult to keep your emotions from interfering with the process, and Emries hold is strong. But you did very well."

Pike swallowed hard.

"I felt myself resist."

"Everyone resists, regardless of how badly they want the results. In fact, I have found that the more you want something to happen, the more resistance you will find. The one constant I have learned through the eons of my life has been conflict, resistance, and change."

"So," Pike said, his patience with Shau-ling's continued vagueness slowly wearing thin, "what is this story you had to tell me?"

Shau-ling sighed and then began the tale that had haunted him through every generation of his life.

"I was the one of the first creations of the being known as the Creator. In my infancy, I became attached to the power of life itself, and the different forms it expressed itself. I grew with the plants and the animals on a hundred different worlds. They became my friends. I learned everything from them about the different aspects of creation; its desires, hungers, and drives, and I also learned how to feel the power that ran through it. This power was called the Blaze, an aspect of the power of Creation made manifest. It is of the Creator, but the Creator did not make it. It was without uniformity, simply existence. And so I tied my power to it, the power granted me by the Creator, and thus I became the master of the Blaze on every world throughout creation. It is an eternal green fire that burns under every rock and through every tree, feeding on and nourishing the life-forces of every plant and animal. The planet sustains itself by promoting the growth and death of each and every species. But the Blaze is a fickle master, and when threatened it can express itself not only through the promotion of life and death, but it can also fundamentally change the nature of those things it lives within."

Shau-ling paused, a deep sadness clearly evident in his voice.

"When Emries began his tyrannical reign of destruction on this world, the Blaze ached to fight back. It changed some of the denizens into its first protectors, you know them as Kalbraks. But these soldiers were not enough, they needed a leader. And so when I came to this world, I was standing by the side of Exeter Lake, and Emries had just rebuffed my warnings to stop his perversions of the Creator's laws. Standing there, considering how to make Emries pay for his arrogance, the ground beneath my feet began to shake. Suddenly there was a groan like thunder, and when I looked down into the lake, I saw a green fire bubbling up from the bottom of the lake. Then, as though it saw me, a tendril of the fire rushed through the water to where I stood and erupted in a geyser twenty feet tall and ten across. As I stood there watching the fire dance before me, I knew what I had to do, what I had to become. So, I touched it, and let it enter me. At that moment, I felt as though I had been immersed in joy. The radiant energies of the Blaze filled me to overflowing and kept going. Just when I thought I would burst, the energy began to withdraw, but never completely. From that day on, my fate has been tied to that of this world."

Again, Shau-ling paused, rolling his next words over in his mind before he let them drip from his tongue.

"Emries gave me no choice in what came next," he continued. "Emries was not interested in this world. He only saw this place as a land he could turn into his utopia, a place for his children to rule. It was then that his progeny began to follow the short-sighted and violent mandate of their god. These men looked to Emries as though he was the Creator, and never were allowed to know the true Creator. However, Emries was not prepared for the punishment that the Creator would levy upon him for his arrogance. The Creator gave him the curse of the *Coromor*, removing all divine protection from him. Literally translated from the language of the gods, *Coromor* means 'He who brings destruction.' Emries used this curse to his own devices, and gave it the meaning that people know today."

Shau-ling shook his head.

"But the Creator was not without a sense of mercy, and so the Creator gave Emries one last chance to prevent what would happen. Emries was told by the Creator that the time had come for him to give the Creator's laws to his children, to make them respect all that He had created. So, he gave to Emries a book of laws to give to his people. Emries took the book from his master, and indeed he did give them to his people. However, he tore many of the pages from the Book of Knowledge and then presented the laws as his. The Creator was so angry about this that he cursed the progeny of Emries to death. Not an immediate one, but a slow lingering death. They would be born and then start to die over a long series of years, suffering at times, and then finally they would leave this life and cease to exist. Upon hearing this, Emries was furious. He blamed the Creator for the problems of his people even though the fault was his own. The Creator gave to me the same book of laws that he had given to Emries and told me to make them known to all who wished to know them. So, I had a church to the Creator built in a little church outside of vast forest on the edge of the ground of Emries' sprawling palace. On a podium before the dais, I put the book and covered it with a magical glass box. This box would keep the pages safe for the rest of time. The box was also made light and nearly insubstantial so that anyone could lift it to read the book. As you would expect, Emries was not pleased by this, so, he told his people that the book held ancient secrets that human eyes were not ready for, and when the time was right, the glass box would lift so that all could examine it. He knew of course that that day would never come. He instead opened the book to a passage he knew well, the life-joining ritual that you refer to as marriage. He professed that this was a ceremony decreed by himself, the Creator, that must be followed, and so it was that the then holy city of Aradon was founded beside that old church."

Pike listened to the story with contained doubt. Much of what Shau-ling said made perfect sense, but it went against everything that he had ever believed. Pike knew that he would have his beliefs tested while in Shau-ling's presence, but he never dreamed that it would ever be like this.

"That was how it began," Shau-ling said, the sadness and regret so thick in his voice it could not be ignored. "The Creator called me before Him and told me that my days as the peaceful Halicon were over. I was to punish my brother, Emries, and to make him see the error of his ways. He then stepped with me into the minds of men and showed me what it was that they most feared. In all cases, the large black lizards of old, creatures called dragons were the most feared in all the men. Dragons were a myth to the men of this world, but a powerful one. So, when the Blaze came to me that day beside Exeter Lake, a dragon was the form I chose. Then, the Creator gave me the permission to change the very animals of the wood as well as trees and mountains into my servants. Then, He gave me the one order that has haunted me to this day. He told me that my destiny was to exterminate the plague that was human life, and to kill my brother for his treacherous acts against the Creator. To this I said that I would obey, and from that day on, I became the Living Nightmare, otherwise known as Shau-ling."

At this point Shau-ling fell silent. He did not look at either Nightwing or Pike, but Pike somehow felt that Shau-ling was waiting for something. Perhaps he wanted recognition that they understood.

"And that was when the phasia and the *Erieal* were created?" Pike asked already knowing the answer.

"Yes," Shau-ling responded in the same dejected voice, "and that may have been my greatest mistake. I created the phasia in the image of the worst human beings that I could find. I thought that the way to destroy them was to use their own weakness against them. The lust, greed, and vengeance that drove them would be perfect fuels to kill them. But I soon found that the phasia were as frail as the humans and as prone to failure and weakness. They began to squabble amongst themselves and were more worried about killing each other and me to worry about their mission. I then became too wrapped up in the affairs of the phasia and my personal war with Emries to do anything about my mission. The Creator I know is displeased with me, and it may be too late now to save any of us from the fire that is coming."

It was Nightwing's voice that interrupted the dreadful silence.

"SHAU-LING," Nightwing asked, "DO YOU KNOW ME?"

Shau-ling nodded and sighed.

"I do indeed Nightwing, I know the person you are as well as the creature you are. Draven did well in recruiting his Dark Riders, using the creations of his brothers and sisters against them, but I believe he made a fatal mistake with you. The other members of the Dark Riders are tools that Draven can bend to his will, though as with all things he overestimates the lengths to which their abilities can be employed. They are flawed because their wills are weak, and they will do what they are told, even the Flame, who is but a shadow of what he once was. But you, your heart cannot be subjugated so easily by this war, and the Creator has given you a place with the angels when you die. Perhaps you will be my brother in the heavens when this world is consumed with fire."

If Nightwing reacted to the words, there was no way to tell it, as the brilliant red slits for eyes conveyed no emotion.

"SHALL I REVEAL MYSELF?"

Shau-ling nodded.

With that, Nightwing stood very still and concentrated. Pike had seen this trick before when Nightwing had been revealed as Aryx, and his palms began to sweat in anticipation of the identity of the new host. There was a twisting in the pit of his stomach, an expectation that had been aching in his heart since he had battled the creature in Brea. Then, the pieces of black armor began to peel away and retract into human skin. The faceplate was the last to go, and when the person beneath the armor was revealed, Gwydeon and Pike stood eye to eye, both armed and ready for a fight. But it was not the old crippled Gwydeon that Pike had met in Brea. The man that stood before Pike was a young strong man with that same gleam in his eyes that had been there from the very beginning of the first quest.

"Gwydeon," Pike intoned slowly, with a knowing dread creeping into his voice, "is that really you under the armor, or is this some kind of trick?"

"It's me, Pike," Gwydeon responded, "but I'm not exactly the man I used to be. The powers that Nightwing gives me magnifies my own skill ten or fifteen times, and I am faster and more agile than anyone in the world, except for maybe Draven and Shadow. I feel almost like I've been reborn."

Pike scratched his chin, but did not relax his grip on the haft of his axe.

"So that's why you didn't attack me in Brea."

"Yes, Pike," Gwydeon answered. "I couldn't bear the thought of harming you or Midarin, but I had to keep up the appearance that I was doing what Draven told me to. I knew that he could strike at Midarin or Nathaniel any time that he wanted, so I had to get them away from him and to relative safety. Unfortunately, there was nothing I could do to save Sabrina. I'm afraid that she will have to deal with Draven on her own for a while. I do however intend to remedy that situation soon enough."

Shau-ling stepped between the two old friends at that moment, drawing their attention immediately to him.

"Draven should not be the focus of your thoughts or your vengeance at this moment my new if not ironic allies, he will be busy enough shortly. Draven has decided to start the War for Power by challenging the twins Rael and Trece to a battle. I have no doubt that Draven will be victorious, but that gives us more time to formulate a battle plan. As usual my children underestimate how much I know about their plans, and we must use that to our advantage more now than ever. There are gears within gears rotating in the world, and it is time that you stop being driven and start driving the wheel."

"No offense," Pike said, "but I don't care about Draven or the War for Power, or driving a wheel. Right now the only thing I care about is saving Sabrina."

"I hoped you would say that, Pike," a voice said from out of the darkness. "I would have been disappointed if you would have turned into a self-absorbed bastard while I was gone."

Pike spun and watched as the owner of the voice walked out of the shadows into the light. As soon as Pike heard the voice, he knew the owner of it. It had been twenty-five years since her death, and Pike could still hear her voice as she died because for him it had been but weeks prior. Eldar was a beautiful woman to say the least. Her long golden hair was braided in the back, and the braid hung over her left shoulder. The clothes she wore were very common, a pair of black pants and a white shirt that laced up the front. In her right hand she held her sword loosely at her side, but Pike knew that it could become deadly at a moment's notice, and the smile on her face, equally deadly, made Pike's soul light up in a way he had not felt since her loss.

"Eldar?" was all that Pike could manage.

"It's me, Pike," she said after a moment, stopping about ten feet from him. "Shau-ling brought me back not long after my death. He began teaching me the truth about the war, and he essentially made me a member of his phasia. He did not give me any of their powers so to speak, but he has given me access to the Blaze, and it has made me much stronger. I knew that you were alive through the Blaze, and I was waiting for you to wake up. When you finally did emerge on the Island of Mist, I begged Shau-ling to bring you here so that I could see you again, and he did out of respect for me because I have never tried to harm him as the phasia did."

"She has been a wonderful student, Pike," Shau-ling commented. "Everything I taught, she learned and wanted to know more. You humans were always more wise than I gave you credit for, and now that you are here, I can do for you what I did for her."

Pike looked up at Shau-ling and then to Eldar. He had been tormented by her death, but perhaps it was the long sleep that had driven that rage or desire from his heart. She was not a temptation for him. Then it hit Pike. Shau-ling was trying to cloud his vision by bringing Eldar back to life. This was the trick that Pike had been waiting for. As quickly as he could manage, Pike rounded on Shau-ling with his axe *Fury* and slashed a hard downward stroke at the reptilian-featured man. The axe seemed to hit Shau-ling, but then the blade passed through his body. The next thing he realized, Eldar stood before him with her blade poised for battle. Shau-ling reappeared behind her, a shocked look on his face. Eldar, not thinking, struck out to protect her new master. Pike spun away from the blow and retaliated. The blow from *Fury* would have taken the head clean off of her body, but the metal clawed hand of Nightwing crossed the distance just a second earlier and intercepted the blow. There the three of them stood for a moment or two just looking at one another. They were three old friends that had gone through amazing transitions, and were not the same as they were when they were friends. Pike's anger began to ease, and as Nightwing release the axe, Pike let it fall to the ground.

"You must learn to wait and ask questions before resorting to that type of violence, Pike Rhuiden." Shau-ling chided. "I brought Eldar Merin back because I was fascinated by her strength and bravery. My purpose in reviving her was not to tempt you. That is the way of the phasia. You must accept that I am not my creations, and that their ends are not mine. They are an outdated and outmoded response to the viciousness of my brother Emries, and I had no choice but to fight his wickedness with greater wickedness. That was my mistake, one that I hope through my alliance with those of you who can be made to see the truth, to rectify."

Pike nodded and then picked up his axe. When he looked up into Eldar's eyes, he tried to find that spark about her that he loved. However, when he looked deep into her eyes, while he saw intensity and power, along with the famous tenacity, there was very little of the compassion or love left. It was almost like all she cared about any more was doing the job that Shau-ling asked of her. But Pike too had other goals, other motivations. Old love and regret would have to wait. Pike's focus now was getting Sabrina back from that fiend Draven. There was nothing more important than that.

"Where did you leave Sabrina?" Pike asked turning to face Nightwing.

"SHE WAS LEFT IN THE ROYAL BEDROOM IN THE PALACE OF SCALLA. WHEN DRAVEN RETURNS FROM HIS BATTLE WITH RAEL AND TRECE HE WILL GO THERE EXPECTING TO FIND HER. IF SHE IS NOT THERE WHEN HE RETURNS, DRAVEN WILL TAKE HIS ANGER OUT ON MIDARIN AND NATHANIEL. THAT IS NOT ACCEPTABLE. I MUST PROTECT MY FAMILY EVEN WHEN I AM NOT WITH THEM. DRAVEN THOUGHT HE BEAT ME WHEN HE MADE ME INTO THIS MONSTER, BUT HE WAS A FOOL. WITH THE POWERS OF NIGHTWING AT MY DISPOSAL, I WILL BE ABLE TO BATTLE HIM ON HIS OWN LEVEL."

"That is true, Gwydeon," Shau-ling responded, "however, there is a large danger that you are overlooking. Remember, Draven has full control over the group that he calls the Dark Riders. Now, Draven has learned the secret of Nightwing, and in learning that, has learned to manipulate it. Unless you are free from the bond that Draven has imposed on you, you will not be able to use your new-found abilities against him. If you wish, I will take that burden from you, and make you as I made Eldar. A phase but not a phase."

"WILL I BE FORCED TO BOW TO YOU WHEN MY TASK IS OVER?" Nightwing asked.

"You will be connected to the Blaze. The Blaze is connected to my essence, but it is not me. I am not the Blaze, but neither can I exist without it. Long after I am gone, the Blaze will still burn. Therefore, in answer to your question, no."

"THEN DO IT."

Shau-ling nodded and closed his eyes. The lights in the room flared one by one as the columns of light exploded into the air and slammed against the ceiling in violent collisions. A murmur began in the room as Shau-ling began to chant in a low nearly incomprehensible voice. Nightwing, not powered by his own wings, began to hover in the air, and wisps of white-lit smoke began to circle around him. The smoke entered and left Nightwing's body slowly at first, and then sped up as the moments passed. Within a matter of seconds, it looked as if Nightwing were totally consumed by the white smoke. Nightwing was only partially visible, but as Pike looked on, he could easily see that the black armor slowly changed colors. The colors cycled through the spectrum from white, red, blue, black, and all the other colors of the rainbow. The colors sped up as the moments passed until they became a flickering mass and Pike had to look away. Then, there was a bright flash of light, and the room went dark for a long minute before a green glow filled the room. Pike looked back to see Nightwing bathed in the glow, his body covered in the scorching flames known as the Blaze.

"You are now free from the bond of Draven," Shau-ling said in a straining voice. "You may now go to fight him and gain revenge for your family. Go now, and rescue the girl Sabrina and take her to her mother. Then, you may rejoin your family without fear. Your redemption and place in the heavens has not yet begun Gwydeon Sandar, but you have taken your first step."

Nightwing did not answer, but a swirling blue portal appeared behind him. Nightwing bowed to Shau-ling after a moment of reflection, and then saluted to both Eldar and Pike before stepping through. After the portal closed, Pike rounded on Shau-ling again.

"What about me?" Pike growled. "Sabrina is my responsibility. I promised her that I would keep her safe, and now you're not even going to allow me to go after her?"

"Be still, Rhuiden," Shau-ling responded in a weak impatient voice. "You have business to attend to that far outweighs this situation. And the matter of Sabrina Binosear is not yours to meddle in. As usual, there is more at work then the eyes of one human could ever see. The Creator has doomed us all because of my arrogance and the arrogance of one of my own. In order to reverse the damage done, we must help the forces of the Shadow to overwhelm the forces of the Light so that Emries does not succeed. There is one true way for us to accomplish this feat, and that is to go to the other reality, the reality where the Light is dominant and remove one single man from the equation. This man is not a member of the phasia, nor the *Coromor, Chosen One,* or a member of the *Erieal.* He is simply a man, but a man so special that the fate of a reality rests on his shoulders. He has already begun to discover the truth, but he cannot make it known because it would mean his death. I have foreseen that he is the only force that will be powerful enough to destroy Draven. So, Pike Rhuiden, Eldar Merin, I charge you with the task of retrieving the boy named Wolf Ranthall, the son of Logan Ranthall and Elwyne Tamerlane."

Pike stood in utter shock for a moment, and then after the shock wore off, he could not convince his mouth to utter the words that he was thinking. In the other reality, Logan and Elwyne had both lived long enough to have a son, and he had grown to be a powerful man. Pike sighed and nodded in ascent to the mission. Shau-ling nodded, but when he spoke again, the sadness had returned to his voice.

"I am circumventing the will of the Creator by sending you in my stead. I am interfering without interfering, and I know not what this act will cost me in this reality. Be careful, there are forces there that will try to destroy you at every opportunity, including yourselves. It will not be easy to get to the man Wolf Ranthall, but you must succeed at all costs. The fate of all of the lives in both realities rests on what you do next."

Shau-ling then took a deep breath and raised both of his hands into the air. Sweat beaded on the ancient man's face, and his expression spoke of the extreme pain the exertion was causing within him. Suddenly a swirling white portal appeared above Shau-ling's head. The portal was small at first, and then with increased exertion on Shau-ling's part, began to grow bigger. Shau-ling was breathing very heavily, and his eyes were squeezed shut so tightly that he began to cry tears of blood.

"Go!" came the raspy reptilian voice of Shau-ling.

Eldar took Pike's hand and led him in a leap toward the portal. The instant they touched the outer edge, the two disappeared in a flash of light.

Shau-ling then fell to his knees and released the portal. He held his eyes closed for a moment and then opened them. Shau-ling was shocked to see that there was a pair of boots before him. Shau-ling looked up, the blood trickling from the corners of his eyes at the man who stood before him. His shirt was light and flowing, the purple color bright against the backdrop of black. The cruel smile on his face was only out-shined by the fire in his eyes and the glowing blade in his hand. The golden symbol of a striking viper glowed an angry crimson, and Saurn looked as though he were a vengeful god ready to unleash his wrath on an ungrateful subject.

"You look tired, old man," Saurn said with venom, "perhaps it is time for you to go to sleep."

* * * * * * * * * *

A cold wind blew through the abandoned city of Brea as the thunder of marching troops filled the air. The army of red skinned Jeresei came to a halt at the frontier of the kingdom and watched, waiting for the signal torches to go up on the walls of the palace, signaling for the defense to take their positions, but no torches went up. The twin generals of this evil army, the phasia Rael and Trece Starlin looked at each other puzzled but still gave the order for the army to advance. The Jeresei hesitated for a moment. Many clans had been extinguished by the defense mounted by the Order of the Sword, and there were several clan leaders that had fallen to the blade of the commander of the Order, Gwydeon Sandar. It was not that the Jeresei were afraid to fight the Order, but they were cautious to know the power of the enemy they were about to engage. Suddenly, the screams of rage went up from the clan leaders of the army, and the Jeresei began their quick march toward the city. After several moments, another volley of screams hit the air, and the Jeresei broke into a flat sprint, ready to destroy everything that got in their way. The generals of the army however stayed behind the ranks of advancing Jeresei, waiting for the slaughter to begin, but no hail of arrows rained from the walls of the palace. There were no signal fires or shows of typical Sandar defiance. It was as if the city were dead.

"I wonder where they are," Rael said almost to himself.

"If they were smart, brother," Trece answered, "they would be hiding."

There was a loud crash of thunder, and lightning flashed all around. The next sound was that of something being whipped around in the breeze. When Rael and Trece looked up, they saw their younger yet very powerful brother Draven floating above them. Draven looked down at the siblings, and then slowly descended until he was hovering just in front of them.

"Draven," Rael spat in hatred, "what an unexpected surprise."

"To what," Trece continued, "do we owe the honor of your presence?"

"I came to tell you that you are too late," Draven said smiling. "Thanks to my cunning and strategic brilliance, Sandar and his pitiful army have abandoned Brae. The fight is over. You can have the lands, they mean nothing without resistance."

Rael glared at Draven and then drew his sword.

"What of your challenge to Trece, Crow?" Rael challenged. "Our enemy hovers before us. If we kill you, not only do we get Brea, but Scalla and Trelon also."

"Not to mention," Trece continued, "years of peace and quiet where we do not have to listen to your incessant cawing."

Draven smiled.

"Then, let the War for Power begin."

Depths of Evil

Creator's Calendar Year 1205; Light Reality

The normally quiet town of Aradon vibrated with the sound of church bells as the massive and ancient iron carillon rung five times in honor of the dead. In each home, the grieving would continue until the sound of the bells faded away completely. These were the most special moments of the burial ceremony in Aradon, the last few moments to say goodbye before their life would begin again in a world without the departed. Each death in Aradon was met with a measure of respect and a measure of sorrow. After the ceremony was over however, the grieving would end, and the sorrow would disappear. The best tribute to the life that had been extinguished was to live each day to the fullest. Joy was a better tribute than tears, and the Book of the Creator taught that life was sacred, and to dwell upon death was to sin against life. Such was the way of Aradon.

On the field outside the large graveyard, a group waited. They had all come to pay their final respects to a woman that the world knew and loved, not only for her bravery in the war which had brought her fame, but also for her caring heart that had garnered her the loyalty and love of commoners and royalty alike. After the final toll of the bell, Lissa Terian waited for Wolf Ranthall to emerge from the old church. Part of her longed to hold him, to somehow take the pain of his loss away, but as she looked into the eyes of her adopted sister, the princess Sabrina Binosear, a part of her wanted to crawl under a rock and hide. She knew that part of

Sabrina was still in pain, a pain that they both struggled to understand, but Lissa could not deny the feelings of her own heart. Finally, the man she waited for emerged from the old church. Something was wrong though. He seemed to be disturbed about something, and he was not wearing a shirt. He took three steps out of the church doorway and waived for everyone to come to him. Lissa only hesitated for a second before dashing up the hill toward the church, and she was followed quickly by one of the newer members of the group, the man named Jared Vale. The shocking secret had been made known that Jared was the son of the infamous phase Caris Vale and the legendary Lord Lion, Cedric Binosear; a secret that would take months to come to grips with. His lineage gave him powers beyond that of even the *Erieal*, but Lissa knew that it also filled him with a sense of doubt and uncertainty. Lissa had felt the same when she learned of the exploits of her so-called father Aryx Terian, the man known throughout the world as White Lightning. When they reached the crest of the hill, Wolf turned away and re-entered the church. Lissa and Jared only hesitated for a moment before following, and when they finally caught up with Wolf, the scene that greeted them was one that they never expected, and Lissa could to prevent the wince that twisted her features.

Wolf was kneeling beside a woman, holding her in his arms like a protective father holds a new-born child. Her blond hair, while beautiful and shimmering was matted with blood and sweat, dulling its brilliance. A large cut was open on her forehead, but Wolf was doing his best to dab the blood away with his shirt that was wrapped around the shivering woman as a makeshift blanket. When Lissa looked down at the woman, she immediately averted her eyes realizing that the woman was naked. The embarrassment passed after only a moment concern winning out over modesty, and Lissa knelt at the woman's side alongside Wolf. Jared only took a moment before removing his own shirt and covering the woman's hips and legs. He grimaced a bit when he saw her face, and when Lissa looked she was shocked as well. A cut had opened above her left eye that had sent blood streaming into it, making it almost impossible to see. Her eyelid had swollen as well, and it looked as though she couldn't have opened her eye even if she wanted to. The condition of her other eye showed nearly the same amount of damage. The skin around her right eye was puffy and the coloring was black and blue. Her bottom lip was split as well, but the bleeding from that wound appeared to have stopped. When

Lissa had looked at the woman's body she had noticed other cuts and bruises all over her, but none of them as serious as the ones on her face, save perhaps around her ribs, which could have been the indication of broken bones. Without a word, Wolf and Jared slowly began to lift the woman, and with each little move, she groaned in pain, but did not cry out. Lissa helped to brace the woman in the two men's strong arms, and then the three of them carried her out of the church.

When the three exited the church, they noticed that the rest of the group had made it to the crest of the hill. Midarin immediately rushed to aid the woman, followed quickly by Gwillim. Sabrina and Cairyn held their ground with Nathaniel, and Aryx seemed to watch the entire scene with a detached air about him. Liette seemed to be the only one not paying attention to the woman. Her mind appeared to be elsewhere, scanning the horizon for something. Gwillim took over for Lissa carrying the woman. Wolf took the lead, directing the makeshift litter back down toward Aradon. In a matter of minutes, they arrived at the small house just outside of the perimeter wall that surrounded Aradon itself, the same one that had been the home for first Logan and then Wolf Ranthall. Upon entering the house, Aryx was hit with a strange sensation. Something did not feel right about the house. It was almost as if someone was watching their every move. Wolf, Jared, and Gwillim carried the woman to the back room of the home, and carefully laid the woman on a small bed that was situated against the back wall of the house. This had been the room where Wolf had spent all of his nights growing up, and the bed that he himself had slept in only a few nights earlier. Leaving the injured woman's side for a moment, Wolf went into another of the back rooms and fetched a blanket. The woman seemed to have lapsed back into unconsciousness by the time that Wolf returned, and he made sure that the pillow and covers were situated properly. Satisfied that she was comfortable, Wolf reached into a wardrobe near the door and emerged with two gray shirts in hand. He threw one to Jared and then pulled the other over his head. Wolf motioned for Gwillim and Jared to follow, and they joined the rest of the group in the front room of the home.

"Hopefully she will be able to rest," Wolf remarked in a quiet voice. "One of us should go get Mayor Sandar and Erin Rhuiden. The mayor needs to know what is going on in his town, and Erin should be able to heal whatever wounds this woman has. She has been a great comfort to many people here in town while they were sick."

Midarin nodded in ascent.

"I'll go get them, Wolf. Torris will probably be better to get Mrs. Rhuiden then I would be, but my relationship with Torris is better than anyone here. After all, he is Gwydeon's father."

After a moment, she turned and left. Liette still seemed distracted by something, and after whispering something to Aryx, he nodded and the two of them quietly excused themselves. Jared watched the two go for a moment and then shook his head.

"There is something that makes me not like that little girl," he said almost in a whisper as if Liette would be able to hear him, "she makes me nervous."

"You're not the only one," Wolf commented aside. "I think it's that, 'I'm going to kill you' look that gets to me."

Wolf chuckled to himself after the comment and Jared smiled in response. Cairyn and Sabrina seemed too concerned about the young woman to react to the comment, and Lissa just shook her head.

"Liette takes some getting used to," Lissa responded, "once you get to know her, you will understand why she is the way she is."

"Well, I'm not going to take the chance," Jared said finally, "especially with Aryx Terian at her side."

Lissa scowled for a moment at the mention of her father's name, and then sighed deeply. Wolf could tell that the situation was grating on her, and it would only be a matter of time before she snapped again as she did in the forest. Wolf prayed that if there was a next time, cooler heads would prevail again. There was a low moan that came from the young woman, and the group returned to the bedroom. This time, it was Cairyn that knelt at the younger woman's side and brushed her hair lovingly away from her face.

"I think she's coming around," the queen said softly.

Sabrina took a step back and waited. It was almost like she expected something bad to happen. Lissa seemed to be on guard too, but Wolf could sense no evil coming from the woman.

"Where am I?" the woman's voice croaked out.

"You are in Aradon," Cairyn replied softly, taking hold of the woman's hand. "What is the last thing that you remember?"

"I was in Rama, with my newly-born son. We had just gone to sleep for the night, and then suddenly there were figures all around me. The next thing I knew, I was here. I remember a man in a church."

Wolf stepped forward, he knelt at the other side of the bed, but kept his distance.

"That was me. I found you in the old church on the hill badly beaten and bruised. There is a healer on the way, and before too long she will have you back to fighting shape."

The woman smiled meekly and then sighed heavily.

"Thank you for rescuing me, my name is Susanne Praen. I should probably tell you why it is that I ended up in your church."

Cairyn shook her head and stroked Susanne's long blond hair.

"Stories can wait until later," Cairyn said softly, "wait for the healer and then we can talk later."

"No," Susanne said as strongly as her body could manage. "There may not be time. The hunters will no doubt be after me now, and I must tell my tale so that you will know the depths of danger that is about to befall this world."

Gwillim leaned toward Wolf and whispered.

"I feel a Shau-ling story coming on. Nathaniel and I are going to see what Liette and Aryx are up to. I don't like them being away this long without one of us watching them."

Wolf nodded absently. Gwillim's candor as to his concern about Aryx Terian was more than disconcerting. How was it that the forces of the Light had become more like the phasia in this generation? Where was the love and trust that had held the People of the Dragon together all those years ago? As the two brothers left, Susanne began her tale. Her voice was strained, but the more she spoke, the more Wolf could hear the pain and resentment.

"After the Army of the Dragon left Rana and Rama in pursuit of the Jeresei that had attacked them, the religious leaders in the city began to form a secret sect. This sect became known as the Creator's Torch Society. They endeavored to find the truth behind the war between the Light and the Shadow and bring peace back to the world. The leader of the sect, a man named Dei, began his studies into a group known as the Moridon. From what he uncovered, the Moridon were a race of people who were the first beings to ever walk the face of the world under the rule of the Creator. They were the first men, and those gifted with a strange power known as magic. All of the books and history found about the Moridon told of them wielding strange powers over the forces of nature that were so destructive that several of them together could move a mountain. The greatest stories of the Moridon came from the pen of a man known as Aralias Imstra, the same man whose pen gave us the prophecies of the *Coromor*. Imstra himself was a member of the Moridon and he gathered under him a group of Moridon warriors so powerful that the world would shake if they wished it too. This army was called the Hand of the Light. The Hand fought against the Shadows in whatever form reared its head. They battled the phasia in epic clashes that spanned whole kingdoms. However, when the war was entering what seemed to be its final stages, the Hand of the Light was defeated by a man named Saurn, and the Moridon seemingly disappeared. They were only to reemerge years later under the command of Lord Cedric Binosear and the great Arathorn Geoffrey. But while the Moridon were great warriors and had power beyond those of normal mortals the act of fighting the Shadow so openly was not consistent with their teachings."

Susanne paused, taking a breath and swallowing hard. When she spoke again, her voice was raspy.

"Dei, under more intense study, found some of the religious scripture relating to the beliefs of the Moridon. At heart, they were a very peaceful people, dedicated to the preservation of life, and the championing of everything that is good about the human race. They believed in using their powers to heal the sick, help those in need of money, food, and shelter, and using their powers to protect those that could not protect themselves. However, there is nothing within the teachings of the Moridon that made them a war-like people. However, when the threat of the Shadows was upon them, hundreds of thousands of the Moridon left their homes to seek out the phasia and their twisted followers. There was no provocation for any of these attacks. The Creator's Torch society began to adopt the teachings of the Moridon in an effort to understand why these great people fought the Shadows with such vigor and disdain."

"It was probably because they saw the threat to humanity that the phasia posed," Sabrina answered in a matter of fact tone.

"No," Susanne said strongly, shaking her head. "That was not the only part to the equation of the Moridon. It was not just those who were in the Moridon homelands or the most capable. Those who were working within kingdoms healing the sick, and even the infirm were mobilized to combat the threat. It was like the shadow spawn were an affront to the very existence of the Moridon and they would do whatever they could possibly do to destroy all of them."

"So you were a member of this Creator's Torch Society?" Lissa asked.

"Yes," Susanne responded nodding her head slowly. "Dei was my teacher, and I was one of his best students. We were taught that the Light and the Shadow were two sides of the same coin, but that we were to determine for ourselves which was evil and which was good. However, there were times when those who worked for the Shadow were not evil. Dei often pointed to the example of Basille and Jerrard Mystic. He said that they had seen the error of their ways and had not let their breeding dictate their sense of goodness. The Torch, as they are called by all who know them, is methodical about the practices and any in the group who does not live up to the physical or mental rigors that they are put through are violently disposed of."

Cairyn and Sabrina both cringed at the terminology.

"Is that what happened to you?" Wolf asked.

Lissa looked at Wolf crossly for a moment and then smiled. She realized what it was that he was doing. There was something that Susanne was not telling them and he was doing his best to pull it out of her. Though neither of them truly wanted to press the wounded woman for information, they would not allow themselves to be trapped by their sympathy for her. She was the one who pressed to tell her tale, so they had to make the most of the opportunity.

"No," Susanne answered mildly shocked at the question. "I was one of the best of the Torch. I was physically fit beyond all of the other women of the group, I was a perfect student, and one of the favorites of all of my teachers. I made the mistake however of falling in love with another member of the Torch, and man who called himself Toren. Toren and I were nearly inseparable from the moment that we met, and before long many of the Torch believed that we would be married and become the parents of the first Child of the Torch. However, while there was a child born of our union, there was no marriage. It was after the birth of the child that Toren revealed himself as the phase Erdric Yarrow. He killed Dei during one of the meetings of the Torch and then fled, laughing at us all as he stepped through his portal. I was blamed by the entire society for bringing Erdric close to Dei. Then my son became the target of hatred as those in the society knew he would have the powers of a phase. A new leader was proclaimed, Dei's former lover, a woman named Seraphina. In a long speech, Seraphina denounced the teaching of Dei saying that the peaceful nature of the Moridon had robbed them of their security and after a tragedy just like the murder of Dei, the Moridon saw the error of their ways and struck out. While there was no historical backing for this accusation, the entire Torch agreed and decided to follow the path of the Moridon to its fruition. Seraphina preached that the world had shifted away from the teachings of the Creator, and that even the great heroes had walked away from their responsibilities. Logan Ranthall had forsaken his duty, Pike Rhuiden was a more interested in accumulating power than serving the Light, and Midarin Rice was nothing more than the dutiful shadow of a fallen hero. The Torch then began the reformation of the Hand of the Light under its new leader, Seraphina Masile, a replacement for the broken and fading People of the Dragon. I was kept around to raise my son to be used as a weapon for the Hand. When Michael, my son, was old enough, Seraphina ruled that I was no longer needed in the Torch and that I was to be cast out. She said that I had given my heart to the Shadow and from that time on I would be considered and enemy to the Hand. The cuts and bruises that you see were my parting gifts from the Hand as I was made to run a gauntlet of all of my oldest friends, each of them beating and cursing me as I ran."

Wolf felt his blood boil. The memories of the Blaze began to fill his mind again. The Hand of the Light had been a powerful opponent to the members of the phasia and the forces of Shau-ling. They won many battles against the likes of Warron and Zarsi, however, their trampling across the face of Shau-ling's will was thwarted by Saurn. He single handedly destroyed the Hand of the Light and killed Aralias Imstra. It was then that Aerith Seth was captured and the prophecies began. Basille's own memories of Aerith Seth then entered Wolf's mind and he saw the way power hung on the man so that it was nearly a palpable aura around him. Now the Hand of the Light was reformed, and they had a tool that could rival nearly anything that the phasia could send up against them in the personage of Susanne's son Michael.

"Did the Torch have enough time to uncover the teachings of the Moridon magic?" Lissa asked apparently on the same page as Wolf.

"Yes," Susanne said straining, "They have learned everything that the Moridon sought fit to write down in their teachings. The magic wielded by the Torch may not be as powerful as the original Hand, but in a fight I am sure that it will be most effective."

Susanne groaned again, and Cairyn held her hand tightly and stroked her hair.

"That's enough questions for now," Cairyn said quickly, "after the healer has looked at Susanne, then there can be more, but that is probably too much for now as it is."

Wolf nodded his ascent and grabbed Jared by the arm and led him out of the house. Lissa followed, and after a moment Sabrina joined them. Just as Wolf was about to speak, he saw Midarin approaching with Torris Sandar and Erin Rhuiden.

"Midarin," Lissa said quickly to the older woman, "keep my mother busy for a little while, and then we'll let you know what we found out."

Midarin looked at the red haired girl for a moment and then smiled. She knew the secrets that were kept from Cairyn. It had been a necessity up to that point, but Midarin knew that there would be a time when all the secrets would have to come to light, and the battle then would be on such an emotion level that some would be irrevocably changed by it. After watching Midarin lead the others into the house, Wolf led Jared, Sabrina, and Lissa over near the border of Logan's Wood.

"Ok, Wolf," Lissa said almost immediately, "what's on your mind?"

"Jared, being the son of a member of the phasia, you have access to the memories of the Blaze, and partial access to the memories of your mother Caris. You have to open yourself up to these thoughts and just let them come to you. See if you can find anything about the Hand of the Light or Aerith Seth in those memories."

Jared nodded and closed his eyes. For a long time he had held the gifts of his birth closed tightly and never used. But now he opened himself up to the Blaze. In Wolf's mind he felt the power flooding into the young man and watched as like a flower the Blaze bloomed inside of him. Suddenly the memories hit Jared's mind. He saw wars between Jeresei and men and women dressed in flowing white robes wielding staffs and spears that appeared to be made out of pure white light. He saw the woman that was his mother, Caris standing in the tower of a castle looking down onto the battlefield with her eyes locked on one man. He moved gracefully through the combat, a sword in each hand, striking down Jeresei as though they were immobile practice targets. One by one all of his enemies fell, until the battle was ended. But there were more of his mother's memories about the man named Aerith Seth. Jared saw the scene change to yet another castle. There was a large grim man dressed in gray seated on the throne. The Blaze told Jared that this man was a member of the phasia and that his name was Grawn. Caris moved passed this man into a different chamber of the castle, a bedroom where she intruded upon a man and a woman locked in the throes of passion. The man was Aerith Seth, and the woman was another member of the phasia, Bryn Aplee, the wife of Grawn. The memories then stopped trickling into Jared's mind, and as he opened his eyes, he could see Wolf smiling.

"I take it you found something."

"Well," Jared said after a moment, "Aerith Seth was a very interesting person. Not only was he the best member of the Hand of the Light, second in command to Aralias Imstra himself, but he was also the lover of a member of the phasia, Bryn Aplee."

"And," Lissa added, "he was the first *Chosen One* of the prophecies, and his death at the hands of Shau-ling started the cycle of the *Coromor*."

"So," Sabrina asked, "what does this tell us?"

"It tells us that we are in way over our heads ladies and gentlemen. I think we should find Nathaniel and Gwillim and put our heads together on this one. I am really starting to not like this. The Hand of the Light is a variable that I am sure none of us thought of."

There were nods all around.

* * * * * * * * * * *

When Gwillim and Nathaniel exited the little house, they saw Aryx and Lissa just disappearing into Logan's Wood. Not a word was spoken as the two men followed quickly and quietly into the wood. For a long couple of moments, Gwillim and Nathaniel stayed silent as Liette and Aryx spoke quietly between themselves. It was then that Liette whirled around and spoke loud enough for all to hear.

"There is someone else here."

Aryx and Liette were both looking in the direction opposite from Gwillim and Nathaniel. After a moment, two figures emerged from deeper in the forest. The first was a man of about average height with short brown hair. He was dressed all in black and appeared to be unarmed. His companion was a beautiful red haired woman with sparkling green eyes dressed all in white. She too was unarmed and was smiling. Aryx tensed at the sight of the pair and quickly drew his sword and held his gauntlet ready for a fight. Liette too drew her sword, almost as though she too recognized the pair. Nathaniel closed his eyes for a moment and then felt the strings of Blaze-fueled power coming from deep inside both the man and the woman. He mouthed the word phasia to Gwillim who had his sword ready.

"Well if it isn't Aryx Terian, White Lightning himself," the man said proudly.

"It has been a long time Aryx, or should I call you Nightwing?" the woman added.

Nathaniel and Gwillim were both a little shocked at the revelation, but they held their ground waiting. Liette did not seem to react to the words of the couple, but when Nathaniel closed his eyes, he saw something that he never expected. Liette was bathed in a white glow unlike anything Nathaniel had ever experienced. It was not like the powers of the phasia nor any of those who served the Light. However, it was not as though she were drawing on the power, it was like she was the shell that incased the power. Perhaps that was the explanation for her incredible growth and development.

"It has been a long time, Rael, Trece," Aryx said slowly, "a very long time indeed. The last time I saw the two of you, I did wear the mantle of Nightwing, but that time is over. Why are you in Logan's Wood?"

"You are direct as always White Lightning," Rael began, "but you are very rude to not introduce us to your lovely friend."

"The name is Liette, phasia scum. Learn it well, because I am the one who will seal your fate."

Liette's voice was hard. There was a viciousness there that neither Nathaniel nor Gwillim had ever seen in her.

"Do delusions of grandeur run rampant in the forces of the Light?" Trece asked laughing to herself. "Little girl, you could not last more than two minutes against the weakest of the phasia let alone against one of us. However, against both of us, the fight would be over long before it started, and your old companion there knows it to be true."

Aryx ground the hilt of his sword between his hands, waiting for the opportunity to strike. The twin phasia were as dangerous as they were boasting, but he knew that he could probably survive long enough for help to arrive if the talking did turn to battle. It was then that Aryx heard the rustling in the bushed behind him, and turned his head slightly to see Gwillim and Nathaniel emerge. Gwillim was holding his sword ready to strike, and Nathaniel was bathed in the glow of the powers of the *Coromor*. Now the tables had turned and the phasia were at the disadvantage. As if sensing this, Rael and Trece both took a step back and waited to see what the new arrivals would do. It was then that Trece felt a surge of power from elsewhere in the forest. It was something they had been trained to feel, but it was old, almost as old as the Blaze itself. The power came from the very fabric of time and reality, and that meant only one thing, Aerith Seth.

"Perhaps, dear brother, it is time for us to withdraw and allow these puny heroes an opportunity to live a bit longer. Their time will come soon enough to be sure," Trece said quickly.

"Only a coward runs away from a fight," Liette answered stepping forward.

"And only a fool fights when he does not have to," Rael replied.

That next moment, two portals opened below the feet of the phasia and they dropped through, the portals closing instantly behind them. The children of Shau-ling had escaped again, and when Liette turned to face Nathaniel and Gwillim, she had the fires of anger raging in her eyes.

"What are you two doing out here? We had it under control, and if you hadn't shown up, we could have taken two of the phasia out. Because of you, they now know where we are and they are going to take that information right back to Shau-ling."

Before Gwillim or Nathaniel could answer, Aryx chimed in.

"The twins wouldn't have been here unless Shau-ling sent them. He knew that the forces of the Light wouldn't be able to resist coming to the funeral of Elwyne Ranthall, and he sent them to gather information that he already basically knew. Shau-ling knew who would be here and what they would be doing, he just wanted confirmation so that he could stay one step ahead of us. Now he knows for sure that Pike is with the Enforcers in Kandor and that he is marching on Lakestone. The trap has been set to be sure, and unfortunately I think we have probably seen the last of Pike Rhuiden."

It was half-way through his rationale that Wolf, Lissa, Sabrina, and Jared emerged into the clearing. When Lissa heard what Aryx had to say, she was nearly devastated. Nathaniel turned immediately sensing more phasia power, but he relaxed when he saw it was only Wolf and Jared.

"So you think the Enforcers are as good as dead?" Lissa asked.

"I am almost sure of it," came Aryx's gruff reply.

"Then we have to get going as soon as we can," Sabrina chimed in. "Pike needs us with him, and I am sure that our powers will be enough to get him out of whatever jam that he is in. Besides, with Wolf and Jared, we should be able to get there in no time. They can open up and portal and set us down right in Pike's lap if they wanted."

"Hold it right there, princess," Wolf answered trying not to sound too hurtful, "there is no way that I am going to ally myself with Pike. All he will do is try to use my powers to fuel his reckless quest to fight a war that is not his to fight. The battle that needs to be fought is not in Lakestone. Sure there are phasia floating around. Rane Larion is one of the perfect examples of that fact. She was out here looking for Jared. I can understand why now that I know he is Caris' son. Then we have Susanne Praen laying there in my house. Her son is also a child of a member of the phasia and he is about to be used by the newly reformed Hand of the Light to do exactly what Pike is trying to do."

Aryx's jaw dropped open at the revelation of the reformation of the Hand.

"Both of these courses of action are a little too reckless for my tastes, and I believe that the path we need to follow lies toward the city of Barer and the kingdom that is usually ruled by Grawn and Bryn Aplee."

"You're just a coward," Liette shot back, her sword hefted high in the air. "Pike is a brave man fighting the war that the light destined him to fight."

"He is fighting a war that his pride and vengeance has destined him to fight," Wolf countered. "He is reckless and everyone that follows him will die in a futile attempt to avenge the dead."

"You're out of line," Sabrina said rounding on Wolf. "Pike is doing what he feels needs to be done to win the war for the Light. He's fought this war before, and this time he knows what it takes to win. It doesn't matter how he does it so long as Nathaniel and I make it to Shau-ling's throne room and take care of Shau-ling in this generation and continue the prophecies. If you are standing in the way of that, you are more of an enemy than you are a friend."

Sabrina's tone was vicious, and a fire ignited in Wolf that he could only imagine was coming from Basille and the Blaze.

"If you want to die," Wolf said, "I will be happy to put you right down in the middle of whatever Pike is doing. But if you want to win, I would suggest that you come with me and try to unravel what part Aerith Seth is playing in this war and what the reason is that the Hand of the Light is mobilizing again. Susanne is right, something about this doesn't figure. Something happened to the Moridon just like something is happening to this Creator's Torch Society. I think that is more dangerous right now than whatever is in Lakestone."

The next few moments was a stalemate. There were no words spoken, and there were accusing looks from members of the little group to other members. Liette was the first to break the silence.

"Maybe the part of you that is a phase is getting to your brain and making you work against us. Perhaps you are trying to lead us into a trap in Barer and your phasia friends are planning an ambush. I should kill you now."

She took a step forward with her sword ready for a fight, but Aryx restrained her.

"Now is not the time for this Liette," Aryx chided. "Wolf has the path that he wishes to follow, and so he cannot be restrained from that. The fact that he is a Ranthall grants him that right. I personally do not want to travel to Lakestone either, but if it is my mistress's wish, I will do so. Midarin will be the final judge of my fate in that case. Liette you are free to do as you wish, as are the rest of you. But I would make your decision quickly for I feel that time for them is growing short."

"I'm with Wolf," Jared said quickly. "I think that Barer is the best chance for me to find out exactly who I am and what part I play in this war. I don't know who Pike Rhuiden is and I have no intention of fighting when there is no reason."

"I'm with Wolf too," Gwillim replied. "Pike has been good to me for as long as I can remember, and he took great care in teaching me how to use my powers. But it was a Ranthall that saved me, and a Ranthall that found the right path in the last war. I don't know if we are going to find anything in Barer, but it is a better road for us to travel than the one to Lakestone. And as Wolf has said, family has to count for something."

"The *Coromor* should not be risked on meaningless battles," Nathaniel spoke confidently as if her were much older than he really was, but to Wolf's ears the words did not feel as though they were coming from the young man. "Pike has his Enforcers to do what he needs to do, and if he needs help, Jerrard and the Raven's Wing will be there to help him. If he is in danger, there is nothing that we can do to stop it. So, my vote is with Wolf as well."

"Lissa?" Wolf asked looking directly as the red-haired girl.

"I owe Pike a lot," she said after a moment, "he taught me and took care of me when things were rough for me. But I think you're right. I don't think that we will be able to make much of a difference if we are there with the Enforcers. I don't even know what Pike is looking for there. He has been so secretive since Logan died that none of us has been able to pry anything out of him. All he cared about was putting the Enforcers together and making sure that everything was ready for the war."

"Lissa!" Sabrina chided.

"It's true Sabrina. How long has it been since we have spent time with our dear father anyway? Eight months? A year? Two? How long has it been? Plus Duncan will be coming back to Marcwell soon, so Cairyn will be wanting to get back and stave off any problems that he causes. He is dangerous and you know it Sabrina. He wants the throne of Marcwell so bad that he can taste it, and I can see Pike fighting him for it. If we go to be with the Enforcers now, we will become part of a civil war fighting our own friends and brother over a broken deal. I say we go with Wolf and fight the real battle that needs to be fought, against the phasia and Shau-ling, not against the memories and grudges of an old man. Besides, if Aerith Seth is involved in this, then you should be interested too. After all, you're the *Chosen One.*"

Sabrina stood silent for a moment and then nodded. She knew that Lissa was right, but she did not like thinking that way about her father. He had been so good to her over the years, taking care of her when her mother only showed passing interest. But as the years ran on, he had become more and more distant, treating the Enforcers more like his family than a group of warriors.

"I guess I'm in too," Sabrina said.

"Well, Liette," Wolf said in the most condescending tone that he could manage, "should I send you to Lakestone. Please?"

"No," she answered. "I want to walk into this trap that you are planning just so I can be the first to turn my sword on you and spill that phasia tainted blood of yours. I don't care if you are a Ranthall. If I even get a hint that you are in league with the phasia, I will turn on your so quickly it will make your head spin, right before I lop it off."

Taking the threat in stride, Wolf smiled and turned away, heading back to his house just outside of Aradon. Once again a Ranthall was leading a group toward the evil Shau-ling, and as Aryx sheathed his sword he could not help but wonder if he was truly doing the right thing.

* * * * * * * * * *

Deeper in the forest, two more people watched the clearing, listening to every word spoken. They had seen the two phasia Rael and Trece and heard the taunts and arguments that had followed their departure. It was the comments about the Hand of the Light that caught Evan Sinn's attention the most, and as all the people left the clearing, Evan stood and sighed deeply to himself. Meredith stood also and looked Evan deeply in the eyes before sighing and speaking.

"Well, you said that we needed to get close to Wolf Ranthall. It looks like he's going to Barer. Does that mean we are going too?"

"Yeah," Evan answered, "but we still have to keep our distance. If Lissa or Sabrina find out that we are following them, they are going to get really suspicious. I guess we are just going to have to operate in the shadows for a little bit longer. They are trying to find out what part Aerith is playing in the war, but I think that someone else is acting in Aerith's name, and I don't mean me. If that's true, maybe we can find some answers in Barer. I guess we better get going. Aerith told me not to stick around in one place for too long."

Meredith smiled and then waited as Evan pulled a green stone from his pocket and pulled it open to form a portal. As the two stepped through, another portal appeared. This one was white and full of sparks. As the sparks and light receded, Pike Rhuiden and Eldar Merin looked around quickly getting a gauge of their surroundings. They could see the plumes of chimney smoke rolling off in the distance, and on a hill to the east, the spire of the old church rose above the trees showing the massive church bells. Pike smiled to himself. He was finally back to the place it had all started all those years ago. He was home.

The Love of a Father

Creator's Calendar Year 1205; Light Reality

Before the wars that claimed most of the civilized world, the kingdom of Scalla was a place where peace and freedom were not ideas or ideals, they were reality. This was all because of a man named Basille Mystic. Lord Basille was loved by all of his subjects and revered by everyone that he met. Most of his subjects knew that he was not mortal like the rest of them, but because of his kindness and protection, they did not care. From lifetime to lifetime, generation to generation he ruled with a love and grace without compare in the world. He knew all of his subjects by name, and many times knew their parents and was present at their birth. He touched the lives of every subject in a personal way. Most kings who were at some point Basille's contemporaries saw only the numbers of population, army size, and servant count. They saw their subjects only as a means to an end, be that end political or military. Basille saw something more. He saw the people and the problems that they had. There were servants who worked for him that had been injured and could not continue in their chosen field of work. One example was a blacksmith who had been caught in a terrible accident and lost use of one of his arms. Basille put him to work in the palace as a handyman of sorts. He was not the fastest on the job, but Basille knew that the position made the man feel as though he still was worth something. This kind of kindness was an everyday occurrence for

Basille, a trait that was counter and nearly incongruent with what he was born to be.

The truth of Basille's situation, while not frightening for the people who knew him, would have shocked the rest of the world. Basille Mystic was a member of the Brotherhood of Phasia, a son of the mighty Lord of the Shadow, Shau-ling. Basille was embroiled in one of the worst wars that the world would ever see, and yet the Kingdom of Scalla would remain untouched by it for hundreds of years. However, Basille could not keep the evil away from his beloved kingdom forever. The first foray of the forces of the Shadow into that sleepy little kingdom created the tragedy that would forever haunt Basille. He had taken a wife during one of the many generations that he ruled Scalla, a common woman, and he hid her away from both his enemies and his friends. For a few years they were happy together, and together they had a son. But then tragedy befell the Mystic family. For too long Basille's enemies in the War for Power had overlooked his kingdom, but when they found out about his wife and son, they could not help but strike. The battle raged for many days, with numerous lives lost on both sides of the battle. When the siege was finally over and the city was saved, Basille went back to his little house in the country and found it burned to the ground. He thought the worst and knew in his heart that both his beloved wife and infant son were dead. In Basille grew a great hatred for his brothers and sisters inside the phasia. It was then that Basille hatched his plot to bring the phasia to their knees.

For generations, Basille had been seen as the bastard child of the phasia, the lowly last-born. The members of the phasia each had glaring weaknesses, but they also had their overwhelming strengths, and over the years, Basille had found them all. So, in an effort to make up for all the years of being last in his master's eye, Basille began to devise ways to destroy each of his brothers and sisters by using their strengths and weaknesses against them. Basille began to win battle after battle, and was fast becoming the favorite in the War for Power until the prophecies began to come full circle. Basille found himself face to face with the man named Aerith Seth, the first *Chosen One* of the prophecies. But, he underestimated his opponent and found himself dead. When Basille was reborn in the next generation, he began to study the prophecies very diligently. While at many points the prophecies made perfect sense, most of it was utter gibberish.

There were contradictions at every turn, vagary wherever you looked, and what seemed like utter blind stupidity at times. It took Basille nearly fifteen years of intense and constant study to begin to make heads or tails of it. Then, it finally began to make something close to sense.

There were references in the prophecies to blood lines and birthrights that never seemed to make sense to Basille. But then he realized that everything had to start with Aerith Seth. So, he began to look into Aerith Seth's bloodlines. Strangely enough, he could not find any records of who Aerith's parents were. Even Saurn's information about the man seemed to be filled with inconsistencies and blatant lies. Saurn's records indicated that Aerith had a brother who had died in childbirth, but Basille knew that was simply misinformation. The children who were sent to the mines of Quea early in life often were mistaken for one another and the record keeping was spotty at best. Then Basille's memories began to fill in many of the pieces to the puzzle. He remembered that Bryn was extremely upset when she learned that Aerith had slept with Lady Christina Trelis during her journey to her wedding with Lord Wolfric Binosear, Cedric's father. Wolfric had been a good friend and ally to Basille over the years, and so Basille had no problems getting close to Cedric and his sister Anabel. It was obvious, once Basille got close enough, that Cedric and Anne were actually Aerith Seth's children, not Wolfric's. Having made this stunning discovery, one that none of his contemporaries within the phasia had discovered, Basille began to chart the bloodlines marked by the prophecies. Before too long, he had a rough sketch of the seven generations that would lead to the downfall of Shau-ling. There were no names attached to it of course, but there was enough information inside the prophecies to have a pretty good idea of what would come to pass. What concerned Basille the most was that the prophecies were so transparent in the ultimate course of events. If Basille didn't know any better, he would have thought that Shau-ling had created these prophecies himself in order to ensure that his enemy, Emries, would be vulnerable. No matter how much he studied, there were still passages in the prophecies that were oblique or impenetrable, and so to continue his studies he created a place where he could conduct his research undisturbed by the petty world outside. He had records on everyone that he deemed important to the prophecies tucked away below his palace in a secret vault. A vault whose location was only known to one other living person, his son Jerrard.

When Jerrard was a young boy, his father gave him a medallion to wear. On the back of the medallion was an inscription hidden by the mysterious force known as the Blaze. Basille had hidden the inscription, but decreed that if he were to be banished by either the Light or the Dark, the veil over the inscription would be lifted so that his son could continue the work that he started those many years ago. Jerrard had never noticed the words until the fateful morning after his return to Scalla from Shau-ling's palace. Once he was reunited with his bride Erika, they began to rebuild the kingdom that had once been so proud to fly the banner of the Raven. When the city was finally rebuilt, and a palace was erected for Jerrard to rule from, a banner bearing the symbol of the Raven was proudly raised from all of the palace's towers, and Jerrard would adopt his father's banner as his own. However, Jerrard swore that he would not venture into his father's crypt until such time as the world needed the information. Jerrard then met with Logan Ranthall just days before his death. Logan guessed that Basille indeed had information about the prophecies and the times to come, but he told Jerrard that to reveal the knowledge too early was too dangerous, and that any knowledge about the crypt should be forgotten. Logan had said that there were secrets, one in particular that could not be known. If it were, then it would jeopardize everything they fought for. To that end, with Jerrard's permission, Logan used what remained of his powers to seal those memories away from Jerrard's mind, but they were locked with a key. When the war began again, and Elwyne had passed away, Jerrard would remember his father's crypt and use the knowledge found there to aid in the destruction of Shau-ling.

Without the distractions of the coming war, Jerrard and Erika were able to lead a happy life. Together they had a son and a daughter. The son, Storm, was a proud young man and was nearly an exact duplicate of his father. He was the older of the two children, and by the time Taya was born, Storm had already reached his third birthday. Storm instantly became protective of his baby sister, and as they were growing up, the two were nearly inseparable. Sometimes though, this was not by Taya's choice. There were times when Storm was too protective of his sister, and it became very evident when Taya reached the age when she began to notice men. However, because of Storm, as soon as any man would talk to her, Storm would interject himself and scare the man away. While this was very frustrating for Taya, she very rarely would scold her brother. This of course led to Taya sneaking out of her room to speak with people, or she would wait until Storm was asleep to steal away to the inn to have a drink with one of the men from her father's army. This was normal life. However, normal life would change on the day the letters arrived from Aradon and Marcwell.

The morning audiences had just ended when the courier arrived. Jerrard and Erika were seated on their thrones discussing some of the morning business between themselves, and Storm and Taya were locked in a discussion with a member of the Army of the Raven discussing the day's training exercises. It was then that the doors to the throne room opened and a page hurried into the room.

"My lord Jerrard," the man said panting, "I bring an urgent message for you from both the city of Aradon and the city of Marcwell."

Jerrard's ears perked up instantly. There would not have been an urgent message from Marcwell unless something was very wrong, and to hear from Aradon at all could only mean that there was an emergency of the gravest importance.

"Read the message, quickly," Jerrard replied in an eager yet fearful tone.

"Yes my lord."

The page cleared his throat and then pulled out one of the letters that were protruding from his overfull pocket. After unrolling the parchment, he cleared his throat again and began to speak.

"To Jerrard Mystic, Lord of the Kingdom of Scalla and member of the People of the Dragon. It is unfortunate that this news must be delivered in this way, however, it cannot be helped in this case. On the third day of this month, the Lady Dragon, Elwyne Tamerlane Ranthall was found dead in her home. She was found peacefully in her bed, and it has been concluded that she died in her sleep. We could only hold off the funeral for six days, but we fear that by the time you receive this letter it will already be too late for you to attend. I hope that you can take solace in the fact that she lived her life in the way that she wished, and that you can take comfort that she was at peace when she left us. Her greatness and love have been a blessing to the world, and it is with some regret and some awe that I pen these letters that will be read by leaders of the greatest kingdoms; people that

Elwyne called her close friends. May the Light of the Lord and Lady Dragon comfort you in their absence. Signed, Torris Sandar, Mayor, City of Aradon."

Jerrard felt his heart sink when he heard the words that spoke of Elwyne's death. He did not know her well, but as the Lady Dragon, she touched him in a way that could only be understood by those who were at Logan's side in the throne room of Shau-ling. While everyone there was fighting for the lives of the world, they were also fighting to protect one of their own, Elwyne Ranthall. Jerrard had grown to admire Elwyne over the years, and their friendship had grown over time, and that made the news even harder to take. Trying to hold back the emotion in his voice, Jerrard spoke.

"What of the other letter?"

"Yes my lord," the page replied.

The page put away the letter from Aradon and pulled out the other sealed parchment. He quickly broke the seal and cleared his throat again before speaking.

"To my longtime ally and friend, Lord Jerrard Mystic of Scalla. Jerrard, please excuse the informality of this letter old friend, but time does not permit me to have Cairyn proof this before sending it. By this time you have probably heard about Elwyne's death, and I hope that this letter does not find you before word from Aradon does. As we have discussed many times over the years, this has been the sign that we have waited on as far as the fate of the Enforcers and of the Order of the Sword. By the time you read this, I will have already departed with the Enforcers to your neighbor Lakestone in an effort to determine Shau-ling's influence there. As you know he has always started his attacks on the fringe kingdoms, and one of his favorites is Lakestone. Some of my scouts have reported movements by Jeresei in the area, so my Enforcers and I will check it out. If we get in trouble or need to resupply, we will use Scalla as our base of operations. Secondly, the Order of the Sword should begin dismantling within the week. A detachment will be headed your way some time after that. I expect that Midarin will be attending Elwyne's funeral at this time, and her plans after that are not mine to know. I expect that she will return to her kingdom to oversee the split of the Order of the Sword, but you know how Midarin is, so it is anyone's best guess. Oh, by the way, remember what Logan said about Wolf. We are not to interfere with his path, whatever that happens to be. I will be in contact after Lakestone. Goodbye old man. Signed Pike Rhuiden, Lord of the Kingdom of Marcwell."

Jerrard sat back after that and exhaled slowly. The block imposed by Logan Ranthall had been lifted, and the memories of the secret vault returned to Jerrard's mind. It was not an invasive flow of information, it was just like suddenly remembering something. Jerrard stood and took hold of the hilt of his sword without a word. It was not that he was angered with the situation, exactly the opposite. He remembered the day when he found out that Basille was his father and the struggle that he went through trying to cope with the fact that his father was a member of the phasia. Now, with the help of his father's notes, he would be able to use Basille's knowledge to cripple the phasia.

"What is it, father?" Taya asked with deep concern.

"The throne room is to be cleared, and the palace is to be sealed. Send word throughout the kingdom of Scalla that today is to be a holiday in the honor of Elwyne Tamerlane Ranthall, the Lady Dragon. There is to be no business, courtly or otherwise done today or tomorrow. Also, ready the Army of the Raven. They will be marching in a matter of days. Send word far and wide that the forces of the Shadow have risen again, and it has come time to take the battle to Shau-ling."

The page faltered for a moment before responding to his lord's commands. Once the shock finally began to wear off, the page quickly bowed, turned on his heel, and left the throne room. Storm by this time had made it to his feet and there was an intensity in his eyes that Jerrard had never seen before. For years Storm had basically lived on the stories that his father had told him about the war with Shau-ling and the fact that Storm's grandfather was a member of the phasia. These stories had fueled a desire in his heart that he had never believed he would ever be able to fulfill. He knew that his father was a hero in the eyes of many throughout the world. Storm had always wanted to be a hero, but with no war to fight in, and no great evil to fight against, the chances to become a hero were very slim. Now though, Shau-ling and the phasia were back, and it was time for a new generation of warriors to take their place in the Army of the Light. The fact that Storm was a grandson of a member of the phasia almost destined him to fight, and now, it was time for that fight to begin. But as he looked at his father, out of the corner of his eye, he saw the look of concern on his sister's face. Storm knew that though Taya was a very strong woman in her own right, she was not the warrior that Storm or Jerrard were. If she were to go into combat against the forces of Shau-ling she would not have much of a chance. So, Storm resolved inside himself that when the Army of the Raven marched out of Scalla, Taya would be watching from a palace window with their mother Erika.

After a few moments, the words of the Lord of Scalla began to take shape. The throne room was cleared of people except for the royal family, and when the huge wooden doors were pulled shut, Jerrard exhaled again slowly, the pain in his mind from the sudden recall of lost memories subsiding, and sat back on the throne. The look on his face was one of stalwart thought, and after a few minutes of reflection, Jerrard stood again and addressed his family.

"Taya, Storm, the two of you will follow me down to the bottom of Basille's tower, there are things there that I must show you. There are stories from the war, and certain events that happened after which I have never told you. Those tales must be told now, and we must unlock the secrets left by my father. Erika, my beloved wife, you must come with us also, as it is you who can open the door to the past."

Erika stood and nodded. She knew this day would come sooner or later. Logan had told her during their last visit to Aradon before his death that there were dark times coming. She was one of the last of the first generation of heroes that still lived, and she was special in that regard. Old heroes were a rare commodity in the war, and in times to come, their knowledge and advanced age would give hope to the new generations. But there was something more to her role than just moral support. When Logan looked into Jerrard's mind and found the knowledge of Basille's hidden library, he also found the knowledge of Basille's attachment to Erika. As far as Basille was concerned, Erika was his daughter. To that end, there were secrets inside of Erika that no one would ever be able to guess at. Logan had tried to scan her mind after he had put the time release block on Jerrard's knowledge, but found Basille's mark hovering before him. Erika was protected in ways that Logan had never seen before and had no way to circumvent. Logan did know however, that the key to unlocking what Basille knew lie with Erika.

Erika stood and smoothed her dress before taking her husband's arm and walking with him out of the throne room. Erika had nearly reached her sixty-first birthday, and she was almost twenty years older than her husband. However, one of the gifts of being the adopted child of a member of the phasia was the rejuvenating touch of the Blaze that allowed her to age at a much slower rate. She had the look and the health of a woman half her age. Jerrard often found himself impressed at the ease and grace that his wife moved with, and this day, when the weight of the world was heavier than ever, was no different. Storm and Taya trailed behind the practiced and even steps of their mother, their thoughts lost to the words of their father. Together the four of them descended from the throne room down into one of the back corridors of the palace.

When the kingdom of Scalla had been decimated by the attack of the creature known as Nightwing, the palace had been one of the greatest losses. Fortunately, Jerrard knew that there was a blueprint that existed under the house where he was born. Jerrard found the blueprints and a map of the town which showed each and every house, and the name of the family that occupied it. There was also a journal with the events of the city of Scalla, day to day for all the years that Basille ruled it. Jerrard for a whole year took the time to read the journal and familiarize himself with man that had been his father. Jerrard was captivated by the attention to detail his father had. There were records of every birth and death in the city for the entirety of Basille's rule. There were also several cases where the speech done at a person's funeral were included in the book, because they were written and spoken by Basille himself. It was the blueprints though that received the most attention from Jerrard. He poured over every single inch of each page of the blueprints until he knew them like the back of his hand. Then, he contracted the best stoneworkers, carpenters, and craftsmen in the world to recreate the palace that Basille had called home for so long. Jerrard personally oversaw each step in the construction and checked and rechecked each and every measurement. If something were just a fraction off of the original specifications of the palace, Jerrard had it redone.

Overall, the construction of the palace took three years. However, when it was done, there was no end to the amount of comments as to how perfect it looked. No one could even tell that there was a difference between the old palace and the new one. There were some visitors who had not known that the original palace had been destroyed, who, when told, never believed that there had been a disaster that wiped out the palace. Now, as the family descended through the familiar halls and passageways, they began to take on a new an ominous presence. It was like they were walking back in time as they descended. They were going to unearth the thoughts and life of a man who had been dead for twenty-five years, in the very palace that he had ruled in for lifetimes.

Finally, the family reached the bottom of the tower known as Basille's tower. It got its name because for years Basille had used that tower as his own private residence. There was a bedroom just off the throne room, but that was only used for the momentary diversions that Basille had found himself occupied by over the years. It was also used for guests of high regard. Basille used his tower more as a place of refuge and solace. He could go there to hide, for years at a time if need be, and never be disturbed. This was where he conducted most of his research and wrote his books. Unfortunately, the books that Basille was working on just before his death were lost forever in the fires of the Blaze that Nightwing rained down upon the palace. There was a small steel door which lay at the very bottom of Basille's tower. No one knew how to open it though, because there was no handle and there was no keyhole. It was almost as though it were not a door at all. However, Jerrard knew differently. This was the door to the secret library of Basille, where his lifetimes of knowledge about the forces of the Light and the Shadow were stored. Now that the knowledge was back in his mind, Jerrard began to realize that there was more information in his head than there should have been. Logan had added knowledge to that which Jerrard already possessed.

In the days and weeks before Logan's death, Logan held many meetings with his old allies. Midarin and Jerrard received most of Logan's attention, and it was odd that Pike was almost excluded except for one fateful meeting. Most of the time Logan would talk about the visions that he was receiving from Aerith Seth, the person that had given him the mantle of the *Chosen One*. Logan's mind continued down a strange road as the days leading to his eventual death passed. He became obsessed with the war against Shau-ling and preventing what he called a 'disaster of such proportions that the war would never be the same, if there was a war at all.' His thoughts at times would go from the sublime to the simply nonsensical. There were times when it would be almost like he was arguing with himself trying to figure out what he would say next. Perhaps that was most of the reason that Midarin and Elwyne stayed with him almost all the time. They seemed to exert a type of control over him that no one else could. Jerrard could understand why Elwyne was able to talk to Logan, but Midarin never really figured in. Maybe it was because of Gwydeon, but there was no way to be sure.

As the new thoughts ran through his mind, Jerrard began to recognize the conversation. He and Logan had been talking about the phasia when the subject of Basille came up, and then the sermon started. Jerrard found himself lost in the torrent of words that came from Logan, a powerful somber look at the status of the world to come.

* * * * * * * * * * * *

"Life runs in a circle Jerrard, a circle created by the Creator and maintained by Emries. However, there are very few alive who understand the way the circle works, and the needs that the circle itself has. Basille understood more than any of us will ever know, and for that reason, his library will become the text by which the rest of our lives will be decided. The phasia, despite their demonic ways have to bow to the same circle that we do, and in truth their lives are more dominated by it than ours. We know that they are spun out again and again, destined to live the same lives in the quest for something that they can never have. We mortals bow to the circle, but whether we will be reborn or not, no one can say. But we are not mere mortals are we? Does that mean that we are doomed as the phasia are? I don't have an answer to that."

"Basille has studied the phasia since his birth, and I know that much of his information has come from the older phasia, Grawn, Bryn, and Ellis. I know that it was those three phasia that are responsible for writing the prophecies and giving them to Aralias Imstra. They devised the way to destroy their own master. However, I have a problem with that entire situation. Why would Shau-ling allow his own children to plot and plan a way to destroy him? There had to be someone else involved, someone of such power that Shau-ling could do nothing against him. I do not believe that Shau-ling is stupid. I think he knew all along what was going on, but because of the laws of the Creator, he had no power to intervene. Who that force was, I have no idea. But this much is clear. There are other agendas at work here, agendas that Aerith Seth is concerned about but has no true way to act upon. He has become frustrated with the war. He does not think that I can hear him, but I still can. When you enter the library of Basille after I am gone, you should concern yourself with finding out the history of the phasia. There will probably be some very unusual things there, things that will make you wonder what the truth is. I am willing to bet that some of the things you have always believed to be true may turn out to be a lie. Do not let this sway you from the path that you have chosen my friend. The truth is something that can only be seen through the right eyes, and a lie seen through the mirror of truth is a lie nonetheless."

* * * * * * * * * * * *

Jerrard had been confused by that last statement the entire night, but it was blocked from his mind the next morning with the rest of his knowledge. Logan had not wanted to hand any advantage to the forces of the Shadow. All they needed was another advantage. However, if Jerrard waited to open the vault until after the phasia had revived, then the forces of the Light would have a better chance at winning. The reason for that was that the phasia by nature were extremely arrogant. Once they began to take root, they would start to become buried in their own agendas, and stop paying attention to things they thought were harmless. Once their claws were hooked into other meat, they would not see Basille's library as a threat. However, if they found out about it while they were still hiding, they would have time to study and find the true threat behind the information and try to destroy the library and the people who had learned the information before they reemerged. Then, when the phasia did come back, they would be able to take the fight to the forces of the Light without the fear of what their former brother had left behind. But now the waiting was over. The prophecies had begun to take the center stage again, and the phasia were going to grow in power as the time passed. Already Pike was mobilizing his army against enemies that may not even be there, and time was growing short. The time to open the library of Basille had come.

"Erika, my dear," Jerrard said lightly turning back to his wife, "if you would do the honors."

Erika nodded and knelt down in front of the round metal door. She examined it for a moment by running her hand slowly across the cold metal, and then sighed deeply. Then, she removed the necklace from around her neck and held it in clear view of her family. There was a small piece of a black metal that for some reason did not shimmer like metal when the torch light hit it. Jerrard immediately recognized the metal as the same kind that composed his father's sword. Basille had always been a collector of odd or unique things. This metal was no different. It was at one time steel, but it had been treated several times with different magical and natural techniques. When Basille found the metal, he had it made into a sword, but decided that he would assist in the forging. So, he stoked the blacksmith's fires with the Blaze to the point where the sword became a conduit of Blaze energy.

Erika lowered the piece of metal to the metal door and touched them together. There was a flash of green light, and Erika was forced back and landed on her back. Jerrard, Storm, and Taya were also forced backwards, the shock of the brightness making each of them take a back step. When the light faded, the door to the library had swung open, and below it, there was another door, one more like the doors that would be found anywhere else in the world, complete with a handle and keyhole. Erika looked down at the keyhole for a moment and then lowered the piece of metal, and placed it in the hole. After a short breath, she turned the metal key and heard an audible click. Erika then took hold of the door handle and pulled. Slowly, the door creaked open, and a torch sparked to life revealing a stairway down into the library. The torch burned with an angry green flame which Jerrard instantly recognized as the Blaze. Together they all carefully walked down the narrow steps single file. As Jerrard reached the bottom of the steps, another Blaze torch sparked to life marking a corridor that stretched on before them. Jerrard looked back to see if everyone had made it through the door. By the time he looked back, he saw that Storm had just ducked his head through when the door to the library slammed shut.

The sound shocked Storm for a moment, but he quickly regained his balance and kept himself from stumbling down the narrow steps. Jerrard watched for a moment longer to make sure his son was alright before continuing down the corridor.

After a few minutes of walking, several more torches sparked to life in the distance, marking the edges of a huge room. The light in the room was barely enough to see by, but as Jerrard crossed an invisible boundary, a fountain of Blaze fire erupted to life in the center of the chamber. The room instantly lit up as if a small sun had appeared. As Jerrard looked around, he saw the rows and rows of book shelves and the desk that his father had probably used as a work bench. There were several scrolls of paper and open books on the desk, obviously the matter that Basille was working on prior to his death. Jerrard was pensive for a moment before continuing, but then slowly walked over to the desk and sat in the oversized seat and began to look over the papers left by his late father. Erika, Storm, and Taya stopped at the precipice of the chamber and were marveled by the fountain of Blaze fire. While Erika walked to Jerrard's side, Storm and Taya began to examine the books on the shelves. As the two perused the titles of the books, Taya stopped suddenly and waved to Storm. There was an urgency in her eyes, and her motions demanded immediate attention. Storm hurried over to his sister and looked at the books that she had been so shocked by. Storm was taken aback by the titles. The spine of the first book read 'Storm Mystic' and the second read 'Taya Mystic'. Storm and Taya then began to look closer at the titles of the books. Most of the books had people's names on the spines. There were names like Pike Rhuiden, Logan Ranthall, Midarin Rice, and Gwydeon Sandar on the books. Many of them were heroes in one of the wars against the Shadow. However, there were other books that had the names of members of the phasia on them, but they were all grouped together in a separate section of the library.

"Father," Taya said slowly, "I think you should come and see this."

Jerrard looked up from the rather confusing text about the powers of the Blaze to where his children stood. Seeing the looks of amazement on their faces, Jerrard stood and led Erika over to the bookshelves. When Jerrard arrived at the bookshelf, he saw the books that Storm and Taya were pointing out. He also saw a book with his own name on the spine, and without thinking, he pulled it from the shelf and began to look through it.

Jerrard was amazed to see that every single moment of his life had been recorded in the pages of that book. From the moment of his birth to his marriage to Erika and the birth of their two children was right there in front of him in black and white. As he flipped through the book, he found the last entries that detailed his trip down to the depths underneath Basille's tower to the very discovery and reading of the book with his name. Jerrard was shocked momentarily by the discovery, but then smiled to himself and closed the book. Somehow, his father had discovered how to keep tabs on all of the people he deemed important in the world. Satisfied that there was enough knowledge to tip the scales between the forces of the Shadow and the Light, he went back to Basille's chair and began to study more of the inner workings of the Blaze as written by Basille himself. Storm on the other hand began looking harder at the books, and finally found one that seemed interesting. It was entitled 'Lineage of Power, Generation to Generation'. As he began to leaf through the book, he found the stories of the passing of the mantle of the *Coromor* and the *Chosen One* from generation to generation. He also took note that there was a section about the *Erieal* in the book as well. Satisfied with his new discovery, Storm closed the book and carried it with him as he walked to join his sister.

Taya watched her father with interest for a moment as he examined the book with his own name. She had looked over his shoulder to read some of the words and figured out that it was his life in the book. She was then suddenly glad that Storm had not been nosy enough to read the book about her. Confused as to what she should do, she began searching around. It was just a matter of random luck that she ended up in the section that detailed each and every member of the phasia. As she was looking, she noticed that each member of the phasia had more than one book. She thought to herself that each book probably represented a lifetime and a rebirth. They had no individual markings on them that would tell the casual observer which lifetime the book chronicled, but she was sure that before long she and her father would sit down to read them. Storm was strong of body, but not exactly the smartest man. He excelled in feats of strength and physical prowess, which made him a natural choice for lieutenant in the Army of the Raven. However, what he had in physical prowess, Taya had in the way of intelligence and savvy. Taya was akin to her father in ways that Storm would never be. Storm did not have a knack for strategy or tactics, nor did he care about history or anything of the kind. Taya on the other hand soaked up all the information that she could, and would gladly sit with her mother and father to have deep intellectual discussions. Storm was ready to take the fight to the phasia and stand against them one on one on the field of battle. Taya knew that she was not able to stand up to a member of the phasia, but she knew that if she could learn to think like them, she could out think them. That was why, when scanning the titles of the books, naming each of the phasia to herself as she read each book, she was shocked to find four names that she did not recognize. She called out for her father as if she had just been struck, and Storm made it to her side first, followed quickly by her father and mother.

"What is it sweetheart?" Erika asked softly, holding her daughter and stroking her hair.

"The names on these four books. They're coupled here with the phasia, but they aren't names that I recognize. Rane Larion, Stryfe Cadre, Grimm Salde, and Cash Griffon. It looks like we have four more phasia to contend with father."

"Yes, dear," Jerrard said shaking his head and sighing to himself.

It was bad enough when there were fourteen of the phasia out there, but now there were four more of the bastards that no one knew anything about. There would be the contents of the books and that would be all, but there would be no notes from Basille. These new four would be more dangerous than anyone could ever imagine.

As her father was lost in the moment, contemplating the situation that would soon befall the forces of the Light, Taya shook off the shock of the situation and continued to scan the books that were on the shelf with the books of the phasia. She was struck by the fact that there was no book about Shau-ling, but then she consoled herself when she realized that gods may be above the kind of magic or power that a mortal, or a simple creation of a god could wield. Then two books again caught her eye. The first book was bound in black leather, much like the rest of the books. However, unlike the rest of the books, there was no simple title. The title on the spine read, 'Aryx Terian – First Incarnation of Nightwing.' She had heard her father's stories of Nightwing, so this book was no surprise. However, as she continued scanning, she found another book, a book that was not there before. She swore to herself as she looked at the large brown book with golden lettering that the book wasn't there a second before. The title of the book read, 'Aryx Terian – Son of Shau-ling.'

Chapter XXXIII

Strike Fast, Strike Hard

Creator's Calendar Year 1205; Dark Mirror

Logan walked away from his meeting with Midarin with a heavy heart. A part of him wanted to stay and comfort her over the loss of Gwydeon, but the other part of him remained a cold, battle-hardened soldier. Ever since Elwyne had been killed in Shau-ling's palace, part of his heart ceased feeling, almost as if he had one foot in the grave already. But he shook off the unpleasant thoughts of the past and finally looked up to see where he was in the palace. Shock ran through him when he realized that he was standing in front of the doors to the armory. Somehow the Elder had drawn him to them, and it was time for answers to be revealed; the kinds of answers that Logan had waited a long time for. After taking hold of the large iron ring on one of the doors, Logan pulled, but the door would not budge. He then took hold with both hands and used all his strength in the attempt, but again failed. Then he felt gentle warmth heating his left leg. Looking down, Logan noticed the Dragon Sword glowing again, but not a brilliant white like before, it was more like a light green. The color was very familiar, but he could not place it. Then it struck him. That was the same color as the Blaze flames he had seen in the Hall of Terrors and then again in Shau-ling's throne room during the final battle. Then the bright flash of light consumed Logan again, and he found himself standing in the armory right beside the huge cauldron that served as the home to the Elder. The astonishment wore off slowly this time, and Logan soon realized that three of the huge red worm-like creatures had risen from the molten metal and were facing him.

"Welcome Lord Dragon," the Elder said in a different voice then he had heard in the previous lifetime. It was not in the back of his mind this time, but assaulting his ears like the roar of a Jeresei. "This is a drastic time for the world, and it is time to tell you the truth of your existence. However, as it is the will of the Creator, we may only tell you this with the provision that our lives will be forfeit. Do you understand this?"

Logan thought for a moment. The Elder had always been mysterious creatures, even more mysterious at times than Emries and Aerith Seth. If they were going to sacrifice their lives to make sure Logan had this information, it must have been extremely important. After a deep sigh, Logan nodded.

"Very good. We are pleased to see that you are still alive Logan Ranthall, but that is not true, is it? Shau-ling's touch is upon you as sure as it was upon Aryx Terian in the previous generation. Remember Logan, there is nothing that we do not see, and there is nothing that you can do to prevent the course that you have laid for yourself."

"I don't know what you are talking about," Logan said defiantly taking a step back.

"Do not lie to yourself, Logan," the Elder chided. "We watched as you knelt beside the body of your wife Elwyne Tamerlane and scooped her into your arms. We heard the cries in your mind as you searched for some way to save her. All of the powers given to you by Aerith Seth were not enough to bring back the dead, but there was the whisper in your mind. The source of the Blaze was so close, and you had seen the kind of power that Shau-ling had wielded. You had seen him create life out of nothingness with his phasia, and the temptation was too great. You reached into the Blaze and wielded it as though it were your own. You gave yourself over to the side of the Shadow as soon as only a trickle of its power entered you. You surrendered to your pain and to your need just as surely as Cedric Binosear had in his battle with Shau-ling a generation before."

Logan's heart dropped and so did his eyes. All he could do was stare at the floor and listen to the words of the Elder. He knew them to be true, but that did not help his situation. He had used the Blaze to try to bring back Elwyne, but he must not have been skilled enough because she was still dead. Maybe it had been the will of the Creator that he suffer.

"That is a foolish thought," the Elder said glumly.

Logan immediately looked up in surprise. He had forgotten that it was a simple trick for the Elder to read the minds of those with power.

"The Creator had nothing to do with either the death or the failed resurrection of Elwyne Tamerlane. The blame for both lay elsewhere. This is the tale that we have traded our existence for, so listen well to what we have to say for we may only repeat the tale once. For all the evil that Draven has been endowed with, his is amazingly honest, and to that end we say that he was correct when he said that Shau-ling was not responsible for the death of Elwyne Tamerlane in the previous lifetime."

Logan was shocked. He had never expected that.

"Hold your anger and shock for a moment Lord Dragon, because this tale has just begun to turn in new and different directions. Cedric himself was not even responsible for his actions, just as you were not responsible for your touching of the Blaze. There is another power behind this, and he has been at the core of this war, the beginning and the end of it. It was by his will alone that this war perpetuated itself, and it is his will and trickery that continues to thwart that of the Creator. We can see the formation of thoughts in your mind Logan. You are seeing now for the first time what you were prevented from seeing, and what you must now see clearly."

Logan thought hard. The voice in the back of his head there in Shau-ling's throne room had been a familiar one. The identity was illusive, slipping away from his thoughts like an eel through murky water. But suddenly where there was haze, the Elder imposed clarity. The voice could have only belonged to one person. Emries. The revelation was like an explosion going off in his head. Emries had been there from the very beginning of the war against Shau-ling. He was the one that had steered

Logan and his friends down the path to Shau-ling, and helped bring the prophecies to fruition.

"Very good, Lord Logan," the Elder said before the thoughts in Logan's mind spiraled too far out of control. "But we have not yet finished. There is grave danger imminent for both the forces of the Light and the forces of the Shadow. Soon this world may come to an end, and there may be nothing you can do to stop it. The phasia have been plotting for a long time to overthrow their master, and perhaps this is the generation where it will happen. Also, the forces of the Light may be strong enough to strike a blow at Shau-ling's heart. However, I tell you that the real enemy is the man named Emries. It is he that ordered the death of your wife Elwyne, which spurred you to fight harder and kill Shau-ling. Without that edge you might not have been victorious. Emries does not care about you or about anything. He will stop at nothing to see his brother Shau-ling vanquished. And this is but a fraction of the machinations at work at Emries' hand."

There were many questions that Logan wanted to ask, but as he opened his mouth to speak, the Elder cut him off again.

"Our time in this dark world is at an end Logan, but there is more that we must say, so listen closely. You are the link to finding a way to save all of time and reality. This war is no longer about Emries and Shau-ling, the Light, or the Shadow. You must keep your mind open and follow the path that your heart sets for you. You have touched the Blaze, there is nothing that can be done to reverse that now. If Shau-ling calls, you must answer. But no matter what his orders may be, you will still have a bit of the free will that your Creator endowed you with. Therefore, remember this. While you may not be able to directly act against Shau-ling, you are still able to influence the battle. We know your mind Logan Ranthall, and we know the way that your heart burns over the loss of Elwyne. No matter what, do not forsake your position in the prophecies and strike at Emries directly. You will die faster than you could ever imagine and none of the powers that you have been granted will help you against him. He is one step down from the Creator, but we do not know how much of a step that is any more. Remember your patron, and remember your true role in this war. Go now. Our time is ended. Be wary in Sador. Nothing is ever as it seems."

Those last words spoken, the worm-like Elder retreated back into the molten metal. Then, slowly the cauldron began to melt in upon itself until there was nothing left but a smoldering ring of ash on the floor of the armory. Logan stood there in guarded disbelief for a few moments before turning to exit the armory. There were thoughts in his mind that he could not control and a hatred building in his heart that he knew would soon be beyond containment. Emries would pay for what he had done, even if it took the sacrifice of Logan's very life to do it.

* * * * * * * * * * * *

The Order of the Sword mustered out not thirty minutes after the assault by Draven's army, one of the advantages of keeping a high level of combat readiness at all times. The majority of the army marched in the direction of Sador, while a detachment guarded the wounded and those unable to fight on their travels to the mountain caverns that would protect them. The nightmare of Nightwing still plagued many of their minds, but the Order had won the day. They watched a stranger, a man called Pike Rhuiden by some, the missing hero from the previous generation, stand toe to toe with the metallic monster and survive. Though they had lost a leader in Gwydeon Sandar, Midarin Sandar still stood and still gave the orders to march. Alongside her was the legend himself, the Lord Dragon, Logan Ranthall. Most of the Order of the Sword knew that Logan had led a strike on Trelon to recover the captured members of his army as well as Queen Cairyn Binosear and Princess Sabrina Binosear. The raid had been successful, and now there was a pocket of the Army of the Dragon that marched side by side with the Order. Early the next morning, the banners would rise, and it would signal the beginning of a new age for the forces of the Light, an age where victory was not a hollow word. Sador would fall, and it would mark the first in a long line of victories for the Order of the Sword. However, as the marching soldiers took comfort in the power and courage of their leaders, Midarin Sandar was not as sure of their fate.

The horse Midarin rode had been a present from Erika Mystic Viruci on the occasion of her marriage to Gwydeon. The horse was from the lineage of the one that she had ever since she was a little girl in the kingdom of Scalla and Erika said that it would bring Midarin luck in the days to come. Even as Midarin stroked the mane of the fine animal she could not help but let her mind wander to all of the friends that she had lost in her short time as a member of the forces of the Light. She was a mortal, nothing more, just like her husband Gwydeon, and she had survived some of the most gruesome and pivotal battles that the world had ever seen. Battles that she, by all rights, had no business even being close to. But she fought anyway, and when the forces of the Light were victorious, she celebrated. But it was never without a price. First had been Eldar Merin and Lane Toridon. Then it was Arin, Jerrard, and Talon. Even the mighty Korrd Ranthall and the beautiful Elwyne Tamerlane were not safe, as they met their end at the feet of Shau-ling. And that was victory. But the worst losses for Midarin would come after the war was already long over. Scalla was the first struck, and Erika met her death. Then it was Gwillim in the battle to save Aradon from destruction. And now the Princess Sabrina, Pike, and her own Gwydeon were numbered with the dead. Only Midarin, Gideon, and Logan were left now from the original People of the Dragon, and she could not help but wonder how long it would be before that number was lessened even more. Who would be the next to fall? It was then that the horse and rider beside her caught Midarin's attention. Rachel Core had been a comfort through all the years that she had been with the Order of the Sword. She had the tendency to be a little hot-headed at times, but without Pike around, that was needed. She was a good warrior and an even better friend, but there were times when Midarin needed more than just a friendly ear, and Rachel had always been there through the uncertainty and the bouts of depression. Midarin didn't even know if she would have gotten through all the rough times without the help of the fiery redhead.

"You don't look very well."

Midarin smiled at the statement and shook her head.

"You are the master of the obvious as always Rachel. You must have something on your mind."

"Why do you say that?" Rachel asked smiling.

"You're never talkative unless you have something really important to say. It's just not like you to chat. So, tell me what you are thinking."

"I know this is going to be difficult on you Midarin," Rachel started sighing hard, "and if you want, I will take command of the unit of archers so that you will be able to stay closer to Logan and Nathaniel. With Gwydeon and now Pike gone, things are going to be a little more difficult. Sol, Ebios, and Evan have been talking and they don't know if Gwydeon's plan is really going to work. Now, I know we have all been together for a very long time, but without Gwydeon here, it's not the same."

Midarin guarded her first response for a moment and then shook her head. Part of her wanted to lash out at Rachel for the narrow-mindedness of the other generals, but that would not be warranted. Midarin knew that the fight which lay ahead would be the most difficult that any of them would ever fight, and the time would soon come when there would be a balance between the possibilities for victory and defeat and only doubt could swing the balance against them. As Midarin opened her mouth to speak, she spotted Evan riding back from the lead of the army. She held her tongue a moment longer, knowing the message that was to be delivered.

"Sador is in sight my queen, the time is now to split the archers from the advance. That is if you still intend to use Gwydeon's plan of attack."

"Yes, Evan," Midarin growled, "I still do intend to use the plan that my husband devised. Keep in mind that while he is not with us, his brilliance is. There is nothing wrong with the plan. I will take the archers down the path, and Rachel will go with you to command the advance through the paths. Logan will be responsible for the northern assault and then he will fall back to cover your advance to the western and southern gates."

Evan nodded. He turned away, but then turned back.

"I take it that Nathaniel will be accompanying you and the archers?"

"No Evan," Midarin replied shortly, "Nathaniel will be by Logan's side throughout this little endeavor. The archers will be fine without his help. Now, issue the separation order."

Evan nodded and rode back toward the front of the advance. Midarin watched as each unit of archers split off from the main group and started the advance toward the secret path through the mountains. Midarin turned back to Rachel the next minute and smiled.

"Everything is going to be alright Rachel," Midarin said slowly, "you'll see. Just stay close to Evan and make sure that he does what he is supposed to, when he is supposed to, and everything will be fine. I'll see you in the palace."

Rachel smiled and leaned forward to hug Midarin. Midarin was caught off-guard by the embrace for a moment, and then surrendered to it. Midarin could feel something different coming from Rachel in that moment, a dark chilling feeling like that of death. Perhaps she was just imagining things, but when she pulled back Midarin had the strangest feeling that she would never see Rachel alive again. Rachel smiled and rode away, leaving Midarin to sit in her puzzlement.

* * * * * * * * * * * *

The march finally over, Logan Ranthall sat perched on his horse and waited for the two signals that would start the most important battle that he had ever fought in his short life. The first signal would be the low moan from signal horn Evan had constructed during the trip. The moan sounded more like that of a baying wolf than a horn. The second would come from the young man sitting to Logan's left. Nathaniel Sandar was not the frailest man in the world, but his physical size almost made Logan worry. But as Logan looked at him, he could feel the hard echoes of power raging from inside him, almost so powerful that it made Logan's insides quiver. Suddenly the horn blared through the air, and Logan tensed, waiting for Nathaniel to give the signal that the archers were in place. Logan looked back to the young man, whose eyes were closed but moving back and forth rapidly behind the closed lids.

"They are ready," Nathaniel said in a low voice.

It was much like the voice that Logan had heard Aryx use all those years ago during his teachings of the powers of the *Coromor* and the *Erieal.* The sound made Logan feel a little stronger, but then it also made him afraid. If the young man ever learned how to see the strings of Blaze flame and how they tainted another's soul, Logan's secret would be revealed, and all that the Elder had told him would be undone. Nathaniel was the current incarnation of the power of Emries, and he would most likely be driven to destroy Logan if the truth came to light. Logan drew the Dragon Sword from the scabbard that hung at his side and cried out in the loudest voice that he could manage.

"Death to the Shadow!"

The din of the forces behind him echoed down the winding passages of the forests of Sador, and soon the answering cry from Evan's detachment hit the air. With the banners of the Army of the Dragon and the Order of the Sword raised high, the charge began. Logan could see the northern gate of Sador and the garrison station that lay before it. It only took a matter of moments from the beginning of the charge before the northern gate slammed shut and hundreds of Jeresei streamed from the barracks on either side of the gate. The fight would begin in seconds, and it would take all the tenacity that Logan could summon up to make it out alive. Suddenly Logan could feel a surge of power beside him. Nathaniel became bathed in a golden glow as his horse glided effortlessly in time with Logan's. The two of them would be upon the force of Jeresei well before the combined forces of the Order and the Army of the Dragon following a several paces behind, the gap growing larger with every heartbeat. Then it began. Logan felt a tendril of power emerge from his companion and snake its way into the void in Logan's mind, feeling for the powers that he had been granted as the second *Chosen One* of the prophecies. The golden tendril suddenly found what it was looking for, and Logan could feel a rush of pure power enter him. Some reflex within him wanted to grab for the Blaze, but Logan restrained himself and let the power of the *Coromor* and the *Chosen One* combined fill him to nearly bursting. Nathaniel was filling with power to, and when Logan looked down, he realized that he and the boy had floated off of their mounts and were hovering in the air before an astonished group of Jeresei. Never in all of his time had Logan ever seen Korrd or anyone with power be able to do what Nathaniel was doing, and only the great Aryx Terian had ever come close. Nathaniel began speaking, but it was not in a voice that Logan recognized. The voice was deeper, more powerful, and very angry.

"The Kingdom of Sador has long been known as a kingdom control by the Shadows. Even now I am sure that a member of the accursed phasia sits cowering in his throne room waiting for a chance to escape. I challenge you, whoever you may be coward."

The Jeresei stopped in their tracks, and so did the army that followed Logan and Nathaniel. They were all in awe of the golden aura of power that radiated between the Lord Dragon and Nathaniel. It was like nothing any of them had seen before. Over the next few seconds, a murky black liquid appeared to ooze through every crack and crevice of the walls of the palace of Sador covering the entire structure with a black film. Out of the film emerged a face that Logan recognized from the stories Gwydeon had told of his time in Sador. The face was pale with long white hair falling around it to cover the ears. Green eyes broke the monotony of white, but the jagged red scar on the side of the face was the most telling feature and an instant clue to the identity of the phase before them.

"Zarsi," Logan said smiling.

"Ah, Logan Ranthall and his pathetic Army of the Dragon. It is so nice to finally get to meet you, Lord Dragon." Zarsi's voice spat with pure sarcastic venom. "I must say you are looking very healthy for a dead man. And who is your charming young friend that can't seem to keep his mouth in check? Surely courtly manner has not been sacrificed by the forces of the Light. It was one of the few things that made you quaint in your pathetic rhetoric."

"I am Nathaniel Sandar, son of the same Gwydeon Sandar that killed so many of the phasia in the last generation. I am also the Lord Ram, the third *Coromor* of the prophecies. Your master was deceived, and you shall pay for his shortsightedness."

Zarsi seemed surprised for a moment, but then the cruel smile slowly emerged on his face, and after a moment he let a cautious laugh slip, but it did not touch the hatred in the phase's eyes.

"Come then, Nathaniel Sandar. I shall wait here in my throne room for you. If you make it this far I will be sure to end your pitiful little existence. Oh, and I'll make sure to send you to see your dead brother. If you are good enough, I will mount your head on a pole right beside his."

The huge visage of Zarsi disappeared a moment later, signaling the continuation of the charges of the Jeresei and Army of the Dragon. Logan could feel the anger begin to boil within Nathaniel, and he let loose a primal howl unlike any demonic sound that Logan had ever heard. As the boy thrust his hands toward the onrushing army of Jeresei, Logan could feel the surge within him that would release all the power that Nathaniel had stored. Instinctively, Logan pointed the Dragon Sword at the Jeresei and commanded a release of power as well. The beam that erupted from the Dragon sword was like a ray of sunlight piercing through the blackest of mornings. Jeresei that were not burned to a cinder where they stood were greeted with severed limbs and holes piercing all the way through them. Nathaniel's release came a few moments later, and it was unlike anything that Logan had ever seen. A wave of pure molten fire poured from Nathaniel's outstretched fingers until it flowed like a river and crashed down upon the ranks of the Jeresei. To say that the attack was devastating to the Jeresei would be an understatement, as the survivors of the assault numbered less than thirty. However, they were too close to the Army of the Dragon to retreat, and they were cut down a moment later without a single loss suffered by the forces of the Light. A moment after the massacre of the Jeresei, Nathaniel let himself and Logan gently descend from their perch above the battlefield. Logan turned and quickly rallied the troops, sending them to meet up with the rest of the army in the paths of the forest. When Logan turned back to find Nathaniel, he saw the young man standing transfixed, his eyes locked on the palace. Nathaniel had a different look now, he seemed older and more powerful than his feeble form had during the travel to Sador. It was as if the powers of the *Coromor* had aged the boy and nourished him with pure unadulterated power. But there was something else there, and Logan could feel it hanging like a shadow over the young man. Hatred had entered Nathaniel's heart. He hated the man that was waiting for him in the throne room of the palace, and Nathaniel would stop at nothing to see Zarsi's broken body lying at his feet.

"There's more to be done, Nathaniel." Logan said quickly, "stick to the plan and you'll have your taste of Zarsi soon enough. Remember what your father taught you and don't let your hate or your new powers take advantage of you."

For a moment the comments didn't seem as if they registered, then slowly Nathaniel turned and locked his eyes on Logan so hard it made the older man shiver.

"I want him dead, Logan."

The voice was filled with power and hatred. It was not the voice of a twenty year old young man who had never known life outside of his sieged kingdom, but more like the voice of a man twice his age who had fought wars. Logan remembered the same behavior and voice tone from his brother Korrd during the final acts of the battle in the previous generation. It had something to do with Emries, Logan was sure of it, but that had no bearing on the moment. If he could not find a way to exert some kind of control, then all could be lost.

"We need to help your mother, Nathaniel. The rest of the army needs us for the plan to work properly without too many losses on our side. This was the way that your father wanted it, and I'm sure if he were here you would want to do everything you could to help him."

"Stop treating me like a child, Logan Ranthall," Nathaniel snapped back in defiance. "My mother and father are dear to me, but they are not my only motivations in life. You go, old man, and do what you can to salvage the army that you created. I have other business to attend to, and by the time you are done with the pathetic Jeresei, I will have Zarsi's head."

Nathaniel started to walk away when Logan grabbed him by the shoulder and roughly spun him around. The young man seemed unfazed by the turn of events and struck Logan square on the shoulder as he turned. Pain rocketed through Logan's arm as the old wounds from the many previous battles were reopened. The punch was much harder than it should have been, and Logan suddenly saw the flows of earth coating Nathaniel's hand. He glared down at Logan with a look of disdain and power in his eyes.

"That was unwise, Logan," came the malevolent aged voice. "I could kill you with a thought and yet you still resist. Are you trying to save Zarsi from his fate? Have you given your allegiance to Shau-ling? You know that you have powers within you that defy all description and yet you refuse to use them. Why? You saw how I completely obliterated that huge force of Jeresei, and I know that you are capable of the same type of destructive power if you will just open yourself up to what you are. Use what you have been given, Logan. If you desired it, you could destroy the rest of the

Jeresei on your own without a single member of the Order or your forces from Trelon being scratched, much less dying. But you are content to merely fight amongst the mortals like one of them, only using your powers in the most dire of situations. I hate to tell you this Logan, but the situation doesn't get much more dire than this. The game is nearly over, and we are losing badly. Now wake up and use what you have been gifted with or curl up somewhere and die. Either way, get out of my way before I have to kill you."

Nathaniel turned away again and started his slow walk to the closed northern gates of Sador. The pain in Logan's shoulder was immense, but he forced himself to his feet and took hold of the Dragon Sword which lay on the ground beside him. It was agony gripping the sword and raising it into the common defensive position that he had used so many times in the past. If the road to Emries led through this boy, then that was the way it had to be.

"You're just going to have to kill me Nathaniel," Logan said as strongly as he could manage. "Because I'm not going to let you throw your family and your father's dreams away."

Nathaniel stopped in his tracks, sighed and shook his head. When he turned back around, Logan saw a different look on the young man's face, one that resembled pity. The look faded after another sigh, and Logan watched as a beam of white energy emerged from Nathaniel's right hand that formed itself into a sword.

"My father taught me well, Logan," Nathaniel said slowly. "I'll try to make this quick."

"Your father was never that arrogant," Logan answered trying to stifle his pain, "and taught me well also. Let's just see who the better student was."

* * * * * * * * * * * *

Evan and Rachel heard the roar from Logan's detachment of the Army of the Dragon and they both sighed before ordering the advance of the Order of the Sword. Sol and Ebios would be keeping the pace of the rest of the group until the first fork in the paths was encountered. Only a few yards into the forest, the first group of Jeresei reared their ugly heads. The Order held their ground and kept their ranks against the wild and formless assaults of the Jeresei. One by one the red-skinned beasts fell under the superior skill and numbers of the Order, and when it was all over, only a few members of the Order had fallen. Evan and Rachel had not seen any combat because the assault had taken place in the middle ranks. Evan saw the attacks as a sizing-up battle, probing the army trying to find the weak points in the ranks. While the attack had been unsuccessful, Evan and Rachel both knew that it would only be the first and the greatest test was soon to come. The charge through the forest was difficult as the path narrowed from time to time down to nearly nothing. Jeresei would seemingly pop up out of nowhere to attack making the pace even slower than it could have been otherwise. Rachel and Evan led the charge, cutting down whatever got in their path. When the fork in the path was just ahead, Rachel led one charge toward the southern gate while Evan led the charge toward the western gate. It was then that they heard the resounding cheers of the Army of the Dragon as they came up quickly to join the ranks. The stories were quick and garbled, but it was obvious that something extraordinary had happened. With a new found confidence, Evan and Rachel led their individual armies into the fray.

Evan's detachment was the first to encounter resistance as the western gate opened and Jeresei and Kalbraks poured through. The charge of the Order was immediate, and Evan raised his sword high and began to strike all that crossed his path. Blood flew everywhere as the feral nature of the Jeresei began to take command of the battle reducing it not to a war of skill but of strength and number. The Order was scattered by the unpredictable attacks of the Jeresei, and Evan found himself isolated, fighting enemies in all directions as the waves of enemies continued to crash over them. More and more members of the Order fell, but the bodies of the Jeresei and Kalbraks seemed to be twice that number. Finally the monstrosities stopped coming, and the Order rallied behind their blood-soaked leader. Evan led what would be the final charge as the remaining creatures were crushed under the weight and might of the Order's advance. After a quick cheer of victory, Evan sent out a battle cry and ran headlong toward the open western gate that would lead to their final objective, the palace of Sador.

CHAPTER 33

* * * * * * * * * * *

As soon as Rachel and the rest of the Order of the Sword emerged from the southern path, they could see the masses of Jeresei pouring out from the southern garrison, charging toward them with reckless abandon. Rachel told her troops to stand their ground and she waited for the inevitable. Suddenly the sound of a hundred bowstrings snapped all at once, and a hail of arrows plunged into the ranks of the Jeresei dropping many of them as the deadly metal tips penetrated heads, throats, and other vital organs. The second deluge was nearly as deadly, and the force of Jeresei was reduced by more than half in a matter of seconds. Gwydeon's plan had been a resounding success, and Rachel smiled in spite of herself as she raised her sword and ordered the charge of the Order. In a matter of moments it would all be over, and Rachel found herself gleefully taking strikes at the remaining Jeresei. Suddenly there was a sharp pain running through her as red claws ripped at her back. She fell to the ground and rolled in time to see the grinning face of a Jeresei perched over her. Lost in a sea of bodies and carnage, Rachel knew that her time in the world had ended and she waited for the strike that would bring her life to an end. The Jeresei howled and then dove and Rachel with its claws extended. At nearly the last moment an arrow slammed into the side of the Jeresei's neck, sending it sprawling to the ground screaming in agony. A second later another arrow pierced its heart, and after it finished thrashing around, Rachel took her sword and looked around. The battle was nearly over, but still she had been surrounded and no archer should have been able to make that shot. Then she saw the woman emerging from the old mountain path leading the rest of her archers behind her. Midarin Sandar was a sight for sore eyes, and as the last of the Jeresei were finished off by a combination of swords and arrows, Rachel met Midarin half-way, and quickly embraced her.

"I'm glad you're alright, Rachel," Midarin said first, "but I'll get a healer to look at that wound on your back. I need you in good condition because we still have a long way to go."

"Yes Queen Eagle-eye," Rachel said smiling, "whatever you say."

Midarin took a step back as if struck. She had only been called that once in her life, and that was by the daughter of a visiting dignitary all those years ago when she was still a princess in Brea. She tried to remember the name of the girl or of her parents, but the name would not come to her. Rachel did not wait for Midarin's response, and went to gather her forces for the next advance and to find the healer. Midarin issued her orders in a bit of a haze, and as they waded through the carnage toward the palace of Sador, Midarin was left in wonder.

* * * * * * * * * * * *

Logan and Nathaniel stood face to face with weapons ready for a fight. Logan did not want it to degenerate to this, but it had to be done. Something had come over Nathaniel, something that Logan could not explain, but he was sure that it had something to do with Emries and the mantle of the *Coromor*. The arrogance and malevolence of the boy was not something that he ever could imagine coming from the son of Gwydeon Sandar. It was the weapon being wielded by the boy that bothered Logan the most. The sword of energy had been forged purely out of the string of Order. That string was supposedly lost, but apparently Nathaniel, probably with the help of Emries, had found the string and was going to put it to its most lethal use. Then suddenly Logan felt as though he were struck as memories flooded his mind. He had been toe to toe with Cedric Binosear and had been able to rob him of his powers with the string of Chaos. Charged by those memories, Logan dove into the blackness of his mind and found the mass of congealing blackness that composed the string of Chaos waiting for him. He felt the slippery substance in his hand, and just as he was about to take hold of it, the string slipped out of his grasp. Suddenly the blackness of the void in his mind was filled with the green flames of the Blaze. The sight shocked him so much that he was left dazed for a moment.

Nathaniel had begun circling Logan when the confusion hit, and it was only Logan's reflexes that saved him from the long downward slash of the Order charged sword. However, in opening himself up to let his reflexes take control of his body, he opened himself up for the remnants of the *Chosen One* left inside of him to take control. Logan soon found that he was merely a spectator as that part of him that was still one with the *Chosen One* began drawing deeply from the Blaze charging him with the near limitless energy. When Logan regained control of himself, he felt as though he had been immersed in power and had held all he could while still being fed more. Nathaniel had taken a step back, and when Logan raised the Dragon Sword again, this time the blade glowed an eerie green, and the dragons that formed the hilt were no longer gold but a black color that made them almost look alive. The two opponents began to circle one another, each with a heavy respect for the powers at their disposal. Finally Nathaniel tired of the circling and lashed out with his glowing white blade. Logan easily blocked the attack. As the two swords connected, sparks of green and white flashed and hissed. Then the duel truly began as both attacked and blocked, slowly at first, and then increasing in speed. Each feint and strike was blocked and countered. Powers flowed through them, making their movements impossibly fast and dangerous. Thrusts blurred into blocks and counters, which blurred again into feints and slashes. Not a single hit was scored and yet they continued to whirl faster and faster in their deadly dance. It would only take one missed step or one unblocked blow for the battle to be over. The crash of steel and the sizzle of power filled the air as the combatants continued to flail at one another, only their skill and their tenacity keeping them alive. Finally, Nathaniel broke from the combat, a long jagged slash across his chest. Blood poured from the wound, and he breathed heavy. Logan stood perfectly still, watching the younger man out of the corner of his eye. His muscles screamed in defiance, but the powers of the Blaze were sustaining him. The sword in Nathaniel's hand disappeared, and he turned to face Logan, the blood covering his chest, stomach and legs. Logan had never intended for the cut to be that deep, but the speed of the combat had not allowed too much for the pulling of punches.

"It's over, Nathaniel," Logan said finally, trying to suppress his heavy, labored breath. "Stop this foolishness and let's get back to what we came here for. We make it into the palace together as a force fighting for the Light, not as individuals."

Nathaniel began to chuckle softly to himself.

"You are a fool, Logan Ranthall."

The voice changed again. Emries had only been angry once in front of Logan, and his voice at that time had been cold, hard, and vicious. He spoke of the future as if he already knew it was going to happen and all of the arrogance within him faded into quiet confidence. That was the quality that Nathaniel's voice took on. It was as though Emries had begun to embody the boy.

"The time of the Dragon ended many years ago, and you yourself said that you would never fight again. It was your vanity that brought you back into the fray, and it is your vanity and carelessness that will end your life permanently. Do not think that I do not know what powers you are wielding. You have touched the Blaze, and you have become a servant to Shau-ling just like the phasia have. For that alone I should end your miserable life. But I will let you live on this condition. Forget about trying to stop me and forget about this war. Stay where it is safe and keep my mother with you. Otherwise, I am afraid that she will be harmed. Do this, and I will never tell your secret. If you refuse, I will use all of the powers at my disposal to strike you down."

Logan stood and watched as the gaping wound in Nathaniel's chest slowly healed itself. The jagged edges of the open skin pulled themselves together and resealed themselves as if the blade of the Dragon Sword had never touched them.

"And what about the prophecies, Nathaniel?" Logan replied after a moment. "I have enough power to kill you, even if you kill me in the process. If you die, the prophecies will be broken and Emries will have lost."

The look on Nathaniel's face never changed, and the haughty smile remained.

"If I believed for a moment that you would be able to kill me, I would believe that you were threatening me, not telling a pathetic joke. Your time is over Logan, and if I have to kill you to prove it, so be it."

The next second, the sword made of the string of Order reappeared in Nathaniel's hand and he leapt at Logan. Thanks to the Dragon Sword, Logan was able to parry the blow, but was not able to counter. The stalking was slower this time, but Logan knew that this would be the last collision with the boy. Their swords crossed again, sending a shower of sparks into the air. There was a sound of thunder rolling in the distance and storm clouds began to gather overhead. Logan couldn't tell if this was Nathaniel's work or some random will of the Creator. The stalking continued as the soft cold rain began to fall. The look of determination on the young man's face did not change, and as he lashed out with his next strike, Logan could feel the powers of the Blaze surge within him. It was as though the rain was charging him somehow and tightening his control. The block and parry came effortlessly from Logan as his mind opened to the Blaze and the training of Gwydeon Sandar began to become part of him rather than just lessons in his mind. The speed inevitably increased again, as the two moved faster and faster through each form. Steel met flesh again as the Dragon Sword ripped at Nathaniel's flank. However, as soon as the blow was landed the wound healed itself and the boy continued fighting. The storm grew in intensity almost in time with the battle that raged on below it. Logan suddenly felt a stinging pain as he realized that the sword made out of the string of Order sped through his defenses and thrust directly into his gut. The spasm that ran through his body made him stop all movement, and as his muscles involuntarily tensed and relaxed, he lost the grip on the Dragon Sword and it fell to the muddy ground. Pain racked Logan's body as he felt death creeping up on him. Blood mixed with the water and mud at his feet and as he collapsed to his knees, Logan knew the end was close. In a few moments the loss of blood would overtake his desire to live and death would come quickly.

"I guess we see now who the best student was," Nathaniel said quietly to himself as he turned back toward Sador's northern gate. "Now it is time to introduce myself to Zarsi, and show him what pain really is."

With a simple use of the string of fire, Nathaniel melted the huge metal gate and stepped into the common courtyard just below the palace leaving the bleeding and broken hero of the second generation, the Dragon, Logan Ranthall to die.

The Shadow's Own

Creator's Calendar Year 1205; Light Reality

Storms rolled in over the city of Illimar, darkening the grandeur of the City of Lights. A feeling of dread and despair began to enter the inhabitants of the proud city, and each felt a shiver of fear wash over them. The signals that the wars between Light and Darkness would soon start again were apparent, and no one would sleep peacefully again until the war was over. However, deep in the bowels of the castle of Illimar a meeting was about to take place; a meeting that would help to shape the future of the world. The dungeon that lay under the castle had been sealed ever since the mad queen Saris had been overthrown by an unknown assassin. However, when it was revealed that Saris was actually the phase Caris, many feared that she would one day return to reclaim her throne. None would have ever believed that in the depths of the dungeon the very woman they feared had returned to await an old friend and sometime enemy.

Caris paced slowly across the stone floor of the dungeon, now and then stopping to examine the forgotten pieces of torture equipment. She had been happy in the kingdom of Illimar, strangely content with the power and prestige that it brought to her with very little effort. When Korrd came along and upset the balance, it was time for her to move on and take a new place in the war. It was her involvement that very nearly brought the prophecies to a premature end and victory to her master Shau-ling. However, things were never easy when dealing with the *Coromor* and so

Caris met her end thanks in no small part to her own sister Bryn. But that was in the previous lifetime, and there was a new threat to deal with. A new *Coromor* was soon to rise to battle Shau-ling, and it was up to the phasia to prevent that occurrence at all costs. Just as Caris began to get impatient, she felt the familiar twinge of power in the back of her mind. A portal was forming near her. She turned in time to see the portal open and a man dressed in black step out. Jeroch Yetre was a man that very few of the phasia could stand personally, and very few would ever dare to deal with privately. He was the most dangerous and favorite of Shau-ling's family, and to trifle with him usually meant death. It had only been a fluke in the last generation that he fell to Gwydeon Sandar, and a similar freak occurrence that had ended his life in the first generation. An outside observer might say that Jeroch had bad luck, but others might say that Emries hand had been in both of those fights. Things would be different this time around if Jeroch had anything at all to do with it. The two silently regarded each other for a moment. Caris knew Jeroch better than just about any other member of the phasia. He was cruel, calculating, and never modest about his abilities. He had more power than any of the other members of the phasia, but his control had never been honed to the fullness that it could have been. Shau-ling usually kept Jeroch back away from the battles until absolutely necessary, and that had caused Jeroch's skills to never fully evolve. But what Jeroch lacked in experience, he more than made up for in tenacity. There was something more though that Caris had always suspected. At times it seemed like Jeroch was holding himself back, unwilling to display his full potential to anyone. He preferred to work in the shadows, like his title, strengthening the capabilities of the armies at the disposal of the Brotherhood of Phasia and their master.

Jeroch's eyes instantly locked on Caris as soon as he stepped through the portal. She was one of the most dangerous of the phasia because of her unassuming stature. She was beautiful beyond compare, but her temperament and evil tendencies showed through to those who knew her true nature. She was cold, calculating, vicious and devious. She knew more ways to accomplish her goals without bloodshed then most of the other phasia combined. Jeroch's fascination with her was not only physical but mental. He knew that her abilities to read minds and direct the thoughts of others was without compare within the phasia, and that had always intrigued him. In the past he had tried to get her to teach him, but she refused citing the War for Power as her primary reason. She never forgot that he was the first born and that all roads to power led through him. However, if it did ever come down to Caris against Jeroch, it would be a long drawn out battle because they could predict the others actions.

"I came as you asked, Caris," Jeroch said trying not to sound overly cold.

"I know it is difficult for you to remain out of master's sight for too long, Shadow, so I will not take much of your time. I wanted to discuss Hawk with you for a moment."

"And Natalie I assume," Jeroch added.

Caris nodded.

There had been a time long ago when many of the phasia believed that the road to the throne of power required phasia children because of the restrictions on the power of full members of the phasia. However, Shau-ling's law only really permitted Jeroch to have children because Shau-ling believed that only Jeroch was truly loyal to the cause of the Shadow. This sanction caused jealousy within the ranks of the phasia, and reduced the ability for Jeroch to find a mortal to bear his child. Any mortal foolish enough to attempt to carry Jeroch's progeny would be hunted down and both she and the child destroyed. To that end, Jeroch and Caris launched a plan together in one of their more memorable alliances. They decided to have a child together and train that child in the powers of the phasia to use as both a spy and a tool against the other phasia and Shau-ling himself. The plan worked out beautifully, and before long, Caris was pregnant. However, when the baby came, there were two children, one boy and one girl. The boy was named Hawk and the girl Natalie. Jeroch instantly took Hawk under his wing and started to teach him everything about his new powers and the abilities granted to him as a child of the Brotherhood. Caris took charge of Natalie and raised her to be devious, seductive, and controlling like her mother.

Hawk turned to conquest through power of arms and eventually took control of the kingdom of Sador. However, that rule was short-lived as first Zarsi and then Gwydeon Sandar came calling. Hawk's death was hard on Jeroch, and that was one of the motivations for his duel with Gwydeon Sandar in the Hall of Terrors. However, that battle did not end in Jeroch's favor either. Natalie on the other hand had learned her lessons well from her mother and put them all to good use. Her travels took her to the seats of power in Trelon and in Marcwell where she gathered information for Caris and passed along everything she could about the movements of the forces of the Light. Natalie's greatest triumph however was her seduction of the prominent lord Alfred Merin. Alfred and his wife Ariel were in Trelon with their children Eldar and Eldric. Natalie used her prowess to pull Alfred away from his wife. She possessed a common woman by the name of Valerie Conor and seduced Alfred into committing adultery. Ariel discovered the couple just as Natalie returned control of Valerie's body to her. Ariel left Alfred taking their daughter Eldar with her. It was later discovered that Valerie was pregnant, and to save face, Alfred took her as his wife. Caris was pleased to see this, as that the destruction of a life is a wonderful thing to orchestrate. However, it served a better purpose later when the same Eldar Merin became very close with Logan Ranthall and the rest of the soon to be People of the Dragon. In order to keep the flow of information about the forces of the Light, Natalie seduced and married Eldric Merin, Alfred's son. Caris was able to keep tabs on the Merin family as well as most of Aradon through Natalie until the attacks began and the forces of the Light left Aradon under the direction of Cedric Binosear. Caris had her own means of spying on the Kingdom of Marcwell and all who came and went from that place, so she had no further use of the network that Natalie was slowly building. But the progeny of Caris Vale' and Jeroch Yetre continued, and a year or two after their marriage, Natalie and Eldric had a baby boy that they named Rand. The boy was the very reason for the meeting that Caris had arranged on this occasion.

"You remember that Natalie had a son?" Caris asked coldly.

"Yes, the boy's name was Rand as I recall. What of it?"

Jeroch's tone was unnecessarily harsh. The years of war between the members of the phasia had made Jeroch bitter and slow to let his guard down, especially in one on one meetings with another member of the Brotherhood. The last two face to face meetings that Jeroch had ended in the death of two other members of the phasia, the first being Saurn, and then Basille. Neither were pleasant by any stretch of the imagination, but Jeroch survived by his distrust.

"Well," Caris continued, "Ellis has brought me some very interesting news about our grandson that I thought you should know considering you have never bothered to ask about him. Whether you know it or not, he has your temper and your short fuse, but strangely enough he has a sense of loyalty. To keep a leash on him, Ellis and I arranged for him to marry Ellis' daughter Jessica."

"You mean the one with the fascination for bats?" Jeroch asked looking around the room, barely able to suppress a wince. Caris had always suspected the identity of Jessica's father, and Jeroch's reaction was all the confirmation that she required.

"Yes. As I recall she does have a fondness for the flying rodents. But Ellis and I thought it would be in our best interests that he be kept control of, and Jessica has a very strong will and has him well in hand. So much so in fact that only two years ago the two had a child. The boy, which they named Devlin, is the perfect collar for Rand. Now he would do anything to protect his wife and son, and therefore he is under our control."

It was obvious to Caris that Jeroch was losing patience with the meeting. He had begun pacing, and he did not look comfortable around the torture devices. From the look in his eyes, Caris did not need to read his thoughts to know that he was wondering when this little meeting would become a battle whose outcome would leave him stretched on the rack.

"Not to sound shallow, my dearest sister, but what does this have to do with me. I want nothing to do with Natalie or her son, I left her to you a long time ago. And, after the pain I went through after Hawk was murdered, I do not know that I want to have another child in the world."

Part of Caris was a bit wounded by the harsh words, but she let them slide past her, the pride over the information she held sustaining her through the insults.

"I went to visit Rand as well as to visit Natalie and Ellis when she and I started to talk about this war. You know how Ellis is, she always has a plan in motion. However, as intelligent as she is, she sometimes forgets that the rest of the phasia are not as brilliant as she is. She was very happy with herself when I arrived. She has discovered something that she said was so obvious she was disappointed that she didn't see it earlier. After several minutes of her rambling, I finally got it out of her that Rand is a member of the *Erieal* for this generation."

Jeroch immediately paid complete attention to Caris.

"I thought that would interest you," Caris said confidently. I don't have to tell you what this means to us, Jeroch. You and I, along with Ellis unfortunately, have control of one of the members of the *Erieal*. That is not as unstable a situation as Saurn was in the last generation when he thought he was in control of the *Chosen One*. We can steer our little puppet to do whatever we want so long as we hold his wife and son over his head. He will be helpless to act against us."

"Brilliant strategy Caris," Jeroch said after a moment of reflection. "Shall we go to meet with our grandson and pay our respects to the newest addition to our family?"

Caris was about to chide Jeroch for his sudden change in position over Rand and Natalie when a ball of black and white energy floated into the room through the ceiling. Only a moment later a ball of green energy penetrated the wall of the dungeon and floated in front of Caris.

"I suppose that will have to wait," Jeroch said, his eyes fixed on the floating ball before him. "Master summons us, so we should not delay."

With that Jeroch touched the ball of white and black energy and watched as it stretched itself into the form of a portal. Without another word, Jeroch stepped through, leaving Caris alone in the musty dungeon. At first, Caris wanted to ignore the summons, but she knew she had been away from the Council too long as it was. This was the first official meeting of the phasia in this lifetime, and it would be the beginning of a new era for the Shadow. Caris could feel a little bit of fear within her as she touched the green ball of energy and watched as the swirling green portal appeared before her. She swallowed hard and then stepped through, hoping that she was not stepping into the middle of a warzone.

* * * * * * * * * * *

Shau-ling stood in the empty council chambers waiting. It would only be a matter of moments before the entire council of phasia would arrive, minus a few members, he hoped. Taron had been sent as a gift for Pike Rhuiden, but part of Shau-ling knew that Taron would never peacefully allow himself to be destroyed no matter what Shau-ling demanded. Stryfe would also probably be missing from the meeting. Taron thought that he had kept his alliance with Stryfe a secret from Shau-ling, but there was very little that huge lummox could hide. Stryfe was still a young phase, he had many lifetimes left to learn who was the most powerful of the Brotherhood and who he should listen to. Taron most definitely was not at the top of that list. Shau-ling let his thoughts wander for a moment until the first of the phasia appeared. Jeroch stood proudly in his appointed place at the head of the Council. One by one the rest appeared, until finally the Council was whole. As Shau-ling had expected, Stryfe and Taron were missing.

"My children," Shau-ling started before any of the phasia could make their voices heard, "I have called you here for several reasons, and not the least of which is to discuss the scourge of the *Coromor* which once again fouls the lands with its presence. But the first order of business is to introduce you to three of the newest members of your ranks. There is a fourth new member, but his stupidity has caused him to ally himself with Taron, which should bring a quick end to his existence."

There were a few chuckles around the room.

"The first of my new children is Rane Larion. Step forward Rane and let yourself be seen."

The woman dressed in green stepped forward and received a snort of defiance from Caris. Rane could have been Caris' twin except she was a bit taller and her hair was fine and shiny. Rane's green eyes sparkled, and her body was impressive beyond any in the Council. She was not muscular, but appeared as though she could fight if she wanted to.

"Rane's beauty is not nearly as complete or as dangerous as yours Caris, but it is seductive nonetheless. However, my newest daughter here has a penchant for blood, and lots of it. I believe that all of you will find her a very interesting addition to the Brotherhood."

As Rane stepped back into her appointed place on the Council she was greeted with glares from Trece, Bryn, and Caris. Ellis did not seem to be phased by the newest sister to the family, but then again Ellis rarely was phased by anything.

"Next is Grimm Salde. Step forward son."

The hulking man that stepped into the light was a monster in every sense of the word. His size would have been equal if not more impressive than Taron's and his musculature was almost as defined as Warron's. The huge ax that rested in his left hand would have been enough to fell the oldest and largest trees in a single blow.

"All of the mistakes that I made with Taron, I have corrected with Grimm," Shau-ling said smugly. "Size and strength are a wonderful combination, but without a mind steering the body, you are fodder in this war. I believe that Grimm with soon make himself well worth the time I put into crafting him."

Grimm looked around the room as if sizing up his new brothers and sisters. After a coy smile came to his lips, the huge man stepped back and continued smiling.

"The newest lastborn to the circle is another impressive woman, however, Cash Griffon will not be running in the same circles as Bryn and Caris. No, she will be in battles alongside Trece and Grimm. Step forward Cash."

The blond that stepped into the light was by no means plain. Her face was attractive by most standards, but it was her body that was most impressive. She was very muscular and well built. Not only were her muscles well defined, but there were almost too large for her frame giving her an ominous presence. The sword that was on her hip was a less than subtle reminder of what she was bred for.

"Now my children," Shau-ling said as Cash stepped back, "three more of my children have been asked to rejoin the Council. This war requires that the circle be complete, and to that end, I have summoned Grawn, Bryn, and Ellis back into the Council. They have been forgiven of all their past crimes and those dark times are never to be spoken of again."

"But master," Jeroch said after a moment.

"Never, Shadow," Shau-ling bellowed. "The damage was done, and that is all that will ever be said. Do you all understand?"

Silence filled the room.

"Good. I see you are getting wiser in your advancing ages. Now, the reason that you were called here is this. No matter the infidelity you have shown to me in the past, I am willing to forgive. However, let this be known. If any of you openly act against me ever again, you will be banished just as Basille was in the last lifetime. My patience and forgiveness is at an end. This stupidity that you call the War for Power ends now. If any member of the phasia is killed by another member of the Brotherhood, that phase will be cut off from the power of the Blaze and hunted with the same ferocity that I have hunted the forces of the Light in the past. And before you allow your arrogance to get the better of you, consider my next words. I have recreated Nightwing to do my bidding and my bidding alone. It will not take orders from any member of the phasia. Nightwing will be keeping an eye on all of you, so be wary. An attack on Nightwing is an attack on me, and that will be revisited ten times over. If you break this law, I will personally hunt you down and destroy you with my bare hands. Do you understand?"

Again the silence was deafening.

"As I said, your increasing wisdom is heartening. Now, I expect reports from some of you. Rael? Trece?"

The twin phasia stepped forward in the next moment and bowed before speaking.

"My lord Shau-ling," Rael began. "As you requested, we traveled to Aradon for the funeral of Elwyne Tamerlane to keep tabs on the remaining members of the People of the Dragon and the Ranthall boy, Wolf."

"As we initially suspected," Trece continued, "Midarin Rice, and her brood from Brea made the trip to Aradon, as did the group from Trelon led by Cairyn Binosear. Gwillim Sandar and Midarin's son Nathaniel Rice were present along with Sabrina Binosear, the daughter of Pike Rhuiden. A man by the name of Jared was also present."

Caris tried not to let a frown slip past her well-maintained defenses.

"However, the anomalies at the funeral were our very own Aryx Terian, his daughter Lissa and a little girl by the name of Liette," Rael finished.

Shau-ling's face contorted into a scowl. While Caris did her best to try and hide her smile. She knew much about this interesting family, but she had not yet had the time to devise and plan to put her information to use.

"But worse was the fact the Emries himself was at the affair."

The frown became a scowl.

"Continue," Shau-ling said as calmly as he could manage.

"The ceremony was without incident," Trece continued, "but before the bells were rung as is . . ."

"The tradition due to the Old book in the church," Shau-ling finished, "yes I know, continue."

"The boy," Rael said, "Wolf Ranthall discovered a woman in the church. When she was finally able to speak she told the tale of her rather painful expulsion from a group known as the Creator's Torch Society. From what she said, it is a group that takes its teachings from a people known as the Moridon."

"A people we helped to eradicate," Erdric said proudly.

"As long as a people's beliefs are still being taught," Ellis commented, "that people will never be completely gone."

After a momentary pause, Trece continued.

"The little girl named Liette somehow sensed our presence. And it was because of her that we had to abandon our posts and flee. However, just before we left the area, we felt a string of power much like that of Aerith

Seth coming from somewhere in the forest. That is all that we have to report Master."

Shau-ling regarded the information for a moment before speaking.

"It is ours to know that one of the descendants of Gwydeon Sandar is the foil to our existence in this generation. However, I believe that he is not the target that we should be most concentrated on. My order is this. Aryx Terian and all related to him must be destroyed. However, whatever you do, do not raise a hand to harm Wolf Ranthall. He is not a danger to us. In fact, in time he may become the greatest ally that we have in this world. Also, the little girl named Liette must be dealt with. Do not let the frail exterior fool you, inside her is a power nearly as great as that which you possess. Remember the words that I have spoken today. There are other matters that I must attend to, so I will leave you now. Do not take it upon yourselves to attempt to start this War for Power again. That time in the history of the phasia is over. Ignore this order, and you will suffer the consequences."

After a long hard look at each of the phasia, Shau-ling disappeared.

"All of you have heard what the master had to say," Jeroch said proudly, "we should..."

"You should just shut your mouth, Jeroch," the irascible Saurn shot back defiantly. "Shau-ling has always had you on a tight leash, so naturally you will be threatened by him. It is just a ploy to keep us in line a little longer so we will kill the *Coromor* and the *Chosen One* and free him of the prophecies. Once that is done he will be free to destroy us one by one. I came back to this supposedly august body to prove to the master that I have not completely left my senses behind as many of you suspect. However, my aims and goal have not changed, and any of you who believe that following blindly as the impotent Jeroch does will result in anything other than your own extermination deserve that fate."

"And what do you propose?" Aldridge countered. "Start the War for Power, fight amongst ourselves, and then let the forces of the Light pick us off one by one like we did in the last generation? Sorry Saurn, but I'll pass."

"Aldridge is right for once," Zarsi added. "Last generation we were too passive sure that we could be easily victorious. But in the end we lost once again, and even our best fell to the sword of a mortal."

Jeroch frowned. He knew that Gwydeon Sandar had gotten the better of him in the last generation, and it did not help his pride when he was constantly reminded of the fact. His blood boiled every time that he thought of that battle. He knew he was better than that mortal.

"Jeroch had been weakened by his battle with the Flame," Farax said quickly in his high pitched voice. "Though I do not normally defend Jeroch, Gwydeon Sandar was far from a mere mortal. And coupled with the might of Pike Rhuiden and the rest of the People of the Dragon, it was too much for one phase to stand up to."

"And that is the point," Grawn said gruffly. "Shau-ling needed us to realize that as long as the forces of the Light work together as a cohesive unit, they will always beat us when we are divided. Rael and Trece always did well against the People of the Dragon, until they were split up in a futile attempt to defend the palace during the final assault. That was our downfall. We did not work as a group, we worked as individuals, and that is what lost us the war."

"You all talk too much," Warron said finally.

Everyone was caught off guard by Warron's comments. Warron was usually the last to speak, but his words often carried the most weight.

"Shau-ling's threats mean nothing to me. Your words mean nothing to me. This is a war, plain and simple, and we have a job to do. Make whatever plans you want to make and do whatever it is you think you need to do, but I will tell you this. If any of you get in my way, I will kill you. No matter what Shau-ling says, there is and will always be a War for Power, and I intend to win it. There will be no truces, no bargains. Stay away from me and you just might live a little longer."

With that said, Warron created a portal and disappeared.

"The same goes for me," Saurn commented. "I got very close in the last generation only to be cheated out of it due to the meddling of other members of the phasia. You are all on your own, and I will stop at nothing to sit on the throne of power."

Saurn's disappearance was a breath of fresh air for many.

"I had that bitch Lissa Terian in my hands, only to be cut short by Midarin Rice and her pathetic children. I can assure you that I will not fail again. We newest phasia will prove ourselves worthy if it is the last thing we do," Rane said coldly.

Grimm and Cash followed her through the portal.

"I am afraid that I have my own methods to get close to that little group, and as you know I work alone, so I shall see you all at the next one of these wonderful meetings. Oh, and if any of you see Warron, tell him that he can start his killing spree with Rane," Caris said stepping into a portal.

"I'll be sure to tell him," Bryn said just before Caris disappeared fully. "Well, all of my angles are closed at the moment, but I have a question for you Rael, Trece. What was this about feeling something that was like Aerith Seth?"

Grawn growled to himself and mumbled under his breath as he created a portal and left the Council chambers. Bryn ignored the hasty departure, but Ellis quickly created her own portal and headed through.

"There was a trickle of power flowing though both the land and the air, and it felt much like the powers that were given to the *Chosen One* however they were more detached, and seemed to have a much more potent power," Trece answered.

"Due to the memories of the Blaze," Rael continued, "we believed it was Aerith Seth."

Bryn smiled to herself and walked over to the twins.

"Why don't we go to Aradon, and you can show me."

The twins looked at each other for a moment and then agreed. As the three new allies disappeared, the remaining phasia looked hard at one another. The five remaining phasia had never been the closest of allies, and in many lifetimes past they had been some of the most bitter of enemies.

"I have business to attend to in Sarmeel," Farax said finally. "Most of you I am sure will like what I have been cooking up over the last few years."

After a hideous laugh, Farax disappeared leaving the other phasia grateful that he was gone.

"Well, Aldridge," Erdric said finally, "I am afraid that I am the one who needs your help this time around. You and I have a date with the Rice family too, only this time, you and I are going to be victorious."

Aldridge looked at Erdric puzzled for a moment but then followed. Erdric had done Aldridge a favor in the last generation, and Erdric was calling in his marker. As much as Aldridge hated it, he did owe Erdric a lot. Finally, there were only two people left in the council chambers. For many lifetimes they had been the most powerful forces in the war for power, but now, they had to find a way to be allies. Never before had they been left alone, face to face. In the past it had been too risky of a proposition, and as Jeroch stood there looking at Zarsi, he was not sure it was at all better now.

"I don't like you," Zarsi said after a moment of silence, "but Shau-ling is right. We need to work together to defeat the forces of the Light. I have a bit of an army still waiting for me in Sador. If you want them, my army and I are yours to command, Shadow."

Zarsi extended his hand. After a moment, Jeroch crossed the room and took Zarsi's hand in his own. It was a momentous day. The bargain that could end the war for good had just been made in the very heart of the Council chambers, and as the two phasia left through a portal, Shau-ling reemerged from his hiding place at the edge of the chambers with a mixed feeling in his heart. He knew there would be resistance to his commands, but he never dreamed at the amount of dissidence from Warron and Saurn. They would be the most difficult to break into the new system, and they would probably be the first to be excised from the new Council. He was happy to see that his newest phasia were at least somewhat loyal, but he was sure that Rane and her companions Grimm and Cash would be begging the older phasia for their assistance soon enough. However, it was the wild cards out there in the world that Shau-ling worried about. And naturally the plans of Caris, Erdric, and Bryn were things that Shau-ling could not completely anticipate or control.

What worried Shau-ling the most was the name of Aerith Seth, not the *Chosen One,* but the true Aerith Seth floating around again. He was a wild card personified. But as that Aerith Seth was the beginning of the war between Shau-ling and the forces of the *Coromor,* it was only logical that he would be there at the end. However, the only problem was that Aerith Seth gave his loyalties to neither the Light nor the Shadow, and so when all was said and done, the only winner in a war in which Aerith Seth fought was Aerith Seth. These thoughts were more than just a thorn in Shau-ling's side, they were a major worry. In a game were the balance between good and evil was a delicate thing, there was no room for those who could not see past their own interests, and as much as Shau-ling tried, he would never be able to breed that out of his phasia. Their shortsightedness would soon prove to be his undoing. As Shau-ling's mind drifted across the planes of time and reality, he could not help but wonder how much time he and the world he had grown to love had left.

The Definition of Courage

Creator's Calendar Year 1205; Dark Mirror

Lightning flashed, illuminating the darkened sky around the abandoned city of Brea. Upon the desolate battlefield surrounding the city lay the still warm bodies of both humans and Jeresei, marking the site of one of the most recent and bloody battles between the Light and the Shadow. There had been no clear victor of the battle, as the forces of the Shadow had retreated at the order of their commander. However, a new army had taken the field, hoping to find some resistance that they could crush. This army, led by the twin phasia Rael and Trece Starlin had found a different form of resistance waiting for them, their evil younger brother Draven Batoe. The challenge made and accepted, the twins dismounted their horses and watched as Draven levitated down from his perch in the sky and touched down on the blood-soaked ground. For a moment the three stood staring at one another. The first blow of the War for Power and the Battle for Ascension would be struck in a matter of heartbeats. Draven was the first to make a move, lashing out with a stream of fire that leapt from his hands and sped toward his enemies. Both of the twins were able to dive out of the way, and as Rael rolled through and popped up onto one knee, he unleashed an attack of his own, sending shards of black energy toward Draven. Trece too quickly recovered from her dodging dive, forming a bubble of Order in her hands and rolling it toward her distracted younger sibling. Draven sidestepped the shards of blackness easily, but was barely able to dive out of the way of the bubble of Order. Much to his surprise, the bubble turned to follow him, and before he could mount any defense, Draven found himself encased in a hard sphere of translucent pulsing energy. All of his attempts to break through the field were thwarted, and Draven watched as the twins pulled themselves off the ground and walked slowly towards their trapped prey, smiling brightly.

"For all his talk," Trece said wickedly, "Draven proved a very easy prey to catch."

As the twins laughed in unison, they took their eyes off the imprisoned phase long enough for him to draw the Sword of the Ram from his scabbard. Focusing his powers from the string of Chaos into his blade, he sliced at the hard shell that surrounded him. The sound that shook the twins was that of breaking glass, and when they turned their attention back to Draven, they saw that he had broken free and was brandishing the Sword of the Ram and smiling. Wordlessly, Rael and Trece each created swords out of their own strings. Rael's Chaos sword was a slimy concoction of black masses, while Trece's Order sword was perfect in form, weight, and beauty. Again there was a standoff between the three phasia, but this time, it was Rael that broke the silence as he roared with a feral battle cry and charged at Draven. Trece followed her brother's lead and together they slashed at Draven. With his heightened reflexes, Draven was able to block both of the attacks, but as that he sensed he was in a bad position, Draven leapt into the air and flipped backwards, resetting himself some twenty feet away from his assailants. With a look to one another, Rael and Trece slowly traversed the distance, waiting for some form of retaliation from Draven, and when none came, they struck again, this time with more fury.

The combination of blows came at Draven almost too fast for him to respond. It felt as if Rael and Trece had the same reaction speed as he had, which was nearly impossible considering Draven was wielding the Sword of the Ram. As he thought about it, Draven realized that while we was fast it was possible that Rael and Trece were faster. Rather than the added advantage of the *Coromor's* sword pushing him significantly past the abilities of his opponents, it was only barely keeping Draven ahead in the game. However, he knew that if he stayed on the defensive for too long, his older siblings would get the better of him. After blocking a blow from Rael's blade, Draven lashed out with a beam of ice which struck the man square in the chest and sent him sprawling backward into a pool of congealing blood. Left with only one opponent to face for a few seconds, Draven blocked the hard downward slash by Trece and countered, opening a wound in her right side. The redhead fell backward, stung by the harsh pain, but not letting her guard down. Rael had recovered by this time, rushing to his sister's aid. When the two touched, Draven could see an arc of power rush between them, and watched as the wound in Trece's side closed itself. It was not a permanent fix, but it would aid her in getting through the battle. Rael's look changed in the next moment. There was a hatred in his eyes, and as Draven watched, he was mesmerized by what he saw.

The very human blue eyes of the man named Rael started to take on a different appearance. The pupil widened and then elongated vertically. As this was happening, the blue of the eyes became sharper and brighter. Within a few moments, Draven was staring at a pair of cat's eyes. Rael's short black hair then began to grow longer, and the pores in his face and his arms also began to sprout thick black tufts of hair that almost resembled fur. The sword of chaos was quickly discarded as Rael's hands grew wider and his finger's shortened and got fatter. The hard callused hands quickly formed huge powerful paws that were armed with hard black nails that gleamed with a sharpened point. The change took only a matter of seconds, but where Rael had stood now stood a huge muscular black panther. There were hints of Blaze energy around each of the cat's extended claws, and though it was a beast, the beast had the look of intelligence in its eyes, and evil most certainly destined only for the phasia. Once that metamorphosis was complete, Draven looked to Trece who also had begun to change. Her piercing green eyes became more beautiful as they morphed into cat's eyes. Draven then watched as the color retreated from her hair and was left stark white, much like Ellis'. The slim frame of the beautiful woman widened and grew muscles atop muscles as the form of the huge white tiger became prevalent. The tiger also had powerful paws whose claws glowed green with the powers of the Blaze. Draven began to fear the combination, and he stood steady, waiting for the assault to come. The panther was the first to move, stalking in a large circle around Draven. It became obvious what the two creatures were trying to do. They wanted to divert Draven's attention so that the other could strike. Draven took several steps backwards, attempting to keep both the tiger and the panther in view. However, the tiger had begun to move and when Draven looked, he realized he had lost track of the tiger, then when he looked to where the panther should have been, it was gone also. Several times Draven spun around looking for the beasts, but they were nowhere to be seen in the advancing night. There were too many shadows and darkness filled holes to search, and Draven was left out in the open, practically begging to be attacked. A low deep growl filled Draven's ears the next second, and it was answered from a growl elsewhere in the night. Draven clutched the hilt of the Sword of the Ram tightly, knowing that the attack would come at any second. Scanning the desolation around him, he caught a glint of motion out of the corner of his eye. He swore to himself that he saw a white form moving out in the darkness.

Behind Draven, a pair of sharp blue eyes approached slowly. Each time the phase would turn and look, the panther would close its eyes and wait. Rael knew that Trece was keeping Draven busy, and he could hear her thoughts echoing in his mind. She knew exactly where Rael was, and she was doing her best to keep Draven jumping at shadows until the panther could get into position. Draven had turned again, so Rael opened his eyes and continued to crawl forward, inching ever closer to his prey. Only a few more steps would be needed and then a powerful leap would take the panther the rest of the way.

Draven spun again looking for the movement out in the blackness of the night. He had caught mere glimpses of the tiger out of the corner of his eye, and he was sure that the panther was just out of his field of vision playing with him also. Then, just in front of him, the tiger appeared. It stood straight and tall, looking at Draven with those impossibly bright green eyes. Before the phase could realize that the tiger was alone, the panther leapt from behind him and raked his huge set of claws across Draven's ribcage. The phase howled in pain and let the sword drop from his hand. The tiger was on him the next moment, clawing at Draven's face and arms. Draven had been able to get his hands up in time to defend his throat, but was not able to concentrate to activate his defensive powers. The jaws of the tiger descended and took a powerful hold on Draven's left arm, ripping and tearing at it, almost as if it were trying to rip it off of the phase's body. The panther was just recovering from its leap and was moving in for the kill. If Draven did not act soon, his road to the Throne of Power would be a dead end. With all the power that the phase could manage, he channeled ice into all of his limbs and tried to create sharp jetting ice daggers from his pores. He could tell his success when the tiger released its hold on his mangled arm and yelped in pain. Draven scrambled to his feet and concentrated on his defensive powers. Now any direct attack against him would be diverted and reflected. So long as he was able to keep both of the monsters in view, he would make it out of the battle alive. As if sensing something had changed, the tiger and panther backed away from Draven, sizing him up again.

The pain in Draven's body was immense. Blood flowed from a variety of cuts on his face, legs, arms, and side. His right arm was practically useless as it hung limp at his side, looking more like shredded meat than a human limb. He would have created a portal, but he knew that would require him to drop his defenses. He was too weak to maintain both uses of power. Besides, he was not fighting an ordinary tiger and panther. He was fighting two members of the phasia, and losing badly. He had gotten the fight to a stalemate, but that was a tenuous one at best. If the beasts regrouped and split up again, the chances were good that he would not survive the next assault. He had to figure out a way to get enough time to create a portal and still keep his defenses up. However, time was against Draven as that he was slowly bleeding to death.

The Blaze energy that was coupled with each of the claw strikes from the beasts was eating him up from the inside, and it would kill him before the loss of blood would. Even though the Blaze infused and sustained the phasia, in its raw form it was a vicious parasite that devoured everything it could. It poisoned the blood, rotted the flesh, and burned everything it touched until there was nothing left but the Blaze.

The twins seemed to be plotting their next attack as they stood looking at the wounded phase. Suddenly there was a howl from another animal. It sounded vaguely like a wolf but with a much different pitch and timber, higher and discordant like that of a female wolf. Just as suddenly, Draven felt pain rack his body again as a set of sharp teeth buried themselves into the back of his right leg, severing his hamstring, sending him to the ground flailing his one good arm helplessly. His immediate reactions taking precedent, Draven dropped his defenses and opened a small portal on the ground he was rapidly falling toward. It was only at the last second he saw the gleaming hilt of the Sword of the Ram out of the corner of his eye and made a lunging grab for it with his remaining good arm. Sensing the creation of the portal, both the panther and the tiger leapt at Draven that next instant. While their claws were able to rip more of his flesh, they were not able to stop him from going through the portal. Draven had escaped his death with his precious weapon still firmly in his possession, and as the portal sealed behind him, the twins were left facing their unexpected ally, a petite gray wolf.

The tiger and panther stood looking at the wolf for a moment, but did not know what to do. It was obvious that the wolf was trying to help in its attack against Draven, but only a member of the phasia would do something of that nature. In the next moment, the twin's silent question was answered as the wolf stood up on its hind legs and began to change. The legs and feet of the wolf straightened and elongated to form an exquisite and very feminine pair of human legs. The same was true of the arms and the body. The hair from the wolf form disappeared leaving only the beautiful bare skin of the woman behind. It was obviously soft and well pampered skin without a single flaw or wrinkle. The last part of the woman to revert to human form was the face. There was very little change to the stark blue eyes, other than the color fading a bit. When the human hair returned and fell down upon the woman's naked shoulders, the formation of the face was only cursory. The twins knew the phase who stood before them very well. She was the seductress of the Brotherhood, the phase Caris.

Caris stood naked for a moment before the two creatures and then allowed the tight green dress form around her body. She waited and watched silently as the twins resumed their human forms. Caris giggled a bit to herself noting that their transformation was not as graceful as hers, but then again, no member of the phasia ever was as graceful as she. The silence was broken the next moment by the obviously irate voice of Trece.

"We had him under control, Caris," Trece said with venom, "and it was your interference that let him get away. I hope you have an explanation for this, otherwise Rael and I will take out our frustrations on you."

"Calm down little sister," Caris replied smoothly. "There will be other days for you to take your measure of flesh out of Draven. You know that you can beat him in a fair fight, that is good, and a psychological edge that you can hold over his head. It will change his tactics the next time, make him more desperate and timid, and it will also force him to cheat. All of those things you can manipulate and use to your advantage. But now is not the time for him to be taken out of this little game. He is serving his purpose, of that you can be sure. He has flushed Midarin Sandar out into the open, and I have a little bit of a score to settle with her and that pitiful Logan Ranthall. I need your help in getting to them, and when we succeed, I'll help you take out Draven."

Rael and Trece looked at each other for a long moment, the unspoken conversation raging before Trece silently nodded and Rael returned his gaze to their older sister.

"It's a deal Caris," Rael responded, "we help you get Logan Ranthall and Midarin Sandar, and then you help us get Draven."

"But after that," Trece added, "all bets are off, and you and I will have a score to settle over this little incident."

Caris laughed.

"My darling little sister, you're so cute when you're angry. You should have followed the example that Bryn and I put forth and become a seductress like us. You have the body and most certainly the mind for it."

Caris reached forward and laid her hand on Trece's shoulder.

"You and I could grow to be great friends if you just gave me a chance."

"Said the spider to the fly," Trece recited as she brushed Caris' hand from her shoulder. "There are no friends amongst the phasia during the War for Power, you know that. We will honor our end of the bargain, just make sure that you honor yours."

Caris nodded and then created a portal that would lead the three of them to the city of Sador.

* * * * * * * * * * *

Deep in the bowels of the palace in the kingdom of Scalla, Princess Sabrina Binosear huddled herself in a corner wondering what would happen to her next. After walking through the portal with Pike in Brea, Sabrina had found herself dropped through another portal into a black room with a throne on one end of it. She had only a moment to get acclimated to her surroundings as a woman with white skin and hair, wearing nearly nothing walked into the room and took hold of her. Sabrina was immediately locked in a dank dark room just off the dungeon and left waiting for something. She knew in her heart that Nightwing had not honored the deal that Pike had made for her, and that soon she would be face to face with Draven again. She shivered to herself whenever that name or his face entered her mind. The horrible night that she had spent in Trelon under his 'care' had been the most horrible nightmare that she had ever experienced. She was trying to shut out the pain, but no matter what she tried, the nightmare still haunted her. The only peace she found was in her thoughts of Pike Rhuiden. He had been her salvation in Trelon, and she knew in her heart that he would come to save her once again. She had no reason to believe it, but somehow she knew she would be saved. Then there was a stirring somewhere inside of her. There was a power rushing into the room unlike anything that she had ever felt before. In the far wall of the room, a single pinpoint of blue light appeared. The point of light slowly grew, and within it Sabrina could see the cyclical pattern as the waves of light circled in on themselves. She had seen phasia portals before, but she had never seen one form so slowly. Then, a man stepped gently through the portal. Dressed in black pants and a white shirt, Gwydeon Sandar was a stunning man. To Sabrina he looked more like an angel with a glow around him like the sun itself. She wanted to shout at the top of her lungs with joy, but the familiar calming voice in the back of her mind made her hold back the cry and slowly get to her feet. Gwydeon put a finger to his lips as soon as he locked his eyes on the girl and then turned his attention back to the portal. He closed his eyes for a moment, and the portal disappeared as though it were never really there to begin with. Sabrina was a bit surprised, knowing that phasia portals always closed the same way they opened. The puzzled look was answered by Gwydeon's famous smile. He extended his hand to the girl and she walked quickly over to him and put her hand in his. Suddenly a powerful sensation ran through her. It was like a cold chill, but harsher. The girl shrank back away from him as if struck, and Gwydeon did his best to silently reassure her. He knew what she was feeling, but there was nothing he could do about it. Nightwing was still a part of him. She would have to make peace with that. After a moment, Sabrina fought through the feeling and took hold of Gwydeon's hand. He smiled warmly down to her and made his way toward the door of the room. Sabrina wanted to resist, knowing what was on the other side of the door, but she followed, trusting that Gwydeon knew what he was doing.

The door opened, and Gwydeon stuck his head out looking around. To his right he saw the exquisite form of Vengeance. She was standing with her back to the door, and apparently Gwydeon had been quiet enough to keep her from hearing him. After waiting a few moments, Gwydeon kicked the door hard, sending it slamming against the stone wall, alerting anyone within earshot. Vengeance spun around quickly, the lightning blade materializing in her hand almost instantly. That was what Gwydeon wanted to see. Her reactions were no quicker than that of a normal mortal, and despite the speed at which her weapon materialized, it was enough of a delay to be exploited. Given the opportunity, he would have enough time to kill her before she could use her powers to alter reality. It would have to be a concise and powerful blow that she could not recover from, otherwise the battle would be over. Vengeance did not ease her stance when she saw Gwydeon emerge from the room with the girl in tow, in fact she took a step forward and readied her sword for a fight.

"Step aside Vengeance," Gwydeon said in a voice that was strong and full of hate. "Draven will be back soon and he will want Sabrina as soon as he arrives."

Vengeance did not move.

"I'm sure that you do not want to disappoint him," Gwydeon added after a moment.

After taking that into consideration, Vengeance lowered the sword and let it fade into nothingness before stepping out of Gwydeon's path. After a cruel, very unnatural smile, Gwydeon led Sabrina into Draven's throne room. The rest of the Dark Riders had already assembled, and most of them took a shocked notice to Gwydeon. They knew Gwydeon Sandar as an enemy while they knew Nightwing as a friend. It would take them all some time to get used to the duality. Neither Gwydeon nor the Dark Riders had time to react before a portal appeared in the middle of the room and a very tattered Draven spilled out onto the floor. Holocaust and Shadow were quick to aid their fallen master, and when Gwydeon got a good look at Draven's mangled form, he cringed. Claw marks covered both of Draven's cheeks, and there were many more on his arms and legs. One large set of marks dominated each of his sides, and the blood still trickled from the jagged wounds. His right arm and right leg however showed the most damage. The teeth marks on his leg and the huge protruding tendon rolled up to the back of his knee showed why Draven was unable to walk. Someone or something had bitten though Draven's hamstring and calf, freeing the tendon from its moorings at the base of his ankle. Because of the tightness of Draven's muscles and his lean build. The tendon had rolled itself into a ball which ruptured the tight skin and collected itself at the back of his knee. Most of the blood loss had occurred from this wound, but Draven had somehow managed to stop the bleeding. His right arm was also badly damaged. The bite marks on his upper and lower arm merged into a mess of bloody punctures that had reduced the arm to mincemeat. In fact, the tendons of Draven's shoulder were barely able to support the dead weight of the limb. With the help of two of his Dark Riders he was able to hobble his way to the throne. Vengeance immediately went to work, slowly transferring the wounds to Wrath, trying not to shock either of them too much in the process. Each wound would take time, and none of them would be easy.

"Those bastard children Rael and Trece did this to me. I had them beaten until someone else interfered. Holocaust, Shadow, Flame; find out where they are, and who helped them. Then, when you find that out, kill them all. And Shadow, nothing cute this time. This is not an assassination, this is revenge. Make is messy, painful, and permanent."

Holocaust threw back its skull head and cackled loudly before the three of them disappeared into a portal. Gwydeon smiled to himself. The numbers were down to three against one, and Gwydeon actually felt like he had a chance, especially without Draven at full strength. Part of him though could not help but feel sorry for Rael and Trece. They had no idea of the war they had started. Draven looked directly at Gwydeon and then smiled.

"Nightwing good. I see that you followed orders. I also liked the way that you led my army. However, you should have let Brea be destroyed."

"That was not what you ordered Draven," Gwydeon answered. "You wanted me to get the girl for you, so I got the girl."

Sabrina pulled away from Gwydeon and looked up at him in horror.

"Just putting the pieces together are we my sweet?" Draven said laughing. "Gwydeon is no longer an agent for the forces of the Light. He is now my little puppet, Nightwing."

Gwydeon did not flinch and kept his eyes locked on Draven. After a moment he looked down to Sabrina and mouthed the words, "trust me."

"Nightwing, take the girl to my bedroom. I will pay her a lengthy visit as soon as Vengeance is finished with her duties healing me. Then I will have you pay my respects to a few members of the phasia with Wrath's help. The two of you should make a good team."

Wrath chuckled.

"Now go."

"No," Gwydeon answered.

"Good boy it nice when you're . . . what?" Draven said sitting up. "Did you say no?"

Gwydeon stood defiantly.

"You cannot defy me Gwydeon, remember our deal. You do what I say and I don't harm your family, remember? You don't want me to send Wrath here after Midarin and Nathaniel do you?"

Gwydeon continued to stand silently.

"I thought not. Now, take the girl to my room as I have ordered and then report back here."

Gwydeon did not move.

"No Draven. Our deal is now null and void."

In a split second, the Nightwing armor burst through Gwydeon's skin and fastened itself around him. No one in the throne room was able to react fast enough to counter what Nightwing would do next. He opened his mouth wide and let a single beam of white death erupt toward Vengeance. The beam hit her, and a moment later she was reduced to a smoldering pile of ashes.

"NOW WE ARE EVEN, DRAVEN," Nightwing said in a cold metallic voice. "THAT WAS FOR GWILLIM."

"Now you are dead," Draven said in such anger that it was obvious it was consuming him to the very core. "Wrath, destroy Nightwing."

The huge monstrosity named Wrath raised its scimitar, which stood as tall as Nightwing, and took one thundering step forward. Nightwing took to the air the next moment, taking Sabrina in his arms and flew toward the domed ceiling of the throne room. A beam of white fire erupted from his widened jaws the next moment, searing a hole in the ceiling large enough for him to fly through. Wrath stood watching for a moment and then looked over to Draven.

"What are you waiting for?" Draven screamed. "Get him!"

Wrath took to the air the next moment, his huge leathery wings flapping and raising his massive bulk into the air. The roof of the throne room shattered as Wrath's horns and hard head butted their way through. Nightwing watched as the massive beast rose into the air and Nightwing waited. In a matter of seconds the monster would be upon him. Resolving a battle plan, Nightwing created a portal below where they hovered and dropped Sabrina into it, praying that she would make it to safety. Then, he pulled two of the bladed feathers from his wings and waited for Wrath to arrive. The two Blaze creations hovered before one another, sizing each other up. Wrath charged in, slashing hard with his massive blade. Nightwing blocked the assault, but the sheer power behind the blow sent the metallic creature tumbling through the air, out of control. He was able to recover in time for the next attack by Wrath, a quick thrust with the curved point of his scimitar. Nightwing dove under the blow and sped toward the exposed stomach of the massive beast. The tip of Nightwing's sword penetrated the thick hide of the monster, but instead of crying out in pain, Wrath laughed in a low bellowing voice. The sword was extracted and the piece of metal discarded like a person would discard a toothpick. Nightwing hovered there for a moment marveling at the impressive creature, when he began to recall memories from the Blaze. Nightwing had faced difficult opposition in the past, and Wrath was no different. All it would take was opportunity. Nightwing would have to use his speed to get through Wrath's defenses to make the plan work. Suddenly another slash fell toward Nightwing, and he darted out of the way in enough time to strike at Wrath's hand with his remaining sword. The blow broke the flesh on the massive clawed hand, but it did not cause enough of a wound to make the huge creature drop his sword. However, the retaliatory strike with the back of Wrath's other hand sent Nightwing tumbling again, this time though when Nightwing righted himself he barely had time to breathe before he was struck again. This strike consisted of a huge fist pounding the metallic creature down toward the ground. By all rights, the blow should have shattered Nightwing's armor, but the fact that it was forged out of *Debuisa* metal made it able to withstand more punishment. The ground rushed up at Nightwing at an amazing speed. It was only by mere inches that he was able to pull out of the uncontrolled and tumbling descent and set himself down gently on the ground. Wrath still hovered high in the skies above Nightwing, laughing down at him. Nightwing knew that he had very little time left in the battle before Wrath's strength would completely overwhelm him. Pulling another two of the bladed feathers from his wings, Nightwing concentrated a moment and using the elemental nature of the *Debuisa* metal changed the composition of the blades to that of a dense compound that had a tendency to explode when introduced to fire. Armed with his two new weapons, Nightwing launched himself straight upward and zoomed toward Wrath with as much speed as his wings could manage. The timing would have to be perfect, and Nightwing would risk that he would not survive this attack. Wrath hovered in the same position, waiting for Nightwing to veer away. However, Nightwing had nothing of the sort in mind. The collision would happen in only a matter of seconds, and Wrath had no time to evade. The tips of the two swords stuck Wrath's chest, and in that split second Nightwing channeled all of the control he had over the primal elemental string of fire into the *Debuisa* metal until the metal itself was wreathed in white-hot flame. The searing heat activated the explosive element of the swords and a massive explosion ripped through the body of Wrath and created a massive fireball in midair that shown brighter than the full moon that hung low in the sky. Large chunks of the massive body of Wrath began to fall from the sky, hitting in various places around the city of Scalla. When the smoke cleared in the air, the only creature still left was Nightwing. There were no holes in his armor, and as he flew back toward the throne room of Scalla, all he could think of was taking his revenge on Draven.

* * * * * * * * * * * *

Draven watched as Wrath sped after Nightwing, and he knew it would not be long before Nightwing came back looking for him. It was not that he was doubting the abilities of one of his Dark Riders, but he made the mistake of underestimating the resourcefulness of Gwydeon Sandar once, and he did not intend to make that same mistake again. Vengeance was not completely unsalvageable, her sword still remained intact, so it would only be a matter of time before she was able to warp reality to bring herself back to life. However, he could not wait that long. Using his powers over the Blaze, he manipulated the reality altering properties of Vengeance's sword and began to repair his body. He had just repaired his leg when he heard the explosion rip through the heavens. Time was short, and it was apparent that the battle between the two members of the Dark Riders was over. He concentrated the last of the powers of the sword on his arm, and by the time Nightwing launched himself back into the throne room, Draven was almost completely back at fighting strength. Nightwing regarded Draven for a moment, and then the armor began to retract, showing the man beneath.

"Well, Gwydeon," Draven said moving his newly repaired arm around, checking its strength and movement, "I must admit that I am impressed. Not only did you last more than a minute against Wrath, you were able to save the girl and kill the beast in under ten. Next time I will have to make sure that I pattern all of my Dark Riders after you."

"There won't be a next time, Draven," Gwydeon said proudly. "I'll make sure of that."

"Oh," Draven said drawing the Sword of the Ram, "this is the part where we're supposed to fight and you're supposed to kill me. Sorry hero, that's not how this story goes. Remember, the bad guys win this one, and that means me. So, get ready for a lot of pain Gwydeon, because I want to take my time and remember every bit of this."

Draven leapt from the dais the next moment and took a long hard slash at Gwydeon. The veteran warrior was able to dodge the blow easily with a simple sidestep and he turned to face where Draven landed.

"Don't forget, Draven," Gwydeon said smiling, "you made Nightwing part of me, and so you made me into a demon like you. Like it or not, I am better than you. I'm stronger, faster, more agile, and simply better."

"I made you, Gwydeon Sandar," Draven shot back, "I made you, so I can destroy you."

That comment was accompanied by a hard slash from the Sword of the Ram. Gwydeon again easily sidestepped that blow, and then ducked under the wild slash that followed. Two rapid thrusts came next, and Gwydeon dodged them as though they were three times too slow.

"This is fun Draven, but when are you going to start trying."

Gwydeon never had a history of being cocky, but this was different. Revenge had turned on a different part of Gwydeon, and his hatred was manifesting itself in the form of pure contempt for Draven's life and abilities. Finally, Gwydeon drew the Lion's Sword from the scabbard at his side and took a defensive position. The time for playing was over. Draven attacked again, and steel met steel for the first time in the duel. Each combatant edged into one another, making the crossed blades into a fulcrum for a test of strength. Gwydeon pushed hard and sent Draven sprawling to the ground. Without a word, Draven leapt back into the fray with a thrust that carried him through Gwydeon's defense. However, thanks to Gwydeon's increased speed, he was able to spin out of the way and disarm his opponent. Draven went stumbling down onto the floor, and the Sword of the Ram clamored to a rest beside him. Gwydeon turned and waited, enjoying the duel to its fullest. It had been a long time since he had let his emotions dictate a battle, and he wanted to get a full measure of pleasure out of this one. Draven stood up slowly, his eyes locked on his opponent. It was time to stop taking the man lightly and use all of the powers at his disposal. Draven recovered his sword and focused all of his energy into the blade. The sword began to glow with power, and Draven could feel the echoes of energy inhabit his body. His reflexes began to get sharper as did his control over his powers and his muscles. In just a matter of seconds he had become a single focused weapon. As the next attack came, Gwydeon noticed that Draven's movements were more fluid and sharp. Each attack was harder and harder to block, and Draven began to move at a faster pace. Each thrust and slash was immediately followed by another regardless of counter or block. Gwydeon found himself blocking two or three blows at a time before he was able to counter one. After another minute, Gwydeon had gone completely defensive. Then the pain it. A single slash had penetrated the perfect defenses of Gwydeon Sandar and a huge slash opened a gaping wound in his chest. Blood flowed freely, and Gwydeon recoiled from the pain. However, as the blood ran away from the wound, Gwydeon noticed the cold hard armor of Nightwing was still undamaged. The cut had been hard and deep, but not deep enough.

"First blood to the victor," Draven said proudly. "This is fun."

Draven's haughtiness had returned, but the cockiness was not reflected in his movements. He was fighting very cleanly, and there was a crispness to each step and movement. Gwydeon concentrated again, opening his mind to his new powers. Suddenly he felt a warmth from the sword in his hands. There was another power guiding him, a power that he had never felt before. It was like the Blaze, and yet it was different. There was more clarity to the power, like it came not from another source, but from inside himself. That was when he felt the Lion Sword change. The twin lions melted in his hands, and the sword itself disappeared. Then there was a burning under his skin, like an itch but magnified ten thousand times. He tried to resist, but the pain was so intense that he felt as though he could claw his skin off. But as he looked down he noticed that his skin was peeling off, leaving only the shell of Nightwing behind. Draven had stopped in his tracks, transfixed by the scene that played out before him. It was then that the first pain rocketed through Gwydeon. It was a white hot searing pain that flooded all of his limbs at the same time. Then he heard the clanking of metal as shards of the Nightwing armor fell to the floor.

When he look at his left arm, he saw that some of the armor had fallen away, but he did not see skin below his armor. What he saw was a pure white light. More and more of the armor fell away, leaving only the bright formless light below it. In only a matter of moments, everything had fallen away except Nightwing's bladed wings. Draven watched in horror as the bright white light began to pulse with power. He had never seen anything like this, and the memories of the Blaze also had no clue what was happening. The force of the light where Gwydeon's left arm had been suddenly intensified, and solidified in the shape of a human arm. One by one each of the appendages reformed, and in a matter of moments, Gwydeon the man, not the beast Nightwing had reformed. Only the wings of Nightwing still remained visible on his back. Suddenly the light consumed the wings as well. The metal flaked off in large pieces, but the form of the wings remained unchanged. The light again intensified and began to pulsate with power. Then, as the light receded, the glowing angelic wings that were revealed made Draven fall back in horror. Each feather of the new wings was perfect in form and the brilliant gleaming white was flawless. The last part of the new Gwydeon to form was his weapon. The golden hilt formed in his hand, and a crystalline blade slowly emerged. When the process was over, Gwydeon stood looking at himself for a moment and then smiled. Memories and thoughts began to flood his mind. The Creator had made good on Emries' promise to make him a Brother of the Angels. His purpose had not changed, but the Creator had decided to intervene.

"You can't win now, Draven," Gwydeon said slowly. "The Creator has given me the gift of angelic existence. I am more powerful now than you could ever imagine, and my agenda is to make sure that his interests are served in this war. That requires your death."

"Then come, Brother of the Angels," Draven said holding his sword high in the air, "cross blades with the King of the Devils."

Chapter XXXIV

A Bitter Pill

Pike stood with his eyes locked on the man that had called himself Stryfe. The pale blue skin of the phase glowed with a type of power that Pike found very familiar, and the sword in his hand moved like the flame of a candle being blown by the wind. The phase's hair was black as midnight and hung long down his back. His eyes were a dark blue, and every now and then Pike swore that he saw flashes of lighting around the pupil. Stryfe was a very intimidating sight, but Pike's anger would not let any fear creep into him. Their comrade was wounded and barely hanging on to life, and he would be damned if he was going to let her bleed to death when he had the power to stop it. Just before Pike could answer the words of the phase, Ren stepped forward and pointed his sword directly at Stryfe's black heart.

"You are the coward, Stryfe. All of the phasia are cowards. You hide behind your powers and your armies of Jeresei and Kalbraks. However, in a fair fight, you will always fall to the superior strength of purity instilled in all of us by the Light. I challenge you to a duel, Stryfe, and I will defend the honor of my lord Pike Rhuiden. If you do not accept, I will not be surprised, and I will know you are more of a coward than Taron."

Stryfe took a moment to reflect before dismounting. He smiled down at the man in full plate armor and held his sword aloft.

"Very well fool," Stryfe replied in a haughty yet powerful voice, "I will end your life and then I will turn my blade on the coward that you owe your allegiance to. Oh, and just to make sure your friends don't go anywhere, my little army will keep them nice and busy."

With that Stryfe leapt from the top of the building and propelled himself downward toward the waiting Ren. At the same time, Jeresei emerged from the shadows and attacked the remaining Enforcers. Turok took a moment to gently lay Celina on one of the building's porches and stood over her, brandishing his sword ready to give his life to save hers. Pike and Valin paired off, back to back with axes ready to spill Jeresei blood. Zak was also ready, crouched low, nearly at the level of the water that still flowed through the streets. Something was happening to Lakestone, almost as if the island were slipping further into the frigid waters of Exeter Lake. Ren brought his blade up in time to block Stryfe's flaming sword, but the burning blade passed through Ren's steel and etched a dark black streak down the gleaming breastplate of Ren's armor. Ren took a back step, shocked by the attack, but then stepped forward again, waiting for his opportunity to retaliate. The battle cry of the Jeresei echoed through the air as more and more of them poured from the shadows toward the wounded band of heroes. The first blow would be struck in a matter of seconds, and the fates would decide who would live or die.

Pike clutched *Fury* tightly, and as the first of the Jeresei came into range, he lashed out with all the rage built up inside of him. The red-skinned beast was split in two, but another and another came bounding toward him. Rachel appeared the next moment, her whirling blades impaling two Jeresei as she danced from fight to fight, killing anything and everything that got in her way. Valin also began to fight as hard as he could. Disregarding his wounded arm, he waded deeper and deeper into the ranks until only the glint of his axe and plumes of blood could be seen to mark his progress. Zak, his mobility severely hampered by the wound in his leg used the water to his advantage, hamstringing all of the Jeresei that got close to him. Pike waded close to Zak and the two fought hi and then low, cutting down each of the beasts that approached. Turok was incensed. He stood with his shoulders squared and a defiant look in his eyes that could have stared down the Great Dark One. Several Jeresei rushed him at once, and each one of them met a quick death under the assault of steel. The battle so far had gone in the favor of the Enforcers, but it would only take one single lucky strike to change the flow of battle for good.

Stryfe stood looking at Ren for a moment before lashing out again with his flaming blade. Again Ren's attempt to block was thwarted as another burn mark appeared on Ren's armor. This time though, Ren could feel the searing heat of the blade as it contacted his breastplate. It would only take one or two more strikes before Ren's armor would be totally useless. The phase began to get haughty. His strikes became slower and more predictable. In a matter of moments, Ren had his timing down and lashed out with a focused strike toward the phase's chest. The point of Ren's blade should have pierced Stryfe's heart, but instead there was a flash of light, and a surge of energy flooded through the steel blade and attacked Ren. The surge of electricity flashed through Ren making him drop his sword. His nerves then began to react erratically, causing his knees to buckle which made him fall face first into the cold water. It was this cold that saved Ren's life, shocking him out of near unconsciousness and bringing him back into the fight. He scrambled to recover his blade, and after a moment was standing toe to toe with the surprising phase again. As if the jolt made Ren's eyesight clearer, Ren noticed that Stryfe's armor appeared to have tiny bolts of lightning jumping from one ring to another. His entire armor was electrified, making any attack with a metal weapon perilous.

The war with the Jeresei was still progressing well. Turok was holding his own against the on-rushing Jeresei, but they were coming closer and closer to striking him. Pike and Zak were starting to get tired, the sheer volume of Jeresei sapping their strength and the increasing numbers making it difficult to move without leaving themselves open to possible counterattack. The water in the streets was red with the blood of the beasts, but also with the blood that streamed from gaping wounds on every member of the Enforcers. Zak was beginning to feel the pains in his leg grow stronger with each move that he made. As Zak turned to defend the blow from another of the red-skinned monsters, he saw Pike's side split wide open, and the blood still flowing from the wound. Rachel's movements had also slowed to nearly nothing. The dance of death was now something akin to a funeral march as more and more of the Jeresei fell before her. However, she showed the wear of the battle on her body with huge slashes of claws across her stomach and back. Valin was trapped deep into the Jeresei ranks, his axe chopping them down like young trees and his back pressed firmly against the wall of one of the buildings. His legs were threatening to give out, and only the firm structure of the wall was keeping him standing. Time was running out for the Enforcers, and if the onslaught didn't end soon, it would be the last battle that they ever fought together.

Ren looked at his opponent more carefully this time. Stryfe proved to be more dangerous that Ren had initially anticipated, but that would not stop him from defending the honor of his lord and master. Ren lashed out again, this time aiming for the phase's head instead of his torso. The ghostly flame blade flashed upward and suddenly the metal sword that Ren wielded struck something solid. The flame blade melted through Ren's sword and set half of it toppling down into the cold blood stained waters. Ren backed away from Stryfe, sensing that the battle would be at an end in a matter of moments. Then, out of nowhere, and man leapt in between Stryfe and Ren. He was dressed in commoner's clothes and was armed only with a simple staff. The stranger faced off with Stryfe and motioned from Ren to move back.

"The fight is now with me, child of darkness," the man said in a proud voice. "Give me your best."

Stryfe laughed at the new arrival and then struck out with a fairly simple blow. Ren knew that any person in the world could have blocked or dodged the attack and Ren assumed that Stryfe was just toying with the stranger. However, as Ren watched the stranger made no moves at all until the very last second when he sidestepped to the left and then launched himself toward the phase. The staff struck Stryfe in the chest the next second, knocking the wind out of the phase and sending him stumbling backward. The stranger followed up with a hard blow to Stryfe's right knee and then the back of his left. Stryfe fell backwards into the water. Suddenly there was an explosion from the water as the lightning of Stryfe's armor escaped its confines with an eruption of light and fire. Stryfe screamed in agony as the power rushed through him. The ghostly flame sword remained lit within the water, and as the man poked the fallen phase with his staff, Ren recovered the sword and held it aloft. Ren could feel the power emanating from the blade and then as if the blade had communicated to him in some way, Ren instantly knew how to use the powers within the blade. He put his hand on the stranger's shoulder and smiled.

"Thank you for the assistance my friend. I would like the pleasure of your name but I am afraid that introductions will have to wait. My friends are in danger."

The stranger did not turn around and stayed focused on Stryfe.

"He's not dead," the stranger said quickly.

"That doesn't matter now. My friends are in trouble and with or without you I must help them."

Ren didn't wait for an answer before turning and launching himself into the battle.

* * * * * * * * * * *

The battle was looking bad for the Enforcers. Rachel had fallen back to Turok's position, and the two of them were barely able to keep the Jeresei at bay, let alone inflict any damage. Pike and Zak were in a similar situation. They were surrounded and totally defensive. Suddenly they heard a scream of pain and watched as Valin's axe was tossed out of his hand and the Jeresei left his position, his bleeding body floating in the water. Pike could tell that he was still breathing, but he was not sure how long that would last. Then, Ren emerged from his battle with Stryfe with a new weapon in hand. The flaming sword gleamed with malicious intent for a moment before striking a Jeresei, splitting it effortlessly in two. As though possessed with the fire from the blade, Ren moved hurriedly through the Jeresei cutting down any that got in his path. The spectacle energized the Enforcers, and Pike ordered a second charge. Rachel and Zak followed the command and slashed through Jeresei moving toward Ren. When the three met in the middle, they were greeted by another throng of red-skinned demons. Within seconds they had all fallen. Suddenly one of the Jeresei leapt from behind Ren. The blow would have taken the proud man's head completely off had the staff of the stranger not descended rapidly on the creature's skull, caving its head in. After a roar of defiance, the Jeresei retreated, leaving the Enforcers to tend to their wounded comrades.

Pike rushed to Valin's side and gently moved the man through the flooded streets over to where Celina still lay. Turok looked as though he would pass out from the exertion, and Zak's movements were obviously slow and labored. The cut on his leg was deeper than Pike had first anticipated, and it was a wonder that the thief could walk at all. Rachel fell to her knees the moment that the Enforcers had a moment to rest, and as Ren approached, he willed the sword in his hand to extinguish itself and he fastened the hilt of the sword to his belt and helped tend to his friends. The stranger was the last to approach, gently picking his way through the fallen Jeresei bodies. When Pike looked up at the man he cringed slightly. Where his eyes should have been were blackened marks as though his eyes had been seared shut in some way. It was a wonder the man could move about at all, let alone strike effectively in a battle. However, Pike had learned many years ago to never underestimate anyone.

"Thank you sir, for aiding us in our fight against the Jeresei," Pike said clutching his side as the pain racked his body.

"You have wounded."

The statement was pointed and charged with an energy that Pike could almost feel. Suddenly the stranger dropped to one knee and laid his staff aside. A golden glow gradually enveloped both of the man's hands and he held them over the Celina's chest. Turok almost stopped the man, but he had no strength left in his body for fighting. After a moment, the golden glow began to fade, and Celina's eyes opened and she started to sit up slowly. Turok, finding new strength in his love's revival, helped her to sit up. It was obvious that she was still weak, but the fact that she was conscious and mobile was a start. The bleeding from the wounds on her back had stopped, and it almost looked as if they had started to heal a bit. While everyone had their attention turned to Celina, the stranger's glowing hands floated over Valin. The glow weakened even more as Valin began to stir, and by the time Valin sat up, the glow had vanished completely from the man's hands. After a deep exhale, the stranger recovered his staff and used it to balance himself as he stood.

"I have done all that I can for them," the stranger said, "that should sustain them long enough for you to get them to the nearest healer. There are several in Scalla that should be able to help you. I would recommend that you go now before those vile beasts return."

"May I have the honor of your name sir," Ren said turning toward the blind man. "You saved my life and now you have saved the lives of two of my dearest friends. For that I owe you a price that I could not possibly pay in one life time. I would at least like to know the name of the man that I am indebted too."

"My name is Galen," the man answered proudly, "Galen Pryde."

Suddenly there was a laughter resounding in the air. It was a deep bellowing laughter that Pike recognized from his worst nightmares. It was Taron. He had been watching the entire fight with his gleeful evil smile painted on his face, and Pike was sure that he had enjoyed every second of it. After a moment, the monstrous phase appeared, his hand still clutched around Elizabeth's neck. She was not struggling, and appeared as though she had given up all hope of survival. Taron strode over the body of his fallen comrade Stryfe and then looked at Pike with the evil grin still firmly affixed to his face.

"It is a pity that you were able to so easily defeat Stryfe. He is new to the Brotherhood, but I had such high hopes for him."

A portal appeared under the unconscious phase, and he fell through.

"But I guess when everything is said and done, if you want something done right, you have to do it yourself. So, Pike. How did you like your little trip to Lakestone? I hope it was everything you expected it to be and more. Ah, I see you have a new friend. One more person for me to kill, how lovely."

"For the last time Taron," Pike said holding his axe, "let the girl go. She doesn't mean anything to you. It's me that you really want, and you know it. Just let her go and you and I can finish this for good. That's what you want."

Taron sighed and shook his head. The smile was gone, replaced with a disappointed frown.

"No Pike, that isn't what I want, not at all. You just don't get it do you? Must either be all those blows to the head or all the drink. Maybe both. Who knew you would become so pathetic as you've aged? In the last generation you were just a little annoyance that was very fun to play with. I killed your little wife, and it made you predictable and reckless. I thought it would get you killed, but you were just too stupid and stubborn to die. Then, you made it personal by coming after me in Dreamscape. You humiliated me in the way that you ended my life in the last generation. So, when I was reborn, the only thing I could think of was making you feel so much pain in your life that you would rather kill yourself than go on. So, I devised this little strike on Lakestone knowing that you would just come running for a chance to get back at me. So Shau-ling tried to stab me in the back with that overgrown parrot of his, but I am too smart for both of them, and here I stand with one of your precious little Enforcers in my hand, her life hanging by the thinnest of threads. It wouldn't take much pressure and her neck would snap just so easily. That would make you hurt, wouldn't it Pike?"

Pike didn't answer, but stood his ground with his axe held high.

"I thought so. Once I kill this little girl, I can move on to the little redhead over there, and then I can go to women a little closer to you. Perhaps your fine little wife Cairyn first, then maybe your foster daughter Lissa, or maybe your real daughter Sabrina. Or maybe I should just start on your little mistresses. There are enough of them to keep me busy for a few months."

Most of the Enforcers were able to stifle their reactions, and Pike could feel his blood begin to burn. Hatred was coursing through his veins and he could feel his powers grow with every second. The rage was igniting the powers granted to him as a member of the *Erieal* and it would be only a few more moments before he could strike Taron down where he stood. As if sensing the assault that was about to be targeted at him, Taron contracted his hand tighter around Elizabeth's throat. The movement broke Pike's concentration, and Taron's laughter rolled from his chest like thunder. Before Pike could say anything, Galen stepped forward and steadied himself on his staff.

CHAPTER 34

"The life of an innocent is nothing to be wasted. I would trade my life for that of the woman that you hold in your hand, and so I make you this offer Taron. I challenge you to a fight to the death. You against me, no assistance from anyone. If you kill me, you may do as you wish with the girl and Pike and the rest of his Enforcers will do nothing to stop you. However, if I win and I am able to kill you, the girl will be saved and you will have to wait until the next generation to exact whatever vengeance you wish on Lord Rhuiden."

Taron laughed.

"You wish to fight me? You must be joking. I refuse this ridiculous request."

Galen stood proud and tall.

"Are you afraid of a simple blind man?"

That caught Taron completely off-guard. Pike smiled to himself. He knew that Taron could never decline a challenge when his honor was on the line. While Pike could not completely trust the abilities of the blind man, he really did not have a choice in the matter.

"Very well," Taron said shaking his head. "This should be worth the two or three minutes it will take to crush the life out of your pathetic body."

Taron then opened his left hand and a bubble of energy appeared around Elizabeth. The bubble extended until Elizabeth seemed to be floating. Taron then pulled off the red shirt that he wore and moved his head from side to side until the joints in his neck cracked loudly. Then, closing his hands into massive fists, more cracks and pops of knuckles sounded off into the air. Galen did not move, and stood firm with the staff point buried into the ground. Taron took two steps forward and stood toe to toe with Galen, towering over the blind man. Pike watched the bright red aura materialize around Taron, and Pike knew the battle could be over quickly if Galen was not good enough to feel the attack coming. Taron quickly brought one of the massive fists crashing down upon Galen, and the blind man moved out of the way just as quickly, diving to his left and smashing Taron's knee cap in the process. Taron howled in pain, and the aura flashed for a moment before Taron turned to face Galen again. This time, Galen was holding his staff like a weapon. The next blow was a straight punch from Taron. In one fluid move, Galen spun through the punch and buried the tip of his staff into the huge phase's gut. The blow knocked the wind out of the phase and sent him backwards. Galen was not content with one strike. The next blow slammed against Taron's face, wrenching his jaw and sending three teeth flying from his open mouth. Next came a thundering strike across Taron's back that shattered the staff and sent Taron toppling forward. The aura around Taron flashed again, and as he struggled his way back to his feet, Galen waited for an opportunity to strike again. After an angry growl from the wounded phase, Taron charged Galen and was met with a palm strike to the chest that wilted the phase like a flower in the hot sun. Taron collapsed, breathing heavily. The time for playing was long over, and as the aura intensified around Taron's hands, the massive fingers began to grow larger until the fists had doubled in size. Galen was unprepared for this tactic and as he dodged the first in a new series of punches, the extra girth of the hand struck the blind man square in the shoulder and sent him flying backwards. Galen's head collided with the ground so hard that he appeared to be unconscious.

"Too easy," Taron chuckled to himself.

The huge phase gloated over the fallen body of his victim for a moment, until Galen's arms shot up and took hold of Taron at the knees. After kicking his legs forward and pulling hard, Taron was knocked off his feet and sent sprawling face first into the dirt. Galen stood quickly and turned back toward the phase. Taron got up slowly, a new respect forming for the blind man. Taron charged the next moment, and Galen charged as well, diving toward Taron's knee, causing the hulking man to once again lose balance and end up face first in the dirt. When Taron made it back to his feet this time, he was obviously in pain, and Pike could see that one of the bones of his lower leg had broken free of its moorings and ripped through his skin. Blood was flowing from the wound, and Taron was trying his best to balance on one leg. However, his massive weight and bulk were also straining that leg.

"You are beaten, Taron," Galen said proudly. "I could hear the tendons in your knee snap and the rip of your skin as you fell. I figure that you aren't able to move very well now, am I right? It should be simple enough for me to take away the rest of your mobility and then crush your oversized skull. How does it feel to have been beaten by a mortal?"

Taron laughed despite the pain.

"There is a time to talk, blind man, and a time to act. Remember that the dear little girl is still very much in my hands, and it takes only a thought to kill her. First we finish this battle and then I finish her. You will pay dearly for what you have done to my leg, and she will pay dearly for the humiliation I have suffered at your hands."

A stream of fire erupted from Taron's hand, claiming Galen full in the chest. The blind man cried out in agony and then slumped to the ground. His breathing was slow and erratic. It seemed as though he were barely hanging on to life.

"It appears that I have won the little challenge. It was fun toying with the blind man, but I fear that I have other business to attend to."

Taron extended his hand and the bubble that contained Elizabeth floated over to him.

"Say your last good-byes, Pike, for this is the last time this little girl will breathe."

It was at that moment that the wind began to howl. As if from nowhere a storm appeared, and lightning and thunder rolled through the skies. A portal appeared high above Taron, and the black metallic form of Nightwing sped toward the ground. The beast hovered before Taron in the next moment, its eyes red and full of obvious anger.

"YOUR LIFE IS NOW FORFEIT TARON STEEN. YOU WILL RELEASE THE GIRL AND BOW BEFORE ME. THEN YOU WILL SUBMIT TO THE WILL OF PIKE RHUIDEN WHO I AM SURE WILL END YOUR LIFE VERY QUICKLY. IF YOU DO NOT COMPLY WITHIN THE NEXT TEN SECONDS, I WILL BE FORCED TO TAKE MATTERS INTO MY OWN HANDS."

Taron laughed and pulled the bubble of energy close enough to him to take hold of Elizabeth's neck. Pike screamed at the top of his lungs but nothing could prevent what happened next. In the span of a blink, Taron squeezed his hand shut, crushing Elizabeth's spine, instantly killing her. There was not even time for a single word to escape her lips before her eyes rolled back in her head, and her lifeless body slumped to the ground. Rachel screamed in agony and the launched herself at Taron. Zak was quicker, diving toward Rachel and pinning her to the ground as Nightwing unleashed a beam of energy at Taron that knocked him to the ground, melting the skin of his chest into a congealing pool. Taron screamed, but still had sense enough left to create a portal that would pull him out of harm's way. Nightwing dove after Taron, and was able to get through the portal before it could close. Pike and the other Enforcers stood in disbelief of what they had seen. Another member of their ranks had fallen, and as Pike stood looking at the dead body of Elizabeth, Rachel fought her way free from Zak and ran to where her sister lie. There were no tears from Rachel's eyes, but when she looked up at Pike, the look could only be described as one of utter hatred. After a moment, Pike broke the silence.

"We'll regroup in Scalla. With the Raven's Wing's help, we'll cleanse every last piece of shadow spawn out of this city."

There were no words from any member of the Enforcers as they began their long walk toward the kingdom of Scalla. There were no answers for what had happened to them in Lakestone, and there would be no way to account for the three losses that had been presents from the forces of the Shadow. What was worse was that the elite fighting force known as the Enforcers were not the cohesive unit that they once were, and in the heat of battle the emotions that consumed them had threatened to pull the group apart. It was only a matter of time before the tensions became so great that the group would turn on itself and the Enforcers would cease to exist, and so perhaps too would the chances of the forces of the Light in their seemingly never-ending war with the hated Shau-ling.

Patterns in the Wind

Creator's Calendar Year 1205; Light Reality

The City of the Gods stood empty as Emries walked down the perfect long white pathways smiling to himself about all of his accomplishments since the beginning of the third generation of the prophecies. Despite the possible horrors that could come from failure at the hands of the Creator, Emries was confident that it would not come to the destruction of the embattled world below. Things were going well for the forces of the Light in both realities, but not nearly well enough. In the Dark Mirror, he had needed to give Nathaniel Sandar a gentle nudge to realize the power that he was capable of, much as he had with Cedric Binosear after the murder of Erika Belnosian.

Each and every generation, Emries had found himself having to push those who were supposed to be serving his interests to their true purpose. Cedric would have been content to sit in his palace as the world fell down around him. For the child of Aerith Seth, he was remarkably timid. If he had it to do all over again, perhaps he would have selected Cedric's sister Anabel to carry the mantle instead of Cedric. That branch of the Binosear family seemed to be made of much sterner stuff. Once Cedric raised his banner however, the warriors of the Light flocked to him like moths to the flame. Even the strong-willed Arathorn Geoffry was quick to bend his knee to his lesser. But that was the first generation of the prophecies, and there was little known about the evil they were facing. It had been hundreds of years since any mortal had heard the name Shau-ling, an intelligent ploy by his sometime brother. Then when his phasia and his minions struck, there was more shock and desolation, much like there had been during the first war when the phasia were a true force to be reckoned with, not this collection of spoiled and neglected children. Though he had not needed to ignite the instinct to fight in Korrd Ranthall in the previous generation, it had been necessary to give the new members of the *Erieal* something to fight for. Arin Domae had been led easily enough. He was a creature of duty, so pushing him into situations where his duty came first simply reinforced the role he was supposed to play. Pike and Talon only needed to be shown danger, and they would fight. Tipping the forces of the Shadow to the fact that the People of the Dragon were staying in that little port town on their way to Marcwell had yielded unexpected results, but all of it benefited Emries' goals. Of course it had cost them two members of the People of the Dragon, but in the long run, the gains more than made up for the losses. But this generation was proving to be far different, and those who supposedly fought for Emries were spending more time fighting amongst themselves than they were the enemy.

The Dark Mirror reality was becoming a quagmire of conflict. While the Creator had thwarted Draven's plans for Nightwing by making Gwydeon Sandar into the Brother of the Angels, as much as it impact the goals of the phase Draven and ultimately Shau-ling, it did not help Emries. Nathaniel Sandar was moving along nicely, and it would only be a matter of time before he could be molded into a weapon far more powerful than his processors. But Shau-ling was no fool. He knew the stakes as well as Emries did, and he was not going to sit idly by and watch as his plans were dismantled. He had subverted the Creator's mandate of non-interference by recruiting warriors of the Light to do his bidding under the paltry veil of free will. Pike Rhuiden and Eldar Merin had been sent to the Light reality, and that was not acceptable. They would most surely interfere with all of the plans that Emries had so perfectly laid out. The old and stupidly self-righteous Pike had fallen into the trap at Lakestone which would make him fight even harder against the Shadow, and perhaps in time he would be needed to destroy the incursions from the Dark Mirror. But for all of Emries' manipulations, forces of fate still conspired against him leaving loose ends that could not so easily be sewn up.

Aerith Seth still floated about, using his powers however he saw fit, which made it very easy for him to stop either Shau-ling or Emries. Emries had never liked the man named Aerith Seth, and he liked the nature of the man's powers even less. Aerith had been the only danger to Emries in the time before the prophecies. He seemed to be willing and able to fight for anyone and anything he wished, and he showed an amazing if annoying tendency to see though all forms of manipulation. There had been many times that Emries considered simply killing the troublesome lout, but after being brought into the Hand of the Light, Aerith became an asset. Emries would tie Aerith's death into the destiny that would end the life of his hated brother forever. Though such an intervention brought Aerith more fully to the attention to the Creator and inextricably tied Aerith to the powers of both Emries and Shau-ling, it was a small price to pay for the thwarting of one's enemies. And now the Hand of the Light lived again, with a new breed of warriors that Emries could bend to his will.

It had been far too easy to introduce the teachings of the Moridon on the religious fanatics from Rana and Rama. If nothing else, Logan Ranthall's zealous adherence to the role that was not his to play had created a massive pocket of devotes warriors to the cause of the Light. All anyone had to do was hold up the Dragon Banner, and they would come running, frothing at the mouth, and screaming the praises of a man who was nothing more than a pretender who happened to be in the right place at the right time. The group's appointed leader, Dei, had been easy to control until he was getting too close to the truth about the origin of the Moridon. Of course, Emries could not allow something as insignificant as the truth to get in the way of the usefulness of the resurrected Hand, so the little man had to be exterminated. Erdric was perfect for that purpose. He was so easily duped into believing that the death of the man named Dei would somehow help his master that it took only a little push to make the assassination a reality. The phasia were proving to be more useful tools for bringing Emries' will to fruition that the *Erieal* were. Liette Forer was another of the Creator's little distractions that Emries had to worry about, but it appeared that her sights had already been set in the right direction. It was fairly obvious that she would dispose of the Rhuiden boy for Emries and that he would not have to dirty his hands. Basille had thought he was so cleaver tying his powers to Wolf, but all it did was made the boy a target not only for the phasia, but for the more fanatical elements in the forces of the Light as well. No one would truly trust him, and whatever message he was trying to spread would be drown out by questions as to his loyalty. However, as Emries ruminated on the issue, he became suddenly sorry that he had allowed so many elements of the People of the Dragon to continue to exist after the last generation. All they would do was distract Nathaniel and the new warriors from their true purpose. At least the petty little girl Sabrina was proving to be nothing like her predecessor. In the Dark Mirror reality she was a frightened child, terrified into submission and inaction by a monster. In the Light reality, she was petulant and easily distracted, a benefit of her upbringing by Pike. In both cases, Sabrina would never be the kind of threat that Logan Ranthall became in his later days.

As Emries continued to walk, he heard the thoughts of the man named Logan Ranthall from the Dark Mirror echoing through the empty stone structures of the City of the Gods. The words were of growing hatred for his creator. Emries laughed to himself. He had taken great pleasure in watching Nathaniel kill Logan, but when it became obvious that the man was too stubborn to accept that he was dead, Emries felt there was no choice in what he would do next. Logan would have to pay for his actions. Though he had only violated the spirit of the law and not the letter, Shauling had already interfered in the Light Reality by sending Pike Rhuiden and Eldar Merin, and so Emries would set foot onto the Dark Mirror and teach Logan Ranthall the true meaning of power, and that everything had a price.

* * * * * * * * * * *

In the fields outside of the kingdom of Scalla, Aerith Seth sat watching the wind blow through the leaves of the trees and ruffle the tall grass around him. This was the most peaceful that he had ever been, and it was about time that his old body had been given peace. It was clear that Evan Sinn was going to do the job that was required of him, and that he would unravel the mystery of the war between the darkness and the light. Inwardly Aerith wished things would have been different. He had a life once, before the entire war started. He had a home with Bryn. Though they both had to live in fear of Grawn, it was obvious that he knew she was in love with Aerith. They had fought together many times, and Grawn himself had given Aerith the blessing to try and handle Bryn if he could. Besides, Grawn was having his own affair with Ellis. Even though Bryn was a member of the phasia, she was still able to love, and Aerith was sure that she had found that love with him. But life was turned upside down when somehow Ellis discovered the prophecies that would bring down the reign of Shau-ling and turn the world over to the phasia. Ellis gave the prophecies to a man named Aralias Imstra, eventually forcing the expulsion of Grawn, Bryn, and Ellis from the Brotherhood of Phasia and starting the true Battle for Ascension and the War for Power. It was only a matter of time before the understanding between Grawn and Aerith had eroded and Aerith was forced to make a choice. It was that choice that would forever change the world as he cast his lot in with the Hand of the Light and would become the martyr from which the entire war would begin. Of course, death was not the end for a man like Aerith Seth. How could it be? The fate of the world falls down on your shoulders and then someone other than the Creator gets to decide your time is done? Of course, Aerith had not expected what had happened after his death. He wasn't sure what he expected, because he never had given it one moment of thought.

Looking back on his life, Aerith recognized that he was neither a subtle nor a self-aware man. In fact, he probably would have called himself a blunt instrument. He had been trained to be nothing more than that by Saurn. It simply reinforced what Aerith had already become by necessity; a survivor. He had survived the cruelty and the brutality of the orphanage. He had survived the horror and the hazards of the mines of Quea. When Saurn came to him and brought tutors and opportunity, Aerith was determined to not let anything pass him by. He soaked up as much information as he could, barely sleeping except when exhaustion could no longer be ignored. As a student Aerith worked harder than he ever had in his life, and soon found that knowledge was every bit as dangerous as the monsters that lurked in the darkness of the mines. Then he was turned loose on the world. Of course, it wasn't really freedom, it was only the illusion of freedom. He understood now that he didn't choose that little town, or that tavern, or the woman who shared his bed. He had been a tool, nothing more, put in the right place at the right time by forces he wasn't aware enough to know existed, let alone smart enough to understand the motivations of. Days later he found a new purpose, another designed for him and not of his choosing. He was a general, a soldier, a lover, and a foil. All of the roles he took on as voraciously and unrepentantly as any he had in his life to that point. Of course, he had never counted on feeling something for the woman who shared his bed, and he never counted on looking into those deep and wise eyes and finding love staring back at him. Perhaps that had been the moment he had started to question. Perhaps it was just the romantic sentiment of an old and tired man trying to find meaning in his long life. Either way, it was Bryn, her love, and her budding and unfamiliar sentimentality that pushed Aerith to his ultimate fate in the Hand of the Light.

When he had reached the Other Side after his execution, Aerith had been told that he was no longer a mere mortal but akin to the gods, and as such he was not truly dead. He didn't belong on the other side any more than the gods or Emries did. Emries had wanted Aerith to take a position in the City of the Gods and continue his war against Shau-ling, but Aerith refused, only passing his mantle because it was the will of the Creator, not because of Emries' words. It was at this point that the suspicions began to grow within Aerith. He had spent his entire life surviving, moving from the will of one powerful person to another. But the time for that was over, and if he were going to have to spend eternity wandering the world, it would be on his terms and no one else's, certainly not Emries'. Part of him wished that he could see Bryn again before he died, but that would not be able to happen. Eternity without her ultimately was not worth living. That was when Aerith hatched his plan. He would find someone to give his powers to, someone who could do what he could not. Aerith would get the answers that he so desperately wanted, and he would get them on his terms. But those answer would come with a cost; a very high one. Upon giving his powers to Evan Sinn, Aerith had given away his life, only keeping enough power to make sure that the job would be done, and of course enough in case an emergency should arise. As Aerith relaxed back into the soft grass he laughed to himself and expended some of that remaining power to change the shape of one of the clouds that floated above him to resemble Bryn. He smiled to himself, looking upon her beautiful face, and felt at peace, nearly content enough to let the last bits of his life slip away. Soon enough he would be able to let go of the world that didn't seem to want to let go of him. There were still a few places left to go, a few goodbyes to be said. Reaching into his pocket he pulled free one of the portal stones that he had kept for himself. The places he needed to go were not for his successor, they were for Aerith alone. A moment later, Aerith was gone. As a stiff breeze blew in from the south, scattering the cloud formations, down in the fields below the clear blue sky, only the flowers and the trees felt the wind.

* * * * * * * * * *

As the Erin Ranthall worked on the bruised and cut body of Susanne Praen, Midarin Rice was left to her thoughts about the future. She had survived a war in which many of her friends had died, and yet she stayed close to the war waiting for the next in a series of battle to begin. It was only now, sitting in the house that they had made into a quiet sanctuary on the precipice of the next stage in the war that she realized why Logan and Elwyne had wanted to stay away. Perhaps if Gwydeon had survived she would have done the same. But as she thought she wondered if she would have the strength and conviction that Elwyne showed to stay away from the trappings of power and fame. Elwyne could have been the most powerful woman in the world, a queen in the kingdom of Marcwell, the mother and inspiration to a whole generation of heroes. Instead, she settled down in a common town, with common concerns, and in common and very desirable peace. Midarin had the easier and less fulfilling role. She became exactly what she never wanted to be. She was a queen. She had power. And yet at the same time she was beholden to the office that she had been bred for. Treaties, pacts, alliances, and all manner of courtly matters were her stock and trade, and at times they were her only sustenance. She loved her children deeply, even the child that was not her own that she had taken into her home and made part of her family. Now however, looking around the room that had belonged to the simple and yet complex and steadfast woman, Midarin began to remember some of the strength that she had in the days of the People of the Dragon. She was not the Queen of Brea. That may have been her title, but that was not who and what she wanted to be any longer. She did not want any longer to let the tides of battle dictate her actions. Her life was not supposed to be run by the whims of others.

She thought she had stayed in Brea for love; love of a man that could never love her back because of his own loathing of love. But she knew now, and perhaps she had always known, that it was not love but rather the echo of love. Pike Rhuiden was a powerful man and a gentleman when the mood struck him. However, it was his passions and his strongly charged emotions that ran his day to day life. Midarin could no more love him than he could love himself. Pike was the study of thwarted ambition, and a man who constantly dreamed above his station. Even being the lord of three major kingdoms was not enough, and his reach continued to extend far beyond his grasp. His family was nothing more than a means to an end for him, and it was that very feeling that had destroyed any relationship that he could have ever had with his son Duncan. That boy would be trouble, but it was trouble that Pike brought on himself. Pike's stubbornness would be his undoing and his inability to love himself would make him a greater enemy to himself than any member of the phasia would ever be. Midarin, in the years after the final battle with Shau-ling had drifted, taking the roles that were meant for her. At the time she thought that she had fallen in love with Pike because they were kindred spirits, and they could be together to end to feelings of loss and isolation. Pike would never be a substitute for Gwydeon, but Pike was a man that could sympathize and help through the long and sorrowful nights. But Pike was not what Midarin needed. He never would be and never could have been. Midarin had not truly known who she was until she had fallen in with the rag-tag band of misguided adventurers with the laughable mission of saving the world from the Shadow. She was not the pampered princess who saw her kingdom as nothing more than a gilded prison. She was not the mourning wife of a long-dead hero. She was not the chaste queen who sacrificed all of herself for the people of her kingdom. And she certainly was not the doe-eyed girl mooning over a married man that she could never truly have. No, she was truly the woman that she had found after that day in Illimar. She was a warrior, an archer, a hero for the Light, and now she needed to be what the world needed most, the leader of the People of the Dragon.

* * * * * * * * * * *

The Creator watched from his perch in the Heavens with detached disappointment. The fragile balance between the two realities in the crucible testing his children was coming apart even as he watched, and the degradation of the ephemeral wall between the two realities was weakening. Before too long, the interference by both Emries and Shau-ling would be too much to control, and there would be nothing to stop the two realities from combining back into one. It had all been so simple in the beginning. There had been no wars and no deaths. It was only the peaceful co-existence between the Cosmos and the Creator. Then the ideological wars between the Creator's children and the scourge of man appeared to question the very nature of their existence and everything beyond. Emries' children which he dubbed the Moridon, forerunners to the beings that would become known as the *Erieal* harnessed the powers of nature in a way that was so unnatural that it began to slowly kill the world. But the fate of one ball of dirt mattered little in the grand design of the Creator. What could not be abided was the disrespect that Emries had shown in proclaiming himself the Creator to the men of this world. That insult had led to Shau-ling being created, and it led to the war that raged now. For thousands of years the children of the Creator had squabbled, trying desperately to prove that their view of the nature of the Cosmos was the right one. They had presided over the birth and death of hundreds of worlds in an effort to be the victor. And even when those ideological battles became more practical ones, the conflict rarely escalate past the level of sabotage. At least not until the lost and destroyed world of Loinn. The carnage and horror there would have ramifications that would echo through the whole of the cosmos, and perhaps that more than anything had led to the arrogance that Emries now displayed. But the Creator knew that even if the world of Onea was sentenced to fire, there would be other worlds, and the battles between his children would only escalate. The Creator began to formulate a new plan. A plan that would once and for all determine which of his children were superior.

* * * * * * * * * * *

Pike and Eldar sat in the clearing just outside the city of Aradon taking a rest from their long travel. This was the world that should have been, according to Shau-ling, and in a way it still felt wrong to Pike. While he was overjoyed that the city that he had been born and raised in still stood, and the old woods were still very much alive, there was still a part of his heart that was heavy. Granted that part of him was worried about Sabrina, but that was not the only feeling of pain in his heart. It was more as though there was a longing within him, and need to find the truth. Suddenly he caught sight of the spire of the old church again. Then he remembered the story that Gwydeon had told about the fact that the old church had not survived the attack on Aradon, but the book with the marriage ritual had. Without a word, Pike began a slow walk through the paths of the forest leading back to the very church that he had sealed his love for Eldar in.

While she was not the same woman that he had been in love with all those years ago, his feelings were still as strong as they were on that day. She hesitated a bit when she saw where they were walking, and while she was content to hang back from Pike, she still felt as though she needed to follow.

Pike hesitated at the door of the church for a moment, the feelings and memories washing over him again. He could see himself, young and foolish, stealing away with Eldar to take the vows at the old church during the spring tournament. And even while they made love there on the dais in front of the book, it had felt as though something was hanging over them, a power that could not be explained. It had clouded Pike's thoughts then, and now that he had returned, the feeling came over him again. Pike's eyes instantly locked on the book that sat open under the glass box on the dais. He remember the stories from his younger days, his father telling him that the greatest secrets of the world were stored in that book, and when the time was right, the box would lift and the book would be able to be read by everyone. Somehow Pike had always doubted those stories.

Pike walked down the length of the carpeted aisle and ascended the dais so that he looked down on the large open book. The pages were still a crisp white and the black ink was flawless on the pages. He could see the red edges of the cover with the golden binding evident even in the sparse light of the church. Eldar remained in the doorway, watching from a distance as Pike ran his hands over the top of the glass box. Pike looked down onto the words of the open page, re-reading the vows to himself as he occasionally looked up at Eldar who was slowly walking toward him. As he read the words to himself he could feel his heart pound a little faster. He didn't realize that he was mouthing the words until Eldar began to repeat them with him, as though they were etched in her memory forever. As they finished the words of the vows of marriage together, Eldar stood in front of Pike, her eyes locked on his, a look of passion and love filling her bright blue eyes. Unable to help himself, Pike ran his fingers through her blond hair, and then closed his eyes and quickly touched his lips to hers. It was as though time had stopped. They were both so struck by emotion that Eldar had to take a step back and in doing so, she and Pike both bumped the platform where the Book of the Creator rested.

Near the smoking and desolate ruins of Aradon, on a simple marble pillar, a book stood encased in a glass box. Prophecy told that one day the box would be removed so that the truth of the Creator would be told and life would enter an era of peace that would reign forever. The darkest days had come to the world, with it lingering on the edge of falling into Shadow for eternity, and yet the box did not move. But, on a still spring morning, with only the birds around to witness it, the glass box shifted.

* * * * * * * * * * *

For a long few moments the kiss between Eldar and Pike continued. Their love had been sparked in a way that they never realized was possible. And in their hearts the love began to grow. A rat scampering across the floor caused Pike to trip and the two moved down the dais. Again Pike bumped the pedestal, thinking of nothing but the woman before him and the passion in her kiss.

* * * * * * * * * * *

Birds chirped loudly as the strange motion from the old pedestal continued. The glass boxed lurched again, this time shifting the box even more. The book remained fixed in position, but the box had been moved almost enough for a human had to touch the book. A very curious bird landed on the box and began to walk across it. Normally the box would have been a good perch for the birds that chose to remain near the smoldering ashes of Aradon, but as the bird approached the side of the box that hung slightly over the edge of the pedestal, the bird felt its weight shift. The box had tipped when it had walked too close to the edge. Immediately the bird lifted off again, and as it watched the glass box settle back into its awkward position, the bird landed.

* * * * * * * * * * *

The two rejoined lovers had found their way to the floor of the church and had returned to the very position that they had been during their last visit to the old church. Pike smiled down at Eldar before beginning their kiss anew. Suddenly there was a crash, and the sound of breaking glass filled the old church. Pike leapt to his feet and spun around to see the old book, uncovered, with its pages being ruffled by the light mid-day breeze.

Blood is Thicker

Creator's Calendar Year 1205; Dark Mirror

Bryn was in a bad position and she knew it. Inwardly she cursed herself for being the focal point of a power play in yet another lifetime. Last time it had been her devotion to Aerith Seth that had gotten her to betray her master, and now it seemed that it would be her devotion to her family that would result in the same end. Ellis was on her knees a few feet away, laboriously dragging breaths in and out of her tormented lungs. Bryn could see the look of triumph on the girl Taya's face, and strangely enough, it was a look akin to the ones that she had seen on the faces of the phasia after a kill. Taya was enjoying the torment and torture that she was inflicting, and Gideon looked pleased as well. It was coming down to another act of treachery against her master, and Bryn felt an uneasy twist in her stomach at the thought of betraying Shau-ling after all of the second chances she had received. Even in the last lifetime, it had been she who led Korrd Ranthall and the rest of the forces of the Light through the palace and into the throne room, and then in the next life time she was welcomed back into the council after so many years in exile. She, Grawn, and Ellis had been accepted back into the bosom of the Shadow as though nothing had happened. Inwardly, Bryn wondered how many more chances she would receive before she met the same fate as Basille.

"I'm waiting, mother," Gideon said coldly.

Bryn sighed hard and slowly nodded her head. This was not going to be an easy or a quick explanation. She knew what Gideon wanted to hear, but that was only the beginning of the tale. Gideon just wanted to know who Nightwing was and how it came about, but that opened the door to the origin of Nightwing and the eternal and ultimately confusing question of why. It was a question that truly had no answer, at least not one that was ever satisfying.

"Release Ellis, and I will tell you everything."

Gideon hesitated for a moment. If he allowed Ellis to be freed, it would place him and Taya at an extreme disadvantage. Where before they had the element of surprise with Taya's powers, now that they had been revealed, the two phasia were more than capable of shutting those powers down. However, there was a look in Bryn's eyes that Gideon had never seen before, one he didn't think a member of the phasia was capable of...remorse.

"Taya, release her."

Taya stared in her father's direction for a moment, not believing what she was hearing. The phasia were their enemies, and their death meant the salvation of their world. For years, Taya had watched as the phasia ripped apart kingdom after kingdom leaving only those alive that suited their purposes. Others became examples of what happened to those who rebelled. Taya's mother had been one of those examples, another casualty quickly forgotten by the phasia. For a long moment, Taya waited, not certain if she should obey her father's wishes or follow the will of her soul and take more revenge for her mother's murder. It would be easy for her to simply contract the flows of air around Ellis' throat, stifling her and snuffing out her life.

"Taya . . ."

Gideon was starting to grow impatient. It was as though he could feel Taya's thoughts, and it scared him that he agreed. It would not bother him one bit to see Ellis die at Taya's hands. There had never been a time that Gideon could remember not looking at any of the phasia and feeling hate in his heart. Maybe it came from the fact that he was a member of the *Erieal*, or perhaps it flowed deeper than that. Gideon had always felt close to the father that he never knew, Aerith Seth. Some of the emotions that he felt were so alien to him, and despite all of the resentment he felt towards Bryn after she had left him in the hands of Basille, he still loved her. She was his mother, and no matter what manner of monster she proved to be lifetime after lifetime, he could not forget that she was responsible for his birth. While the rest of the phasia could burn, he believed in his heart that he would risk his life to save Bryn if he could. In the last generation, Korrd and Gwydeon had done that for him.

"Let her go, Taya."

A deep sigh escaped Taya's lips, and she released the flows of Air that surrounded Ellis. Relieved, the pale phase rose back to her feet and unconsciously rubbed her neck, trying to push away the memory of the pain that had been inflicted upon her.

"Now, mother," Gideon said turning back to face Bryn, "I have lived up to my part of the bargain, now you will live up to yours."

Bryn swallowed hard and then nodded.

"How much to you know?"

Gideon sighed.

"Not as much as I wish I did. A man like Gwydeon Sandar does not just disappear, that much is obvious. I have always known in my heart that if he were ever to die, it would be something spectacular that everyone in the world would know about. He is not the kind of man that just curls up and dies."

"That much is certain Gideon," Ellis chimed in, her voice scratchy and strained. "For a mere mortal, he was a huge thorn in the side of the Brotherhood, and particularly for Jeroch. But that is why your People of the Dragon were extraordinary, not for the powers at your disposal, but for your humanity and your tenacity."

Gideon sighed, but kept his focus on the topic at hand.

"Then I couple that with the knowledge I have about Nightwing. Aryx Terian was not Nightwing that much is certain. As much as I hated Aryx, I cannot forget the stories of his valor and strength that Basille told me over the years. When Shau-ling created Nightwing, large amounts of the Blaze held it together, and I think the Blaze became conscious inside of Nightwing like it did in the Flame, and so Nightwing became a living creature. Unfortunately for it, there is not enough of Nightwing that it can exist on its own, so it needs a host. Somebody either tricked or forced Gwydeon to become that host, and I have a sinking suspicion as to who that someone is."

Bryn and Ellis were both impressed at Gideon's knowledge of the subject. Ellis was sure that most of the information had come from the teachings of Basille. What neither of them could have guessed were the rest of the insights that Gideon had been able to glean.

"I think it was Draven."

Bryn silently nodded and then sighed.

"As Ellis said, Draven is one of the most impressive of the phasia, and he has been able to fight us to a stand-still on many fronts. The battle with Gwillim Sandar still stands out as one of the most impressive acts ever accomplished by any of us, with the sole exception of Jeroch's murder of Aerith Seth. Draven somehow found the secret of Nightwing and devised a way to resurrect the metallic monster. Though it would not have been easy, I suspect that the Flame had something to do with it. The Blaze is the life force of the very world that we inhabit, while it may seem that we wield it simply and with no thought, it is exceptionally difficult. We are merely the instruments and the conduits through which the Blaze flows. It is almost as if it uses us for its purposes. Shau-ling on the other hand derives his life and all of his power from the Blaze because he has surrendered to its powers. He is not the Blaze, but he is part of the Blaze, and they are equally immortal. The phasia were gifted with an ability to tap into this limitless power, but each time we do, we are weakened."

"Bryn!"

Ellis was incensed by the information that Bryn was giving away. The most intimate secret that the phasia shared was the weakness that followed drawing deeply on the Blaze. For Grawn, Bryn, and Ellis, the weakness seemed more pronounced because of their advanced age, and the length of time that they were away from the Council. Jeroch seemed to be the only member of the phasia that was not affected by his drawing upon the Blaze.

"It doesn't matter now, Ellis. There is more that I will tell, and you know the secrets that I hold inside of me. It is time that this silent war was given a voice."

Ellis felt the sting of the words deep inside of her. The secret wars inside the phasia and the true secrets of the Brotherhood had never been given voice, even in the dark days when the War for Power was more than just a name. Back before the splintering of the phasia, when there were only six children of Shau-ling.

"The Blaze is more than any of you mortals could ever envision. While it gives power unlike anything else in this world, there is a terrible price for its gifts. The more you open yourself up to it, the more it takes control of you, and weakens your mortality."

Both Taya and Gideon stared blankly at Bryn.

"I can tell by your looks that I am speaking over your heads. You mortals who supposedly serve the Light, all you ever want is answers. But you aren't prepared for the price you pay for those answers. You want it easy, and quick. That is why Cedric was so easily manipulated. That is why Logan and Korrd took so long to find their true paths. But your father, Aerith, he knew one day he would pay for what he had done. The phasia for all of their arrogance and all of their fire, know the price for their knowledge and their actions. In the end that is all there is for us. Duty, honor, and the price for our sins. And now you stand before us asking for answers, and you want to understand. But for you to understand this, you must first understand what the phasia are."

Ellis cut Bryn off hard.

"You realize that by doing this you could upset the covenant handed down by the Creator of balance. Remember what happened the last time, with Aralias Imstra."

Bryn nodded silently and then sighed.

"Yes, Ellis, I realize what I am risking. But as you well know, the Creator has already intervened on several occasions in this generation, and I don't think once more will plague him. There is no more time for games."

"As your friend," Ellis began, "I will not stop you from continuing with your tale. But as a member of the Brotherhood of Phasia, after the story is concluded I must challenge you to combat. You do realize this?"

"I know Ellis," Bryn answered. "Do what you have to do, and so will I."

Ellis nodded and motioned for Bryn to continue.

"The phasia were created in the time when the war against the mortals and their patron Emries was in its infancy. Shau-ling didn't know how to fight against these men, and so he created a group designed to use his gifts, the powers of the elements, and the Blaze against his enemies. But after his first creation, the one you know as the Flame, Shau-ling realized that something was missing. There was too much power and not enough substance. So, Shau-ling tried again, this time using more of his own innate abilities as well as those shared by Emries. The next phase that was produced was Jeroch. Blindly loyal, Jeroch had power at his disposal that would be unmatched, and yet there was still something missing. There was no purpose to the power other than following orders. Like a true inventor, Shau-ling had set backs. After all, he was not the Creator, and even the Creator seems to be fallible. So, Shau-ling secretly watched his enemy, saw the way that man reacted. He saw the pain and anger, the depth of emotion. It was the 'negative' emotions that fascinated Shau-ling the most though. Hatred, rage, lust, greed; these were the very emotions that the phasia would come to embody and exploit. In his next children, Shau-ling infused these human emotions into the lifeless forms created from the mass known as the Blight, and watched as they came to life. Grawn, always bitter and cruel; he used jealousy and greed as his motives. As you know, Water was his weapon of choice. The Flame originally had a name, Kamen, and his massive size and power centered in the string of Earth. In those days, Jeroch was imbued with the powers of Chaos, and so he was truly Shau-ling's child. Ellis, cold and calculating as she ever was, also had a greedy nature, but not for power. Her greed was for knowledge, and she used such knowledge to destroy all that opposed her. Vanity is also something that my dear sister is known for, but the ice-cold demeanor is only rivaled by her powers over Wind."

"And of course for my dear sister, Bryn," Ellis countered with more venom than information, "lust was more of a game than it ever was a tool. And saying that I am vain in comparison to her is like saying that a lightning bug shines brighter than the sun. Fiery nature is not lost on her, neither in temper, desire, nor power."

"That flattering depiction aside," Bryn continued not missing a beat, "we come to the sixth member of the initial council. Remember though that Shau-ling used the forces of nature sparingly and treated them with a great reverence, making sure that he did not tamper with the Blaze. The sixth member, while a disappointment to all of us, seemed to fill Shau-ling with the most joy. He and Jeroch were almost like twins in the way that they acted, except while the loyalty and strength were there, there was something else. We would learn to call those emotions bravery, and valor."

Gideon brushed his hair back out of his eyes and then refocused his puzzled gaze on his mother.

"I never thought I would hear those two words connected with a member of the phasia, certainly none of them that I have ever faced."

"And there is certainly no bravery in the way that Jeroch and Draven have been descending on wounded kingdoms and killing helpless women and children," Taya added.

"Your venom is lost on us Taya," Bryn said coldly. "We have seen many wars in the lifetimes that we have been among you mortals, and we have seen your own people kill women and children in pathetic wars over land that had nothing to do with us. However, your point is valid in that these emotions are not part of the Council any longer since their initial possessor was purged from the Council long ago. That man was none other than White Lightning himself, Aryx Terian."

While Taya seemed taken aback by Bryn's words, Gideon just silently nodded, as if he had known the whole time.

"You're not surprised."

Ellis' words expressed her shock as best she could. This had been the most carefully guarded secret of the Brotherhood, known only to those five members of the Brotherhood who were Aryx's contemporaries, and yet this mortal nodded as though he had just been asked if he was hungry.

"I've known for many years, I just never had all the pieces of the puzzle until now. You weren't part of this war when we were assaulted in Taren, so you probably don't know about the meeting between Jeroch and Aryx that happened in the *Inn of Good Faith* that night. After we discovered the shape shifter after the siege of Marcwell, Logan and the others surmised that the real Aryx had been taken during our meeting at Falke. I had always had my doubts, but kept them to myself. Now I know the truth. Shau-ling exerted his power over Aryx through Jeroch, just as he did with Cedric. He called Aryx home and turned him into Nightwing. The switch could have easily been made during the fighting in the palace when Jeroch's army attacked."

"My son, you have made me proud since the day you were born, and you are a credit to both your father and myself," Bryn said in a quieter tone, "but you have only guessed at the beginning of the story. While Aryx was one of us, in both form and substance, he was also restless and inquisitive. He wanted to know everything. There had to be purpose to his fighting, and he was never satisfied with mere orders to kill."

"Aryx constantly questioned Shau-ling's orders," Ellis continued, no longer worried about her bond to keep the secret, "trying to find a deeper meaning to the war. Yes, Emries was the enemy, but that was not good enough. Before long, Shau-ling tired of the constant questioning, and Aryx had openly begun to revolt against the orders he was given, refusing to kill innocents who knew nothing about the war, merely caught in the middle of it. At that point, Aryx was stripped of all his powers and exiled. More than that, Shau-ling showed mercy on his child, sealing away a large portion of his innate powers and allowing his heart to beat like that of any human. Aryx would also age, just at a greatly reduced rate."

"Basille suffered the greatest humiliation that the phasia can endure," Bryn added, "in that he was Banished, his life essence erased from existence. This fate could have easily befallen Aryx, but Shau-ling still loved Aryx as his child and could not bear to strike the blow that would end his life. He was content with the knowledge that he would age and die as a mortal. However, Emries, the cruel and manipulative creature that he is, turned Aryx against us sealing all of the memories away about his true nature and his true identity, making him a member of the wretched *Erieal*."

"Just like he did to you Gideon," Ellis concluded.

Gideon nodded his head again, taking it all in. Everything had begun to fall into place in his mind. Basille had planted these seeds long ago, but it had taken all of the years and the battles for them to finally begin to sprout. Perhaps Shau-ling wasn't the enemy in this war, but his servants were. They had taken the battle to the extreme out of his control, Draven being the perfect example.

"Then as the rest of the phasia were born," Taya said quickly, "they became more and more like the mortals they were trying to kill. They became the embodiments of rage, anger, jealousy, and pain. Shau-ling couldn't control them because he made them too much like humans."

Bryn's coy smile returned.

"I was right Gideon, she is more like her mother."

Gideon smiled again and took a step toward Bryn with arms extended.

"It was good to see you again mother," he said hugging her tightly and then stepping back. "I hope you and I will have other opportunities to speak. I would like to learn more about my father someday."

"The Creator willing, we will."

Gideon turned and took Taya by the arm, leading her back toward the gates.

"You should make for Scalla. You know why…"

Gideon nodded to himself and continued walking. The horses were waiting on the other side of the gate, and Gideon was trying hard not to think of what came next. Bryn against Ellis was an even fight, and there was a good chance that neither of them would live through it. As they mounted, Taya gave her father a long hard look.

"Do you think Bryn will be alright?"

Gideon just straightened in his saddle and eased his mount forward, trying to avoid the thoughts that he had just seen his mother for the last time.

* * * * * * * * * * *

As Gideon and Taya began to ride away, Ellis rounded on Bryn, her eyes filled with uncharacteristic emotion.

"You could have merely told them what they wanted to know about Nightwing, but you couldn't leave it at that could you? Didn't you learn anything from your little fling with Aerith Seth?"

Bryn simply smiled and continued to watch her family depart.

"Look at me when I am talking to you," Ellis said grabbing Bryn by the chin and wrenching her neck, pulling Bryn's face toward her. "You had to have Aerith Seth, no matter what happened, but that wasn't enough for you. You had to make a statement by telling him that he was the lynch pin on which the fate of the world would hang. You handed him over to Aralias Imstra and the forces of the Light without a care or a thought. Now you just handed the phasia to Gideon on a silver platter."

Bryn slapped Ellis' hand away and then countered her with as much venom as she could manage.

"Strong words from a hypocrite like you. Or do I have to remind you of your little plan to give birth to the *Coromor*. Unlike me, you actually succeeded in the plot, but you felt so in love with Arin Rhuiden that you couldn't kill Korrd before he was able to grow up and kill Shau-ling. You even named the boy and kept tabs on him while he was growing up. Of course I was in love with Aerith, how could anyone who knew that heart and that soul not be? But wasn't that what you said about Arin Ranthall? It had to please you secretly that in your way you were bedding Arin to get a taste of what I had with Aerith, because of that part of him that was Aerith. You are no better than me."

Ellis stood straight and smoothed her gown.

"You're right Bryn, but I have to challenge you anyway. It is the law of the Council."

"I wouldn't expect anything less," Bryn replied.

For a moment, the two sisters stood looking at each other, a battle of wills and a fitting last moment before the battle would begin. For centuries, they had been the staunchest of allies, never once aligning against the other, but times had to change. Ellis lashed out first, a beam of pure blue light erupting from her fingers in a heartbeat, Bryn rolled away from the strike, and the beam collided with the doors to the palace, freezing them.

"So much for courtesy..." Bryn said as she popped up to a knee and loosed a stream of fire at her younger sister.

Ellis easily dodged the blow, almost as if she knew it was coming. The two knew each other's favorite weapons and so the battle would go to the person who was the most innovative the quickest. The temperature in the courtyard began to cool, and Bryn could feel the droplets of water in the air begin to freeze. It was merely an instinct that brought up the shield of fire, but the next moment, shards of ice began to fall from the sky. They were sharp as daggers, and as they hit the shield of fire, they hissed as their transition to steam completed. Once the assault had ended, Bryn released the shield and hurled a ball of fire at Ellis. Ellis sidestepped the blast and began to channel another beam of ice, but Bryn's feint had pulled Ellis into the trap. As the beam of ice launched from Ellis' hands, Bryn channeled fire into the ground at her younger sibling's feet and a column of fire engulfed Ellis. For the next few moments, all Bryn could see was churning flames, then suddenly the fire became a wall of steam, and from it emerged a ball of ice that moved so quickly that Bryn was unable to dodge it. The blast took her full in the chest, and she was slammed to the ground by the force of the impact. Ellis stepped from the wall of steam, her clothes badly burned, and the skin on her face showing the signs of blistering. Bryn fought hard to breathe, the impact having broken several of her ribs. She could take the few seconds to channel water and wind into the wounds to heal them, and earth to the bones to solidify them, but there was no time. Any hesitation would give Ellis the opening she needed for the final strike.

"Combat never was your strong suit, Bryn," Ellis said looking down at her battered sister. A single trickle of blood fell from the corner of Bryn's mouth, and Ellis knew she was hurt more than Ellis had initially anticipated.

Bryn coughed a little, sending blood splattering to the ground.

"I really wish that just once you would stop analyzing things Ellis. Just finish me and get it over with."

"Conceding defeat so easily dearest sister?" Ellis chided. "That is not like you. The proud Lady Fox, defeated in her own kingdom? What would your precious Aerith Seth say about that?"

"He would probably say you talk too much..."

At that Bryn kicked her feet and smashed Ellis' knee with a hard strike. Ellis toppled to the ground, and in the next moment, Bryn was on her, a dagger of fire pressed to her neck. There was no hesitation, and Bryn slit Ellis' throat, ending her lift quickly, and as painlessly as possible. For a moment, Bryn was frozen, her eyes not leaving Ellis' shocked face. Then, slowly, she rose and smoothed her dress. A pain hit Bryn suddenly as she tried to take a deep breath and it nearly forced her back to her knees. With a thought, the flows of wind, water, and earth began to weave throughout her body, knitting the damage done in the battle. Satisfied she could breathe again, Bryn looked down at her tattered dress, and in the next moment, the gown was replaced with another of equal decadence.

"Stone."

The word resounded through the courtyard. A few moments later, two of the massive forms lumbered into the courtyard, responding to the summons of their master.

"Bury Lady Ellis and Lord Grawn in the garden, and make sure they have well marked and fitting headstones. I doubt anyone but myself will grieve for their loss, but they deserve to be remembered regardless."

With that, Bryn walked away from her fallen siblings and with a purposeful stride headed for the stables. It would not take much for her to catch up with Gideon and Taya, and a part of her welcomed the thought of being with family, for as much time as she could. She had cast her lot in with the forces of the Light once again, and she inwardly wondered if it had always been that way.

Chapter XXXV

Brother of Angels

Draven had watched Gwydeon's transformation with both interest and awe. He had seen the power of the Creator at work before, but never in such a focused way. Things were going to be different now. Up until a few seconds ago Draven was sure that he could overpower Gwydeon Sandar even if Nightwing was a part of him, but now with the Brother of Angels, there was no such certainty. In the back of Draven's mind, he was trying to shut out the fear and uncertainty, letting the bravado of his birth and power fill him, but this was a different atmosphere. The battle was not just about the Light versus the Shadow anymore. This was Gwydeon versus Draven, the Creator versus Shau-ling.

"Then come, Brother of the Angels," Draven said holding his sword high in the air, "cross blades with the King of the Devils."

Gwydeon let the taunt pass over him. He could feel the tension in Draven's voice. This would be the battle that would hold sway over the rest of the war. If Draven were defeated, the battered forces of the Light would have a chance to mount an offensive not just against one kingdom but the entire phasia-controlled landscape without fear. Draven was by far the most dangerous of their number, and a victory against him would send shock waves through all of the phasia-controlled kingdoms. But if Gwydeon lost, if he were struck down by this monster, he was sure that

Draven's first targets would be Midarin and Nathaniel. With Sabrina in his clutches and Nathaniel dead, there would be no prophecy strong enough to protect the people of the world from the darkness that would eventually befall them.

Draven's charge came the next moment, the sculpted blade of the Sword of the Ram coming down in a long hard slash. Gwydeon brought up his new crystalline blade and the two weapons struck with a sound like breaking glass. At first Gwydeon thought he was dead; that the Sword of the Ram had sliced through and ended his life, but when his eyes opened after the powerful impact, he saw that Draven was just pulling himself to his feet across the room from where he had been moments earlier. The crystalline blade now pulsed with a strange white energy, seemingly charged by the impact with the Sword of the Ram. Draven reached down to recover his blade, but pulled his hand away suddenly as though he had been burned by the metal, but as Gwydeon looked, he saw ice on the polished metal blade and easily guessed the truth. The Sword of the Ram had been chilled to such a temperature that it burned whoever was stupid enough to touch it with bare skin. Draven stood still for a moment reconciling what had happened. There had been a flash of light from the very core of his enemy's blade a split-second before the actual blow was struck. The power then seemed to be released in the form of a wave of cold that assaulted Draven more soundly than a hard blow to the chest. The transformation had given Gwydeon some interesting new tricks. But as Draven was regarding Gwydeon, he saw something in the man's eyes that he had never seen before. Was it fear? Surely not after the blow he had just struck. It had been enough to level Draven, and that was not an easy feat to accomplish, especially with the Sword of the Ram in his hands. No, it was apprehension and uncertainty. Then Draven guessed at the truth. The blow had not been directed by Gwydeon, it had been merely a reflex. That brought a whole new dimension to the battle, and made Gwydeon more dangerous than he was when Nightwing had been a part of him. A man like Gwydeon Sandar was dangerous when he was in control of all of his faculties. However, throwing in an unknown that neither combatant knew the full nature or power of was like throwing a torch in a darkened room that you knew was full of powder kegs, you just didn't know where. One slip from either of them in the presence of these new powers, and they could both easily wind up dead.

Cautiously, Draven reached down again, this time channeling the simple flows of Fire into his outstretched hand. He felt the numbing, burning cold pound his flesh again, but this time it was easier to hold on, and within a few heartbeats, he was brandishing his weapon again, ready to rejoin the battle with his enemy. Gwydeon was standing very still, his crystalline blade showing its inner power with that white hot glow, ready to block whatever attack Draven saw fit to launch against him next. Draven felt the rage surge within him, but he held it at bay and slowly approached the man who could easily be called his equal. With several long, yet carefully considered strides, he stood before Gwydeon again, his blade in a ready position, but the leverage in his body not ready for a quick decisive strike. Gwydeon regarded the devil's body language and saw the casual ease with which he was walking, trying not to be unnerved by it. If Draven was trying to get to him by his matter-of-fact treatment of this duel, it would not take much more. Then, just as Gwydeon began to drop his guard, the blade of the Sword of the Ram lashed out in a quick arch and Gwydeon sidestepped and brought his own sword to bear. Draven had been testing his resolve, and Gwydeon has nearly failed.

Draven smiled to himself at the small victory. Gwydeon had been thinking too much, and it had almost overpowered his ability to act. So, the hero of the battle in the Hall of Terrors was not as invincible as he wanted everyone to believe. There was now doubt in his mind thanks to all of the new abilities. Draven began to feel that he had gained an advantage in this battle and was ready to take his full measure of revenge against Gwydeon for what he had done to his Dark Riders. The first blow of a new assault came quickly raining down on Gwydeon as the hard downward slash struck the flat of his blade. Gwydeon's parry was quick and concise, exactly as one would expect from a master of the sword. Draven recovered and continued with two quick thrusts, jabbing the point of the large weapon directly at Gwydeon's heart. Reflex took over from Gwydeon's clouded mind and parried each of the blows harmlessly away. The pace was too slow for Draven, and quickly the flurry of attacks escalated in speed and intensity. Gwydeon shook away the thoughts about his new powers and the true weight of the outcome of this battle, and let his mind focus on the blade that lay in his hands. One by one, each of Draven's attacks were blocked and harmlessly parried aside and Gwydeon remained on the defensive, blocking every long slash and hard thrust. Finally, the game began to wear on too long, and it was making Draven sloppy.

Gwydeon countered a lazy slash and stepped into Draven, locking the guard of his blade against the woven golden horns of the Sword of the Ram. Draven dug in and let all of the power within the altered musculature of his legs show as he tried to gain the upper hand in this test of strength. Gwydeon too began to exert force on the crux of the two weapons, testing the new powers given to him. They had reached a stalemate, a balance of power. But Gwydeon could hear the tensed muscles and the gritting of Draven's teeth, he was putting in everything that he had. With a single additional push, Draven was sent sprawling across the floor. The Sword of the Ram was still clutched tightly in the phase's hand, and as he dragged himself back to his feet, it was obvious to see that the battles with Rael and Trece coupled with the earlier duel with Gwydeon were beginning to take their toll on the phase. But Draven was far from done. Gwydeon could see him channeling the limitless powers of the Blaze into the Sword of the Ram, allowing that power to help sustain him and give him more than just a fighting chance. With a scream of rage, Draven charged, and Gwydeon charged too, letting his battle-cry ring loudly in the throne room. The two blades flashed and then there was a plume of blood that erupted from the side of one of the combatants as they passed. For a moment they stood, their pass finished. As each turned, the looks of the determination were etched on each face, and when Draven looked down, he saw the blood flowing from the wound newly opened in his side.

Gwydeon smiled as he saw his handiwork. Draven's blow had been parried and the counter had taken the crystalline blade and ripped the flesh of the arrogant phase. As Gwydeon looked down at the blood covering his new weapon, he was intrigued to watch as the blood flowed not off the flawless surface but into the blade itself. Now the blade began to take on a different look. Where originally the blade was a clear flawless crystal like diamond with a powerful white glow, now the blade darkened and the glow changed intensity. Once all of Draven's blood had been absorbed by the crystal, the change in the blade was complete, and the blade looked to be made of ruby, rather than diamond. The glow also had a more reddish hue, like that of the *Debuisa* gauntlet that Aryx Terian once wielded in battle.

Draven chuckled to himself after the little show. It was a simple trick to duplicate, at least in the mind of the phase.

"Well, Gwydeon," Draven said trying to sound like he wasn't breathing hard or in pain, "now that you have some of my blood, I want some of yours."

With that, Draven launched himself at Gwydeon again, this time with more fury. Blow after blow rained down on Gwydeon, and each one was parried in turn. But Gwydeon was not content to just parry this time around. The parries quickly became counters, and Draven had to block more blows than he was attempting. In only a matter of seconds, Draven was totally on the defensive, and was stumbling backward against the flashing assaults of the ruby blade. Gwydeon felt a rage building inside of him like he had never felt before. In the back of his mind, he began to see all of the horrors that Draven had done in his short perverted existence. He saw the fires leaping up from the burning buildings in Aradon and heard the cries of anguish from people that he knew from when he was a child. He saw the broken and headless form of the man who should have been his son lying tattered on the battlefield, the red armor scarred forever by Draven's blade. Then the palace of Scalla, where the execution of Erika Belnosian took place, and he saw the moment Draven turned her own dagger against her to slit her throat. It was Sabrina's face and the look of her abused body that lit the fire in Gwydeon the most. He saw her still, heaped in Pike's arms battered and shaking with fear after what that devil Draven had done to her. The taunts and threats to Gwydeon's family rang loudly in his ears, and the fires were stoked to their highest intensity. Gwydeon in that moment sent a crushing blow down upon Draven. It sounded like thunder when it struck the blade of the Sword of the Ram. Draven reeled from the impact, but was able to bring up the blade in time as the next hard downward slash hit. Draven was nearly forced to one knee. The third slash was powerful enough to put Draven down on one knee, one hand on the hilt of the Sword of the Ram while the other braced the blade in an effort to block the continued onslaught. Over and over, the hard crystal blade slammed into the polished steel of the Sword of the Ram, the intensity of the thunder echoing in the hall like a storm was about the brew in the center of the throne room. Gwydeon continued the assault, unrelenting as he pounded down upon the nearly defenseless phase over and over again. A cry of rage tore from Gwydeon's throat as he brought the ruby blade crashing down again. Draven braced himself for the impact and then heard a sound unlike any that he had ever heard before. That was when the pain hit.

* * * * * * * * * * *

Emries stood quietly and took a breath of the crisp evening air. The time had come for him to rectify some of the mistakes that he had made in the past and once and for all defeat his brother Shau-ling. No one would stand in his way this time around. Emries could still smell the burning flesh of the Jeresei from the assault launched by his newest protégé Nathaniel Rice, and he grinned to himself that the boy was taking the fight to the phasia the way it had always been intended. The first and second generations had been too soft, and now this dark mirror was the result of that lax treatment of the future. Fate had not been kind to this world, and a high price would have to be paid. There before him on the ground lay the beaten body of a man that Emries wished he could have respected.

Logan Ranthall had been a thorn in Emries' side for far too many years. Too many times he should have just laid down and died, but his will was too strong. But that will had almost been broken with the death of Elwyne Tamerlane. It was only the hatred for Shau-ling and the rest of the phasia that had kept him going. Emries had thought that the hatred would have made him a powerful enough pawn to be used in the war, but instead Logan went into hiding only to be taunted out by Draven. A second time, Emries nearly had control of Logan's mind and his powers, but it was not to be as those damned Elder got in the way and told Logan the truth about the war. But what did it matter what his motivations were? Emries was still right. Men were at risk of being totally decimated by the will of Shau-ling. Why did it matter what caused that will? Emries was doing what he could to protect his people, and this pathetic lout was standing in his way. The judgement was already passed, and the punishment would be severe. However, thanks to Nathaniel, Emries doubted that Logan would feel a thing.

Emries raised his hand and could feel the power collecting within his clenched fist. It would only take a bit of the power that he wielded, but Emries wanted to be sure that Logan would not be able to recover from the blow that was inflicted. *That should be more than enough*, Emries thought to himself as he brought down his glowing fist and regarded it for a moment. He then pointed his hand at the limp figure and willed a bolt of energy to erupt from his outstretched fingers. Suddenly, a terrible pain ripped through Emries like a scythe. His insides were on fire and he felt the pain radiate through him as though he had been struck by a mountain. The bolt of power missed the mark by a wide margin, but Emries could barely keep himself conscious enough to care. The pain was slowly beginning to ease, but all of the power and energy had been sapped from his body by the incredible pain. His eyes had trouble focusing. Was Logan moving? Suddenly he realized that something had woken the former hero from his pain-induced slumber. Had he screamed when the pain hit? It was then that Emries realized that a huge cut had opened in his stomach and blood was soaking the front of his normally bright white clothing. It took only a minor thought to seal the wound and stop the bleeding, but there were other concerns now. The opportunity for a quiet execution was now long gone. Logan was indeed moving, and it looked as though he was ready for a fight. Emries wondered two things as the impudent mortal forced himself back to his feet. Whether he was still strong enough to take the mortal apart with his bare hands, and what the cause of the immense pain had been.

* * * * * * * * * * *

Gwydeon had never expected his rage to be that powerful. He had been lost in the thoughts that were consuming him, and could not help but pound over and over again on the unrelenting steel of the Sword of the Ram. But then suddenly there had been a sound like a thousand wolves baying at the moon mixed with a thousand more screams of agony and anguish. Gwydeon had to blink twice to make sure that he was not seeing things. The Sword of the Ram was broken and, no it couldn't be... The single downward slash had continued into the flesh of the most hated member of the phasia and had cleaved Draven in two. It must have been his blood coating the severed ends of the sword. So, Gwydeon kicked the pieces of the sword out of the dead phase's hands. The two pieces clattered to a stop next to the golden throne and Gwydeon eyed them intently for a few moments to make sure it had only been a trick his eyes had played upon him. But as he waited those next few heartbeats, he realized that it had not been a dream or a trick of the light. His eyes watched as the pools of blood by the severed ends of the sword grew every second. The Sword of the Ram, the birthright of the third member of the *Coromors* of the prophecy had been cut in two and it was bleeding.

Gwydeon pulled his gaze away from the sword and let it fall back on the badly broken body of the man he had known as Draven. The impossibly strong strike from Gwydeon's sword had first struck Draven's head, and death Gwydeon was sure, had been quick. Draven had been spared the worst of it. Gwydeon inwardly wondered if it should have been a longer and slower death considering what Draven had done over the years to the people that Gwydeon loved. But the nightmare was over, and the world would be able to rest again now that Draven's reign of terror had been ended. The slash had made it all the way down to the middle of Draven's chest, exposing the cavity where Draven's black heart lay. It too had been divided in half, a fitting testament to the actions of one of the greatest heroes remaining in the world. But Gwydeon could not stand around and compliment himself on a job well done. There was still much work to be done and still many more answers to be found. The disposition of the Sword of the Ram was one of those questions. Carefully, Gwydeon recovered the two pieces of the sword and wrapped the 'wounds' so that the bleeding was stopped. He then wrapped the two pieces together and held them tight to his side. After putting his sword back in the scabbard that hung at his side, Gwydeon decided it was time to get Sabrina and start making plans to move against the rest of the phasia and to let Midarin know that he was still alive. But how would she react to the way that he was now? Maybe the time was not yet right for Gwydeon Sandar to reappear in the world. The problem of transportation entered Gwydeon's mind for the first time. His ability to use portals had been taken away from him, and flying with his new wings would make it easy for anyone to see him. Suddenly the knowledge entered his mind. The huge white wings began to glow, and as the feathers receded away to pure white light, they wrapped around Gwydeon and in the next second, he was gone.

* * * * * * * * * * * *

By the blood covered golden throne, the lightning blade of Vengeance lay discarded. Draven had used it to heal his wounds before the battle that would end his evil life. A long spark leaped from the twitching blade and touched the burned mark where Vengeance had been obliterated by the power of Nightwing. The spark receded after a moment, only to be followed by two more. The sparks searched the ground for a few moments and then returned to the blade. Four sparks lanced out the next few moments, and as they covered the charred palace floor, one of them touched a fragment of metal left over from the clothing of the former member of the Dark Riders. The piece of metal was lifted into the air the next moment, held aloft by the sparks of lightning. A single drop of blood fell from the metal and splattered to the floor. Lightning covered the drop of blood the next second, and the activity was fast and furious. From the floor up, the lightning sparks began to rebuild the body of Vengeance piece by piece. In a matter of mere minutes, Vengeance stood whole again; her body surrounded by the lightning from her blade. After a quick blink of her pupil-less eyes, Vengeance was clothed in her normal garb, and the lightning sword floated from the ground and rested its hilt gently in her outstretched hand. For a long moment, the stark white female stood surveying the scene. She could feel the power from the battle that had just taken place, and the residue of the power of Gwydeon Sandar hung like a fog in the air. That was when her eyes fell on the body of her master, Draven.

The body of the phase looked like a deflated mass of skin lying in a pool of blood. His head was split wide open, and Draven's right shoulder had nearly been sheared off by the might of the blow that had ended his life. Vengeance stood silently, her eyes locked on his fallen form. The blade of lightning began to flash the next moment, the sparks leaping from piece to piece of the phase. As Vengeance stood looking on, the huge vicious wounds on the body of the phase began to seal as Vengeance slowly began to reverse the flows of time around the body of her fallen master. After all of the wounds sealed, Draven's chest began to rise and fall in a normal pattern and the sparks of lightning faded away back into Vengeance's blade. Suddenly, Draven's eyes opened, and he sat up. His breathing was erratic the next few seconds, and Draven looked around, still trying to comprehend what had happened. It was only when he saw Vengeance staring down at him that he guess the truth. Gwydeon had won the battle and struck Draven down. Not only that, the Sword of the Ram was gone, apparently stolen by Gwydeon Sandar. Brother of Angels indeed, he was nothing more than a common thief. Rage began to build within Draven. Now there were a few more names added to his list of people to kill: Gwydeon Sandar, Midarin Rice, Nathaniel Sandar, and Sabrina Binosear to name a few. But there were other grudges to be settled that were far more important at the moment. The decimation of the Brother of Angels and his pathetic family could wait a little while, after all, they were only mortals. There was revenge to be served on Rael and Trece and their little helper. But for that, the Dark Riders had to be at full strength, and at the moment, they were two members down.

Draven first took a bag and collected all the discarded pieces of metal from where Gwydeon Sandar's transformation tool place. He was sure that Nightwing could be salvaged from the wreckage and it would only take time and the right person underneath the armor. But Wrath was the most important part of the puzzle. With a blink of an eye, Draven created a portal and found himself and Vengeance out in the middle of a field which lay under the wide evening sky that had served as the battlefield for Wrath and Nightwing. Strewn across the ground were huge pieces of the carcass from the impressive beast once known as Wrath. It took nearly two hours for Draven and Vengeance to compile all of the pieces of Wrath's body, but finally they had them all neatly piled together. Slowly they began to piece the puzzle together, putting every limb and organ back in its proper position. For a normal mortal this would have been sickening and stomach turning work, but Draven's work was filled with purpose. He had been consumed by revenge, and nothing was going to stand in his way. Finally it was done, the massive beast had been reconstructed, and as Draven lowered the head into position, he could see the tendons and ligaments reach out to connect with the large torso, the quick healing still very active even in the decapitated body. Draven's eyes lit up, and a cruel smile crept on to his face as he watched Wrath heal his body into full working condition. Finally, when Wrath stood up, Draven let loose a laugh that would rival the power of the Great Dark One.

"Now," Draven said looking at his two resurrected Dark Riders, "It is time to pay my dear brother and sister Rael and Trece a visit. Hopefully we will get to them before the other Dark Riders have finished with them."

* * * * * * * * * * *

The heap of rubble once called the city of Aradon was a cold and desolate place, certainly beneath the standards of a princess. However, Sabrina Binosear somehow found it comforting. There were many questions that still needed answers, not the least of which was the disposition of the man known as Gwydeon Sandar. The stories about Gwydeon had always fascinated Sabrina while she was growing up, and Logan Ranthall always told them with such passion that they seemed to come alive. Logan would eventually be her new father, Sabrina was sure of that, if life ever got back to normal again. But Gwydeon was not the Gwydeon out of those stories. He was different now, with a wife and children to protect. And yet he still risked his life, battling Draven, not once, but twice on her behalf. Pike Rhuiden had also done everything in his power to save her. Sabrina started to wonder where Pike was, but her thoughts were cut off as a strange power began to fill the room.

Ever since Sabrina was a little girl, she had been aware of the different powers in the world around her. She could see the subtle flows that would weave themselves together in every plant and even in the air itself. Also, she could see this power active in some of the people around her. But it was when she began to see Logan Ranthall that the biggest change in her took place. Being around Logan was like turning on a water valve. Where originally the powers flowed through her in a steady trickle, being with Logan was like a dam breaking inside of her. She was filled with such power and life that she felt as if she would burst. That was also when the voice began in the back of her head, telling her stories of the past, and hopes for the future. It felt the same when she was in Pike's loving arms. The same, but different. She had been hurt deeply by Draven, in places she didn't know she could be hurt. When Pike held her, she felt the power inside of him, and somehow, by opening herself up to that power, she could feel it flowing into her. With his powers inside of her, she was able to knit the subtle wounds of her body, and put her mind at rest, the best she could.

The power began to intensify, and Sabrina readied herself for a fight. She was not sure how to use her powers offensively yet, but if there was ever a time to learn, it was now. She knew the knowledge was somewhere within her, part of her tie to her mysterious patron, but she didn't know how to tap into it. Sabrina kept waiting for the telltale spike in power that would identify the location of the forming portal, but it never came. Suddenly there was a flash of white light in the corner of the room, and when it receded, Gwydeon Sandar stood before her. Only Gwydeon had . . . wings?

Gwydeon emerged from the white light a little shaken. Only the bat of an eyelash ago he had been in Scalla, and now he stood at the heart of Aradon. Portals took much longer than that, a full minute in some cases. Sabrina was right where Gwydeon sent her, in the burned out remains of Logan Ranthall's home. For Gwydeon, the place felt like home too. There was an uncertainty in Sabrina's eyes, and Gwydeon could guess that it was caused by the rather noticeable new appendages he had grown since their last meeting.

"Are you alright?" Gwydeon asked taking a step forward.

The princess nodded. Gwydeon paused and regarded the girl, not knowing what to say, or what to do. He started to open his mouth to speak, but Sabrina waived him off and smiled.

"Draven?"

"Dead."

"And the sword?" Sabrina questioned stepping forward.

The answer came in the form of Gwydeon producing the two wrapped pieces of the Sword of the Ram, which he held out to Sabrina. Something changed in the face of the girl in the next moment. It was as if someone or something else was guiding her actions. She took both pieces of the sword, and took great care in unwrapping them. The blood still flowed thickly from the area of the break, but Sabrina seemed to pay it no mind. When Sabrina closed her eyes the whole sword began to glow, and the flow of the blood ceased.

"That's better," Sabrina said in a distant voice.

Gwydeon observed the incident with a detached presence. He knew that Sabrina Binosear was the *Chosen One* of the prophecies, the direct recipient of the powers of Aerith Seth. Her link to Emries and the prophecies was tenuous at best, but her powers were not to be ignored in the fight against Shau-ling. Gwydeon continued to watch as the glow around the broken edges of the blade intensified. It was almost as if heat was radiating from the polished metal. In that instant, Gwydeon thought he saw the metal of the blade move. Gwydeon blinked his eyes twice hard, and then refocused on the blade. He had not been seeing things. The metal had not only moved; it was still moving, liquefied by the powers of the *Chosen One* in the area of the break. Without a word, Sabrina melded the pieces back together and once again, the Sword of the Ram was whole. However, Gwydeon could tell that there was something different about the sword now. It was almost as if something had been taken away, and now it was only a sword. Even the rams that made up the hilt seemed dim and lifeless.

"There," Sabrina said, admiring her handiwork, "much better."

Gwydeon nodded absently, still chewing on the puzzle of the sword.

"So, where to now?"

Gwydeon thought hard for a moment before answering.

"Back to Scalla. For some reason I have the suspicion that we haven't seen the last of Draven."

Sabrina nodded, and then the white light enveloped them both.

* * * * * * * * * * *

Near the burned out town of Aradon, sat the remains of a church, and in those remains stood a pedestal, which served as the home to the Book of the Creator. The glass case, which had covered the book for thousands of years, lay broken on the ground and the pages of the book were ruffled slowly by the breeze. A hand softly touched the pages and began to skim through them. Finding a passage, the hands held down the pages from the mercy of the wind and a voice read out the words of the passage to the empty countryside.

And the rage of the Creator shall rain down darkness upon the world, and in darkness shall come the very nightmares of men. A civil war fought between the minions of Light and of Darkness shall consume the hearts and minds of every man and woman who breathes, and the fabric of reality shall be woven around this war. When the world is split asunder, man will face its greatest challenge in the arms of death and life. The Chosen Ones shall rise again to lead the people back from the brink, only to be plunged in again by those who would be gods. One rebellious son shall fall, and one shall rise, but they will only rule ashes when the Creator's will be done. The only hope of salvation is to be found in the might of steel, and remaking the old into new. Lions will fall to the might of a feather. Dragons will fly only to attack their own. Rams will have broken horns mended. When each reflection meets itself again, the mirror shall shatter. So it is written, so shall it be done.

Aerith Seth stepped away from the book, letting the words never before spoken by human lips linger in the air like frost on a winter morning. Maybe he had been wrong about the little girl Sabrina. The one in the light reality may have been full of herself; thickheaded like her father, but this one could be the very heir that Aerith had always dreamed of. He had never truly been a father to any of his children, and his time on the world did not permit second chances. But at least, it would be his descendant, the *Chosen One* of the prophecies that would fulfill the words of the Creator. She had mended the Ram's broken horns. And the cycle had begun. Aerith smiled to himself and began walking. There was only one place left to go, and one more goodbye to be said.

Revealing Light

Creator's Calendar Year 1205; Light Reality

Skies began to darken over the little country town of Aradon, a signal that the rains were about to come again. Rain had never been a good omen for the people in this sleepy town, marking the coming of dark times. In a generation past, the rains had marked the start of an attack by the forces of the Shadow; huge beasts whose only thought was destruction, whose only purpose was death. It had taken many years to erase the pain and devastation caused by that attack, and many more before the wounded hearts would begin to heal. But they did heal, and everyone went on. However, the pain would return, as a new generation held the same promise of death, war, and pain. And as the cycle began again, it was marked not only with the death of legends, but with the hard cold rain.

Midarin Rice heard the thunder roll off in the distance and stifled a shudder. It was too early to be jumping at shadows again. For years, she had dreaded the day when she would have to return to the wars between the Light and the Shadow, but in her heart, she knew that her place was beside her old friends. Aryx had come to her many years before, and while they had never been friends, she felt better with the connection to the past close. He was an old warrior, and he had seen more of the war between the Light and the Shadow than any of them had, and probably more than he had any right to see. Despite his advancing age, he was still the equal of any solider in the ranks of any army that considered itself an ally of the Light.

His presence made the enemy nervous and emboldened their allies. He had been the primary driving force behind the rapid acceleration of the maturation of the Order of the Sword. When Midarin found Pike and Jerrard in their post-war incarnations, she held their company like a newborn child clings to its mother. There was a protection and a security there that she needed to survive. There were still nights, when she lay awake talking to the man who had stolen her heart. For some reason, she believed that Gwydeon could hear her. The promise made by Emries that Gwydeon would become the Brother of the Angels almost guaranteed that fact. Midarin had hoped that in some way she could feel Gwydeon in her heart, or in the back of her mind where the most primal of emotions lay, but no answer came. Even in the early moments of the morning, between night and day where sometimes dreams become reality, there was no comfort for her solace. The few times that Midarin and Elwyne had been left alone to talk after Logan's death they had both touched on that palpable sensation of connectedness, the tangible feeling that they were not alone but cloak in love. However, Elwyne was content in that love, that security. But as much as Midarin had loved Gwydeon, her life did not end with his, and her heart would not allow her to confine herself to the memory of a lost love. So, it had been Pike that had filled the void inside of her.

Midarin had thought once that she could understand Pike Rhuiden better than his wife Cairyn, hoping that his brooding and anger had only been an act to keep Cairyn at bay. However, Midarin soon became entrapped, as all of Pike's mistresses had over the years, in the circle of pain and self-destructive anguish. But somehow it had been easy for her to fall in love with Pike, or at least with the idea of what Pike represented. Here was a man full of fire and passion, though they were almost always steered in the wrong direction. His voice echoed with the words of his soul, with a power and timbre that none could match, but the pain and sorrow that sometimes filled the chords of his song were enough to make the most hardened poet weep. If Midarin had to compare Pike to anything in the world, it would be to a dying rose. The fate of the flower is inevitable, as the seasons change and the weather worsens, the flower will die. But there are some flowers, like the rose, that can fight the death, its thorns there to prick those who venture too close, and the scent of the petals becoming more sweet and intoxicating. That was the definition of the heart of Pike Rhuiden. Everyone knew that his recklessness and rage would cause him to meet a violent and bloody end, and yet women were still drawn by his beautiful words, caring heart, and passionate embrace. Midarin had found herself ensnared like all the others, but to a more profound degree. His wars would only be the end of the story to the other women that had shared Pike's bed. A loss to be sure, but their lives would go on. For Midarin, the connection ran deeper. When Midarin had been with Gwydeon, she learned quickly that no matter the trial, no matter the threat of death, Gwydeon would fight. He would fight with every fiber of his being, every beat of his heart because his life meant the lives of others. He lived because he could do nothing else. He did not seek death, in fact he seemed to repel it when everything said that he should not be able to. Pike seemed to actively seek his end, but continue to survive, like the punchline of some cosmic joke. And yet every scrape, every close call, made Pike long for his own end even more. Pike's web of death and destruction had ensnared her too, and she knew in her heart that Pike's death would most likely be the doorway to her own.

Another clap of thunder rolled through the hillside, shaking Midarin away from her thoughts. The sound had also caused the other woman in the house to stir, the stranger Susanne Praen. The healer had left only moments before, saying that she had done all she could. Midarin, of course, had been curious and had gone to sit by the woman's side. All of the wounds had been bandaged, and the woman had been resting quietly in the bed that had once belonged to Elwyne Ranthall. As Midarin stroked the woman's long blond hair, trying to ease her back into sleep, a spark of recognition shot through her unlike she had ever felt before. The woman below her was no longer Susanne, but Elizabeth, one of Pike's Enforcers. The vision was intense and painful, shocking enough for Midarin to pull her hand away suddenly and gasp. Susanne did not take notice of the occurrence, and faded back into sleep. But the vision had shaken something deep inside of Midarin. Old instincts floated back to the surface. She began to think not like the Queen of Brea, but as the banished princess she had been all those years ago, tagging along with the band of men and women who would become known as the People of the Dragon in legends.

Standing slowly, Midarin walked back into the main room of the home, recovered her backpack, and then walked into one of the other adjoining bedrooms. She stripped quickly out of her clothes and then reached into her bag and recovered a brown paper package sealed with a single piece of twine. It had been a long time since she had ever laid eyes on the contents of the parcel, but she knew it was time. Quickly she untied the knot in the twine and opened the package. The clothing lying there before her had been lying in wait for over twenty years. They were the same shirt and pants she had worn after she and Gwydeon had made love the first time in Sador. Midarin slipped the shirt over her head quickly and then pulled on the pants, feeling them pull snug around her hips. Remarkably, she had been able to return to her fighting shape after having two children, another thing she would have to remember to thank Aryx for before it was all over. How many other queens of major kingdoms would have found herself in the practice fields just before first light every morning working on her sword and bow skills? How many other rulers could claim learning the sword under two different sword masters? In the end, Midarin did not want to be remembered for sitting on a throne as the world crashed down around them.

As she admired herself in the long mirror in the room, she smiled and pulled her hair back and tied a single piece of green cloth around it to hold it in a tail. The piece of cloth had remained from Gwydeon's green shirt from the battle of the Twin Towns, one of the few remnants of her days with him. Confident with her appearance, she pulled a small pair of leather gloves out of her pack and slid them on slowly, and then sat down and pulled on her knee-high boots. After another sideways glance in the mirror, Midarin walked out of the bedroom and out the front door of the house to where her horse was tied. It had only been on a whim that she had packed all of her important belongings, and it was obvious her whim had proven important. After recovering her longbow and quiver from her saddle, Midarin looked up to see her young companions emerging from Logan's Wood. Midarin then turned quickly and returned to the house after withdrawing a sword from a scabbard hanging on her saddle. The sword caught the remaining light, drawing the woman's eyes to the golden etching on the blade. It was the sword that had belonged to Gwydeon Sandar, the man that she loved. For many years it had been kept in secret in her bedroom, a last remembrance brought to her by Elwyne Tamerlane. Trying to contain the emotion of the moment, Midarin pushed the blade into the scabbard on her belt and then strode back into the little farmhouse to await the arrival of her companions.

When she returned to the main room, she was greeted by an awakened Susanne Praen. She stood proudly in the center of the room, wrapped in a sheet, staring defiantly at Midarin. Midarin could tell from the blond woman's eyes that she wanted very much to be a part of what was about to happen. She smiled and then spoke softly.

"My friends will be here in a few minutes, and I don't think you really want to greet them wearing that sheet. We found a bag lying in a corner of the church. Apparently you had a friend in the Torch who wanted to make sure you were taken care of, because there were some clothes in the bag as well as food and a dagger."

Susanne looked down at the floor and smiled.

"That would be my sister, Kiara," Susanne said in a stronger voice. "I figured that she would do something like that, but because of the way things happened, she and I did not have very many opportunities to discuss it. Everyone knew that I would eventually be expelled from the Torch, so she must have had this planned for a very long time."

Midarin nodded and fell silent. There was an uncomfortable air that entered the room holding between the two women for a moment, and then faded as soon as Susanne returned to Elwyne's bedroom. There were no reasons for Midarin to trust the woman, but there was less reason to distrust her. The last time that a seemingly helpless woman had been rescued from mortal danger by the forces of the Light, she tried to kill Elwyne in an effort to get to Logan. But Susanne was most likely not another Jasmen Hiedra. Quickly she shook the thoughts of Susanne's motives away and turned in time to see the door to the country home open. Wolf Ranthall was the first to enter the house, quickly followed by Lissa Terian, Jared Vale, and Sabrina Rhuiden. There were quick looks of recognition that passed between all of them, and then Gwillim Sandar, Nathaniel Rice, Aryx Terian, and Liette Forer arrived. Liette looked angry, and most of her stares were directed at Wolf. For some reason, she had been angry with the young man from the moment she laid eyes on him, and Midarin wondered if it was only the powers of the phasia that was motivating her. Aryx had a strange look in his eyes too. It was one that Midarin had seen only a handful of times before. It was the same blank expression that sat on his face every year on the anniversary of his wedding to Diana. That more than anything tipped Midarin to the fact that something was wrong. Gwillim too reacted, but it was more to the attire that Midarin had changed into.

"Mother?" Gwillim said inquisitively.

"I figured it was about time that I stop being the Queen of Brea, and start being Midarin Rice, the former member of the People of the Dragon. Seeing Susanne has reminded me of why this whole war started, and I know that while it may go on without me, I don't want it to. I'm ready to fight and help Nathaniel battle Shau-ling."

There was a sound of something breaking coming from the third and smallest of the bedrooms of the home. Wolf looked back toward the room where he had lived for many years and winced. Moments later, Cairyn emerged from the back room holding the pieces of a shattered glass.

"I knew there was a connection," Cairyn said almost accusingly.

Midarin would have cursed her loose tongue and not knowing who was in earshot of her words, but there was little time or need for it now. How Pike managed information that flowed within the halls of his kingdoms was one thing, but there were greater considerations now. Cairyn's accusations continued though there was not as much venom in her voice as Midarin would have expected considering the level of the betrayal.

"Pike was taking far too much notice of the boy to just be friendly. He swore to me that he knew nothing of the *Coromor* and the other pieces of the war and he was just doing his part for Logan. There is more to this, isn't there?"

Sabrina took a step forward and squared off against her mother.

"Yes, mother," she started slowly, "there is. Pike has been training Lissa, Gwillim, Nathaniel, and I for this war for many years, but we hid it from you because you forbade father from telling us the stories from his time with Logan Ranthall and the rest of the People of the Dragon. Pike has known since he returned from Shau-ling's palace that Nathaniel would be the *Coromor*, but he found out a few years after I was born that I am the *Chosen One*, like Logan was in the last generation."

Cairyn was shocked for a moment, and did not even seem to be listening as Sabrina told of her training and the involvement of Jerrard Mystic and Midarin. She told of Lissa's involvement and Gwillim's role in the situation, but Cairyn gave no other reaction. The queen stood transfixed through the entire tale, and when it was done, she calmly exhaled and then sat down at the head of the meeting table in the center of the main room. Many of the others had already sat down, and Jared among them had been listening intently. No one noticed that Susanne had also been listening from the doorway, and no one would have known she was there had Jared not looked over and whistled at the sight.

Susanne has changed into the clothes that her sister had packed, but she never expected the uniform that was waiting for her. In the time when the Moridon had united as the Hand of the Light, they had worn ceremonial gowns of white. When the original war between the Light and the Shadow broke out, they donned their attire again to follow the *Coromor* in his trials. Dei had intended the same to be the case with the Torch, but under Seraph's teachings the white lost its meaning and became only a symbol of a long dead group of misguided religious fanatics. Kiara had created a new ceremonial gown for Susanne; however, with a single device adorning the left breast. The gown itself had a leather quality, dyed midnight black so that it glistened in the light. A single piece of the fabric draped around the back of her neck, and connected to a bodice that clung tightly from her bosom to her waist. Her shoulders were left totally exposed by the garment, allowing for greater range of motion. Long black leather gloves hugged her hands and forearms up to her elbow, and blackened steel bracelets held them in place. Beneath the leather tunic however were hardened leather pads that shielded all of her vital organs from slashing attacks, and would have only been vulnerable to precise stabs from the sharpest piercing weapons. The pants of the uniform were constructed in much the same way, with thick pads covering her thighs but openings left at the hips to increase mobility. The pads at her calf were thinner, but still would have prevented attacks that would cripple. The finishing touch of the uniform were the high leather boots with a gentle arch and nearly a heel. The looked to be a heavily modified riding boot, and there were clear indications that very light chainmail was woven into the vulnerable area where the boots laced up. By nature the uniform was impossibly form-fitting, creating an elegant almost sensual display, but it was clearly an outfit designed for battle. The symbol on her left breast was done in white, displaying the forehead, face, and horns of a ram.

"That is quite an outfit Susanne," Midarin said quickly. "That is not what I expected your sister to send."

"This is the standard battle attire for female members of the Torch, except for the color. Their gowns are white with the symbol of the torch on the left breast," Susanne replied.

"Clearly," Gwillim said scratching his beard, "the Torch intended to see combat on a consistent basis. A great deal of thought went into that uniform's construction."

Wolf was not happy to hear the foreboding tone in Gwillim's voice, but the implication was clear. According to the memories of the Blaze, the Moridon upon whom the Creator's Torch Society was based was not a militant group, but fought only when necessary. The Torch however seemed intent on being the one to start the conflict. Looking into the eyes of first Lissa and then Jared, it seemed that they shared the same opinion.

"I take it something is wrong," Midarin said, pulling her attention from Susanne.

"Yes, my queen," Aryx responded stepping forward. "Liette and I encountered the twin phasia Rael and Trece in the wood. Their presence here and quick retreat prompted me to assume they were merely here to see who attended the funeral of Elwyne Tamerlane. If that is true, then Shau-ling knows exactly who is in Lakestone, and Pike and the Enforcers are most likely in danger. But it also means that once again the forces of the Shadow appear to be several steps ahead of us."

"But there is more," Wolf added, "it is most likely too late to help Pike, and in my opinion I want nothing to do with him and his fight. My path is pointing toward Barer. Bryn has information that I need about Aerith Seth and his role in this. With Susanne's information about the Torch, we need to track down all leads that could help us in the fight against Shau-ling. Taking the fight directly to Shau-ling's army isn't what is going to win this war. As Aryx said, information and tactics are the only way to stand against an opponent who is ready for you."

Midarin nodded to herself and then sighed. Her place was with her old ally, not with the new band of heroes. She was a member of the People of the Dragon, and though her son was the *Coromor*, she would never be a part of the People of the Ram. Pike needed her there with him, and because of that, there was no choice.

"Well," Midarin said after a moment, "then I suppose this is the point where we part ways. My place is with Pike, trying to save him from himself if I can. Jerrard will also be embroiled in this before too long, and the Order will need a leader with a level head. Perhaps we can keep the phasia's focus long enough for you to do what must be done in Barer, and before you make whatever move comes after. I wish you all the best of luck in your journey to come, and I hope that I'll be right there beside you when Nathaniel takes on Shau-ling."

Wolf nodded, and the rest remained silent.

"If I may, my queen," Aryx said quickly, "I would like to go with you to Lakestone. My steel will be a great help to you in the battles that lay ahead, and, as I am sure you are aware; I do not belong beside the *Coromor* any longer. My master and friend is long dead, and so my tie to Emries' mantle no longer exists. Pike may not be glad of my arrival, but he cannot question the need for soldiers like me in this war, despite how he may question my loyalty."

Midarin nodded.

"I will be very happy to have your company Aryx, because I think this is going to be a very long and dangerous road. Wolf, if you would do the honors and send us to Scalla, I would be very grateful. It might shock Jerrard us traveling by portal, but I think expediency now is more important than adherence to courtly manner."

Wolf nodded and then closed his eyes. In a matter of seconds, a swirling blue portal appeared out of thin air and hovered before Midarin and Aryx. Taking a moment, Midarin turned and hugged first Nathaniel and then Gwillim.

"Be careful," the older man said softly.

Midarin nodded and then turned her attention to Liette. The little girl tried her best to smile, and then hugged her mother. Midarin then waived to Sabrina and Lissa before nodding to Aryx. The two of them stepped through the portal together and then it winked out of existence as Wolf opened his eyes.

"I suppose that I should probably be heading back to Trelon," Cairyn said after a moment.

It was very clear that she had been shaken by the revelations of her family's role in the war against the Shadow, but something told Wolf that she had not been taken completely by surprise. Cairyn was an amazingly astute woman, and it was clear that she had clues for a long period of time, but had not been able to piece together the puzzle correctly. Or perhaps she had, and this was all a ruse and she was simply playing the part that destiny had fated for her. When she spoke again, the regal manner had returned to her voice.

"Duncan will be back into the fold soon, and I can just feel that he is going to make trouble, especially with his father out fighting the Shadow. It would be the perfect time for Duncan to make a grasp for power in Marcwell. Not only that I hear that he got married while he was out on the Frontier. More likely than not, he has his eye on my throne too. It seems like I am always cleaning up Pike's messes."

The last has more barbs to it that were probably intended, but Wolf could see the barely veiled pained expression come to Sabrina's features.

"Should I open a portal for you as well my Queen?" Wolf asked.

"You've earned the right to call me Cairyn, Wolf," the older woman answered smiling. "And yes, I would appreciate that very much. I am not in the mood to ride for three days alone, even if it is through Logan's Wood."

Wolf nodded and then opened another portal. Cairyn kissed Sabrina on the forehead and then smiled to Lissa before stepping through the portal. After it disappeared, Wolf turned to set his glance upon the newcomer to the battle against Shau-ling, Susanne Praen.

"I know that you have your own vendettas, Susanne, but you have heard what is at stake. You are welcome to come with us to Barer," Wolf said his expression as dire as he could make it. "I'm sure soon enough we will tangle with the Torch, and any information you can give us will be appreciated when that time comes. Or is there somewhere that I can send you?"

Susanne shook her head.

"My road leads toward a collision with Seraph and the Torch that much is certain. However, the Torch was created and dedicated to assisting the *Coromor* in his battle against the phasia and Shau-ling. How could I let my own personal quarrels interfere with the mission that I dedicated my life to? In the end, we all have to do what must be done more than what we wish to do."

Jared seemed the most uncomfortable with Susanne's words.

"We should get ready to travel," Nathaniel interjected. "Because we are going into a phasia controlled kingdom, it would not be wise to just portal in. We can take a portal as far as Frontier, and then ride the rest of the way in. That is the safest bet."

"I agree," Wolf responded. "If you will get your horses ready, we can get out of here as soon as possible."

Gwillim, Jared, and Nathaniel were the first three out the door. Liette lingered for a moment, her eyes glaring at Wolf, but she relented a moment later and withdrew. Sabrina also lingered, looking back and forth between Lissa and Wolf before turning and joining Liette in walking out the front door. Susanne smiled to Wolf and then spoke.

"I'm sure we can do the introductions later. However, since you seem to be the one who is in charge of this little escapade, I suppose I should know who you are. You consort with powerful company in the Queen of Trelon and the Queen of Brea. Of course I recognized them immediately. And of course I have my suspicions about the brown-haired woman who just exited, as well as the two men. Dei was very clear that we had to know who the power players were in this war."

Wolf nodded.

"Sorry," Wolf said blushing a bit, "I keep forgetting my manners when introducing myself."

Lissa scowled in Wolf's direction.

"My name is Wolf Ranthall."

Susanne looked shocked for a moment and then recovered.

"You are the one whom the prophecies of the Dragon spoke of."

Wolf was taken aback for a moment and then asked the inevitable question.

"What prophecies of the Dragon?"

When Susanne spoke it felt almost as though she were reciting from a practiced speech, or reading from a book.

"The Moridon have always been able to communicate with others of their kind who reside on the Other Side. Most people would call it speaking with the dead. After Dei left us, Seraph took control of all the communications, delving more into the War of the Dragon, and the last of the Moridon, a man named Talos. It was from the teachings of this man Talos that Seraph pieced together what came to be known to the Torch as the Prophecies of the Dragon. It told that the son of the Dragon would be the doom of the world. He would bring a destruction unlike any that had ever been seen before, and his life signaled the end of the Prophecies of the *Coromor* as well as the life of the patron Emries."

Wolf just stood for a moment somehow taking inner pleasure in the prophecy that Susanne had just spoken.

"That's our boy," Lissa commented lightly, tapping Wolf on the shoulder. "My name is Lissa by the way, Lissa Terian."

Susanne tensed slightly at Lissa's last name, but it passed quickly.

"Pleasure to meet you both. I'm sure that we will have a lot to talk about in the times to come. I should probably go introduce myself to everyone else and try to be friendly. I am afraid that you all have yet to see me at my best."

Susanne walked past Wolf and Lissa and quickly exited the house. Lissa and Wolf stood looking at each other for a moment, and Wolf's eyes began to wander down over Lissa's body.

"Just what do you think you're doing?" she said gruffly.

"Imagining what you would look like in that outfit," Wolf answered, his eyes never being diverted from their path.

"Could you please get your mind on more serious business?"

"Sure," Wolf replied.

Before Lissa could react, Wolf took her in his arms and pressed his lips to hers passionately. The kiss lasted for a few moments before Wolf broke it off. Lissa stood for a moment, blinked her eyes hard once, and then smiled to Wolf.

"Now," she said coyly, "you know we don't have time for that."

Wolf smiled and the two laughed to themselves as they left the little farmhouse.

Prodigal Son

Creator's Calendar Year 1205; Light Reality

The palace of Trelon was exactly as Cairyn had left it when she stepped into the throne room from the portal that Wolf had created for her. It was just as isolated and desolate as she remembered it, and with the news that she had received about Pike and the trouble he had stepped into, she wondered if the palace would ever seem like home again. She had made a life trying to live for everyone other than herself. When she was a girl, she lived in the shadow of her mother and her uncle, and then after the death of her mother, she assumed the role as the most visible ruler on the face of the world. But the world did not revolve around her, it revolved around the mystique of the Binosear family. She did not know her place in that world. Her mother had been an excellent example to follow, but by the time she had realized it, her mother was already gone. Fortunately, the war against the Shadow did not drag on, and picking up the pieces in Trelon proved to be much easier than in other places in the world. Illimar, Scalla, Kandor, Marcwell, and the twin towns of Rana and Rama had seen far more upheaval and would take many more years to recover. All told, the only major kingdoms that retained a thread of connection to a time before the second act of the war against Shau-ling turned out to be Trelon and Brea, though Midarin Rice's assumption of power in Brea was anything but smooth and seamless. In fact, had it not been for Cairyn's intervention, at the request of her friend Elwyne Tamerlane, there could have been civil war in Brea. But however unified the people of Trelon were behind their new queen, Cairyn did not feel comfortable on her throne. It felt too big for her, and she felt as though she never would belong there. Even after she married, things did not change. She had married the mighty war hero Pike Rhuiden, but after the marriage, she still retained the Binosear name. It felt to her as though she would lose the respect of her people and the notice of the people around the world if her name became Rhuiden. In some ways she would be marginalized regardless which name she took. But regardless of that fact, she still lived her life for the man that she had married. Pike was everything to her. And when Duncan was born, all of her energies that had once been turned to the rigors of politics were turned to the raising of a family that would eventually fall apart around her, despite her best efforts and her intentions.

Duncan was not what people would refer to as a well-adjusted child. From the very beginning he was given everything that he wanted, and was taught by his oft-absent father about the war that was to come and the important part that he would have to play in it. Though later Cairyn would resist this teaching when it came to their daughter Sabrina, there was no way that the successor to the throne of Marcwell could be kept in the dark as to the true nature of the world around him. While Duncan would have been a powerful ally for his father in the Enforcers, it was the absence and feelings of abandonment that pushed Duncan down another path. For as long as Cairyn could remember, Duncan had been filled with more rage than a boy should be filled with. But it was not an unfocused rage. It boiled within him every day, simmering and burning his heart and churning in the pit of his stomach. It was a resentment that ran so deep if was as integral to Duncan as breathing. And so, as soon as the nature of things became apparent, Duncan began working on a plan. The plan, neither elegant nor mysterious had been laid out for many years, and Duncan only had to wait until his twenty-first birthday for all of his plans to come to fruition. The best path to revenge would be to take the very kingdom that his 'father' needed to fuel his war against the phasia. The line of ascension had been clearly marked, and Cairyn knew that Duncan would stop at nothing until her was seated on the throne of Marcwell and the kingdom of Trelon was also fully tucked beneath his belt. And that perhaps was the most elegant, if not ruthless part of the plan. In the strictest of sense, Duncan would be the rightful heir to the throne, and thus it would be Pike who could be seen as the usurper who was unwilling to release his grip on what was not his. Though Pike would have the reasonable justification of the on-going war with the Shadow, and his history as a hero in the ranks of the People of the Dragon, it was Duncan whose claims to the throne could not be ignored. To that end, the second phase of Duncan's plan involved a level of political manipulation that Cairyn continued to marvel at. Duncan had been very serious about his ascension, and started planting the seeds of doubt in his soon-to-be subjects early on. He claimed that he would have to leave the kingdom the year before he turned twenty-one, for fear that one of Pike's agents or mistresses would try to kill him to secure Pike's place as king of Marcwell for the rest of Pike's life. Cairyn remembered the conversation when Duncan cut her more deeply than any of Pike's supposed affairs ever could.

* * * * * * * * * * *

Cairyn sat peacefully in her private garden looking out over the carefully tended beds. It had been almost three months since she had seen Pike, and her thoughts were on him most nights, and those longing dreams often made for long and restless days. It was then that she heard a set of hard and firm footsteps behind her. She knew that her son Duncan was in the doorway, waiting as patiently as he could manage to be acknowledged. Obviously that was a trait that he inherited from his father.

"Mother?"

Cairyn turned slowly to face her eldest child. He looked so much like his father, it was almost difficult to let her eyes rest on the boy's face for too long. It wasn't resentment, at least, she hoped that wasn't what Duncan saw. The boy had very wide shoulders like his father, and that stone-set jaw was obviously as Rhuiden trait. His eyes however had come from the Binosear line; stormy and striking. His hair was cut short, shorter than was the fashion of court, but like so many things in Marcwell and Trelon, the royal family was anything but conventional. Unlike his father, Duncan preferred to stay clean-shaven, and to Cairyn's knowledge had done everything in his power to avoid drink.

"Yes Duncan?"

Instantly Cairyn was unsure as to how she addressed the young man. Should she have called him son? He did after all call her mother. Perhaps that was part of the problem. Cairyn though she loved her children did not feel comfortable with them. She wanted so much to treat them as though they were not her relations, feeling it would have been easier to see them with eyes unclouded by blood. There were times when the professional distance of the court intruded on her ability to ever be anything but a queen. Duncan seemed less effected by the distance than Sabrina, and during her early years the girl seemed to have little use for Cairyn. Perhaps that was simply a daughter's prerogative to love their father more. Cairyn had never had that luxury, and so perhaps that was why she gave Sabrina so much latitude. Duncan on the other hand she understood far more. He was far more like Cairyn than Pike. Pike was violent, Cairyn was ruthless. Pike was blunt, Cairyn was measured. Pike could be filled with hatred, and Cairyn could channel cruelty. It was unfortunate that Duncan perhaps would never be afforded the chance to be gentle.

Having been properly acknowledged, Duncan took two steps forward into the garden. He was being overly cautious he knew, but it was necessary considering the circumstances. In his heart, Duncan knew that both his mother and his father were conspiring to kill him, and even the smallest breach in etiquette could mean the end of his life. And while he clearly knew the reasons for the betrayal that his father was waiting to spring upon him, it was his mother's intentions that continued to be unclear. But then again, to Duncan, Cairyn's motivations never made sense. She continued to stay with a drunk, abusive, adulterous husband, putting on airs that everything was perfect in her little world. Surely she could see the advantage of Pike being removed from power in favor of someone more temperate. But then, Cairyn had had power all of her life, and perhaps that was the only control left to her. To give that power up would end her life as she knew it. However, while Pike would gladly do the deed himself, Cairyn was never so direct. She could simply call for her guards and they would be upon him in a second, gutting him as if he were a common criminal. Then she could concoct whatever story she wanted about his attempts to seize power by whatever means were at his disposal. Duncan would rather roast on the Great Dark One's spit in hell rather than give his demonic father the satisfaction of his death.

"I've come to inform you that I will be leaving the confines of the kingdom and I will return when it is time for me to take my place as the rightful ruler of the Kingdom of Marcwell. I would appreciate it if you would give me your leave to go. As you know, I do not require your leave, but I would consider it a gesture of good faith."

Cairyn sat for a moment and let the request sink in. She knew this day had been coming. Sabrina had warned her of it only days earlier. She had to give the girl credit, at times she knew what was going on more than even the queen, but that had always been true when Cairyn was just a princess as well. Her mother Anabel was always asking for information. Maids that were tightlipped around the queen often found that tongue loosening in the presence of the princess. Gossip could always be easily separated from those things that had more truth than fiction. The practiced ear took in all information, never letting on what was important and what was not. The information itself was what was important. Cairyn phrased her response as she had been taught to do, not betraying that she had information preparing her for this eventuality.

"May I ask what is prompting this request?"

Duncan hesitated for a moment before responding.

"As the Queen?"

Cairyn carefully considered her answer in that next fraction of a second. She could see where Duncan was trying to maneuver her, and Cairyn would not allow that. He wanted more leverage to fuel his beliefs, proof that the kingdom was out to get him.

"As a concerned mother."

Duncan's eyes showed disappointment. That was not the answer he had been expecting, but then again, he had never managed to outmaneuver his sister, and Sabrina was no match for Cairyn in a political arena. He would just have to resort to his most comfortable approach. Attack and destroy.

"You should not be concerned about me mother, especially with your husband spending his nights in the arms of another woman."

Cairyn shrank back as if she had been struck. The comment had been a personal attack, and it had cut her deep. Duncan had gone on the offensive, obviously trying to provoke Cairyn, but she coolly ran her fingers through her long dark hair and set her eyes back on her son. Duncan saw that in that moment, something in her eyes had changed. There was no more caring in those eyes, it was like her mind had changed gears and she was now faced with a hostile dignitary from another kingdom. Duncan had miscalculated, and instead of his mother back-peddling, she was about to go on the offensive. Perhaps he would have been better off dealing with his mother, because he knew in his heart he was no match for the Queen of Trelon.

"As you know," Cairyn's cold pure voice said in a very matter-of-face tone, "there has been no proof to Lord Rhuiden's infidelity, and those who choose to casually slander his name will feel the wrath of the law."

The practiced response didn't surprise Duncan.

"Is that to mean you will send the entire kingdom to the dungeons?" Duncan countered.

Cairyn considered that perhaps Duncan had learned some things in the company of his sister.

"With all of the rumors that have been going around, it is only a matter of time before one of these mistresses will step forward and confirm everything."

Cairyn started to rebut, but she was stopped short.

"Perhaps even the high and mighty Queen Midarin Rice of Brea will shed some light on her more-than-casual relationship with Pike. It's not as though she is above reproach like you, mother. After all, haven't you yourself referred to her as a whore?"

The sting of the words seemed to echo in Cairyn's ears over and over again in the next passing seconds. Cairyn had never had a high opinion of the once banished princess Midarin Rice, but she had found a new respect for her after all of the trials in her life. Though they would never be friends, Cairyn still cherished that mutual respect. And in just a few words,

Duncan had nearly torn it all down. He obviously knew that those were the rumors that had scared Cairyn the most, so it was going to be his point of attack. But Cairyn was not the intemperate young girl that she had been when she had uttered those words, she had done a lot of growing up, and had learned the lessons that only loss could teach. Humility had been her diet for far too long.

"That was a long time ago, before the war. I didn't know her then, and all I had to go on was the rumors. The rumors about her were very much like those that are being launched against your father now, and that is why I am less concerned about them since I know the truth about Midarin."

"Less concerned, mother, or apathetic?"

The counter was well planned and well done. Duncan had grown much in the last few months, and obviously he had time to hone his razor sharp wit and tongue. However, unlike Sabrina and Cairyn, Duncan had other fuels for his sharp comments. Cairyn could almost feel the hatred in his voice, piercing her to the very core where her most basic emotions lay. But she could not allow those emotions to come to light, otherwise it would become a personal battle. That was not where Cairyn's strengths lay. She was a polished diplomat, able to keep her emotions out of situations and trained to use the recklessness of others against them. This was going to be her toughest challenge yet, as that this was not a negotiation, but a battle of wills against one of her own children.

Duncan sensed his mother's trepidation. If he could force her hand and crack that cold exterior, he would be able to plant the seeds of doubt that would assist his bid for the throne. It would only be a matter of time before he would be old enough to complete the ascension, and he wanted to have the most support possible, even at the expense of his own family. There was a time that he believed that Cairyn would support him no matter what. But then the Enforcers became a reality, and the consolidation of power between Brea, Marcwell, Trelon, and Scalla. Cairyn's steadfast support of Pike and his policies continued to fuel the doubt growing inside of Duncan until the two were inextricably linked within their son's hatred.

"Never apathetic Duncan," Cairyn said rising. "I care about the rumors that are being spread, and I have done everything in my power to make sure they are stopped . . ."

Duncan cut her off hard.

"Only because the rumors make you look bad. And you have the powerful Binosear name to protect."

That hit Cairyn hard in the pit of her stomach. Not only had he attacked his own father but now he was attacking the legacy of the Binosear family. It was an affront that had usually meant death for the offending person, and it was obvious that Duncan was walking the razor's edge, and if he wasn't more careful he would end up slitting his own throat.

"The Binosear name is your mother's name, your grandmother's name, the name of the first savior of this world. It is also your sister's name. Are you saying that you are any less proud of the legacy you are about to inherit?"

This was the moment of truth, and Duncan knew it. The line had been drawn in the sand, and Cairyn was more than daring him to cross it. At that moment, Duncan felt the little bit of doubt left inside of him resurface. There was part of him that did not want to travel the rest of the way down this road, as it meant that eventually his own family would have to be the enemies of his cause. There would be no one to stand beside him other than the allies he made between today and when his plans came full-circle. However, if he were to back down now, his mother would have more leverage when Duncan made his move for the throne. She could easily exploit that weakness when the time came. So, Duncan swallowed his pride and let his words roll out with venom unlike any he had ever spat before. But inside, the words cut him as deeply as they would cut his mother.

"You call that pathetic collection of legends and lies a legacy? Why do you think I took Pike's last name instead of adopting the Binosear name as Sabrina did? The name means nothing to me other than a means to an end. And the Rhuiden name means even less. He's as much of a pretender and a usurper as half of the so called Lords and Ladies in this world. And why? Because of the prophecies. The Binosears, the Ranthalls; all they have done is brought chaos to everything they touch. But I know the law just as well as you do, mother. I have to have the blood of the sainted Cedric Binosear running through my veins before I could even try to sit upon the throne of Marcwell. More than that though, as the only legitimate heir, I should have been given control of Marcwell as soon as I was ready, and I have been ready for a long time now. Pike has done everything in his power to keep me away from what is rightfully mine, because he knows that he needs Marcwell and Trelon under his boot to fuel his war against the phasia. He has Sabrina in his pocket, and she will do anything he asks, but not me. I will not be led down his destructive path."

"What Pike is doing is a noble purpose, Duncan. Would you have the phasia..."

"Noble?" Duncan said raising his voice dramatically. "Once there may have been nobility in Pike's war against Shau-ling and his children, but now there is nothing but Pike's need for revenge. Everybody knows it mother, it is sung every night in taverns across the countryside. And what is he getting revenge for? What is this virtuous purpose that inflames the world?"

Cairyn braced herself, because she knew what was coming.

"Is he doing it to save the world from the scourge of evil? Maybe. Pike is a fighter, a warrior, and he knows evil has to be stopped when it rears its ugly head. Is he trying to protect his family from facing the terrible phasia? Hardly. He has plans for all of us in the war to come, and if it takes the blood of his children and the children of his allies for him to win, don't think for a second he'll let every drop of that blood be spilled. Is it that he is fighting for the memory of his fallen friends from the last war, trying to bring some necessity to the loss? In a way. And that is closest to the true motivations of the famous Pike Rhuiden. The true motivation for Pike's vengeful quest to rid the world of the phasia is because of his fallen bride, Eldar Merin."

The name struck Cairyn harder than she expected. There was still resentment there, and though she tried hard not to let it show, from the look in Duncan's eyes, that same look of triumph that Pike always had when he won an argument, her emotions had betrayed her.

"You have heard the story about her, haven't you Cairyn?" Duncan said, his voice changing from one of mock respect to a more vindictive and vengeful tone. "How Pike forsook everything, even his heritage as a member of the *Erieal* to hunt down and destroy Taron just so he could avenge the death of his fallen bride. Do you think that with Taron returning that Pike will care one iota about us? All he cares about is making sure that Taron is dead and the memory of his lost love is intact. Pike married out of convenience, not out of love, Cairyn, and for that, you have condemned me to a life where I have an adulterer for a father and a blind fool for a mother."

Cairyn stood cold and hard as the marble beneath her feet and waited for the tirade to be finished. Whatever motherly part of her had protected Duncan from the Queen of Trelon's wrath died with his angry words. Gently Cairyn pulled back her shoulders and squared off against the young renegade. Those last words rung in her mind long after his voice had left the calming wind. Duncan was right, she had been a blind fool, but not where Pike was concerned. For all the years Duncan had been alive, Cairyn had not been able to see the cobra she had been quietly raising, and now he had turned his venom on her, a gift to repay all the kindness she had shown him over the years. The time for coddling was long past, and it was time for the queen to become a mongoose and teach the upstart a harsh lesson in reality.

"I never thought I would see the day when the young boy I raised would prove to be the fool that I always knew him to be."

The insult was stinging, but what Duncan could not know was the fact that the pain was only beginning.

"A fool am I?"

"That's quite enough," Cairyn said in a very calm, hard voice. "I sat by and listened to your ill-conceived words, and you will stand there and listen to my reply whether you like it or not."

Duncan froze. He had not anticipate this response from Cairyn, partly because he had not been interested enough in matters of court to watch. Had he paid a tenth of the attention that Sabrina had, Duncan would have known that the fire he chose to light would burn bright and hot enough to consume him if he were not careful.

"You have chosen to loose your venom on me Duncan, and for that I must not allow myself to sit idly by anymore. For too many years I have taken all of the abuse that you saw fit to spew in my direction, and I took it like the dutiful mother that I have always been, but the time for that is long past. Had you have been this vicious with your father, you would be lying dead now, and quickly forgotten as a stupid rebel who chose to leap before he knew what lay beyond what he thought he could see. Do you think me so weak and frail that I will not defend myself when attacked? Do you have that low of an opinion of my abilities, not only as your mother, but as the queen of this kingdom? Do you see yourself as so superior and without fault in this little drama that none of the stink of it will cling to you? Everything you blame on your father may be true, and yet you don't have the sense enough to transcend his failings and see beyond your own hate."

Cairyn hesitated for a moment, waiting for the reaction on Duncan's face. She could tell from his eyes that he was off-balance, not knowing whether to stand strong and defiant or be frightened. The doubt was there, it was obvious. So, Cairyn rounded on her target, ready for the kill herself.

"That is why you are a fool, Duncan. You let that damned tongue of yours wag at the wrong time, ready to lash at anyone who will listen, regardless of what they have done for you in the past. But then, when it is time to speak and defend yourself, you stand like a mute, silent to the world except for the meek words that echo within your puny mind. It sickens me to know that you are my son, and while I have defended you and nurtured you your entire life, you dare to berate me. Once I thought Pike made the wrong choice making you wait so long to inherit the throne of Marcwell, but now I wonder if he shouldn't wait longer."

Anger swelled up inside of Duncan and he felt it begin to boil inside of him. It was like a white-hot dagger piercing him to the very core of his being. Without a thought, he raised his hand as though he were about to strike Cairyn. His mother was faster, wordlessly she drew a dagger from her belt, a gift from Midarin Rice of Brea, and its blade darted to the boy's exposed throat. Duncan swallowed hard and lowered his hand, careful not to make any more sudden moves.

"How dare you raise your hand to me Duncan Rhuiden," Cairyn growled. "If you were not my own flesh and blood you would now be dead. Perhaps this is the last moment I will see you as such. That quick temper of yours may serve you on the field of battle my dear boy, but in a court, it will get you killed. That is the reason that Pike and I have worked so hard to get you to understand that the life of a king is not one of glamour and ease. There are many things that you will have to fight for, and even more times when you will have to swallow your pride for the good of the kingdom and let insults pass over you as if they did not exist. The hotter you allow your blood to boil, the more mistakes you will make and the more that weak frail women like me will get the better of you."

Cairyn removed the blade of the dagger from Duncan's throat and he took a quick step back. While the queen lowered the dagger, she did not return it to its sheathe. The threat had been made once; it would not be far past the boy to threaten again.

"You asked me about the rumors of your father's affairs. I keep my tongue and my pride in check for the good of the kingdom. I believe in my husband, both because I love him and because he has never lied to me in the past. From the day I agreed to be his wife, I knew where I stood in this relationship. There was no question. It was a marriage of convenience. I would have an heir to take over my throne, and Pike would have the resources he needed to do battle with the forces of Shau-ling. That is what he was born to do, and he does it very well. For a long time, he hoped that you would show interest in his efforts in the war, and help him against the enemies of mankind. But you never showed that interest, and you never seemed to care about anyone, let alone your family, so that is why he withdrew from you. You curse him for being so lost in his aims that he can see nothing else. But Duncan, one day you will come to the realization that you are your father's son, and you are doomed to be just like him."

Duncan turned to walk away, but not before striking once more with his venom-laden words.

"I cared about the war with the Shadow, mother," the word sounding sickening coming from his lips. "I prayed that it would come sooner so that I would never have to look at the bastard I have to call father again."

As he faded into the shadows, his last words rang clear.

"I'll see you again when I come to claim my kingdom."

CHAPTER 35

Chapter XXXVI

Unhappy Returns

Creator's Calendar Year 1205; Light Reality

Cairyn stood in the center of the throne room looking at the golden throne, lost in her thoughts of the past. She was so lost, in fact, that she never heard the doors of the throne room shift and slide slowly open. It was only when the new footsteps echoed through the quiet room that Cairyn realized that she was no longer alone. When she turned, she saw the face of an old friend.

"Yours is the last face I expected to see here in Trelon, especially now that the war has started. Shouldn't you be out with some army somewhere fighting against the Shadow?"

The man smiled to himself and then took a step toward Cairyn.

"An old man like me? War is for the young, Cairyn, you know that. My time fighting in this war is long since over. I just came to say goodbye to an old friend, and to let you know that you won't be seeing me ever again."

Cairyn sighed and nodded. She knew this time would come someday, but resigning never did make things any easier. She had said goodbye to so much in her life, so much that she couldn't account for, and so much she wished she had back. Part of that was just the naïve heart of girl that fought against the reality of life, and part was getting older and seeing less ahead than behind. She was rapidly approaching the age her mother was when she was murdered, and her thoughts had just left a son that would gladly make a martyr of her as well.

"I will miss you very much, Aerith," she said more formally than she wanted. "You have been a comfort to me through all of the tough times with Pike and the children, and I wish you could stay and help me through the upcoming confrontation with Duncan."

"Duncan is not as much of a concern as you might believe," Aerith Seth replied. "His involvement in this is secondary to your husband's. He is the one who will turn this into a disaster, Cairyn, but I think you already knew that."

Cairyn nodded again and turned back toward the golden throne of Trelon. There were hundreds of questions whirling in her head, and most conflicted. There had been too many lies told during her life, and they were starting to unravel each other. When she sat on the throne and locked her eyes back on the man who had been like an angel to her, she could not help but hear Wolf's words in the back of her mind. *"My path is pointing toward Barer. Bryn has information that I need about Aerith Seth and his role in this,"* he had said. *"With Susanne's information about the Torch, we need to track down all leads that could help us in the fight against Shau-ling."*

"Why are you looking at me like that, Cairyn," Aerith asked approaching her. "Is there something wrong?"

Cairyn sighed and nodded.

"Out of all the lies that have been told to me, and all of the liars I must look at every day of my life, I thought at least you would have been honest with me."

Aerith stopped dead in his tracks. Immediately he wondered how much she knew.

"What ties do you have to Bryn Aplee?" Cairyn asked plainly.

The name washed over Aerith's heart like a wave of pure emotion. Every time he heard that name, it tore at his heart. There was still too much unfinished between the two of them, and Aerith knew that much would never be said.

"She and I are old friends . . ."

Cairyn shot up and pointed an accusing finger at Aerith.

"Don't you lie to me!" Cairyn shouted. "After all of these years, you owe me the truth and nothing less than that!"

After a deep exhale and conceding nod, Aerith refocused his eyes on Cairyn. There was a new look now than what Cairyn was used to. It was one of power that demanded respect. The same look her uncle Cedric had in his eyes. The likeness was nearly uncanny.

"You're right, Cairyn. There have been too many lies. I guess it has been easy for me to lie, not to mislead you, but perhaps because I no longer wanted to know the truth. I wish this had come between us in a different way, but I suppose that if I had my choice, it never would have come out at all."

Aerith sighed, squeezed his eyes shut for a moment, and when he opened them again, he nodded, looked back at Cairyn, and began to speak again.

"Sit down Cairyn, and listen. The tale you have asked for is sordid at best and lecherous at worst. But I ask you to please bear with me until the end, and I promise that by the end of my tale, things will be more confusing than they ever were before. Life has a strange sense of humor, and at times I think it has all be directed at me."

Cairyn sat back on the throne and waited for Aerith's tale to begin. Not long after Cairyn ascended to power after her mother's death, the man who called himself Aerith Seth came into her life. He said that he was simply an advisor who would help her through her adjustment to becoming a queen. Cairyn quickly accepted his help, and before long, he began to fill in the gaps in her mother's teachings. However, there always seemed that there was more to their relationship then just advisor and student. During the troubled times when Cairyn was unsure in her marriage to Pike, and she found herself at the point of tears, Aerith was there, like a father. She could cry on his shoulder and find comfort in his embraces. Though there was never more than friendship in his arms, and again, it was like the love of a father.

"My little tale starts, I suppose it's been over a hundred years ago now in a city called Lakestone. That was long before any of the wars started, and Lakestone was one of the major cities in the world. That was the place that I was born. I never knew my mother or my father, and I was raised in an orphanage with hundreds of other boys, all either abandoned or disowned. We were hired out to the shops and the marketplace as labor for cleaning or anything else the shop owners wanted. Most of my days were spent sweeping and scrubbing floors in the orphanage because I got a reputation for being too willful. But luckily for me, my willfulness paid off. I was hired by a couple to help the wife with shopping for the day. My whole chore was to carry the goods for her, load them into the wagon, and then unload them when we got to the house. It was a simple job. However, while traveling through the city, the woman was pulled into an alley by two men. Before they had a chance to do anything to her, I was able to intervene and pull her away in time. Luckily, someone else saw what had happened and called the city guards to investigate. At this time, I was only seven, but I was quick enough to prevent something bad from happening. The woman was very grateful, and she cooked me dinner and said that when her husband returned, they would find a suitable way to thank me. I went back to the orphanage that night wondering if I would ever see the woman again.

"The next morning, I was awakened by the orphanage master. He told me that my services had been purchased permanently, that I was no longer going to be a resident at the orphanage. My freedom had been purchased. When I got downstairs, I saw the woman waiting for me. Apparently her husband had been there during the night and immediately decided that I should be spared. In the middle of the night, he woke the orphanage master and paid for my freedom. The woman said she was sorry, but her husband had left early that morning and would not be back for a long time. I would come to find out, that was the way life was for her. The husband was never home, and when he did return, he would only stay an evening, and then come morning he was gone again. One night when I couldn't sleep, I heard a noise coming from the front room of the house. I went to investigate, and saw a man dressed in armor with a long black cloak. I never got to see his face, but I do remember the long blond hair. The wife came out before I could investigate further."

"What was her name?" Cairyn asked.

"Forgive me if I do not remember her name. I was only in that house for a short time, and we were never very formal. In fact, I don't recall her ever calling me Aerith. It was either boy, or merely a command."

"But I thought . . ."

"What?" Aerith questioned. "That I was adopted and loved and had a family that I could call my own? No, this was not freedom. I was purchased from the orphanage to keep an eye on the wife and do chores for her while the husband was gone. But the reason, I was to learn later, was that she was dying. Not two months after I came to live with her, the woman died in the middle of the night. The healers said that she had been weakening for months and it was a wonder that she lived as long as she did. Immediately I began to fear for my life. I was an orphan again, and the last thing I wanted was to go back to the hell that was the orphanage. But the mysterious husband intervened again, only this time, it was not news that I relished. A carriage arrived the next morning, and the driver had instructions to take me to a town called Quea. I knew the name of the town very well, mostly from the horror stories told to me by the orphanage personnel. Quea was a death sentence."

"The mines of Quea?" Cairyn asked.

Cairyn could not keep the look of horror from coming to her face. She knew the direction the story was about to go, because she too had heard the stories of the mines of Quea.

"Exactly. As you well know, the only thing Quea has are the gold and silver mines that twist and turn for miles underneath the mountains on the edge of the kingdom of Scalla. At this time, the mines were fairly new, and more dangerous because of the mystery involved. I'm sure you have heard the stories of hundreds of miners suddenly disappearing apparently into thin air? Well, it had just started happening when I started my work there. I remember the first day, as it was my eighth birthday. A pick in my hand

and a shovel strapped to my back, I followed the group into the mine and passed a section of tunnel roped off with a simple wooden sign with the word danger printed on it. I would later hear the stories about the disappearances. The old timers would tell me that sometimes during the night shift in the mines you could hear screams of terror and pain coming from deeper in the roped off shafts. I thought it was just a story to frighten the new workers, but then I took my first night shift in the mines, and the sounds I heard still echo in all of my nightmares. I worked in the mines for five years. Hundreds of men died, but somehow I survived dozens of cave-ins, abductions by the things below, mine fires, and explosions. Some said I was lucky and that they wanted to work on my shift, but then I would walk out alone from yet another mishap. This was when I was noticed by the lord of Quea, Saurn Macco."

The name sparked recognition within Cairyn.

"I see that through your husband you know of Lord Saurn. So much the better, it will save time. To put it bluntly, Saurn was more insane than sane, but there was a genius in his insanity. Believe me, it has taken me nearly all of my life to understand some schemes that he concocted in only a matter of days. Saurn knew what I was long before anyone else did, so he took me out of the mines and placed me in a family of his court. Naturally, he was quick to make up a story about me, how I was gifted and had been pampered by my former family, learning everything I could. In reality, I barely knew how to read, enough to mind the right signs in the mine shafts, and I couldn't write my own name. Yet Saurn kept to his story about my wondrous abilities and so tutor after tutor was led in front of me. Strangely enough, somehow I was able to retain everything they taught. Languages that I had never even heard before came to life from textbooks in my mind, and I was fluently speaking six languages and a dozen more dialects within the next year. Art, math, alchemy; all of it was my playground. But then I started listening to the generals of Saurn's army, and there my true love took form. It was my thirteenth birthday when I first picked up a sword, and from that time on my life became totally different. From the maps that the generals showed me, I could see whole battles in my mind and their resolutions a hundred different ways depending on deployment. It was like music in my mind."

"This was when the War for Power was just starting?" Cairyn asked trying to get Aerith back on the subject.

"Yes. It was only in its infancy then, at least that act of it. I was to learn later that it had been raging for many lifetimes before that; a nice private battle. Saurn immediately moved me into one of his armies, but for some reason, we never saw true combat. It was as though Saurn was waiting for something. Don't get me wrong, I make no claims of knowing Saurn's mind or holding his council, but with Saurn, everything was a scheme. When I turned eighteen, I received word that Saurn needed me for a special task. I was to be transferred out of the Army of the Viper and begin working with one of Saurn's allies. I would later discover that this ally was Bryn Aplee and her Army of the Fox. Within a few months I had worked my way through the ranks of the army, and attained the rank of general. It was no secret that Bryn had a hand in my promotions, and it was rumored through the ranks that I would soon be in her elite guard. While that never did come to pass, it was true that Bryn had taken notice of me, and the night I was summoned to her chambers late at night would be a night that would change my life forever."

Cairyn felt a little sick in her stomach as the thoughts of her friend Aerith and the phase Bryn together crossed her mind, but from the look in Aerith's eyes, he meant something different than lovemaking. There was something that he was holding back.

"What happened?" Cairyn pressed.

Aerith hesitated, and Cairyn could swear that he saw color come to his cheeks in embarrassment. But there was a wonder in his eyes that his expression could not contain, something akin to waking up one morning and suddenly understanding the mind of the Creator.

"When I arrived in her chambers she was sitting on her bed with two poured glasses of wine. My thoughts of course went to her physical beauty, but when her eyes caught mine, there was not a look of desire or lust, but one of curiosity. It was as though she were looking into my soul with those piercing green eyes, looking for something deep within. Before I could say anything at all, she asked me a simple question. *'Aerith Seth, you have been special from the day you were born. The gods have smiled on you, and so have the devils of the world. I will ask you a simple question that will change the very destiny of your life and all you have to decide is whether to answer yes, or no. If you answer yes, your life will be difficult and bloody. There will be many hardships and loses, but as many victories and pleasures. If you answer no, your life will be mundane and filled with 'what ifs', but perhaps you will live long enough to see old age. The question is simply this: Do you want to know why?'"*

Aerith fell silent for a moment after that. Every time his thoughts turned to Bryn, his reaction was always the same. The pain in his heart was still strong after all the years of separation, and it still ached during the years of lonely nights that had held him since their parting.

"I still don't know whether I answered right or not. Maybe I will know before it is all over. However, I was at the point in my life when I was curious about my purpose in life and why I was made to suffer for all those years. So, I answered yes."

Again, silence filled the room. Cairyn could tell that Aerith was having difficulty coping with the events of his life and the trials he had been through. She too had pivotal moments in her life, but nothing she had ever been through could have compared to Aerith's experiences.

"For the next few hours, Bryn would tell me of the timeless war between Emries and Shau-ling. How they battled from the beginning of time, through the birth of man, to the present. She told me of the birth of the phasia and their fight against the *Erieal* and the other chosen heroes of the gods. For most, this would have been a tedious history lesson, but I was enthralled by the whole of it. Then she began to tell me about the being known as the *Chosen One*."

Immediately Cairyn's ears perked up. She had heard Sabrina refer to herself as the *Chosen One*, and the words had scared her. Cairyn had never wanted to know the particulars of the war, as that it had claimed too much of her family already, but now it was affecting her daughter, and that changed everything.

"According to Bryn, the *Chosen One* was an entity of neutrality who owed his allegiance to neither the Light nor the Shadow. If he chose, the *Chosen One* could take the fight to either Emries or Shau-ling and win. Rumor was that the *Chosen One* was the champion of the Creator himself. That was probably the most demoralizing fact. I don't think there was ever a point when I didn't believe what Bryn was telling me, but there must have been a look in my eyes that said otherwise. She tried hard to convince me that all of my strength, incredible learning speed, and my retention of knowledge was due to the powers I inherited as the *Chosen One*. She eluded to the fact that I would have other powers open to me, and that in time she would help me to wield them with lethal intensity. For the rest of the night, I was in a daze. The wine flowed freely and so did the lust. The next thing I remember is waking up with her in my arms, snuggled together under the covers of the bed."

Aerith then moved to the window in the throne room and looked out on the square. He knew what was coming and the sacrifices that were being made, but he could not let them affect him now. Too many things were in motion, and most of them hinged on him disappearing. While he had simply come to say goodbye, he felt as though he owed this explanation to Cairyn. After all, her daughter was now trapped in all of this nightmarish normality, and if there was one thing that Aerith could change, he wished that his mantle would not have fallen upon the girl. But again, the cosmic joke seemed to be on Aerith and those unfortunate enough to be his family.

"From that point on, I took full control of the Army of the Fox, only taking orders from Bryn, but most of the time she let me do what I needed to. Under her watchful eye, my powers grew in intensity, and the army's strength seemed to grow with mine. We never lost a battle that I commanded, and before long, we were the most powerful force in the world."

There was a conviction in his voice unlike any that Cairyn had ever heard. She could remember her uncle's speeches about his fight against Shau-ling, and she recalled how they always sounded so rehearsed. Aerith could feel all of his words as they escaped his lips. He felt them in his heart and soul, down to the very core of his being.

"But that is not the part of the story that concerns me now, nor is it the reason I came to visit you my dearest Cairyn. In my days before serving Bryn, I traveled through a small country town whose name has long since faded from my memory before venturing into my fate in Barer. I took my time before following Saurn's orders, and I decided to walk from Quea to Barer, to see the world. I thought I would never have that opportunity again. In that sleepy little town, I met a beautiful woman, a woman whose eyes sparkled unlike any that I have ever seen in any lifetime before or since. The very stars in heaven paled beside her beautiful blue eyes, and I was entranced by her from the first moment. She was dressed like a commoner, but I suspected that there was more to her than just her appearance. After approaching her, we drank at the bar and ended up spending the night together in the local inn. Then next morning when I awoke, she was gone. Later that day I watched as a processional from the kingdom of Trelon arrived and then departed with Princess Christina Trelis. At first I didn't know who she was, but when I looked her square in the eyes, I guessed the truth."

Cairyn was shocked. Christina Trelis was the only child born to the Trelis family, the ruling family of the kingdom of Trelon. In order to cement an alliance with their neighboring kingdom, Lady Trelis married Wolfric Binosear, Cairyn's grandfather.

"I see by your eyes that you have made the connection. But what you could have never known until now, the secret that I have held since Jeroch ended my mortal life almost one hundred years ago, is that I, not Wolfric Binosear sired the great Cedric Binosear. Cedric is my son, and Anabel is my daughter, making you my . . ."

"Granddaughter . . ." Cairyn said looking deeply into Aerith's eyes.

"For so long I've wanted to tell you . . ." Aerith started but was cut off by a raised hand from Cairyn. The woman had disappeared, and the visage of the Queen of Trelon stood in her place.

"You came to say goodbye, didn't you Aerith?"

There was harshness in her tone. It was there to disguise the shock and confusion, the automatic defenses learned through years of ruling.

"My place and time in this war has long since disappeared. It was simply through pride and a sense of obligation that I have remained this long. This war is for the young, and no one needs an old sentinel standing over them critiquing their every move. I have come to say goodbye Cairyn, but I wanted you to know the truth. It was a truth you should have known so long ago and I was too much of a coward to share with you."

The words rang through her and echoed in the emptiness in her soul. There were too many secrets and too many lies in this war, and not all of them were told by the Shadow. The Light was as much to blame. While Cairyn could have let him go with a simple goodbye, she felt compelled to tell him of the situation that Wolf and the others were about to get into.

"Aerith," Cairyn started slowly, "have you been doing anything concerning the war in this generation?"

The queenly demeanor was still very prevalent in her voice, but the quiet concern of the woman was starting to show through.

"Nothing at all."

It was a subtle lie, as that the passing on of his powers to Evan Sinn was not really considered interference. At least, the Creator had not deemed it so yet.

"Well, Wolf Ranthall and the others have reason to believe that someone else is acting in your name, so they are on their way to Barer to speak with Bryn."

Aerith's blood ran cold. He did not know how Bryn would react to such questions, but he was positive that even the mention of Aerith's name could send Grawn into a murderous frenzy. Inwardly, Aerith wondered whether or not he should make an appearance in Barer. Not only that, if Sabrina was with them, and she was starting to connect with her abilities, it made everything endlessly more complicated.

"Why would they think I was involved? What has happened?"

Suddenly the doors to the throne room burst open, and in strode Duncan Rhuiden flanked by a man and a woman dressed in impressive white uniforms. On each of the uniforms was a black symbol of a torch worn over the left breast.

"I think it has something to do with us..." Duncan said proudly.

The Army of the Wolf

Creator's Calendar Year 1205; Light Reality

The city of Alimidar had always conjured one of two images in the minds of people around the world. The first was one of the nobility of the Sacred Swords, the symbol of the ruling family that had been missing for nearly a century, rumored to be lost when the forces of the Shadow sieged the city and killed most of the ruling family. Second, was the reputation of Alimidar as a den of thieves. It seemed at times that the only trained and skillful individuals in the city were the rogues and robbers who aspired to make their fortunes at the expense of the hard working merchants who traveled through the countryside. However, all that had changed in the years following the end of the second generation of the prophecies. A military presence began to make itself known not to long after the War of the Dragon had ended, and while its banner would have been very well known in other parts of the world, the banner that displayed the symbol of the wolf was merely another banner to the people of Alimidar who had seen so many over the decades since the fall. The Army of the Wolf had gathered quickly, its first task to stamp out anyone who chose to defy the laws of the ruling family. It took only a few executions in the town's central marketplace before the long-standing thieving guilds began to take notice and look for safer havens to ply their trade. Roving detachments of the Army of the Wolf, called Hunters, patrolled the streets with impunity that allowed them to act as the judge, jury, and executioner for all criminals that crossed their path. The men of the Army of the Wolf were a collection of castaways and vagabonds from other military bodies, and many of them were surviving members from a previous incarnation of the army from Illimar. They served their generals with undying loyalty, because they knew the power resided in their namesake, the Lady Wolf, Caris Vale'. But there was more to the situation in Alimidar than simply a military state. The control was more complete, refined, and vicious.

Alimidar had been under control of one family for as long as the city had stood, with the exception of a small interruption by the phasia. The occupation of the forces of the Shadow had been cut short thanks to the Hand of the Light, but the aftermath left the city in turmoil and chaos. The claim to rule was the symbol known as the Sacred Swords. However, once the swords were stolen, the court of Alimidar fell into turmoil. The major houses and families began to fight for control. They passed laws against one another, starting a diplomatic civil war that saw much bloodshed without a single physical battle being waged. Court-ordered executions numbered in the hundreds, and it was only a matter of a few years before some of the houses were obliterated. The citizens of Alimidar largely ignored the silent and faceless war of the court, as it gave the thieves more of an opportunity to do what they did best without having to worry about a unified city government hunting them. However, in the later years of the civil war a well-known name from the court of Trelon began to rise in power within the great houses. The name was Merin. However, this incarnation was not the great politician Alfred Merin of Trelon, it was his son, Eldric. Eldric had become a major figure in the reformation of the political landscape in Brea, and left not long after the liberation and the investment of Midarin Rice as the queen. Eldric began to petition and fight for unification within the houses, proposing military strength in an effort to keep the city from being ripped to shreds by their neighbors. He relied heavily on the fate of neighbor Lakestone and the powerful mercenary armies that lay only a few miles away in the fortified city of Askronilka. If a battle broke out again that saw the reemergence of the beasts that turned Lakestone into a submerged no man's land, or if the mercenaries to the north decided they would strike out on their own, Alimidar would be consumed in a heartbeat. The thieves would assuredly survive, as they are creatures of adversity, thriving as conditions worsen, but the politicians would be the first killed as the new rulers established themselves. Eldric's words carried great weight in the existing houses, and before long ordinances were passed giving Eldric the task of building the army that would be the savior of Alimidar. However, the politicians never expected the Army of the Wolf to descend so quickly or so completely. Within a matter of months, the Army of the Wolf was the law in the streets, and Eldric Merin found himself with power and leverage unmatched within the city's political circles. He was soon invested with the title of Chancellor, with powers equal to that of a king. However, it was what was happening behind closed doors and outside the view of the rest of the politicians, which gave Eldric Merin his true power.

As the old saying goes, behind every powerful man is a woman who is driving him to become even more powerful. This was never a truer statement than in Alimidar. The real power in the family was Natalie Yetre. As the daughter of Caris Vale' she was a master manipulator and used all of the powers at her disposal to wrap the politicians of Alimidar around her finger and then securely place them in her husband's pocket. Eldric did nothing without her council and approval, and much of the responsibilities of Chancellor were being fulfilled in the privacy of Natalie's chambers where she drafted orders and proclamations only to have her husband and puppet-monarch sign them into being later. Though Natalie was in control of the city, she too was serving a higher power. Her mother Caris had asked her to secure the city as a training facility for the Army of the Wolf, and that had been easily accomplished through careful manipulation. The other main responsibility had been to make sure that Natalie's son, Rand, stayed far away from the battle between the Light and the Shadow until Caris was ready. Caris had confided in Natalie exactly what the boy was, and as the daughter of a member of the phasia, Natalie understood the unspoken danger very well. Rand could be as much of an advantage as he could be a liability. It was all in the way he was handled. Caris, with the help of her older and sometime wiser sister Ellis had hatched a plan to keep him chained to Alimidar, and thusly to the will of the phasia.

Rand was always treated better than anyone in the city. He was pampered in the city's palaces, and found that anything he wanted was always at his fingertips. But his mother and grandmother would not allow sloth to become a vice of their little pawn. Rand was pushed in every way possible, his mind and body constantly being demanded to exceed higher and higher limits. Every weapon that was available, Rand was trained with. Ax, spear, sword, hammer, bow, fists; it didn't matter the means, but Rand was a master. The same could be said of his mind. Caris knew that the heritage of both phasia and human blood gave Rand an edge mentally and physically; especially when the human stock was from one of Emries' prized marked lines. The Merin line was most assuredly a marked one, even though in Eldric it was tainted by phasia blood, at least in part due to his less than immaculate conception. So, the potential was there to be exploited, and if there was anyone who knew how to exploit an opportunity, it was Caris. She had seen the care that Saurn had taken with the training of Aerith Seth, and that was the regimen that Caris tried to emulate with Rand. Though the speed at which the information was absorbed was significantly slower than that of Seth, Rand still excelled in everything that he devoted himself to. It was only a matter of time before he was one of the most respected men in the city of Alimidar, both by the politicians as well as the members of the Army of the Wolf. Rand would join the army shortly after turning fifteen, and by his twentieth birthday, he was a general with a great deal of respect within the ranks. However, it was obvious to both Natalie and Caris that the boy was growing restless. He had a strong will like the female side of his family, but the pull of the *Erieal* part of him would be hard to resist. So, Ellis devised a plan that would leash the boy once and for all to the service of the Shadow. Ellis too had a child, and while the girl was not known to many in the council, those who did know were always shocked at first to learn the identity of the father. Caris herself had guessed as much that when Grawn finally sired a child it would not be with the aid of Bryn, though their marriage of convenience had lasted many centuries. Her wandering eyes and appetites were never pointed in his direction long enough to accomplish the task. Plus, after her affair with Aerith Seth, Grawn cooled on Bryn as a mate and turned his sights to his closest ally Ellis. Caris though had heard that Aerith Seth had also kept the company of Ellis within her bed and that perhaps he had beaten Grawn to the punch not once, but twice. However, regardless of her dubious parentage, Jessica Chandara would be the literal ball and chain that would keep Rand in line.

Jessica Chandara was a stark contrast from both her mother and father. While Grawn had always had short gray hair in every lifetime, and Ellis' tress of hair was white as the snow, Jessica's long straight hair was a beautiful shiny black. She also had a much fairer complexion than her mother, though that did not take much considering Ellis' lily white skin. However, all of the differences ended in appearance. Jessica was most assuredly her mother's daughter. Jessica was cold, calculating, logical and evil to the core. Schemes whirled in her head that would take normal mortals years to unravel, and the more obscure the fact, the more likely Jessica was to know it. She was fascinated with everything that normal mortals feared and shunned. That was probably why her penchant for bats came about. She loved the rodents more than nearly anything in the world, and she sought to understand them. It took only a simple use of power and manipulation to align Rand and Jessica, and the marriage was one of love, at least that was the emotion that Rand thought he was feeling. The line between illusion and reality in Rand's life had always been blurred, and that was in no small part due to the interference by his mother and grandmother. It was only a matter of weeks before Jessica was with child, and the bind that would hold Rand was tied tighter than ever.

Things in the kingdom had progress very smoothly since Jessica's marriage to Rand, and it was only a matter of time before the Army of the Wolf would be called upon to set its claws upon a target. When Natalie felt a portal begin to form in her room deep in the palace of Alimidar, she began to think that that time had finally arrived. In a matter of seconds, the swirling blue portal had winked into existence, and out stepped the only form that Natalie had been expecting, her mother, Caris. As always, Caris was dressed in a flowing green gown that was cut almost low enough to reveal the full of her breasts. Also, there were no straps that held the dress in place, and it seemed as though Caris had altered gravity itself to keep the garment in place. Natalie smiled to herself knowing that the very possibility was well within her mother's powers, and fit her personality.

"Greetings Natalie dear," Caris said letting the portal close quickly behind her. "How are things in your nice little kingdom?"

Natalie felt the intonation of the word little. Caris was not trying to degrade her daughter, but it was just in her nature to lay what barbs she could.

"They are quiet mother. Your army continues to improve and grow more impressive every day. I am sure when you are ready to bring them to bear, they will topple any enemy that you see fit to loose them upon. Though by the look on your face I am sure you did not come here for a status report."

Caris was impressed with her daughter. Few could read Caris, but Natalie had always seemed to show the skill. Perhaps Caris had trained her too well.

"Is something wrong, mother?"

Caris smoothed her dress and moved over to one of the plush chairs in the corner of the room. After motioning to her daughter, Natalie sat across from her mother waiting for the revelation of her purpose in Alimidar on this occasion.

"As always my dear daughter, you are very intuitive. There is indeed something wrong, and I wanted to come here and see you before the point where that becomes impossible. As always within the Brotherhood there are plans within plans that are always in motion, and I hope that some of them will be coming to fruition soon enough."

Natalie nodded absently.

"Does that mean that the Army of the Wolf will moving soon?"

Caris sighed and shook her head.

"That unfortunately is out of my hands Natalie, I am afraid that order will surely come from your father."

Natalie looked surprised for a moment and then slowly nodded. Caris was sure that there were a million questions running through Natalie's mind, but she had been taught well enough to mind her tongue and learn all that can be learned before venturing to ask questions. Enlightened minds often learned more by listening to the ramblings of others than forcing a conversation with questions.

"I am afraid that I will not be able to travel with you when the Army of the Wolf sets its sights on its target, and it is not possible for me to take you where I am going. I will only be risking my life, and I would not be able to complete my task if you are with me."

"I understand mother," Natalie replied.

"I doubt that," Caris said shortly. "But good girl for not questioning those things you know you are not meant to understand. In time, you will understand why everything has transpired this way. And I hope I am still alive when you do. I will say though that your mother is probably a little too ambitious for her own good this time around, but if I succeed in my task, the coup will be more grand then the one I scored with that miserable Cedric Binosear."

With that Natalie smiled, and Caris would have let out an arrogant laugh had the feeling of a portal forming tugged at the back of her mind. It was not localized in the room, but it was somewhere in the palace. Caris took a brief moment to trace the line of power back and found the origin point had been the kingdom of Barer.

"Ellis is here," Caris said absently.

"Probably doting over her daughter Jessica again," Natalie replied with disgust thick in her voice.

"I trust my dear older sibling has not been giving you any difficulties. She does tend to be overbearing when she thinks she knows more than the people around her."

"Which, if memory serves," Natalie added, "that would be all the time."

Caris smiled and stood, smoothing her dress again.

"I taught you very well my dear…"

Caris' voice trailed off again as another string of power flashed through her mind. Another portal was going to form soon, and it was centered in the room. Obviously, Natalie felt it too.

"Did someone change the location of the Council and not bother to tell me?"

Caris let the facetious comment slide past as she tried to concentrate on tracking the origin of the portal. Unfortunately, the origin led back to the Council chambers themselves, so that meant than nearly any member of the phasia could be making their way to Alimidar, but Caris had a pretty could idea of who it was. It was in that next moment that a portal formed, and mere heartbeats later, Jeroch stepped into the room and locked his eyes on Caris and Natalie. Caris let her guard down only a little when her eyes met Jeroch's. She knew that he was here on the errand that they had discussed in the dungeon of Illimar, but being face to face with another member of the phasia when not in the Council chambers was a tenuous situation at best. Natalie seemed pleased to see her father, which was understandable, considering they would go stretches of years without laying eyes on one another. Caris inwardly had hoped she had bred all emotion for her father out of the girl, but that was apparently not the case.

"I see you came as we agreed, Jeroch," Caris said firmly.

"I was held up in the Council longer than I expected," Jeroch said barely acknowledging Caris. "But I always keep up my end of the bargain unlike some other and newer members of the Brotherhood. I trust you have not done anything that will upset our dear daughter too much."

Natalie looked at Jeroch puzzled by his statement, and then fixed her eyes back on her mother, waiting for a response.

"I leave all the unpleasantness for you Shadow. I know that you surely have plans for my army here, and that is none of my concern. My errand here was simple, I wanted to see my daughter and pay my regards to her lovely son and grandson. My invitation for you to come here was also for that purpose, but I knew immediately upon inviting you that you would turn this into some plan to destroy the forces of the Light. That is between you and Natalie and is none of my affair."

It was a subtle lie. Jeroch wouldn't have come at all without the information that Rand was a member of the *Erieal*, and he was under the control of the phasia. That bait was too attractive to ignore. Unless Caris missed her guess, Jeroch and Ellis would both go with the Army of the Wolf wherever it went, Jeroch to steer and use Rand as he saw fit, and Ellis to keep her hooks in the boy through Jessica. Caris was sure that Jeroch and Ellis would be at each other's throats before too long. But the real positive out of the entire situation was that there were two more phasia that would not be in the way of her plans. Last generation she would have succeeded in her task had it not been for that bitch Bryn, and Caris was going to go out of her way this time around to make sure that there was no outside interference by other members of the Brotherhood.

"Caris, how is it that you and I were ever allies?" Jeroch mused. "You were always the first one to underestimate my intelligence in thinking that you could manipulate me whenever and however you chose. You never thought I could see through any of your schemes and that you could lead me by the nose through whatever hoops you saw fir to throw at me."

Caris's practiced smile did not betray the irritation that Jeroch caused her.

"It was convenient to ally myself with you Jeroch, for many reasons," Caris replied, the slightest hint of venom in her voice. "We were all forbidden to have children after Bryn's carelessness, except of course for the First of the Shadow. You had every advantage Jeroch, and so by allying with you, some of that came my way. Thanks to you, I was able to get close to Cedric Binosear, and I was able to turn him away from the path of the Light briefly, until Basille stabbed me in the back."

"Literally," Jeroch mumbled.

Caris' blood began to boil at Jeroch's impudence. He may have been the first son of Shau-ling, and the leader of the Brotherhood of Phasia, but no one, not even the vaunted First of the Shadow had the right to insult her in front of her own daughter.

"You are treading in dangerous waters Jeroch, and I would watch my tongue if I were you."

Jeroch's tone suddenly changed. To many of the phasia, Jeroch was considered a weakling who hid behind Shau-ling and the laws of the Council. For those who had met him in close combat, they knew better. Caris had seen the evil side of Jeroch surface on many occasions during their rocky alliance, and many times his anger had been directed at her.

Caris could see the change in Jeroch's eyes and braced herself for the onslaught she had just incurred.

"You have a short memory indeed Caris Vale'," Jeroch said his cold, hard stare fixed directly on Caris' green eyes. "Shau-ling has forbidden the phasia from continuing these petty battles in the face of the larger war. The War for Ascension is dead as far as I am concerned, but if you think you want a piece of me, little sister, I am sure that it can be revived briefly. But keep this in mind before you make your choice. If I win, I will most assuredly be forgiven for ridding the Council of a devious, manipulative little whore who does things her own way with no regard for the will of her master. But if you win, Shau-ling will hunt you down for disobeying his decree and make sure that you meet the same fate as your old conspirator Basille. Either way Caris, my dear old ally, I still win."

Caris could feel the anger build in her to the point where she felt as though she would burst. No one, but no one called her a whore and lived. It was a mere thought later that the blade of onyx laced with Blaze flame appeared in her hand. While combat was not one of Caris's strengths, she was still a member of the phasia, and she could still fight with the best warriors the world had to offer. Jeroch only hesitated a moment before stepping back and letting the hilts of his twin blades form in his palms. The pristine sword of Order and the sickening black blade of Chaos pulsed with deadly life. Natalie stepped away from her parents, not wanting to get caught in the crossfire of a battle of full-blooded members of the phasia. As a child of the phasia, she had power, even more considering both of her parents were phasia, but in a battle of this magnitude, she would be stepped on like a bug. However, before the first blow could be struck in what could have been an incredible and bloody duel, the door swung open hard to reveal Ellis and her daughter Jessica. In one deft motion, Ellis leapt across the room, landing between the would-be combatants.

"This is not the time or the place for this battle," Ellis said calmly, alternating her icy stare between Caris and Jeroch. "Master has decreed that none of us, not even you Jeroch, can kill another member of the phasia without his permission."

Jeroch was the first to lower his blades and let them disappear.

"I was merely defending myself dear sister," Jeroch said innocently, "as is my right as a living being."

Ellis stared hard at Jeroch, which Jeroch brushed away with an evil grin.

"Very good timing Ellis," Caris commented as her blade crumbled into dust, "I don't want the burden of being the head of the Council, even if it is only for a few moments."

The three phasia stood silent for the next few moments, tension thick in the air. Finally, it was Caris who broke the uneasy silence.

"Well, I have completed my errand here in Alimidar, and I have other matters to attend to. I trust Jeroch that you will do everything in your power to destroy my army with one of your pathetic plans."

Jeroch dismissed the criticism with a wave of hand.

"As I thought. Well, until next we meet."

With that, a portal formed in the room, and Caris stepped through, bringing a sigh of relief from Natalie.

"Do not get too comfortable yet, Natalie," Jeroch said watching the portal close. "Your mother is not long for this world, that I assure you. And though it may not be me that strikes the final blow to end her life in this generation, I guarantee you that I will have a hand in her demise."

Ellis' stare intensified.

"Safe your wrath for someone who is affected by it, Ellis," Jeroch chided. "You scare me as much as your impotent ally Grawn does. Save your threats and hard stares for him. I have more pressing matters to attend to."

Jeroch pulled himself to full height and then turned to face Natalie.

"I am taking command of your Army of the Wolf. In the morning, we march on Scalla. I intend to make Jerrard Mystic regret the day he turned his back on his family."

Ellis scowled and watched as Jeroch walked out of the room.

"And we'll be right there Jeroch," she added under her breath, "just in case."

* * * * * * * * * * *

Grimm and Cash stood in the clearing just outside the border city of Frontier, watching the people as they came and went. Originally they had agreed to help Rane with her obsession with Lissa Terian, but that had only gotten them this far. Rane wasn't sure if she wanted to assault the group again after her last loss, so she had returned to gather more troops. It was then that Caris had contacted them.

"Tell me again why we are waiting for Caris?" the strong blond woman said to her companion.

"It's simple, Cash," Grimm responded. "Caris wanted us to help her get closer to this group. Rane is intent on raiding the place anyway. So, we use Rane as a diversion, get Caris in close, threaten her a little, and then get scared off. Then when the time is right, Caris will strike at them from the inside and we'll be able to swoop in a mop up."

Cash nodded.

"Sounds like a good plan. Do you really think that Rane will succeed in killing them?"

Grimm laughed.

"Rane may be one of the most dedicated people I have ever met in my short life, but tactics are not her strong suit. If you and I decided to assault this place, we would win. But with Rane, there's no chance."

"Then why don't we do it?" Cash asked drawing her sword.

"Simple," Grimm replied looking down at his companion, "because I have a much better plan."

He Who Brings Destruction

Creator's Calendar Year 1205; Dark Mirror

The din of battle filled the forested pathways around the palace of Sador as men and monsters were locked in a pitched battle whose end would only come at the cost of hundreds of lives. Thus far, tenacity and trickery had proved to give the mortals an advantage over their savage counterparts, but now, in the courtyards of the palace itself, no amount of trickery would be enough to push back the red rage of the Jeresei. Soldiers from the Order of the Sword poured into the courtyards through the broken palisades of the southern and western gates, striking down whatever flagging resistance stood in their way. However, they were not ready for the wave of reserve troops that had been waiting for them. Evan Sinn, one of the generals of the army swallowed hard and hesitated for a moment when he saw the mass of red-skinned devils that stood between the Order and their greatest prize of this war between the Light and the Shadow. Without even a motion toward his men, the Order charged with a feral war cry unlike any he had ever heard before. This war was being fought with the primal and base emotions in the hearts of the soldiers, and it was as though they were pouring every bit of their soul into their screaming muscles. Each second begging their tired bodies to stay steady for just a few more moments until the battle was won. The battle cry rang through the ranks energizing all who heard it, bolstering the wills of the wounded, and making the enemy rock back on its heels. But the advantage was fleeting as the animalistic Jeresei let their own scream hit the air and charged into the fray.

The two armies hit each other with a sound that confounded even the most prolific poet's description. If there was a sound that best fit the word death, then it was the sound made when the two sprinting ranks collided in a mash of color and fury. Screams from man and beast alike pulsed through the intertwined ranks, and blood flowed like wine. Each flash of steel met with hardened claw in a dance of death, some ending with a plume of red blood and the scream of a falling man, others with the sound of shattering bone and tearing sinew with the guttural cry of a dying Jeresei. Evan was at the vanguard of the Order's charge, and though he only had one arm, he fought like the others, damning every force that stood against him, be it heaven or hell. With each stroke of the blade, he moved farther into the ranks of Jeresei. His companions kept pace, some falling along the way to the long sharp nails of the feral monstrosities. As another of the monsters met its end at Evan's blade, he realized that he was alone in the sea of red. The last of his companions had fallen and he was surrounded. Only a few of the Jeresei had taken the time to realize that a human had incurred that far into their ranks as they were too busy picking their way through the dead bodies and moving deeper into the charging mass of humans. But that pause only last for a few heartbeats as four of the beasts moved in on Evan at once. Evan had heard the legends of Logan Ranthall killing whole armies of Jeresei by himself, and his great and powerful lord Gwydeon Sandar standing like a god amidst the battlefield, slaying the beasts by the thousands, but Evan was not a legend, he was only a man. And mortal men die on battlefields. But in the last seconds, arrows flew from seemingly nowhere, striking down two of the advancing Jeresei. The seconds of confusion that the dying Jeresei brought to their companions was more than enough for Evan to kill a third and then make a hasty retreat to the advancing Order ranks. It was then that the shout for another charge went up, and along with the surging ranks Evan moved forward, risking a quick glance back, seeing Midarin Rice and Rachel Core side by side, their bows drawn and then firing. The lethal pair had saved his life again, and Evan was sure it would not be the last time. But the tide of the battle was turning, the Jeresei could only hold out for a few moments longer before the onslaught of the Order would be too much. Then Sador would fall, and the forces of the Light would have their first victory in far too long. But then suddenly the walls to the inner cloister of the palace broke open and the tide turned again.

* * * * * * * * * * *

Away from the clash in the courtyard, a different battle was about to take place in the halls of the palace. Nathaniel Sandar, having left Logan Ranthall to die outside the palace had made his way through the twisted iron gates at the southern end of the central building in the courtyard on his quest to find and kill the phase Zarsi. The entry foyer had been dark, the torches and candles snuffed out. It was as though Zarsi had known they were coming all along and had kept surprises waiting for them. Nathaniel, sensing a trap, kept himself aware of everything around him, as though the stones of the building were living things that would leap out at him any moment. Walking through a long hallway toward a flight of stairs that would most likely lead to the throne room, or at least closer to it, Nathaniel kept his eyes floating from side to side, paying special attention to the suits of armor that lined the hallway. As though his premonition had triggered them, the empty armors began to move, brandishing their weapons as though wielded by human hands. A quick count revealed a dozen of the automatons. One was on top of Nathaniel the second it awoke, slashing downward with its huge axe. Nathaniel rolled out of the way, as the head of the axe continued downward, embedding itself in the floor, and sending bits of the polished floor flying in all directions. Popping up to a knee, the boy tried to send a concentrated stream of Fire flowing back at his mindless adversary, but before his attack could be launched, a sword struck at him, disrupting his concentration and sending him sprawling to the floor again, this time, out of control. The blade of the sword had not struck him cleanly, the blade missing completely, but the flat of the blade clipped his shoulder. Two more large axes came to bear this time, but the boy was ready. A quick almost reflexive movement of his wrist brought a stream of fire erupting from his hand. While this was not a precise attack by any stretch of the word, it was effective. The flash of fire caught the head of one of the axes, melting it into an unrecognizable mass. The other blade was dodged and with another gesture met the same fate. Instinct was beginning to take over inside of Nathaniel, and the powers of the *Coromor* manifested themselves more with every passing second. As though watching from high above, Nathaniel observed as he froze several of the armors in a single attack, rendering them impotent. The three that had escaped this assault found themselves crushed when a web of wind wove itself around them and constricted more effectively than the largest python. To finish the job, another stream of water wove around the frozen suits of armor, the temperature of the metal dropping dramatically with each second. It took only a simple gust of air at that point to send the statues toppling to the floor where they shattered into a million pieces on impact.

One trap had been disarmed, but as Nathaniel looked around inspecting the surroundings again, he inwardly wondered how many still remained on his path to the phase. Beyond that, what tricks would Zarsi have waiting for him when the two were finally face to face? That was a question he was sure that would soon be answered, but Nathaniel could not allow his mind to be clouded. There was only one purpose. The death of a phase was the only way that this battle would be a victory, and without that, the Order of the Sword would have to fight devils and demons until the last of the mortals found death in the palace of Sador.

* * * * * * * * * * *

Time seemed to stop in those brief seconds after the explosion of the wall surrounding the inner cloister of the palace. Rocks and debris hung in the air for what seemed like hours, each grain taking its own time in letting the air guide it in its fall. Midarin Rice watched on through the painful eternity of those few seconds, the horror and despair creeping into her heart. The ground shook again, but this time it was because of the massive foot of a Stone stepping though the newly created opening and out into the courtyard. Several of the Jeresei were caught by surprise and were unable to move out of the way of the massive foot and found themselves squashed under the tremendous weight. But the Stone was not alone in its hiding place. In the next few moments, metallic beasts let their wings touch the wind and rose high above the battlefield. Midarin knew what would happen next. The Shadowwalkers would sit on their high perches, waiting for their opportunity to strike, and then would loose their streams of flaming death upon the already bloodied courtyard, roasting both man and monster for the amusement of their master. Surely only the Stone would be the survivor of such an assault, because Midarin had seen the battle prowess of the gigantic warriors first hand many times over the years. Of all of the forces that the Shadow could bring to bear, the Stone were among the most fearsome. There was so little that could harm the creatures, and it was only their lack of speed and lack of intelligence that held them back from being every bit the match of the Shadowwalkers in lethality. The loyal men of the Order, while braver than most men should have been while faced with the forces of the Shadow, broke at the sight of the gigantic creature, and reformed a generous few strides later. It had taken coordinated efforts of a highly trained and properly prepared defense force to topple the creatures in Brea, but in an open battlefield, the advantage clearly belonged to the hulking colossus.

The balance had returned, and the two forces stood off against one another once again. The Jeresei's will had been bolstered by the appearance of their larger brothers, and Midarin wondered how long it would be before the Shadowwalkers would rain death down upon their ranks. But something was amiss. The Stone stood firm and gazed deep into the ranks of the Order of the Sword, as if it were looking for something. Midarin felt the gaze pass over her like a warm sunbeam. For a moment, Midarin wondered if this were some new weapon devised by Shau-ling to sap the will to fight out of the ranks of the mortals. But as Midarin looked around and saw the clenched fists and nervous stances of the men around her, she realized that she was the only one who had felt that fragile peace for those few seconds. Beside Midarin, Rachel Core drew an arrow from the quiver on her back and nocked it firmly on the bowstring.

"So, I guess they had an ambush set for us after all," she said disgusted as she drew back the bowstring and took careful aim at one of the hovering Shadowwalkers.

Midarin didn't answer, but kept her gaze locked on the Stone. Then suddenly she began to remember her time with the Stone warrior during her time with the People of the Dragon. Stone had been her friend, and her protector, even to its very end. Maybe that familiarity was dulling her senses, causing her to see things that weren't really there.

"Which should I take out, Midarin?" Rachel continued. "Do I have any chance at that big stone thing?"

The waves of peace kept flooding over Midarin, and then she felt a little knot in her stomach. It was the first time that she had felt the child in her womb respond to anything but a sweet song in the twilight hours of the evening. Then she looked up at the Stone, and she thought she saw it smile, though this time she knew it was not her imagination.

"I don't think you have to worry about the Stone, Rachel. He's on our side..."

* * * * * * * * * * *

As Nathaniel ascended the steps to the second floor, he could feel a cold breeze wrap around him. Even his breath had become visible in the next few moments. Carefully the young man extended his awareness to the large hall around him, and was not surprised to find that the mark of Zarsi's power was felt throughout the room. Only this room separated Nathaniel from Zarsi, and the large double doors at the end of the receiving hall seemed ominous. Suddenly the sound of breaking glass filled the room. Nathaniel immediately looked up at the huge stained glass windows that stretched along both sides of the receiving hall. The pictures there depicted huge battles and Nathaniel blinked hard as he realized that the figures in the glass were moving. With a nearly deafening sound one of the huge windows shattered, sending shards of glass spraying into the room, but with the shards were the glass warriors that landed on the wide red carpet that led to the throne room. Now a legion of glass warrior blocked the path to Zarsi, and Nathaniel drew himself up and began to open his mind to the power around him.

The colorful glass warriors began to advance, but Nathaniel had not noticed that some of the warriors, instead of being armed with swords and axes, carried bows. As the young man gathered his powers for the coming hand to hand confrontation, long thin shards of glass launched from the colorful bows and one of them caught Nathaniel in the shoulder. The wound erupted with a plume of blood which broke Nathaniel's concentration. Two more of the glass arrows streaked by, one of them embedding itself deeply in Nathaniel's leg, forcing him to his knees. Laughter filled the room. Nathaniel recognized the maniacal laughter immediately as Zarsi's.

"So, you thought getting to my throne room would be easy, didn't you little boy?"

Zarsi's voice seemed to come from each of the glass warriors. As Nathaniel looked up, he noticed that they had parted in the center, leaving the carpeted path to the throne room doors wide open.

"My warriors have made a path for you Nathaniel, are you brave enough to run the gauntlet?"

Nathaniel stood and stared at the wooden doors. As if commanded, the doors creaked open revealing the golden throne at the far end of the next room. Seated on the throne was the scarred phase Zarsi.

"You see boy, no tricks. I'm right here waiting on you, all you have to do is get to me."

As Nathaniel took a step forward, he expected his foot to rest on the solid floor beneath the red carpet, however, his foot continued to travel downward, and Nathaniel felt a warm liquid rush in around his leg as his foot continued downward. It was then that he realized that the carpet on the floor was no longer a carpet but a long river of blood that flowed to the throne. Nathaniel sank waist deep in the red viscous liquid before he felt the ground firmly beneath his feet. Now the gauntlet had become that much more difficult with the glass warriors on the raised banks of the receiving hall's floor. Thinking better of the road that lay ahead, Nathaniel reached for the raised bank to his right, but as he tried to pull himself up, it crumbled to ash under his touch, sending him face first into the blood that lay below. Zarsi was intent on keeping him at a disadvantage. No tricks, indeed.

"Oh, I forgot to mention," Zarsi said laughing again, "you have to stay on the path."

Smiling to himself as he stood up and wiped the blood off of his face with his forearm, Nathaniel gathered his strength again and sent a wave of wind speeding toward the glass warriors. Where Nathaniel had expected the glass warrior to topple and shatter, he found himself being buffeted by a strong gust.

"Now now little *Coromor*. I didn't say you could use your powers, now did I? It's a good thing that attack of yours was just Wind. I would hate to think what would have happened if you would have tried to channel Earth or worse yet, Fire. Now, little one, shall we stop with these games? Give up and let me kill you quickly, or continue with this charade of trying to kill me, and try to survive my gauntlet. The choice is yours."

* * * * * * * * * * *

Rachel didn't have time to react to Midarin's words before the older woman stepped forward through the crowd of soldiers. Worried for her queen's safety, Rachel followed, inwardly cursing her for being so reckless. In a matter of moments, Midarin had pushed her way to the front rank of the remaining members of the Order of the Sword. Evan Sinn was the first to notice Midarin's presence.

"My lady, it is not safe for you to be here. The Jeresei could charge, or the Shadowwalkers could start their assault at any moment. You should be back in the ranks where you will be safe."

At that moment Rachel pushed her way through the crowd and emerged beside Midarin.

"Rachel," Evan said quickly, "get Midarin out of here."

"No wait," Midarin said after a moment, "you don't understand."

Suddenly Midarin stepped out into the open area between the armies. A quick Jeresei could have crossed the distance and gutted her before anyone from the Order of the Sword would have been able to make a move to save her. Rachel wanted to call out, but Midarin looked back and from the look in her eyes, Rachel could tell that Midarin knew what she was doing. The Jeresei on the vanguard of the other front tensed and looked as though they were about to leap, but the massive Stone took a step forward and the Jeresei laughed and howled obviously mocking the human on the fate she would meet at the hands of their larger ally. Midarin held up a hand and the Stone creature stopped and then stooped down so it was nearly at eye level with the smaller human.

"Do you know who I am?" was the only question that Midarin could muster.

The fear in her had welled up watching the huge creature come closer to her. She had seen firsthand the kind of destruction and pain that could be laid out by one of those monsters, and it had been the Stone warriors that had laid siege to her proud kingdom of Brea and practically leveled it. If she was wrong, if her faith was misplaced, her death would come in a fraction of a second. This could very well be the end of the battle, as the Order would fall without their leader.

"Y...E...S..."

It was the same rolling booming voice that had come from her friend Stone all those years ago, and in hearing it, some of her fears were quelled. But for every fear that was being put to rest there were more questions and still darker fears.

"How?"

"T...H...E...R...E./.I...S./.N...O./.T...I...M...E./.N...O...W./.F ...R...I...E...N...D./.M...I...D...A...R...I...N..."

Midarin was shocked to hear the Stone creature refer to her as Stone had in their time together. But then, Stone were bonded creatures that shared a kind of collective memory. Something else was different too. The Stone said something about time, a concept that the Stone shouldn't have had a concept of. Was it possible that the memories of her and her kindness to the other Stone had transferred to others of its kind?

"Are you here to help me?" Midarin questioned trying to fight through the shock.

As if in an attempt to answer the simple question, the Stone straightened again and turned back on its comrades. Sensing what was about to happen, Midarin took several steps back towards her ranks of soldiers and tried to shield her eyes from the carnage that was about to take place. When the killing began, it was not clear as to who was more surprised, the forces of the Shadow, or the warriors from the Order of the Sword. With a single motion of its huge foot, the Stone slammed its full weight down on a group of Jeresei reducing them to a smear of blood and entrails. One of the Stone's massive hands swatted at the airborne Shadowwalkers, catching one of them and sending it sprawling through the air out of control until it crashed to the ground just on the outskirts of the forest. The other Jeresei broke, caught between their former ally and the mass of humans that were becoming braver at the sight of the huge Stone fighting on their side. Two of the Shadowwalkers dove and loosed a stream of white flame at the Stone. However, just as a man brushes off the sting of a mosquito, the Stone turned and caught one of the Shadowwalkers in its fist and squashed it like a bug, sending the broken body falling to the ground in a heap. The Jeresei not caught by the shuffling feet of the Stone charged the ranks of men, hoping to kill some of them before meeting their own fate. Obviously, they liked their chances against a man far more than they did against a Stone. But the emboldened soldiers would give no quarter to their demonic opponents, and within a matter of moments, all of the Jeresei lay strewn throughout the courtyard, the blood staining the once green grass red. The Shadowwalkers that had not been ripped from the air by the Stone fled to the east, no doubt to inform their master of the treachery against them. But this small part in the battle for Sador was over, and while it gave the forces of the Light their first strategic victory over the Shadow, it also meant that they were now a serious threat. All that was left now was to find Nathaniel.

* * * * * * * * * * *

The blood flowed around Nathaniel and he silently considered his next course of action. Then suddenly it occurred to him. Nathaniel opened himself up to as much power as he could, and then began to send waves of wind through the room. Just as he expected Nathaniel felt the phase exert his influence to reflect the wind. However, what Zarsi had not expected was that the huge influx of power was just a mask to hide what Nathaniel was really doing, and that was creating a portal underneath his feet. Nathaniel fell through the newly opened portal and emerged in the throne room just a few steps from Zarsi, a wide smile on his face. Zarsi could only laugh as the river of blood began to solidify and Nathaniel found himself standing on carpet once again.

"Very good little one. Perhaps I had underestimated your abilities, but I assure you it is a mistake that will only be made once."

"For some reason," Nathaniel said letting a sword made of the string of Order appear in his hand, "I get the impression that you phasia underestimate people a lot."

The phase's expression did not change.

"Impudence does not suit you," Zarsi countered. "Perhaps I should kill you slowly so I get some enjoyment out of the act."

"Try and do whatever you want old man," Nathaniel said letting all of the spite and malice flow into him, "and you'll only get to enjoy your own embarrassment."

Zarsi stepped down from the dais and rounded on his younger opponent. With a motion of Zarsi's hand a pillar of flame erupted from the floor where Nathaniel stood. The boy was fast enough to jump back, and counter with a stream of ice shards. Zarsi moved to dodge the shards and then realized that they weren't aimed at him, but rather at the pillar of flame. The room was quickly filled with thick steam, and before Zarsi could use wind to clear the room, he felt the flows of power from a portal behind him. In a quick motion, the phase dropped to the ground and a second later a beam of pure Order filled the space where his head had just been. Zarsi rolled to the side and then used a quick burst of wind to clear the steam. Nathaniel stood near the throne, waiting, with a bright smile on his face. Zarsi found something odd about the tactics the boy was employing. They were far more lethal and focused, much like a member of the phasia would be in a fight for Ascension. However, a boy, even a boy blessed with the power of the *Coromor* should not have the ability to fight at that level when it had taken the phasia lifetimes to achieve the level of mastery that they currently enjoyed. Something else was intervening on behalf of the boy, and Zarsi's suspicions had only one name, Emries.

"Get up old man," Nathaniel jabbed, "you'll be tasting dirt soon enough after I bury you."

Zarsi suppressed a growl.

"Many stronger than you have tried, but none have succeeded yet. I fought Shau-ling to a standstill for seven days."

"Oh," Nathaniel answered, "and here I thought he let you fight until he got bored. Tell you what, I won't waste our time, and I'll make sure I give you something much worse than a scar to remember me by."

The beam of power that erupted from the boy's hand that next moment moved faster than Zarsi expected. He rolled out of the way and then leapt to his feet. Zarsi couldn't believe what he had seen. That beam of energy had all the elements wrapped together along with one of the forgotten strings. The beam would have been enough to banish Zarsi altogether. For the first time in generations, fear crept into Zarsi's mind. This boy had the ability to revoke a phase's immortality.

"Alright boy," Zarsi's anger pouring through in his voice, "play time is over."

The assault Zarsi launched in the next few moments would reduce the throne room to a shaky foundation. Beam after beam of fire, water, and earth shot from Zarsi's hands, and Nathaniel dodged each one with an unholy speed. Blast after blast blazed harmlessly behind Nathaniel, a half a second too slow to hit the moving target. But where the beam did connect sent debris flying in all directions. Fires blazed throughout the room where tapestries had been the recipients of the wayward attacks. Whole sections of wall blew out after being shattered by columns of water and rock. And yet the assaults continued, with Nathaniel dancing through and dodging each one, and Zarsi firing one after another, aiming becoming optional. Finally, Zarsi let the last beam of fire leap from his hand, and as it missed Nathaniel's speeding form, the boy stopped in his tracks and locked his eyes on his obviously tiring opponent.

"Having trouble keeping up with me old man? If you keep this up, there won't be much of a prize left when the battle for Sador is over."

Zarsi panted. He had not fought a battle like this in some time, and it was taking far more of a toll on him than it should have. There was something else at play here, something that had Zarsi fighting at a severe disadvantage.

"I don't care about this place so long as your dead body is among the rest of this useless debris."

Suddenly Zarsi was encased with the fires of the Blaze. The green flames danced across his features giving him a truly evil and maniacal glow. Unimpressed by the light show, Nathaniel took steady aim and released another bolt of energy meant to banish the phase. However, instead of having the desired effect, the bolt bounced harmlessly off the shield of Blaze energy, launched skyward and sent pieces of wood and tar raining down from the newly pierced ceiling. Again and again, Nathaniel sent bolts of energy against the wall of Blaze energy with the attacks harmlessly batted aside. But then, the aura around Zarsi began to pulse like a heartbeat. Zarsi was drawing deeper and deeper on the Blaze, his only counter to the raw and primal energy that Nathaniel was leveraging.

"Now you will see the true might of a phase."

Zarsi's voice was distant and powerful, like it echoed from another world. Then, before Nathaniel could move there was an explosion like nothing human eyes had ever seen. The room was filled with pure Blaze flame in the next second. After several moments, the flames receded.

There was very little left of the throne room of the palace of Sador. Huge holes in the walls allowed the light from the outside in, and the remaining support beams groaned loudly and threatened to collapse under the uneven weight. All of the tapestries that had once hung throughout the room had been reduced to piles of ash strewn about the shattered rock, wood and glass. Zarsi fell to his knees after releasing the huge burst of energy, trying to drag his labored breaths in and out of his burning lungs. If he had drawn any more power from the Blaze for that assault, it probably would have killed him, but as it was, he would most likely die anyway. Zarsi closed his eyes for a moment, but when he opened them, he saw a pair of shoes before him. Shocked, Zarsi raised his head until he stared the boy Nathaniel in the eyes. The boy didn't have a scratch on him, and he was standing proudly holding a sword of pure Order in his hands once again.

"How?"

"You'll never know," Nathaniel answered bringing the sword crashing down on Zarsi's skull, splitting it in two.

The phase's body slumped to the ground and blood mixed with the rest of the debris. Laughing to himself, Nathaniel walked away from his fallen foe and brushed some of the dirt off the throne before seating himself proudly. A radiant white aura pulsed around the young man's body for several seconds before dissipating into the mass of dust and smoke. He had conquered Sador by himself in his mind, and it was only a matter of time before the whole of the world knelt at his feet.

* * * * * * * * * * *

Logan Ranthall clutched the hilt of the Dragon Sword hard as he watched the man he had known as Emries struggle back to his feet. When he woke and saw the originator of the powers of the *Coromor* lying on the ground, he had first questioned the man's motivations, but the burn mark on the ground near where Logan had passed out answered the question well enough. Emries had come to execute him, but something had gone terribly wrong.

"I never thought you would resort to stabbing one of your own in the back, Emries," Logan said, steadying for battle.

Emries let a scowl curl his lips.

"And I never thought that one of my children would turn on me as you have, Logan. You were given the gift of power and were protected. Your wife and child were protected, and you repay me by taking hold of the very force that I oppose? You have touched the Blaze, Logan Ranthall, and you have tried to use that power to kill the third *Coromor* of the prophecies. For that, you have become an enemy of the Light, and you must die."

Logan laughed.

"I'm an enemy of the Light? If you are the Light, Emries, then I hope that I will be the one to snuff it out forever."

"You impudent whelp…"

"Stop right there," Logan interrupted. "You have done nothing but lie to me from the moment we met, and now it's time for things to be set straight. I know it was you who ordered Cedric to kill Elwyne. I know it was you who turned Nathaniel into the monster he is today. Because of you, I have no son. If because of that you think I am your enemy, you've only got it half right. I was born of the *Chosen One*, my father Arin Ranthall, whose powers came from the Aerith Seth. My mother had the remnants of the power that belonged to Ellis Chandara, a daughter of Shau-ling, your sworn enemy running through her veins. That makes me half-phase by my reckoning. Therefore, I have been betraying my rightful family this entire time by following you. So now, before you and anyone else who can hear me, I give my loyalty and my life to Shau-ling."

"Then, half-phase," Emries answered coldly, "let me send you to hell to meet the bitch you called wife and the bastard you would have called son."

Chapter XXXVII

The Spider and the Fly

Creator's Calendar Year 1205; Light Reality

Susanne Praen stepped out of the little farmhouse and looked up into the bright afternoon sky and let the sunlight wash over her. Even though there were storm-clouds gathering on the horizon the bright light still shown through. It was the first time in many years that she actually felt a feeling of freedom resonate though her. For so long she had been under the watchful eye of practically every member of the Creator's Torch Society, unable to do anything without someone with her. Guards were posted outside her door day and night, she had escorts everywhere she went, and she had been unable to attend any meeting of the Torch since Erdric had been revealed as her lover. In reality, it had been a blessing that the expulsion had come, for she could finally pursue the one man that had destroyed her life and had taken from her everything that she held dear. But revenge would come soon enough. Susanne now would have to try and blend in with this young group of men and women in an attempt to get closer to achieving her goal. Part of her thought it was crazy that kids, which all of them were except for the man Wolf had called Gwillim, were speaking so casually about members of the phasia. Soldiers throughout the world trained their entire lives fearing the forces of the Shadow, but these people were aching for the confrontation. But then again, they were also talking openly about the *Coromor*, the *Chosen One*, Aerith Seth, and Shau-ling. Then Susanne thought a little harder. Wolf Ranthall and Lissa Terian were two names that held a lot of meaning. Wolf Ranthall was the son of the Dragon Logan Ranthall, and Lissa Terian was obviously related in some way to White Lightning, Aryx Terian. Then there was Queen Midarin Rice and Queen Cairyn Binosear, both famous women, but for obviously different reasons. Midarin had been a hero in the People of the Dragon, fighting side by side with Logan Ranthall, Pike Rhuiden, and Elwyne Tamerlane. Cairyn was known because she was the niece of the legendary Cedric Binosear of Marcwell, the Lion, and now the wife of the hero Pike Rhuiden. No matter how ordinary this little band of adventurers might have looked, they were certainly far from it.

The young brunette woman standing outside of the house took notice of Susanne immediately and walked over with a smile. She had a grace and elegance to her demeanor that was obvious to anyone who looked at her, and she seemed to Susanne's eyes to be much more mature than her age might have suggested.

"I suppose my manners have suffered a bit being around these boys," the girl said, her intonation on the word boys being quickly scoffed at by the older Gwillim. "I'm Sabrina Binosear, daughter to Lord Pike Rhuiden and Queen Cairyn Binosear."

Susanne for a moment didn't know whether to bow or not. Luckily, Gwillim saved her from the decision.

"Don't let her fool you, Susanne," the muscular man chimed in walking over with a younger man in tow. "For all her polite talk and courtly way, Sabrina is far less a lady then she would ever let anyone know, and she prefers to be with us boys out here in the country. Suppose you can't blame her considering her father spends most of his time riding all over the countryside."

Sabrina scowled in Gwillim's direction and then let the smile return.

"I'm Gwillim Sandar," he said ignoring Sabrina's reaction, "and this is my little brother Nathaniel."

"Pleasure to meet you both," Susanne said, momentarily distracted by a young girl on a horse a few steps in front of her who was quietly polishing the blade of her sword.

"Oh, I see you have noticed our little sister Liette," Gwillim continued. "She is not the most cordial person in the world, but in a fight she is right at home. I guess you could say that fighting the Shadow is the family business."

Susanne shook herself away from her thoughts about a girl that young fighting with anything other than her older siblings and smiled at Gwillim.

"You seem to be the eldest here," Susanne started.

"Old in form, young in mind," Nathaniel countered.

Gwillim laughed hard and then shook his head.

"And trust me Susanne, they never let me forget it. Yes, I'm old enough to be the father of one of these pups, but the Creator has seen fit to curse me by making me part of this generation. It's a long and boring story to be sure. At the end of the day though, I'm just happy to have my chance to do what needs to be done."

While everyone but Liette laughed at the joke, Sabrina's mirth seemed to end almost as soon as it started. Her smile melted into a pained frown and then she turned her attention to her horse and the preparations for travel. Susanne took a quick look over her shoulder and saw that Lissa and Wolf had finally emerged from the farmhouse and were laughing and talking. Susanne began to guess that the relationship between the two was more than friendship, and the pained expression on the face of the Princess was one of jealousy. Naturally, Gwillim and Nathaniel were oblivious to the situation, but then again they were men, and men very rarely took notice of the subtle hints dropped by women where their feelings were concerned.

"Well," Wolf said as he approached, "is everyone ready to go?"

That moment another young man walked out from the tree line a few feet away and waved toward the group.

"Find anything Jared?" Wolf asked turning his attention to the arrival.

"Well," Jared said walking up and scratching his head, "ever since you told me to open up to my powers, I've been feeling some weird things all around. I was hoping that maybe you guys could help me figure out what it is that I'm feeling."

Wolf wasn't surprised that Jared would have difficulty translating what he was seeing into words. Even with the full memories and the experience of the Blaze at his disposal, Wolf had a hard time understanding what he was seeing or feeling.

"We will if we can," Wolf answered. "Lead the way."

Jared nodded and walked back in the direction in which he came. Wolf followed with Lissa, Gwillim and Nathaniel close behind. Sabrina seemed hesitant to follow but did after a moment, and Susanne fell in step with her. Only Liette seemed uninterested in everything that was going on. Her full attention was devoted to the cleaning and polishing of her blade. Jared led the group to a clearing in the woods and stopped short of where the undergrowth began to get heavier.

"Right here," he began, "I feel a large influx of power, like this was the focal point of something very large but at the same time very controlled. Something targeted this particular location."

Susanne watched as both Nathaniel and Wolf closed their eyes. While she understood little of the type of power that manifested in people like the phasia and those touched by the Creator, she did begin to realize that every use of that type of power left a footprint of sorts in the area. That way, others with power could feel and determine what had happened, whether it was a great battle, or just a parlor trick. Though most of her studies of the ways of the Moridon had ended after the death of Dei, she had learned enough about Moridon magic to know that a similar rule applied to their powers. Moridon magic was more complicated than those who had such abilities naturally, insofar as there were complicated rituals, hand gestures, and incantations that accompanied even the simplest use of magic. But after every use the natural powers, the forces that the phasia controlled, rebelled at the mortal tampering and left the area tainted. The taint was the method to unravel what had occurred.

"Yes, I feel it too," Wolf said first. "It hangs like a fog all over this clearing. It's not a portal, that's for sure, but I do feel similar threads of power in the area."

"That is from Rael and Trece," Nathaniel added. "Their strings of power are easy to separate from this other force. It's like nothing that I have ever felt before, but one thing is for certain. Whoever wields this power is very experienced at covering their tracks. I can feel that this power has not degraded normally, it's like it has been blurred purposefully. That means the power is old, older than the *Coromor* or the phasia."

Wolf opened his eyes and turned to face Sabrina.

"I don't know if you'll have any more luck than Nathaniel and I did, but why don't you take a look and see what you can find. After all, you have a tie to something that old."

Sabrina hesitated for a moment and then nodded. As Susanne watched the young woman shut her eyes, she saw her right eye twitch and then the tremor seemed to continue through her whole body. Sabrina's body shook violently and her knees began to buckle as though a huge weight had begun to press down on her. It looked as though Sabrina was going to pass out any moment, and her face went pale in the passing seconds. Suddenly she collapsed, and Wolf was right there to catch her. After a few seconds, Sabrina opened her eyes and looked up at Wolf. There was a spark there, and Susanne could feel it from where she stood. It was almost as if Sabrina's feelings for Wolf, whatever they were, manifested themselves for that moment when she was unable to keep them behind that well-polished diplomatic exterior. Sabrina clung to Wolf, her face pressed to his chest as though she had been pulled from the brink of death. Then, as though she realized where she was, she pulled herself out of Wolf's arms and straightened herself. Always trying to keep the situation light, Gwillim was the first to say anything.

"I hope you found something, because that was the worst acting I have ever seen."

Sabrina let the jibe pass over her and then nodded.

"I could see the fog that Wolf and Nathaniel described, but there was more to it. There was a huge hole, right here where Wolf is standing, something like a portal but much more powerful. And then a few steps away here where Jared is there's another one. It almost feels like someone created a portal to get here, stayed a few moments, and then created another portal to leave. But the fog isn't the same kind of power that created the portals. It's much more powerful. So much more that it is hiding the true nature of the portals."

"I don't get it," Lissa commented. "How did Sabrina see it clearly, when none of the rest of you could?"

"It probably means that the power that created the portals, if that's what they were, is closer to the powers that Sabrina holds as the *Chosen One*," Nathaniel replied.

"That," Jared added, "and the power that hides the portals has its foundations in the Blaze."

Susanne had been ignoring Jared, but he had moved farther away from the group and had moved closer to the hill that led to the old church on the hill.

"That haze of power seems to end here at the foot of the hill, and so it diffuses a little. From the memories that I have inherited as Caris' son, I can feel the influence of the Blaze on this area, but it is not focused. Probably what happened is that the two forces that either collided or overlapped here are strong enough to cancel each other out. One thing is clear, they were nothing to be trifled with."

Wolf regarded Jared for a moment and then shook his head.

"Well, I think this completes the day. Two phasia, Emries, my mother's funeral, the trap for the Enforcers, our trip to Barer, Susanne, the Torch, and now mysterious portals and clouds."

"Makes me glad my name isn't Ranthall," Gwillim responded patting Wolf on the back.

In spite of himself the younger man laughed.

"We aren't going to solve any of these mysteries here. If the powers here are like those of the *Chosen One* that just makes our trip to Barer even more imperative. Hopefully Bryn will give us enough of a lead that we will know what to do next. Who knows, we may find Aerith Seth sitting there waiting on us."

No one responded but the unspoken sentiment that hung in the air was loud enough for everyone to hear. The danger was just beginning to grow, and the more this group was able to uncover, the deeper into danger they would descend. Mystery and uncertainty were more dangerous foes than any of the phasia, and as long as beings existed who could wield the kind of power that they had felt in the clearing existed without name or identity, there would be nowhere that was safe. Wolf led the group back to the horses where Liette sat quietly polishing her blade. She looked up catching Wolf's eye and glared at him.

"Just let me know when you are through playing so we can get on with this."

Wolf shook his head and looked back a Jared.

"Would you like to do the honors?"

Jared blinked hard and smiled.

"You mean create a portal?"

"You might as well learn now," Wolf answered.

"Alright."

Jared closed his eyes and extended his hand forward. Susanne watched and waited for something to happen, and then suddenly a pinpoint of blue light appeared there in midair.

"Now," Wolf said quietly, "just slowly pull the edges of it outward. But make sure you keep the shape consistent. Don't worry about what is on this side of the portal, keep your mind focused on the country on the other side. This is an anchor and remains a constant."

As Wolf continued speaking the point of light began to grow in size until it was a man-sized swirling blue oval that hang in the air and touched the ground like a doorway to another world.

"Good job," Wolf said patting Jared on the back as the other man opened his eyes.

"I hate to mention this," Lissa said looking at the portal, "but we can't get through that riding our horses."

"First rule of portals," Wolf said looking back at the fiery-haired woman, "is that unless there is no other option, every person or thing using the portal should go through under their own power. It's easier for the person maintaining the portal to control the flow of power that way."

"So," Nathaniel added, "we just lead our horses through and then we'll ride the rest of the way."

So one by one, each member of the group led their horse through the portal and stepped out into a field just outside the town of Frontier, the border town just outside the kingdom of Barer, and the end-point of the rule of the throne of Marcwell. As the portal closed in the little town of Aradon, the sound of breaking glass carried on the light afternoon breeze.

* * * * * * * * * * *

The *Shy Maiden* tavern had seen many visitors since it had been rebuilt and remodeled after the War of the Dragon had ended. For a time, it had been very popular because of the exotic fountain that stood in the very center of the common room. When the news spread of the monument to the victory over the forces of the Shadow had been erected in the quiet town of Frontier, sightseers from towns all over the world came to look at the statue. It was rumored that the figure in the center was the frozen remains of a member of the phasia, and the names carved into the base were of the heroes lost in the war. After the first ten years, the visitors started to slow through the doors of the tavern. Finally, the tourism stopped altogether and Frontier reverted to the quiet place it had been before the war had begun. And so, when eight visitors came in together through the doors of the tavern, the barkeep was more than a little shocked. Several of the men and women barely looked old enough to be adventuring on their own, and the man and woman that did were complete opposites from one another. The older man looked as though he had fought in the War of the Dragon, while the woman looked like she belonged in a temple because of the strange uniform that she wore. But all in all, they were customers, and that is what a tavern needed to keep its doors open.

The group seated themselves near the fountain, and so the barkeeper pegged them for tourists who had decided to pay their respects. Looking across the room, the barkeeper's eyes met those of his newest barmaid and pointed at the table where the newcomers had taken a seat. She smiled, nodded, and made her way over to the table. It had been a stroke of luck that the barkeeper had found her merely hours after his best barmaid had run off and gotten married to some soldier from Kandor. But the girl seemed happy to be working there, and so it was beneficial for everyone involved. Besides that, she was young, pretty, and not overly intelligent. Which meant that he could pay her less, and the patrons would be focused more on her than the watered down ale and wine that he served.

The barmaid approached the table and smiled at the men and women seated there.

"Good day lords and ladies," she said with a little guttural accent. It could have been Alimidarian, but Wolf wasn't able to quite place it. "What can I get fer ye today?"

"A round of ale," Gwillim responded, "and whatever food you have to offer. It seems like it's been a week since we've eaten."

"Of course me lord," the girl said smiling, "where did ye ride in from if I may ask?"

"Illimar," Wolf said quickly. "It's a very long ride, and we were in a bit of hurry. But now it seems like we have gotten to a quiet enough place that we can rest for a while."

The girl smiled wider.

"It doesn't have to be quiet if ye don't want it to be," she replied flirtatiously. "I'll go get yer food and ale, and my name's Felicia if ye need anything."

She started to walk away and then turned back.

"Don't forget now, anything."

She smiled wider and then returned to the bar. It took Lissa only a second the hit Wolf hard on the shoulder.

"Ouch," Wolf said rubbing his shoulder, "I was just being friendly."

"You let Gwillim and Jared be friendly," Lissa replied.

Everyone laughed except Sabrina who had turned her attention to the fountain in the center of the room. She got up from her seat and walked over to it, running her hands over the carved surface of several of the stones, reading the names and inscriptions that were carved there. At one, she paused and closed her eyes, whispering a silent prayer. Lissa by this time had moved to her side, as had Wolf. When Wolf looked down, he saw the name Anabel Binosear.

"I had heard that there was a memorial to my grandmother here in Frontier, but mother and I never got a chance to come here and see it."

Lissa also looked down, saw the memorial for Aryx Terian and scowled.

"Maybe if you're a good girl, we'll put your name right next to his," a strange voice called from the doorway of the tavern.

Lissa looked up and felt her blood begin to boil. The woman in the green dress stood proud and defiant in the doorway, her lips curled into a cruel smirk. Rane Larion was obviously proud of her insult and Lissa was thankful for her chance to exact revenge for the battle in Logan's Wood.

"So, you found the courage to come back and meet your fate?" Lissa taunted. "Good. Shall we pick up where we left off, or should I just run you through and get it over with?"

Rane scoffed.

"You silly peasant. Do you honestly believe that I would face all of you by myself again? You must think I am a fool."

Lissa nodded and smiled.

"Well, I am a member of the Brotherhood of Phasia, and Shau-ling does not give birth to fools."

"No," Wolf replied turning to face the new arrival, "not fools, imbeciles."

Rane growled and then laughed to herself.

"We shall see soon enough young Ranthall. Because this time, I have brought along some of my family."

At that moment the wall behind Wolf, Lissa, and Sabrina exploded, sending the three and everyone else at the table sprawling to the floor. When Wolf made it to his feet, he found Jared and Gwillim at his side with weapons drawn face to face with an impressive duo. The man was tall and powerfully built, much like Taron, except the man held himself differently. He did not flaunt his physical gifts as Taron did, but he stood in a manner that exuded a quiet confidence. The lethal edge was helped by the large double-bladed ax that lay in his hands, and the spiked plate of armor that covered his chest. His brown hair hung loose around his head to the level of his massive shoulders, and his eyes burned with a quiet fury which promised death to any who would wake the slumbering giant.

The second member of the pair was both beautiful and dangerous in the same breath. Her blond hair hung loose and flowed down past her shoulders. The muscles of her arms were clearly visible and very impressive. Her right arm was tensed as she held the hilt of her sword tightly. While her musculature was impressive, it paled in comparison to her physical beauty. Any man would have lusted after her, but no man would have the power to tame her, that much was clear from the fire in her eyes.

"Meet my brother Grimm, and my sister Cash. They are also new to the Brotherhood, but they will have earned their place in the highest echelons after we have rid the world of your pitiful band."

With that Grimm launched himself forward with ax high in the air, ready to cleave whatever got in its path while Cash moved around the side toward the table. Lissa leapt toward Rane, weaving strings of Fire into a single burst that sailed past the phase as she darted into the room. Grimm's axe sped toward Wolf and Sabrina at blinding speed. Wolf dove forward, collecting Sabrina in his arms and pulling her to safety near a recently overturned table. The large phase seemed to know the feint was coming and changed direction faster than a man of that size should have been able to move. He would have buried the gleaming blade of the ax deep into Wolf's back had it not been for the blade of Gwillim's sword rising to meet it. Wolf could see the flows of Earth surrounding Gwillim as he poured all his power into holding off the massive strength of his opponent. Meanwhile Liette and Susanne found themselves face to face with the woman called Cash. Her sword met time and time again with Liette's blade as the two fierce combatants tested each other. Susanne brought her blade to bear and Cash found herself back peddling under the assault of the two women. But that advantage was short lived. Cash parried a slash by Susanne, sending her sword clattering to the ground and Liette leaping to the side to block the retaliation that surely would have ended the newest member of their group's life.

Blast after blast of fire erupted from Lissa's hands, each one closer to the mark than the last, but Rane kept ahead of the assault. Suddenly the phase launched a counter attack, and a beam of fire lanced across the distance and brushed across the side of Lissa's right arm. The young woman was momentarily shaken by the near miss, and that gave Rane the opportunity to go on the offensive in earnest. Bolts of fire, lightning, ice, and rock launched from Rane's palms as Lissa moved to avoid the assaults, but unlike Rane, Lissa was unable to keep ahead of all of them. One blast, and group of ice shards, caught Lissa in the side, ripping the flesh and sending Lissa crashing to the floor, blood flowing freely. Sabrina was over her fallen sibling the next moment, weaving flows of Order into a shield to protect them from the onslaught that would follow. Rane was relentless, and blast after blast of fire and ice collided with the shield. Sabrina could feel the power and control beginning to slip, but help was on the way. Nathaniel inserted himself into the fray, stepping in front of one of the bolts of fire and matching it with one of his own.

Grimm smiled as he stepped back from his newest competitor and then slashed downward again with his axe. Gwillim blocked again, but this time felt the full force of Grimm's blow and found himself staggered. Wolf was up the next moment, channeling the flows of Earth to both himself and Gwillim, steadying them both for the next attack. Grimm swung again, but the power was unlike anything Wolf could have expected, and even with the added power of the flows of Earth, both men were rocked from their feet and sent sprawling to the ground. A huge bellowing laugh erupted from Grimm's chest, and he leaned forward on the haft of his ax motioning for his opponents to get to their feet so the battle could continue. Both Gwillim and Wolf knew that they had no chance to defeat the monster if they kept fighting defensively, so as they stood, they both rushed the larger man and began to gain the upper hand. Slash after slash kept Grimm back on his heels and unable to bring his full power to bear.

Liette kept back-stepping, keeping Susanne out of the range of Cash's long and very accurate sword strokes. Suddenly Cash stumbled, and Liette saw the cause was Jared's scepter. Somehow Jared had gotten behind Cash and laid a hard blow on her back. The phase stumbled briefly and then kicked back hard, catching Jared in the stomach. After another step back, Cash swung hard down at Jared, but the sword met the metal of the scepter and the duel began anew. Liette and Jared both kept the pressure on Cash, and before long began to have the advantage. Susanne, having recovered her sword dove behind Cash clipping her knees from behind, sending her sprawling to the floor. Before Cash could recover her feet, Liette was on top of her, a very sharp sword pressed to the phase's throat.

Rane knew that she was overmatched as soon as the boy stepped into view, but she had to keep the pressure up so that he would make a mistake. It was foolish for any member of the phasia to try to go toe to toe with the *Coromor* but the only way for Rane to gain any power or respect in the Council was for her to win a major battle against the forces of the Light. If she could hold out a few minutes longer, her reinforcements would arrive, and an army of Jeresei would descend on this town and kill everyone and everything that stood in their way. But her opponent of the moment was the boy. Every blast that she sent in his direction was batted away or countered, and Rane was slowly beginning to block more attacks than she was launching. The girl Sabrina was no longer putting her powers into a shield and was actually helping the girl Lissa to her feet, and any minute the two meddling girls would add their power and be enough to overcome

Rane. Out of the corner of her eye, Rane saw Cash fall, and at that moment a bolt of fire came out of nowhere and slammed into Rane's chest. This gave Nathaniel the opportunity that he needed, and he sent a hard ball of ice and stone across the distance and upon impact Rane fell to the floor, her sternum broken and her breathing labored.

Grimm watched as Cash and then Rane fell in succession. He had to do something fast if they were going to get out of this battle alive. It was then that he noticed the barmaid out of the corner of his eye trying to hide from the battle. Ducking one of the blows from the pair of Gwillim and Wolf, Grimm reached down, plucked the girl up from her hiding place and held her firmly in his grasp. Gwillim and Wolf retreated a step and waited.

"Isn't this sweet. You warriors of the Light are all alike. If you were phasia, you would hack through this tasty little morsel here and cut me down, but you can't do that can you?"

Wolf felt the power of the Blaze lurch up inside of him, but he knew that if he took any action against Grimm, the young woman was as good as dead.

"I didn't think so. And that is why you will lose this little war. Now, I'm taking Rane and Cash out of here with me, and then I'll let this little girl go. Understand?"

"No!" Liette answered. "Cash and Rane are dead."

"No little girl," Grimm commented laughing. "If you make one move to harm either of my sisters, the barmaid dies. And I don't think that these poor little whelps here can live with that, can you boys?"

No one answered,

"I thought not. Now…"

With that, portals appeared beneath Rane and Cash, pulling them from danger. Grimm laughed again and then threw the barmaid to the floor before falling through his own portal.

Sowing the Seeds

Creator's Calendar Year 1205; Light Reality

"We had them right where we wanted them, and you just let them go," Liette said in disgust thrusting the point of her sword into the wooden floor where the phase Cash had been lying mere seconds earlier.

Wolf and Gwillim both turned to look at the younger woman, knowing that she was right. However, neither man would have been able to take responsibility for sacrificing the life of an innocent even if it would have sealed the fate of three members of the phasia. But part of Wolf knew that Liette was right, and the trade for the life of the barmaid Felicia might have been a mistake. Liette then drew her sword out of the floorboards and rounded on Wolf.

"I told you all that if we followed Wolf that he would lead us right into a trap. And look what happened. Three members of the phasia knew right where to find us. Kind of a coincidence, isn't it, Wolf?"

Wolf swallowed hard and took a reflexive step back away from the point of the blade that was moving ever closer to his throat. Looking around the room, he realized that he probably seemed as guilty as Liette was making him out to be, but before he could mount any defense, Jared stepped into the fray and parried the girl's blade aside with his scepter.

"There is no time for this, Liette," the man said strongly. "You have no proof whatsoever that Wolf is the reason that Rane and the other two were here. For all we know, it was the information that Rael and Trece took back that tipped Rane to our next move."

Liette stood fast and continued to glare at Wolf. Lissa had risen from where she fell, gripping hard the wound at her side, but with Sabrina's help managed to make it over to a chair where she added her voice to Wolf's defense.

"Jared's right. You wouldn't know this Liette because you were being stubborn as always, but we found a lot of strange energy patterns in the area where Rael and Trece had been. They were the kind of patterns that could not have been created by them. Because the power seemed to have links to the *Chosen One* they probably would think that we would try to find out more information about Aerith Seth."

"And everyone knows," Gwillim added, "that no one knows more about Aerith Seth than Bryn Aplee."

Liette didn't move, but shook her head.

"And who found this power? Jared? Wolf? Both of them have phasia blood and phasia power running through their veins. Either one of them could have created those patterns just to throw you off the treachery that they were planning. Wasn't it Wolf who brought Jared into the party? How do we know that they haven't been plotting and conspiring all this time to lead us into a trap?"

Nathaniel took that opportunity to interject himself into the conversation. Slowly he walked over, took hold of Liette's sword and placed it at his own chest.

"Everything that Wolf and Jared have done since they have been with us has been in the best interest of the forces of the Light and in the best interest of the People of the Ram. I came with him willingly down this path, and I will continue down it. We all knew that there were risks coming to a kingdom controlled by members of the phasia, and it was only a matter of time before Rane found Lissa again and tried to even the score."

Liette tried to withdraw her blade, but Nathaniel held onto it tightly and continued to chide the girl.

"The only one here that has not been working as part of the group has been you, Liette. For some reason you have been holding a grudge against Wolf from the first time you laid eyes on him. Half of me wants to just let the two of you fight it out and get it over with, but I would hate to see my sister get killed for no reason."

Liette growled and forcefully jerked her blade from Nathaniel's grasp. The young man winced for a moment as the sharp metal ripped through the tender flesh of his palm, but the wound cleared as quickly as it had been opened.

"Now, I've had quite enough of this from you, Liette," Nathaniel said turning back to Wolf. "Wolf is not only a friend, but he is family. And if he can look me in the eye now and tell me that he had nothing to do with the attack that was just launched on us, then that is good enough for me."

Wolf hesitated and then stood firm and looked Nathaniel squarely in the eye.

"Nathaniel, I swear to you on the life of my mother Elwyne Tamerlane Ranthall that I had nothing to do with the phasia knowing where we were going."

Nathaniel smiled, nodded and then turned his attention back to Liette.

"Now, put your sword away. We have other things to worry about."

Wolf, having weathered that storm moved quickly to Lissa's side and moved her hand away from the wound that Rane had inflicted. There were several cuts in the flesh of Lissa's side, and the cloth that had been pressed to the flesh was holding the blood back. As Wolf moved the blood-soaked towel away to get a better look, Lissa winced and the blood began to pour forth again. Drawing on the powers inside of him, Wolf placed his hand over the wound and began to subtly weave the flows of Wind and Water into the wound, knitting the flesh and slowing the flow of blood to the area. Sabrina stood close at hand and watched everything that Wolf was doing. The flow of blood from the long horizontal slashes in the girl's flesh had stopped, and Wolf pulled his hand away for a moment to wipe away the beads of sweat that had formed on his brow. He had not expected the work of knitting a simple wound to be that difficult, but as he looked at the newly exposed cuts, he realized that the damage had been done with the addition of the Blaze, make the wounds fester and dig deeper. The healthy flesh would grow weaker as the minutes passed, and eventually any healing that had been done to the physical portion of the wound would give way and Lissa would bleed to death in a matter of hours.

"Jared, I need your help," Wolf said scowling at the pulsing threads of Blaze fire laced into the gaping wounds.

"What's wrong Wolf?" Lissa asked looking down at him.

"Rane was not playing with you, she was going to make sure you died, even if you were able to kill her first. She wove bits of the Blaze into every attack, and when she wounded you, it clung to the wound and is eating its way through your flesh. If it were to just be healed, eventually the mending would give way and you would start to bleed to death again. The only way to fully cleanse the wound is to remove the Blaze energy from it."

"And if any of us were to do it," Nathaniel added, "we would instantly become slaves to Shau-ling."

"Right," Wolf nodded. "But luckily, Jared and I have already touched the Blaze, and because of the way that our powers have been granted to us, we don't have to obey Shau-ling's call. Children of the phasia have the freedom to choose what path they follow, just as the phasia do, and are not limited in their interaction with the Blaze. And thanks to my gift, I have the powers of a full member of the phasia without being a member of the Brotherhood."

Wolf smiled up at Lissa.

"Just relax, it's probably going to hurt."

Wolf looked back at the wound and started to concentrate on the peaks of green fire that highlighted each cut in Lissa's flesh.

"Wolf."

Looking back upwards, Wolf caught Lissa's eyes again.

"I guess you get to be my savior again."

Wolf forced a smile and then looked back over his shoulder to Jared. Nodding, Jared went to one knee so that he was eye level with the gaping wound that was beginning to ooze blood again.

"See the green glow around the jagged areas were the skin was torn?"

Jared nodded.

"We won't be able to fully heal the wound until all of that green glow is gone. When you pull it away, don't let it dissipate into the air, you have to channel it into something else. Probably the best would be to send it into the fireplace."

Jared nodded again, and then after a moment the two began to slowly and meticulously manipulate the powers that they had been granted to pull the remnants of Blaze energy from Lissa's wound. Every time a piece of the living green flame was removed, the two were greeted with a spurt of blood and a wince from the brave woman they were both trying to save. As the process moved from seconds to minutes, Lissa found it more and more difficult to sit still and began to squirm in the chair, fighting the pain. Finally Wolf sighed and took a deep breath.

"Only one more bit to go, but it's the deepest part of the wound. Just hang on Lissa, only a little more."

That next moment, Lissa felt a pain that she had never felt before. It was as though a thousand needles were pressed into her side at the same time and were twisted and ground deeper into her flesh and then suddenly pulled away. All sensation left her body and she began to go numb. Blood flowed freely from the exposed wound, but Wolf put his hand over the ripped flesh again and the torrent slowed to a trickle and then was no more. When Wolf withdrew his hand again, the wound had been mended, and only the faintest traces of a scar would remain. However, the pain had been too much for the strong-willed girl, and she slumped in the chair, unconscious. Gwillim was there the next moment, pulling the girl into his arms and holding her close while Wolf cleaned the blood from his hands.

"We'll need to stay here tonight," Gwillim said trying his best to support Lissa's limp form. "Hopefully Lissa will have her strength back by tomorrow."

Sensing all of the danger had passed, the barkeeper had emerged from his hiding place behind the bar and immediately went to Wolf and shook his hand.

"My boy," he said smiling, "you saved my bar. I was lucky that all I lost was part of a wall, and I'm sure I can have that fixed in no time. Please, stay here the night. Room, food and drink are free for you and your party, it's the least I can do."

Wolf smiled.

"Well, then," he said looking at the hole in the wall, "the least we can do is repair the damage."

Without half a thought, Wolf extended his hand toward the damaged masonry, and the dirt on the floor began to shake. The next moment, pillars of stone began to emerge from the ground and filled in the space that was left by Cash and Grimm's entrance. Only the smallest of cracks remained between the original mason work and the newly erected stone wall.

"I'm sure it won't be difficult to find someone to patch the little bit that remains. But at least this will keep the elements out."

The barkeeper had to take a moment to compose himself before speaking, and even then, he could not find the words. The gruff man could only smile, nod, and shake Wolf's hand again before departing and recovering a set of keys from the bar.

"Here, there are rooms at the top of the stairs, and there should be enough for your group, though some of you may have to share. Thank you again."

The barkeeper locked the door to the tavern and then disappeared into the back room and from the sound of rattling pots and pans, began to prepare a meal for later. Wolf handed the keys to Gwillim, and as he began to head for the staircase, the barmaid Felicia walked over to Wolf, looked him in the eye for a moment and then wrapped her arms around him, pressing her lips to his in a very passionate kiss. The young man was too shocked to resist the woman's advance, and stood dumbfounded for the moments that the kiss lasted. As Felicia stepped back, Jared laughed and patted Wolf on the back.

"I guess you're the designated hero, Wolf."

Blushing, Wolf turned his attention back to the other members of the group. Susanne seemed a little rattled by the experience, but was sitting at one of the tables that hadn't been overturned during the battle taking a long drink from a tankard of ale. Liette had retreated to a table also, and Wolf was met with the same cold stare when their eyes met. Sabrina had a pained expression in her eyes, obviously due to the worry for Lissa. Trying to be a gentleman, Wolf took Sabrina by the hand, pulled her into his arms and hugged her tightly.

"I'm sure Lissa will be fine in the morning," he said softly and then stepped back.

Sabrina smiled the best she could, and tried to quiet her racing heart, thinking that everyone in the tavern could hear it beating like a thunderstorm in her breast. Gwillim by this time had returned from putting Lissa to bed in one of the rooms, and gratefully accepted a tankard of ale from Susanne who had finally risen to join the group.

"How many rooms are upstairs, Gwillim?" Jared asked.

"Six. That mean a couple of us will have to share."

"Someone should probably stay with Lissa just in case she needs something in the night," Susanne commented. "And if no one minds, I'd like to volunteer. Everyone was so nice to me when you found me broken and bleeding, I'd like to return the favor. And besides, I don't think I'm quite ready to be sleeping alone yet."

Jared opened his mouth as if to say something, but thinking better of it took another drink of his mug of ale.

"Well, I suppose I'll stick with my little brother here," Gwillim said patting the younger man on the shoulder. "Besides, there's no reason anyone else should suffer, I'm used to it."

Nathaniel laughed a little and then smiled.

"We should all get some rest. It would be in our best interest if we got an early start in the morning toward the palace of Barer. It gives our opponents less incentive to try again if we are moving through another phase's territory."

"Agreed," Wolf said nodding. "We'll leave before first light if Lissa is able."

As everyone began to make their way upstairs, Jared and Wolf found themselves alone at one of the tables, each finishing off a mug of ale. The day had begun on a strange note, and it was only fitting that they would have been attacked as soon as they arrived in Frontier. However, Wolf could not help but wonder how Rane and the others had known that they would make for Frontier, and why it was that they had attacked alone with no Jeresei or Shadowwalker support. Phasia very rarely took it upon themselves to do anything when they could give the assignment to one of the lesser races. Maybe it was the youth of Rane that was making her reckless, or maybe it was the fact that she wanted to prove herself to the rest of the Council. The fact that she was not acting like a member of the phasia confounded Wolf's mind and the memories that Basille had given him even more.

"I keep waiting for the other shoe to drop," Jared said after a moment. "There is something not right about the way Rane and the others attacked, and it is even stranger that they did not act together to take one of us out. They all seemed like they were waiting for something, but that something never came."

"I was about to say the same thing," Wolf replied thoughtfully. "I kept waiting for the Jeresei and Shadowwalkers to rip this place to shreds, but they never came."

"Maybe Grawn and Bryn have something to do with that," Jared commented.

Wolf thought about that for a moment. It would have been very difficult to move a force of Jeresei and Shadowwalkers into Frontier without Grawn and Bryn knowing about it, and it would have been impossible without their approval. So, the question was now whether they had allies in the palace of Barer, or if they were walking into another trap.

"Don't worry Wolf," Jared said as if he were reading Wolf's thoughts, "if it is a trap, we'll be ready. If this group can take three phasia head to head without any serious losses, I'm not worried about taking Grawn and Bryn on, even if they have their whole army there with them."

With that Jared got up, patted Wolf on the shoulder and headed upstairs for the night. Inwardly, Wolf wished that he shared Jared's optimism. He knew how dangerous Grawn and Bryn were, and if they had wished it, Wolf was sure that Grawn and Bryn could have made quick work of the three younger phasia. Grawn had forgotten more about warfare than Grimm and the others would ever know, and Bryn was one of the most ruthless of the phasia. Wolf lingered in the tavern for a moment, and was joined only seconds after Jared's departure by the barmaid Felicia.

"Is there anything else I can get fer my hero?"

Wolf laughed at the word hero and tried his best to look humble.

"No thank you, Felicia. I think I'll be headed to bed anyway. We're leaving early in the morning as it is."

"Yer going to see Lady Bryn and Lord Grawn, aren't you?"

Wolf hesitated for a moment and then nodded. The girl had been present for most of the conversation earlier, and Wolf had not thought to censor himself with Felicia and the barkeeper in the room. Perhaps that had been a mistake, but then again, after what the two of them had witnessed during the batter with Rane and her cohorts, very little could be hidden from them in the long run.

"Would you take me with you?"

Part of Wolf had expected that question. There was something different about the girl, but Wolf could not quite put his finger on what it was.

Naturally, Wolf was going to object to the request, but before he could, Felicia countered him.

"I was originally a servant for Lady Bryn, and I was hoping to return to her service. I was just waiting fer an opportunity to get back there. I won't be any trouble, I promise."

Wolf opened his mouth to speak, but Felicia cut him off again.

"Besides, even if you say no, I'll follow ye anyway."

Laughing to himself, Wolf conceded defeat.

"Alright. Just be here before first light, and we'll travel together as far as the palace of Barer."

"Thank you," she said smiling.

Felicia leaned in, gave him a kiss on the cheek and then went back to work cleaning up the scattered dishes and tankards that had ended up on the floor during the fight. Wolf shook his head, finished off the last bit of ale in his mug, and then made his way up the stairs and into the last room at the end of the hall. It took only a few moments after shutting the door for him to make his way across the room, strip off his shirt and pants and then fall face-first onto the surprisingly soft bed in the corner of the room. While he was wide awake, Wolf could feel the effects of the ale begin to creep through his body and he knew it would only be a matter of minutes before his eyelids would grow heavy and sleep would take him. Just as he began to get comfortable, there was a knock at the door. Wolf let a groan escape his lips and then fumbled around for his pants in the dark room. As he finished pulling the pants on, the knock at the door was repeated. Wolf hurried to the door, and when he pulled on the handle, he was shocked to see Sabrina standing at the door holding a candle. Wolf realized that he must have fallen asleep, and tried his best to smile at Sabrina.

"Sorry it took me so long to get to the door, I guess I must have fallen asleep even though it feels like I only just laid down a second ago."

Sabrina smiled.

"Wolf," she said sweetly, "do you mind if I come in, there's something I'd like to talk to you about."

A little surprised, Wolf stepped aside and let the princess come into his room. She crossed the room quickly and set the candle on the night table before sitting on the bed. Wolf stretched his neck, rolling it from side to side and then sat at the other end of the bed looking at Sabrina.

"So, what is it you wanted to talk about Princess?"

Sabrina sighed deeply and then focused her eyes back on Wolf.

"Please, call me Sabrina. There's no need to be formal, Wolf. We aren't in court, and I hope we aren't enemies."

"Alright, Sabrina, what would you like to talk about?"

Sabrina inched closer to Wolf and then spoke in a very hushed voice.

"I have a bit of a confession to make Wolf," she said quietly and with a hit of nervousness in her voice. "I have loved you from the first moment I set eyes on you."

At that moment, Wolf didn't know what to do, but Sabrina continued.

"I know that you and Lissa have grown close, but you can't trust her, Wolf. And you can't have her. Her heart belongs to someone else, and so does her soul. So even though you may think she wants you, and she may, she can't have you Wolf, and she'll only end up hurting you in the end."

Wolf stood from the bed, trying hard not to be angry with Sabrina. He didn't know whether she was saying these things to try to spite him, or to try and endear herself to him.

"Please Wolf," she continued standing and pulling him to face her, "I am just trying to make sure that she doesn't hurt you. I'm not asking for any affection from you, but I saw the way you looked at her and took care of her when she was hurt, and I can't stand for you to be hurt by her. So please, just be careful with your heart Wolf."

Silently Sabrina picked up her candle and started walking toward the door. Wolf was too shocked and confused to do anything but watch her go.

"And Wolf," Sabrina said turning back, "no matter what you decide to do, I will still love you."

With that, she quietly opened the door and left, shutting it behind her.

* * * * * * * * * * *

The next morning there was very little said as the group retrieved their horses and set off. A few posed questions about the addition of the barmaid Felicia, but generally no one had difficulty, except of course for Liette. The little girl had begun to question everything as a plot or a trap, and Sabrina was starting to find her interference tedious. While she was not very fond of the new addition, Sabrina was willing to accept Wolf's explanation that it was only for the short trip to Barer, and then after that she would be left to her own devices. Lissa also seemed to grumble a bit with the addition of the pretty blond barmaid, but there were other reasons for that. It had nothing to do with the phantom traps that Liette constantly mumbled about, but rather the flirtatious manner that the woman had around Wolf. Sabrina found that the girl's batting of lashes and gentle touches of Wolf's arm as they talked a little stomach churning as well. However, Sabrina had swallowed her pride over Wolf and Lissa's relationship, and she had sworn to herself that she would not interfere and leave Wolf to make his own decisions. She was trying hard to be happy for Lissa. The anger in the back of her mind and the sorrow in her heart were making that a difficult proposition, and she didn't know how much longer she would be able to keep her feelings a secret when she was constantly so close to the object of her affections. Her few moments in his arms had kept her tossing and turning all night with indecent thoughts that were not fitting a woman of her stature. All in all though, she could not deny the basest aspects of her nature and her desire to be in Wolf's arms every moment of every day. Sabrina had noticed something different about Wolf when he first emerged from his room. There seemed to be a great weight on him that had not been there the previous night. His mood was cooler, and even his greeting of Lissa was not filled with the caring and warmth that Sabrina had expected. They merely embraced for a moment and Wolf did a cursory inspection of the nicely healed wound before gathering his things and heading for the horses. Also, Sabrina noticed when Wolf locked eyes with her that there was a confusion there that threatened to break out from that quiet confidence and shatter his cool and calm facade. He also seemed unwilling to hold her gaze for too long.

The ride to Barer was more of the same, the Nathaniel and Gwillim both commented on how quiet the trip was. Most of the group had expected to meet at least one patrol of Jeresei or a detachment of the infamous Army of the Fox, but instead were greeted by the silent countryside and the rhythmic rapping of their horses' hooves. As Sabrina rode, she found her eyes wandering back to Wolf time and time again, and each time she found him looking as though he were lost in his own thoughts. Something was plaguing him, and no one had been able to provoke him away from his thoughts since the trip had begun. Both Jared and Lissa had tried, but their efforts were met with a very cold and unfriendly response, a response that appeared to hurt Lissa. But after talking to Susanne, Lissa appeared to cheer up. After nearly six hours of the ride, the palace of Barer was finally in sight, and Wolf rode to the front of the group and spoke quietly with Nathaniel and Gwillim. They came to a consensus of opinion apparently and Wolf drifted back again, only to her great surprise, Wolf collected Lissa and moved over side by side with Sabrina.

"I just wanted to let you know," Wolf started in a very monotone voice, "that once we get into the palace, you may start to feel a little strange and have some emotions running through you that you can't explain."

"I know," Sabrina answered quickly. "Every time someone mentions Bryn's name I feel a little lump well up in my throat. I didn't think that Aerith Seth's feelings would manifest like this since I'm a woman, but I guess it doesn't really matter in the long run. He had some powerful feelings about her, and I guess there is no way to deny them."

"Well," Lissa chimed in, "maybe they'll make you think you feel that way about someone else."

Sabrina shot a look of defiance at Lissa, but the comment seemed to snap Wolf out of whatever thoughts had been confining him.

"Lissa may be right," Wolf said, seemingly talking more to himself than either of the women, "you never know how you're going to react with someone else's voice in your head."

Satisfied with himself, Wolf rode ahead, leaving Lissa and Sabrina to try and decipher what had just happened. The window of opportunity was short however, because it was only a matter of minutes before the massive stone warriors that guarded the front gate of the palace of Barer were in full view and moved to block the group from proceeding any farther.

"S...T...A...T...E./.Y...O...U...R./.B...U...S...I...N...E...S...S./. H...E...R...E..."

Wolf dismounted and stepped forward with both hands raised to show that he was approaching without weapons drawn.

"We come to seek an audience with the honorable Lord Grawn and Lady Bryn."

"F...O...R./.W...H...A...T./.P...U...R...P...O...S...E..."

"We seek the wisdom of the Lord and Lady in a matter of great urgency. We would not come if it were not a matter that we believe the Lord and Lady would find interest in. It is as much for their benefit as it is for ours."

The Stone warriors hesitated for a moment and then each took a short step to the side exposing the path into the courtyard of the palace.

"L...E...A...V...E./.W...E...A...P...O...N...S./.A...N...D./.B...E ...A...S...T...S..."

Wolf unfastened the belt that held his scabbard and laid it on the ground at the foot of one of the massive creatures. One by one the members of the party removed their weapons and laid them with Wolf's sword. Jared hesitated a moment before leaving his scepter, and seemed uncomfortable as soon as he realized he would be without it. As soon as the pile of weapons was complete, one of the Stone warriors motioned for the group to proceed.

Upon entering the courtyard of the palace, the group of adventurers was met by what was obviously a detachment of the Army of the Fox. The force numbered in the hundreds, were well armed, armored, and flew the banner of the Fox proudly from all of their standards. Each shield showed the bright device of the Fox, and even some of the blades had the etched figure near the hilt. Three members of the detachment hurried over to Wolf and quickly searched him for concealed daggers. Before they moved on to Jared who was next in line a voice echoed from somewhere in the palace.

"There is no need for that," the man's voice said gruffly. "The weapons that they would possess you could not find in a search. Let them pass and lead them to me."

The men of the detachment snapped to attention immediately and one of them motioned for the group to follow. Sabrina tapped Wolf on the shoulder and then whispered in his ear.

"That was Grawn."

Wolf nodded. Basille's memory had given him the identification of the voice as well, but Wolf was sure that it would be Sabrina's input on behalf of Aerith Seth that would serve them much more fully here in Barer than would the fragmented memories of the Blaze.

It took only a few moments for the soldier to lead the group through a set of large iron doors into the palace. They were led down several winding hallways, up a flight of stairs, and to a set of gold and jewel encrusted doors that would no doubt give them admittance to the throne room. The group had only been standing there a matter of seconds before the doors swung inward and the soldier led them to the presence of his lord and master. As Wolf had expected, an older man was seated on a golden throne, his gray and black robes clashing with his whitening hair. Basille's memories allowed Wolf to realize that Grawn was not aging very well, and he seemed to be creeping along in years much faster than a member of the phasia should. However, the woman that stood beside the throne was a picture of beauty, seductiveness, and grace. Her long brown hair shot through with streaks of red was tied back on this occasion, exposing her bare neck and shoulders, making her even more desirable in the dim torchlight of the throne room. The dress that clung to her body as though it were painted on seemed to reveal more than it concealed while leaving enough a mystery that it did not detract from her beauty. It was Bryn who first spoke, and her voice filled the room like the song of doves on a bright spring day.

"Welcome to the Kingdom of Barer, brave travelers. Lord Grawn and I would like to extend as much hospitality to you as possible, but I must admit that we are both a bit puzzled as to what would cause a fine group such as yourselves to put yourselves at risk by seeking an audience with us."

"Lady Bryn," Wolf said stepping forward, "my companions and I would like to thank you for welcoming us into your kingdom, and for your indulgence with this audience. And as I know you do not take kindly to disturbances, I will try my best to make this brief. My name is Wolf Ranthall. I am the son of Logan..."

"We know who you are," Grawn interrupted. "And that more than anything puzzles us. If you have come here to challenge us to a battle, you may as well leave now. Bryn and I have much more important matters than the petty squabble between the Light and the Shadow to attend to, and we do not have any desire to take a role in this generation's war. But, if you make us fight, we will make sure you do not leave this palace alive."

"My lord," Wolf said taking a step back, "our cause here is not to spill blood. We merely seek information and answers to questions that have begun to plague us. I believe that there is a force growing that is a threat to both the forces of the Shadow and the forces of the Light, and what is more, I believe that this force is being led in the name of Aerith Seth erroneously."

Grawn tensed at the mention of Seth's name, but Bryn seemed more amused by it.

"And so you thought that given our past with Aerith, you would come here to try and make some sense out of the clues you have gathered. While a very logical choice, I am afraid that you have wasted a trip. There is little that either Grawn or I are able to do to help you in this matter."

"But..." Wolf started.

"Bryn said we are unable to help you with this matter," Grawn said standing. "Now, if you will please take your leave, you are beginning to try my patience. I do not relish having my time wasted by children who are trying to play above their station."

Wolf turned, the dejection filling him, but was met by Sabrina's eyes, and as she pushed past Wolf, he was filled with the feeling that someone else was guiding her actions.

"You were never willing to do anything when the name Aerith Seth cropped up, Grawn," Sabrina challenged. "Your jealousy will one day be your undoing."

Grawn turned back and Wolf noticed that his fists were clenched tightly.

"How dare you speak that way to one of the eldest members of the Brotherhood of Phasia little girl. I could crush you where you stand without so much as a thought."

Bryn's eyes locked on Sabrina and then a coy smile curled onto her lips.

"Grawn dear," she said sweetly taking a step forward, "I think perhaps our guests should have a little of our attention. You take care of our other interests and I will entertain these wonderful visitors for a while."

Grawn's stare could have burned a hole through steel. Bryn turned back and the anger in Grawn's features melted. With a bit of a growl, the older man conceded and stomped off through one of the side doors in the throne room. After he had gone, Bryn returned to the throne and took a seat. After crossing her legs and pulling her shoulders back regally, Bryn beckoned Sabrina to approach. For a long moment Sabrina delayed and then took long confident steps up the dais and stood proudly before Bryn. The phase stood the next moment and was eye to eye with Sabrina. Time passed slowly with the two women staring into one another's eyes. Then slowly, Bryn's hand ran across the skin of Sabrina's face feeling its smoothness and tenderness.

"Well, this is quite a different form you have chosen my dear," Bryn said in a voice that only Sabrina could hear. "Though at least you chose a very attractive young woman."

"You knew my tastes better than anyone," Sabrina heard herself say.

"Well," Bryn said smiling a little more, running her fingers through Sabrina's hair, "this will certainly make sharing a bed with you more interesting in this lifetime."

CHAPTER 37

Chapter XXXVIII

What Goes Around

Logan Ranthall stood firmly, the pain rocketing through his body finally beginning to ebb. The wound in his stomach had fully healed, thanks to the power of the Blaze, and though his exhausted muscles screamed with every movement, Logan knew that the battle that was about to be fought would be the most important of his life. The Elder had warned him not to confront Emries, and every instinct within him told Logan that this was not a battle that he could win, but now he had little choice but to fight. Emries would have struck him down where he stood if he hesitated for even a heartbeat. In fact, the man who had once called himself the Creator had even stooped to trying to snuff Logan out as he lay unconscious in the mud. In an effort to survive, Logan would have to use every bit of knowledge learned from Gwydeon Sandar, Arin Ranthall, Aerith Seth, Cedric Binosear, and Aryx Terian. But even that would not be enough. The one factor that had never been kind to Logan would be the force that would tip the balance in this duel, and that factor was luck.

Emries waited until his insult had passed through his opponent before letting the pure crystalline sword that was the physical embodiment of his power spring into existence. This power was like that of the Blaze, just as primal, but was totally devoid of the random element of the string of Chaos. If Logan had not touched the Blaze, Emries could have ended his life and recovered the Dragon Sword with merely a thought, but now

Logan had power enough to rival a full member of the phasia, and possibly enough to give Emries more than a few seconds of competition. Logan stood brandishing his sword his feet set as firmly as possible in the blood-stained mud. In a moment it would begin, and Emries could not see past the first cross of their blades. While his ability to see the future was normally limitless, when he was personally involved the ability to see past the next moments fled from him. Perhaps that was the Creator's way of attempting to prevent his children from directly interfering. But that mattered little now. Logan Ranthall was a problem that only Emries could solve, and he had waited long enough to remove the troublesome mortal from the field.

Logan waited for Emries to make the first move, not knowing whether the ancient being would charge or send bolts of power flying toward him. The Elder were right in saying that Emries was one step down from the Creator and that he was more powerful than Logan could ever imagine. But thoughts began to surface in Logan's mind telling him that nothing was impossible. He had stood toe to toe with Shau-ling, who was at least the equal of Emries, and had come out alive and victorious. Granted that he hadn't done it alone, but the experience was more than enough to help him in this fight. Not only that, but now Logan had access to the seemingly limitless power of the Blaze. It was the one force that Emries feared, but Logan wondered if he had enough control over his new found powers for them to truly matter. Logan knew nearly instantly where the thoughts came from, and for the first time Logan was glad to have the troublesome man's thoughts in the back of his head. Aerith Seth had never seen a challenge that he didn't want to tackle head on, and if the role were reversed, Logan knew that Aerith would be smiling and licking his lips at the opportunity to take Emries on.

Emries charged forward with his flawless crystalline blade high above his head. Logan readied for the strike, and when the clear blade arched down and struck the green hued blade of the Dragon Sword, the sound of shattering glass resounded through the countryside. Heartbeats passed as the two combatants leaned into the cross of the perfect blades. Emries' face was calm and smooth while Logan's forehead beaded with sweat as he poured every bit of his strength into the contest of wills. As the moments passed, Logan could feel the mud beneath his feet begin to give way, and his leverage on the fulcrum of their combat was beginning to weaken. Sensing this, Emries pushed forward with all of his might, sending the mortal sprawling to the ground where he came to rest in a puddle of mud. The child of the Creator lowered his blade and watched as Logan slowly rose to his feet and renewed a firm grip on the hilt of his weapon. The impertinence of the puny creature was starting to grate on Emries' nerves. He did not appreciate the temerity of the man, and he expected that his creation would know when it was dead. But some lessons could only be taught through blood.

The stalking would continue as the two began to circle one another, looking for an opportunity to strike. Suddenly Logan lashed out with his blade, but Emries was ready, easily parrying the long diagonal slash with a block tight to his body. Sensing a weakness, Logan pressed, thrusting deep into the defenses of the white-clad Emries. However, Emries would not let his blood be shed that easily. Using barely a trickle of the power at his disposal, Emries accelerated his movements, and while the point of the Dragon Sword would have pierced the heart of a lesser opponent, in this duel it found merely air. To his credit, Logan was quick to recover his senses and turn to face Emries, and was met not with a gasp of relief, but a knowing smile.

"You have to know you can't win, Logan," Emries taunted. "I can move faster than your mortal eyes can follow or you feeble mind can comprehend. I am merely humoring your pathetic attempt to challenge me. Give up now. Fall to your knees and beg my forgiveness for your o'er-hastily spoken words, and I shall consider ending your life quickly. If you persist with your delusions of grandeur, I shall have no choice but to flay the skin from your bones bit by bit until there is not enough left of you to feed the vultures."

Logan did not respond in words, but rather propelled himself forward with all the might in his body and slashed at the larger man. Emries parried the blow and let the block flow into a quick controlled thrust. Something in the back of Logan's mind told him what was going to happen, and the powers of the Blaze filled him, sending him speeding past where the blade would have pierced his flesh. When the two faced each other again, it was Logan who let taunts fly.

"You are not the only one who has powers Emries, so unless you intend to talk me to death, let's dispense with the preliminaries and find out who the better man is."

Logan knew the words weren't his, but at this point he was far past caring.

"You do not deserve to call yourself a man," Emries retorted, "to think that your weak flesh was to give birth to a savior makes me sick."

The two charged at each other the next moment, their swords meeting with the violent sounds of thunder. The feeling out process was over, and each let the powers flow through them as blocks became parries that became thrusts that became repasts.   Faster and faster the two moved, streaks of green following like ghostly trails behind the movements of the Dragon Sword, and trails of white hanging in the air where the crystalline blade had been only moments earlier.

* * * * * * * * * * *

Three portals opened in the wooded paths outside the palace of Sador, and when they closed, Caris, Rael, and Trece stood looking at the fallen bodies of men and Jeresei that littered the area. Caris was impressed that Zarsi's army could have been so easily defeated by mortals, but then he had never had the best of luck with picking his followers. Granted, he had never lost a major battle in his previous lifetimes against a mortal army, but Zarsi had never been up against the likes of Midarin Rice before. Zarsi was always the first to point out that he had not been leading the battle against Gwydeon Sandar during the battle in the second generation of the prophecies, and that the intention had always been to take the members of Gwydeon's little band alive.

"Do you think the battle has reached its conclusion?" Rael asked kneeling to examine one of the fallen human soldiers.

"If not, it will very quickly," Trece responded. "The signs all point to the fact that the palace has been invaded, and unless I miss my guess, the humans should be able to overwhelm anything that Zarsi might have had hidden there. They have always proven to be quite resourceful when putting down one of our invasion attempts, so it is only fitting that they should be successful in a raid."

Caris nodded.

"Not only that, but where that damn fool Logan Ranthall and Gwydeon Sandar are concerned, you have to give the mortals the edge. They are two of the most frustrating mortals that I have ever had the displeasure of associating with, and they are far more unpredictable than Cedric and his rabble. They know what they are up against, and for some reason are deluded enough to think they can be victorious."

Rael straightened again and closed his eyes. Caris could feel him reaching out through the Blaze. While it normally would have been dangerous to reveal themselves in that way with powerful individuals like Logan Ranthall in the area, it was safe to assume that such a minor use of the powers of the Blaze would be overlooked with a full phase like Zarsi as their focus. Caris felt the flow of power cease, and when she turned to look at Rael, he shook his head.

"Zarsi has met his end," he said softly, "but more importantly is the way he met his fate. The marks of the power of the *Coromor* flood the palace."

"That's impossible," Trece countered. "Gwillim Sandar met his end at the hands of Draven in the fields outside of Aradon. The Ram is dead and only the *Chosen One* remains to threaten the might of our lord."

"Unless we were deceived," Caris commented, smiling, "again. I would not put it past Emries and the Ranthalls to pull the wool over our eyes to make us think that we have won so we will start fighting against one another. It would be a very clever ploy indeed. Both Gwydeon and Midarin still live, so it is only reasonable that they would have had a child together, and perhaps it is that child, and not the man Gwillim that would have been the recipient of Emries' mantle."

"We must return to the Council and warn master of this," Trece said starting to let the flows of Blaze energy fill her.

"No," Caris said closing the portal that had begun to form. "Shau-ling would not take kindly to this information with no proof. And besides that, we have another errand to attend to. There will be time to deal with this possible threat later."

Rael rounded on Caris with Trece quickly behind him.

"Your interference cost us the kill in our battle with Draven, and now you put your personal wars ahead of the safety of our master Shau-ling. We knew that your schemes were ambitious Lady Wolf, but we never dreamed of anything like this."

Caris laughed and flipped her hair back with her right hand before responding to the challenge.

"You are both too young yet to understand what it is that is going on around you. As I said in the fields outside of Brea, Draven is too valuable now for us to lose in this petty War for Ascension. That is no truer now with this revelation that the *Coromor* may be alive and well. So Draven has ambitions to lead the Council. Let him trifle with Jeroch and Saurn, and soon enough he will be taken care of. However, the protection of Shau-ling does not lie with the destruction of the *Coromor* and *Chosen One* alone as so many of the other phasia believe. In the last generation, it was not the great and powerful descendants of Emries and Aerith Seth that were the turning point in the war. No, it was the mortals and those blasted *Erieal* that made the difference. Gwydeon Sandar, and his bitch Midarin Rice in particular."

"I can feel your hate for that woman, sister, every time you mention her name," Trece commented. "What is it that she has done to you that has incited such hatred?"

"She is the only woman who ever humiliated me and lived," Caris said running her finger along the bridge of her nose unconsciously. "If not for her and the woman Elwyne Tamerlane, I would have surely been able to dispatch Logan Ranthall long before he was able to set foot on the Island of Mist. My vendetta against her will soon be rectified, but now I want to concentrate my attention on Logan Ranthall. My score to settle with him is more important than with the bitch Midarin."

Caris closed her eyes the next moment and let her mind probe the Blaze for the powers of Logan Ranthall. She knew that he would be in the area, tagging along with Midarin's army, trying to exact some measure of revenge for his lost Elwyne. Suddenly the powers of the Blaze flared in Caris' mind, a searing pain piercing her temples. Another power clashed with the Blaze in her mind, a perfect power that every phase knew to avoid, the powers wielded by the first *Coromor*, Emries. Forced to release the Blaze, Caris slumped to the ground holding her head. The pain eased over the next few seconds, and when Rael and Trece finally helped her back to her feet, much of it had disappeared completely.

"What is it Caris?" Rael asked with what sounded like genuine concern in his voice.

"Emries is here," Caris replied, her voice straining a bit, "and it feels like he is fighting one of us."

Trece took a step back. While she was still young and inexperienced, the memories gathered from the Blaze were more than enough for her to realize the consequences of going one on one with Emries. It was said that Emries could banish any phase with a thought, and would not hesitate if a member of the Brotherhood was foolish enough to provoke him. The battle between Shau-ling and Emries was older than even the memories of the Blaze would reveal, and it was said that the first members of the phasia, Jeroch, Grawn, Bryn, and Ellis had all stood against Emries at one point and lived to tell the tale. However, that tale was never told, and the knowledge of that time was continually denied to all who followed. It was even thought that the memories of those members of the phasia had been expunged of those memories to prevent them from trying to take on Emries themselves. However, Rael and Trece always had a suspicion that there was more to the nature of the war then they were allowed to see, and if they were ever to one day know the truth, it would rock the foundation of their beliefs. In Trece's mind she could hear Rael's thoughts and the doubt that had been there since his birth. He too doubted the nature of the war, doubted the reason they were fighting, and a part of his heart had no desire for bloodshed any longer. Perhaps the part of them that had been Kamen was manifesting in unexpected ways.

"Which way?" Rael asked.

Caris pointed to a clearing near one of the palace gates. Rael helped support his older sister at first, and then finally Caris pulled away and hurried along at her own pace. When finally the three reached the clearing they concealed themselves behind the dense undergrowth and peered out. They were not ready for the sight that greeted them. In blurs of light and motion, Emries and Logan Ranthall struck at one another with blades of seemingly pure energy. Emries was bathed in the angelic glow of his powers that had been a blessing of the Creator, while the fiery green aura that bathed Logan could have only come from one source, the Blaze. Ranthall had touched the power forbidden to servants of Emries, and was wielding it as though he were a member of the phasia. Whatever had prompted the champion of the second generation of the prophecies to forsake his master and embrace the powers of his sworn enemy mattered little at the moment. What was important was that it appeared to Caris that the man was holding his own against the thing that the phasia feared the most.

Strike after strike flowed between the two, highlighted with bursts of flame and huge gusts of wind that threatened to topple nearby trees. Blood flowed freely from several wounds on Logan's exposed chest, and it looked as though large flaps of skin had been ripped away by the precise strike of Emries' crystalline blade. However, Emries himself was not without damage. His robes were ripped and torn where the Dragon Sword had obvious struck true, but no blood flowed. There were large dark stains around some of the ripped fabric however, leading Caris to believe that Logan had indeed drawn some of the god's blood. Another stroke of Emries' blade fell, but instead of meeting air as the dozen previous had, a plume of blood launched into the air, and a cry of pain ripped from Logan's chest. The mortal fell that next moment, his blade clattering to the ground. Emries towered over him, his clear blade pulsing with power, ready to strike the final blow.

"That must hurt, Logan," Emries mocked, looking down at the massive open wound in the mortal's shoulder.

Emries kicked his foot forward, burying it in Logan's gut, forcing the wind out of him. Logan slumped farther toward the ground, and then Emries lifted his leg higher and dug the heel of his boot into the open wound, drawing more moans of pain from the human.

"I told you that I would make you suffer for your words, half-phase. No member of the Brotherhood of Phasia would be as stupid as to challenge me to a fight. But you, you dull-witted human, you had the audacity to not only challenge me, but to renounce your ties to the forces of the Light. You should have stayed hidden and out of this war, Logan. I would have let you stay behind the scenes, out of the war to sulk and mourn the loss of your precious Elwyne. But you couldn't leave well enough alone. You had to know the truth. You had to fight. And now, Logan, you will die. How does it feel knowing that you will die with the taint of Shau-ling on your heart? How does it feel to know that you have failed everyone you have ever loved? You failed Elwyne when you let her die. You failed your brother when you let him die. You failed your new family when you let Draven take them from you. You have failed in everything you have ever attempted, you pathetic excuse for a hero."

Emries increased the pressure on the wound for a moment and then stepped away and turned his back to the fallen warrior. When he turned back, the crystalline blade was gone, and a ball of molten fire lay crackling and hissing in his hand.

"I give you one last opportunity to make this easy on yourself, Logan. Renounce your claim to serve Shau-ling and I will find forgiveness within myself and kill you quickly. Otherwise I shall encase you within these flames, letting your burn and suffer for years before you finally die. It could be over in a moment, or in a thousand years of suffering, and all you have to do is say the words."

Logan lay motionless for a only another moment and then groped around for the hilt of his sword. Emries shook his head, and with a simple gesture of his hand, the sword slid across the ground until Logan's hand claimed it. Carefully the bruised and battered human fought his way to his feet, using the sword as a crutch until he was back on his feet again. Once standing, Logan pulled his shoulders back proudly. There wasn't a part of Logan's body that didn't sing with pain, but none of that mattered. His mind and more importantly his vision was clear. Emries was the enemy, had been the enemy all along, and more than that, Emries was evil. Evil didn't know how to do anything other than inflict pain, and Logan was through letting Emries inflict that pain. The purpose of Logan's life finally came into full focus, and his head was clear. The guilt was gone. The sorrow was gone. All the pieces had fallen into place, and only his new purpose remained. Logan would kill Emries.

"I no longer serve any force that would call you its patron, Emries. And if I have to suffer a thousand years before dying, I will do it knowing that I die without your taint on my heart."

Emries sighed and shook his head.

"So be it."

The ball of flame hovered above Emries' palm for a moment and then sped toward Logan. The mortal made no move to avoid the strike, but moments before the ball of flame struck, the peaks of fire froze. When the ball finally did connect with Logan's chest, it shattered. Neither Logan nor Emries could fathom what had just occurred until Caris, Rael, and Trece emerged from the undergrowth.

"You dare interfere in this!" Emries roared.

"Logan Ranthall has declared himself an ally to the Shadow," Caris said proudly, "and though his blood is tainted, the blood of the phasia still runs through his veins, and so he is one of us. I Caris, the Lady Wolf and member of the Brotherhood of Phasia extend my protection over Logan Ranthall if he is willing to accept it."

Emries turned his attention back to Logan who was now smiling.

"Looks like things have turned on you, Emries. I gladly accept the assistance of my brethren, and I am sure that if you would like to continue this fight that they would be more than willing to take a piece of you for themselves, Emries."

The man in long white robes regarded the new arrivals for a moment and then laughed.

"My successor will have more than enough opportunities to rid the world of the pathetic phasia and all who call themselves the servants of Shau-ling. Make no mistake, Logan Ranthall, but you and I have not concluded our business. Before all of this is over I will happily watch you die once again, only this time I will not be content to end you quickly."

Emries turned to walk away, but then turned back.

"Enjoy your hollow victory, Logan. But realize now that you have more enemies than could ever dream. The people you once called friends are honor-bound to destroy you, and believe me when I say that I will exert every bit of influence that I have over the forces of Light and ensure that your fate will be filled with pain. You may think you have lifted the veil from your eyes and are seeing this war clearly, but you are as presumptuous as you are foolish."

With that Emries turned again and began walking. With every step, he faded out until finally there was nothing left of him. When he was finally gone, the strength in Logan's legs fled, and he collapsed. The next moment, Caris was at his side, letting the gentle flows of Wind and Water heal the cuts and scrapes on his flesh while the flows of Earth mended the shattered bones in his shoulder and ribs.

"You are more of a fool than I ever imagined you could be," Caris muttered under her breath as she tied off the finals strings of healing power. "What did you think you were doing renouncing Emries and dedicating yourself to Shau-ling."

"I was doing what was right, Caris," Logan answered rolling his head back and locking eyes with her. "Emries is wrong and this war is wrong. If things keep going the way they are, we're all going to die."

"Everything dies Logan," Caris said stroking his hair.

Logan shook his head and let a little chuckle escape his lips.

"You came here to kill me, didn't you?"

Caris smiled and nodded.

"Then end it quickly," Logan said closing his eyes and exposing his throat. "I don't have the power to fight off the three of you, and if you can't see that what I'm doing is right, just do what you think you need to do."

Caris smiled and then brought the palm of her hand crashing down on the side of Logan's face, slapping him with all the force that she could muster. Had she added any of the power that she wanted to, the blow would have easily crushed the bones of his cheek and jaw, but the sting in his flesh was more than enough to get her point across. Logan open his eyes and then rubbed his cheek.

"That was for killing me in Frontier," Caris said rising. "I invested too much time and energy in you in the last lifetime to kill you now that you have started fighting on the right side of this war. While I am sure that other members of the phasia will not be as eager to welcome you into the fold as I am, they will in time see the value of your addition."

Logan shook his head again, and then tried to stand up. The weakness in his body caused him to stumble again, but instead of finding himself back in the mud, the strong arms of the black clad Rael supported him and helped him to find his feet.

"It is good to see you again, Logan," the man said firmly, "and it is good that we will not be enemies. Though it pained me at the time, I grew to have a great deal of respect for you and your friend Gwydeon Sandar when we met on the Island of Mist by Blood Lake. My respect for the both of you grew with each raid that was turned back at the gates of Brea, and after I heard of your victory against Draven's army and your narrow escape from his clutches."

Logan nodded, but could not find the words to match the moment. Part of him was disgusted that he was going to be fighting side by side with members of the phasia against his own kind, but that could not be helped now. The Elder had shown him the true path, and though this may not have been the way they intended for him to walk it, it was the way that he had chosen. He would have to accept that the phasia were his kind now; that he was no longer human.

"Surely," Trece said turning her attention back to Caris, "this is cause enough to return to the Council and inform our master."

Logan shook his head in response.

"There's no time for that. Nathaniel Sandar, the third *Coromor* of the prophecies has already begun his assault on the phasia, and has gotten to Zarsi by now. If we don't stop him, he'll move on to the next target and slaughter the phasia one by one. The four of us have the element of surprise now, and if we strike when he least expects it, before Emries can inform him of our treachery, then we have a real chance of ending his threat for good."

Caris was dumbfounded.

"I never would have believed those words would come out of your mouth, Logan Ranthall."

Logan smiled.

"You'll find I'm full of surprises."

Logan and Caris turned to enter through the melted gate of the palace, but Rael and Trece hesitated. Rael could feel power growing in the area of the forest, and it was a power that was very familiar. Suddenly three portals appeared. Rael and Trece both tensed. Sensing the power Logan and Caris both turned and watched as first the living pillar of Blaze fire, the Flame, emerged from one of the portals quickly followed by two other creatures. One of the creatures seemed to be just a moving mass of shadows, while the other was a large suit of armor with a skull floating above it. The skull rocked back and let forth an ear-shattering cackle before the Flame began to speak.

"Rael Starlin, Trece Starlin, for your attacks on the future First of the Council, the Lord Crow Draven Batoe, you have been sentenced to execution. However, you will first name your accomplice in the ambush during the battle of ascension which left the Lord Crow horribly injured."

Caris stepped forward.

"I was the accomplice, Flame," she said proudly. "The real flame, our brother Kamen, is dead, and you are merely a part of the great power he once held. Who are you to carry out the execution of members of the Brotherhood of Phasia?"

"We are the Dark Riders," the Flame answered, "the personal security force of the Lord Crow, the rightful leader of the Brotherhood of Phasia."

Logan stepped forward and drew the Dragon Sword.

"Remember me, Flame?" he said proudly. "As the new member of the Brotherhood of Phasia, I'll take great pleasure in making you my first kill. Now, feel the wrath of the new Lord Phoenix, Logan Ranthall!"

Bitter Truths

Creator's Calendar Year 1205; Light Reality

Duncan Rhuiden was never more proud of himself than he was when he saw the look on his mother's face, upon bursting into the throne room of the palace of Trelon. For many years, he had been plotting his ascension to the throne of Marcwell and revenge on the family that had treated him more like a beggar than the prince that he was. And now all of the plans were starting to come to fruition. Shortly after leaving the court of Trelon, Duncan had made his way into the wilds of the southern lands, falling in with a nomadic people who called themselves the Creator's Torch Society. The leader of this sect had been brutally murdered several years prior, and so the new leader, a woman named Seraphina Masile, the former leader Dei's lover, was doing her best to hold the people together and keep them from splintering. They had been following the teaching of the Moridon, preparing themselves for a confrontation with the great evil that plagued the world. They had devoted their lives to fighting the evil of the phasia and vanquishing the scourge of Shau-ling from the face of the world. Duncan spoke before the assembled masses of the Torch and gave them something to hope for. The war had always been fought under the flag of the kingdom of Marcwell, and though the great saint Cedric Binosear had fallen by the wayside, the power that was Marcwell was not a force that could be taken lightly in the war that was to come. If anyone was going to mount a successful offensive against the phasia and Shau-ling, it was going to be from Marcwell with the banner of the Lion flying proudly from every tower and every standard. While Duncan did not believe a word that was spewing from his lips, he knew that it was a way to get the forces of the Torch behind him to help him claim the throne that was rightfully his. The Torch immediately consented to help him ascend to the throne of Marcwell and then to strike down every evil force that stood in the way of the forces of the Light. Duncan again fed the group more fuel for the fires inside of them. He told them that the great warrior Pike Rhuiden had been corrupted by Shau-ling, and that it was this corruption that was hanging like a shadow over the once great kingdom that had been the home of the heroes of the first war against Shau-ling. This caused a frenzy in the Torch and they immediately wanted blood. Seraphina Masile conducted the initiation of Duncan into the Creator's Torch Society which also required his marriage to one of the women in the Society. It was Dei's own younger sister that would become Duncan's wife, a woman named Bridgette Dalen. This not only cemented Duncan as a member of the Torch, but also as one of its principle leaders. Soon enough, Seraphina was seen as the leader in all things having to do with the religion of the Torch, while Duncan was the military leader who ruled through his two lieutenants, Seraphina's half-brother Korin Melcab, and the man that the members of the Torch knew as the Messiah, Michael Yarrow.

"Aren't you glad to see me, mother?" Duncan asked facetiously.

The queen took a step back and then composed herself. Too many things were happening too fast, and she did not know how much more she could take. First it was the revelation of her family's involvement in the coming war, then the fact that her great-grandfather was the man she had known as Aerith through the years, and now Duncan and his army had descended upon them like locusts.

"What do you want, Duncan?" Cairyn responded coldly.

"Why my kingdom, of course."

Cairyn sighed.

"You know that I do not have the power to give you something that is not mine. Only Pike can relinquish control of the kingdom of Marcwell to you, and he is currently campaigning against the forces of Shau-ling in Lakestone."

Duncan shook his head slowly, and opened his mouth to speak. However, it was one of his companions who let his voice hit the air first.

"More like conspiring with them," the man behind Duncan remarked.

Cairyn felt a surge of anger flow through her.

"Who is this vulgar man that you have brought with you who does not know how to control his tongue in the presence of a queen? How dare you slander the Lord of the Kingdom of Marcwell in the throne room of his own wife."

While many would have trembled at the thunderous tone, Duncan stood unaffected. He had been preparing for this for far too long to be dissuaded by words alone.

"Save your outrage Cairyn," Duncan replied. "Forgive me if I do not refer to you by your title, as that it will be transferred to my wife Bridgette soon enough."

Cairyn took a step backwards.

"You have given me all the information that I need, and now I shall take my leave of you to deal with my absent father. Keep in mind that I will soon be the Lord of all of this that you once called home, and if you are lucky I may only banish you rather than having you executed."

Aerith took the opportunity to step forward.

"I would not have thought that you would have turned out this way, Duncan," he said, his hand gripping tightly the hilt of his sword. "You were such and lovely and bright child, it's a pity that you turned out to be a spoiled and ugly adult."

Duncan regarded the man for a moment, looking him up and down as if assessing the level of threat that he posed. Seemingly satisfied with what he saw, Duncan smiled and scoffed in the ancient man's direction.

"Don't think I don't know who you are, old man," Duncan said laughing. "And it is only on a whim that I do not end your pathetic existence here and now. However you are not what you once were, and you are not a threat to the new world that I will create. Your evil will soon be wiped from this world without me having to spoil my hands with your blood. You know as well as I do Aerith that you are dying. The world has forgotten you, and even those that you give your power to care not for you but for the quest that the Light has blessed them with. You are nothing more than a means to an end, and for that, you will soon find your eternal home in the pits of Hell with the Great Dark One."

Part of Aerith wanted to draw his sword, but he knew that the time and the place for such a battle was not there and not at that time.

"Goodbye, mother," Duncan said turning his back and making his way toward the door. "If I were you, I would be far away from Trelon by the time I return."

The two men and woman with Duncan smiled wicked smiles and then followed their lord out of the throne room. For a long moment, silence hung like a shroud in the room, only to be broken by Cairyn's strained voice.

"What are we going to do?"

Aerith considered the question for a moment, and then returned to the window to gaze out at the land around the palace of Trelon. If the Torch were going to follow Duncan's lead to the letter, it would take them several days to march from Trelon to Scalla. But there was something wrong. Aerith should have seen Duncan and his army approaching, should have known of their impending arrival. Perhaps this group had a few surprises of their own that made them far more of a threat to Pike's throne than just bluster and talk. What was clear was that Cairyn was no longer safe in Trelon.

"Something about this isn't right," Aerith commented to himself. "Duncan already knew where his father was when he came here. This little visitation was his way to taunt you and throw me off."

CHAPTER 38

Cairyn walked over to the window and stood facing her old friend. The lines on his face seemed to have grown deeper into his skin and the worry on his brow was the kind that no man should have to bear.

"How could he have known that you would be here?"

Aerith shook his head.

"I don't know, but I think it has something to do with the lead that Wolf and your daughter are chasing. They are in good hands with Bryn for now, but I am afraid that the time will come when I may have to interject myself to save them from Grawn. His jealous streak runs a little too deeply for my taste, and the rage builds within him every year. I think that man was built to hold grudges."

Cairyn wanted to ask so many more questions, know so much more about the man whom she now knew was her blood. However, the moment won out over small and selfish desires for truth and deeper connection.

"So what will we do?"

Aerith looked Cairyn in the eyes and tried hard to smile.

"If I were you my dear, I would go as far away from Trelon as you can. Perhaps you should retire to Aradon for a while to visit Pike's family. I doubt that anyone would look for the Queen of Trelon there. Besides, no one is crazy enough to travel through Logan's Woods with the kind of evil intentions that your boy has."

Cairyn let a smile creep onto her face.

"And where will you go?"

Aerith thought long and hard about the question for a moment and then tried hard to come to a decision. Something about the way Duncan was acting was not sitting right in the pit of Aerith's stomach. While the boy had always been coarse and rude, this was too far out of character for him. Aerith had seen the way people would act under control of members of the phasia. While the Shau-ling of this world would probably not willingly be able to help him, thanks to the Creator, there was another Shau-ling that Aerith could pursue.

"I'm going to pay an old friend a visit and try to get some information," Aerith said finally. "I wouldn't worry Cairyn, I don't think that Duncan is going to kill your husband."

Cairyn turned away from Aerith and started walking to her private room. She paused at the door, her hand resting on the handle before she turned her head slightly and let her saddened and pain-filled voice hit the air.

"I still don't know if that would be a bad thing or not."

Softly the doors to the room opened, Cairyn stepped inside, and then closed them behind her. Aerith lingered a moment considering the statement and then let a trickle of power flow from deep inside his body. He knew that every use of his remaining power would make him weaker and that eventually he would fade away, but he had to know the truth, even if it meant dying. He owed that to his family, all of them, even the ones who hated him.

* * * * * * * * * * *

For several minutes, Taya Mystic stood looking at the gold bound spine, the wonder of the title shocking her to the very core. The wonders of Basille's study had helped to prepare her for the new discovery, but the answers that were to be found in that book were obviously not for the weak at heart. As Taya looked around, she saw that Storm was leafing quickly through a book, obviously scanning for certain words and phrases that were important to him. Erika, her mother, was standing close to the fountain of Blaze flame, watching in wonder as the colors within the flames changed from heartbeat to heartbeat. Each peak of flame melded into the next, the rolling torrent of unquenchable hunger feeding on itself time and time again. Looking around, Taya noticed that her father, Jerrard, had made his way back over to the main desk in the room, and was alternating his attention between a dozen scrolls, trying to make some sense of the words written there. It was obvious that the phase Basille was far cleverer and more intelligent than anyone could have ever imagined. Taya was sure that if one had the time to stay and absorb every piece of text in the study that the whole war between the Light and the Shadow would seem petty by the time they were done. Withdrawing the book from the shelf, Taya clutched it to her chest and walked slowly over to her father. She felt as though she were carrying the weight of the world in her arms, but she did not understand where all of this anxiety had come from. It took only a few steps before she was standing beside the desk, and yet the burden on her heart seemed to have grown by factors of ten. There was a great dread and sorrow that entered her as Jerrard looked up into the eyes of his daughter and then smiled.

"Did you find something Taya?"

The young woman could only nod and look down at the book she cradled in her arms like a child. There was more to this book than just pages and ink, it was as though there was a great power tied to it, and the answers to the secrets behind the war itself. Jerrard looked at the book and cleared a place for Taya to set it down. The girl did not budge, and when her father reached for the book, she was surprised when she felt her body jerk away. Jerrard's expression changed. There was genuine confusion in his eyes, but then something in his features changed. He closed his eyes tightly and probed the powers of the Blaze. When his eyes opened again, he no longer saw the rows of books or even the bright face of his daughter before him. Everything in is view was energy, from the bright and shining fountain of pure Blaze, to the outline of his own hands of the string of Chaos that he had inherited from his father. But as he looked at his daughter, he saw a bright golden glow coming from the book that she cradled in her arms. The book itself radiated a power unlike anything that Jerrard had ever seen, except for those times when Korrd Ranthall had revealed the true power of the *Coromor* in the final battle against Shau-ling. Finally, the real world came back to Jerrard's eyes. He saw the colors around him again, as well as his daughter's frightened face. The strong sensation to protect the book had suddenly left Taya's mind and body, and puzzlement and confusion had replaced it. Jerrard smiled in an attempt to calm his child, and as he recovered the book from her arms, Taya felt the weight lift from her heart, and she nearly fell to her knees in relief. Not taking time to look at the spine of the book to read the title, Jerrard opened the front cover and saw the title page. When he read the words printed there in fine golden ink, a great rage grew deep within him. Before he could delve deeper into the volume before him, his thoughts were interrupted by Storm.

"Father," he said running up to the desk, "something is coming."

Jerrard let the anger ebb away from the recesses of his mind and stretched out again with the powers of the Blaze. Storm was right. Jerrard could feel the flows of power from a portal opening in the throne room of the palace, but it would take a few moments for it to finish forming. It was obvious from the amount of power that was being used that the portal originated from a great distance away, but what was puzzling was the fact that the signature of the power was very familiar. It was almost like that of his father Basille, but that was impossible now that his father had been Banished by Shau-ling. Perhaps Basille's string had been reconstituted into a new member of the phasia, or perhaps something else was the cause. Regardless, there was no way to determine whether the impending visitors were friend or foe. Collecting Taya's discovery under his arm, Jerrard created a portal of his own and ushered his family through. They arrived in the throne room only moments before the swirling blue portal appeared near the large wooden doors that led to the receiving hall. After the portal finished forming, Jerrard smiled when he saw the visitor who stepped out. Midarin Rice had always been a friend to the kingdom of Scalla, and their friendship went back to their days in the People of the Dragon. However, the angry scowl leapt onto Jerrard's face when the traitor Aryx Terian emerged only a step behind Midarin.

What happened in the next few moments was a blur. Jerrard took hold of the primal string granted to him as a child of the phasia and snapped the portal closed behind Aryx and then immediately created a sword out of the powers of the Blaze. Storm was also quick to follow his father's lead, drawing the sword from the scabbard at his side. Taya and Erika, shocked at the turn of events, moved out of the line of fire and stood to either side of the throne. Aryx stood firm and without so much as a thought pulled his sword from the scabbard on his back and another from the sheath on his hip. Midarin, whose bow was held lightly in her right hand, quickly recovered an arrow and nocked it onto her bowstring and aimed the point directly at the heart of her old ally.

"Lower your blade Jerrard," Midarin said steadying her aim, "is this any way to treat an old friend who has come to ask for your help?"

Jerrard took a step forward and pointed his finger at Aryx.

"What kind of friend brings a traitor into their friend's kingdom?"

Midarin was shocked, and lowered the tip of the arrow and slowly let the bowstring return to its resting position. Slowly she took a step away from Aryx, and watched as he too lowered his swords and let them clatter to the ground one after the other.

"I no longer have the burden of Nightwing on my heart, Jerrard," Aryx said after a moment, "and you as well as everyone else who was there at the end of the last generation should know that. I sacrificed myself to give Korrd and Logan the opportunity to finish off Shau-ling, and somehow I was spared. I don't pretend to understand it myself, and there is no real explanation I can give that would make sense. But I assure you, I am not a traitor. I am as much a warrior of the Light now as I have ever been."

Jerrard let a little laugh escape his lips and then flung the brown book that he had been holding under his arm across the room at Aryx. It hit the ground mid-way through its flight and then skidded the rest of the way until it came to a stop at his feet.

As Aryx bent down to recover the book, Jerrard said, "Then how do you explain this?"

Aryx opened the front cover of the book and Midarin could see a change in the man's expression. There was a sorrow in his eyes that seemed to grow with every page that he turned. Finally, about half-way through the book, a shadow fell over Aryx's features and he slammed the book closed and let it drop to the floor.

"Where did you find that, Jerrard?"

"It was part of my father's study that has laid hidden for years beneath the palace of Scalla. It even survived the destruction that you were responsible for under the guise of Nightwing."

Silence filled the room again, and Aryx took several steps toward Jerrard before Storm made a move to cut him off. Seeing that there was no graceful way to escape the situation, Aryx stopped in his tracks, fell to his knees and lowered his head.

"If you mean to execute me," Aryx said in a proud voice, "at least give me the honor of killing me quickly and don't humiliate me by exposing me to the world. It would not only tarnish my name, but it would hang a doubt over Lord Cedric and Lord Logan. Cedric was spared the shame of his death in Shau-ling's throne room, he deserves to be spared the shame of this."

Storm took a step forward and then looked back at his father. There was fury in Jerrard's eyes, but the anger that was inside of him was being balanced by an equal amount of curiosity. There were many questions that Aryx would have to answer, and his death would leave the questions burning in Jerrard's mind for the rest of his life.

"I'm not going to kill you Aryx," Jerrard said letting the sword vanish from his hands, "I just want answers, I think you owe us that much."

Aryx looked up at Jerrard and then nodded. Bringing himself back to his feet, Aryx began the story of his past that had never been told.

"First know that what I am about to tell you has been hidden from me for quite some time as well. When I fought at the side of Lord Cedric and then again with Lord Logan I did not know any of what I am about to tell you. However, once I was merged with the creature you came to know as Nightwing, I was infused with the full knowledge of the Blaze, and it awoke in me knowledge that had been blocked from my mind. This knowledge created in my doubt and fear unlike I had ever felt, and though in a way I felt justified in my actions when it came to the extermination of the phasia the command of Shau-ling, I could not bring myself to betray those that I loved and honored."

Aryx paused, and though Jerrard did not want to acknowledge Aryx's preamble, he gave a curt nod and waited for the rest of the tale to unfold.

"When the war between Emries and Shau-ling first started," Aryx began again, "it was simple. It was a battle between brothers, and soon it raged out of control. The creatures that fought for the living nightmare could not be matched by ordinary men. They came slowly to the knowledge of the humans that worshiped their god king, revealing themselves one by one. These creatures of vast power had been molded by Shau-ling to be the vessels of his power. Not creatures of flesh and bone, but rather embodiments of the power that Shau-ling had called the Blaze. Shau-ling had studies his opponent for hundreds of years, seeing the things that all men fear, and the things that drive all men mad. These base drives, these incredible powers of destruction were molded into Shau-ling's children; the emotions and virtues that Shau-ling had observed gave the humans the most power and most drive. Of course, most of these emotions were negative, greed, jealousy, hatred, lust, deviousness, and pride. He called these creatures phasia. But Shau-ling also chose two emotions that were positive, and molded them into one of his new phasia. Those emotions were Valor and Courage. When he was done, Shau-ling was proud of his six children. These phasia, these monsters attacked with such ferocity that they nearly won the war for their master. Emries and his followers were caught so by surprise that Emries was forced to resort to desperate measures. Emries chose his four strongest generals and imbued them with a fraction of his own power. This is how the *Erieal* came to be, a reaction to the devastation wrought by the children of the living nightmare."

Aryx paused once more, clearing his throat. When he began again, a new sadness punctuated his words.

"The first was Kamen, the man that would eventually become the Flame. He was powerful, strong, proud, the perfect combination of strength and intelligence. On the battlefield he was nearly invincible, a mountain of a man who knew no fear and could make the ground shake with every step he took. Next was Jeroch, and you all know him. Jeroch was loyal and proud, but the loyalty was almost to a fault. While it was true that Kamen was born first, because of his eventual fall from the ranks of the phasia it is Jeroch who is regarded as the first born of the phasia. Jeroch was responsible for the creation of the great armies of beasts that serve the Shadow. The fear that he created with his conquests shattered the resolve of any army that was not lead by one of Emries' generals.

"The next to be born were Grawn and Bryn, nearly at the same time, it's because of that they were so inseparable from lifetime to lifetime. Grawn was the embodiment of jealousy and rage, a dangerous combination when you consider that the woman he picked to be his partner through every lifetime was the embodiment of infidelity and lust. Bryn was the perfect seductress and she soon learned that her talents in combination with Grawn's failings could be a lethal combination. She would lure men to her bed, allow Grawn to find them together, and then watch as Grawn ripped the poor victim to shreds. But where they were dangerous in the abstract, like their older siblings, their power was frightening when directly applied. Grawn ravaged the coastal cities, battering them with waves that could reach the stars. Bryn was just as subtle, raining fire down from the heavens, or engulfing armies in columns of flame.

"Then of course was Ellis. If there were ever a person that could be described as too intelligent, it would be Ellis. She was able to see through any scheme, no matter how complex nor how many parties were involved. And, when she put her mind to it, there was nothing that she could not do, or make others do for that matter. She could wreak havoc in a way that the world had never seen, walking into a kingdom alone and have it tearing itself apart by nightfall. Those kingdoms that she could not make destroy themselves were wiped away by tornados and typhoons so terrible that nothing would be left but dust."

Midarin moved to where she could look Aryx in the eyes.

"You're talking as though you were there, Aryx," she said quietly.

Aryx returned the hard gaze.

"That's because I was, Midarin. I was the sixth phase, the last of the original Council."

There was a ripple of disbelief that filled the room. Jerrard, having only looked at the title page could not have guessed that the secret was this deep. In a way Jerrard began to regret his anger, and feel pity for his one-time ally. But judgement would have to wait until the end of the tale. The very core of the phasia was being exposed by Aryx's words. Before anyone could react further to the words, Aryx continued his strange and wondrous story.

"From my description, I am sure that you can realize that I was different from the other members of the phasia. For a time though, we were a family, fighting against the forces that were seeking to destroy us. But along the way, things began to change. The war was no longer simple. Men and women who had no hope of surviving a confrontation against the Jeresei or the Shadowwalkers, were being thrown at us by Emries and his *Erieal*. Suddenly, we weren't fighting against those who wanted to destroy us. We were fighting against those who were told to fight and had no inkling as to what they were fighting for. Emries had lost sight of the true nature of the war and had become obsessed with only winning. So, I went to my master Shau-ling and voiced my concerns. I could not stomach the thought of killing those who did not know why they were fighting. But Shau-ling would not listen to me, and so we went, for years, killing those who stood in our way, men, women and children alike, simply because they threw themselves at our blades. Finally, I could not take it anymore. I could no longer raise my blade or my powers against those who did not have the power to challenge me. And so, in the middle of the Council of Phasia I refused to fight for Shau-ling any longer. I threw down my sword. Shau-ling was furious, and though he wanted so much to kill me, he was still my father, and so he stripped me of my powers as a member of the Council and cast me out forever. He did me the courtesy of repressing most of my power and some of my memories so that I might live out the rest of my years in peace, free from my conscience."

Jerrard could not imagine the faces of the dead that must have plagued Aryx. He also could not imagine the merciful Shau-ling that Aryx was portraying. How could it be that Emries was so ruthless and Shau-ling was so kind? And yet Aryx continued, his somber words making the hearts of everyone who heard them heavy.

"For many years I wandered. I was mortal, for the most part, and so I tried to live as a mortal. I should have realized that would never have been possible, but I again was proven to be a fool. I found my way to a rural little town called Lakestone where I set myself up as a blacksmith and began to live a normal life. I fell in love with a beautiful woman and together we lived happily for many years. But to my great shock, I was not aging, at least, not the way I had expected. Thirty years passed and I watched every day as my beautiful wife got older, but my features never showed so much as a wrinkle or a gray hair. So, fearing that the townspeople would begin to question, my wife and I moved out of Lakestone to a little farmhouse. It wasn't too long before I realized that I had retained some of my powers from my time as a member of the phasia, and I used those healing powers to keep my wife young and beautiful.

"The human body knows though that it is not made to exist forever, and so as the years rolled on, my wife began to weaken more and more. It got to the point that I could not stand to be there, to see her weakened, so I invented errands to run, to keep track of the war that was beginning to grow in intensity with the creation of the new phasia, Saurn, Warron, Aldridge, Farax, Erdric, and Caris. The Hand of the Light was running wild over the countryside, and a man by the name of Aralias Imstra was just beginning to gain a name for himself in some of the lesser kingdoms. However, I knew that I could not leave my wife alone, so I bought the services of a young boy from one of the orphanages to keep an eye on my wife and help her around the house. Not too long after that, my wife died. Her body could no longer go on, and it was her time. I was shattered when the news hit, and I wandered for many years. In fact I went into seclusion in the wilds outside of Lakestone for many years. I was vaguely aware of the defeat of the Hand of the Light, the powerful warrior Aerith Seth, and the creation of Zarsi, Taron, and Basille.

"Finally though, I knew that I would have to choose sides once again. The war was coming to an apex, and I knew that unless someone stood against the forces of the phasia, thousands of innocent lives would be lost. And so, when the Jeresei and Kalbraks descended on the city of Lakestone, I stood with the children and grandchildren of the men and women I had once called friends and tried to defend it and its people. But soon the battle grew hopeless, and I knew that Lakestone would fall. So, I fled."

Aryx stood silent for a moment, obviously trying to sort everything out in his mind.

"My long walk from Lakestone would eventually take me near the city of Askronilka, where I happened to stumble across the tracks of a group of Kalbraks. It was obviously a small hunting party that had gotten separated, either by choice or by necessity, from the main force. I followed the tracks and found the beasts attacking a young woman who had stopped to camp for the night. Of course, I would soon find out that the woman was none other than Erika Belnosian and she would lead me to the service of Cedric Binosear. The rest of course is history."

Jerrard took a step forward and opened his mouth as if to speak. Aryx, sensing the question raised his hand and answered.

"I know what you are thinking Jerrard, and no, I could not sense that Erika was really Caris in disguise. My memories of the Blaze had been completely repressed, first by Shau-ling, and then by Emries when he made me one of his *Erieal*. Besides that, the only way that she would have drawn my attention is if she physically drew on the power of the Blaze, which for some reason in that generation, her shape-changing ability did not require a conscious use of Shau-ling's power."

Midarin took several steps toward Aryx and then stood silently face to face with the taller man. Together she and Aryx had shared many things, and many intimate moments. But the one question in her heart that had once had another answer suddenly seemed wrong.

"She's yours, isn't she," Midarin whispered.

Aryx could only nod. He had known from the moment that he had laid eyes on the little girl lying in her crib that the powers that he had once possessed as a member of the phasia flowed in the blood of the little girl Liette. Though part of Aryx wanted to tell Midarin the truth, there was never a good time or a good way. Besides, Midarin was happy believing that Liette was Pike's child and Aryx was not willing to shatter that illusion. It was only later when he learned that he had a child, one who hated him to the very core of her being, that he realized once again how much a family had once meant to him. Midarin tried her best to smile and took several steps backwards before turning to face Jerrard.

"You got the answers you wanted Jerrard," Midarin said wiping a tear away from the corner of her eye, "and I for one am glad that he had the honesty and honor within him to tell us the truth. I think he has earned our respect and our trust."

Jerrard did not move for a moment and then took several steps down the dais. When he reached Storm, who was still frozen in shock from the revelations in the story, the boy looked him in the eyes and then stepped aside. Jerrard continued forward and then stood face to face with the man that part of him still considered a traitor. But even when Aryx was contained in the shell called Nightwing, he still had the best interest of the force of the Light in his mind. He sacrificed himself to end the battle against Shau-ling and give the Light at least one more generation of freedom from the yolk of the Shadow. Silently, Jerrard extended his hand, and without hesitation Aryx extended his own and the rift between the two sealed. Suddenly the doors to the throne room burst open, and one of the lieutenants from the Raven's Wing, Jerrard's personal army, entered.

"My lord," the man said bowing low, "I am sorry for this interruption but I have urgent news."

Jerrard strode past Aryx and squared his shoulders proudly before the new arrival.

"It is alright. What do you have to report?"

"My lord," the man said straightening, "the Enforcers have entered the kingdom of Scalla. Three of their number was lost during a battle in Lakestone and one of them is badly wounded and being attended to by the healers."

"And Lord Pike?" Jerrard asked, feeling Midarin's silent question.

"He is asking to see you my lord."

"Very well," Jerrard answered. "Take us to Lord Pike, and prepare the Raven's Wing to march on Lakestone."

As everyone followed the soldier out of the throne room toward their meeting with Pike and the remaining members of the Enforcers, no one noticed the brown book with gold lettering in the corner of the room burst into flames and then burn to ashes in a matter of moments, hiding the last of the secrets of the man Aryx Terian forever. As the large wooden doors to the throne room closed, the ashes were scattered in the resulting draft.

Opportunity

Creator's Calendar Year 1205; Dark Mirror

Shau-ling felt the power slowly trickle back into him from the fires of the Blaze deep at the core of the world, but they were not recovering fast enough. Saurn would not wait much longer before using the full extent of his gifts as a member of the Brotherhood of Phasia in an attempt to kill his master. Inwardly Shau-ling wondered how long Saurn had been lurking in the shadows and listening. Saurn had always been one of the most devious and cunning members of the phasia, and while not as intelligent as Ellis or Bryn, he had never found his mind clouded with trivial things. Ellis was a wonder of thought and scheme, but her preoccupation with the love life of her sister Bryn never allowed her to devote her full attention to anything. The proof was with the near triumph over the Ranthall family. Her scheme in giving birth to the *Coromor* had been flawless, but because of all her meddling in the affairs of Grawn, Bryn, and Aerith Seth, she had lost the cold, calculating part of herself and found that she too had emotions that cried out for attention. And so, she let the boy live, and that boy would seal Shau-ling's fate in the second generation of Emries' damnable prophecies. However, in this generation, it was possible that Saurn would finish the game that Shau-ling's brother had started so long ago.

Saurn, to his credit, had picked the perfect opportunity to strike. Shau-ling knew that he had exhausted most of his powers opening the portal for Pike and Eldar to travel to the other reality. While Shau-ling and Emries could make the transition with only a small fraction of the power that they had at their disposal, mortals could not because of their limited existences. Shau-ling and Emries were timeless and boundless in the ways that mortals perceived such things. In the beginning, Shau-ling had existed as Halicon, and was a being as timeless and limitless as the Cosmos itself. Every portion of life flowed through the Blaze, and so whether life was in this world or another, as long as its life was drawn from the forces of the Blaze, then Shau-ling could follow the path. Emries felt the powers of the Blaze too, though he would never admit that he too could have subsisted on that source of power. Long ago, before his war with the Creator, Emries' power was more divine. The Creator had given some of his power to Emries to help create a world. But it was Emries' obsession with the creature man that had created a rift between Emries and the Creator, and so in the end, Emries delved deep into his natural powers as a child of the Creator to conquer his new enemy, Shau-ling. However, the mortals that Emries created had no tie to the powers of the Blaze. They were just empty shells filled with a little of the Creator's power that Emries once wielded with reckless abandon. The first mortals were filled to the brim with this granted power, but after the rift was created, there was nothing left for the generations to come. So, in order to save his precious race, Emries made the bargain that would prove to be the plague of Shau-ling's existence.

Once the war started between Emries and Shau-ling, Emries began to see a change in the mortals that were created in every generation. While the first of their kind had been brimming with the white, pure energies of the Creator, the subsequent generations were a little weaker. Because there was no power left for Emries to replenish his creations, since he had been but off from the divine power through his arrogance, they were slowly weakening. Emries knew that eventually there would not be enough power left to create offspring, and so the human race would fade away, killed by a disease that could not be treated. When Emries finally devised a way to combat this silent killer, many generations had passed. The humans were growing frailer and weaker, and their life spans were shortening. In some generations, the life span was perhaps only shorter by a matter of days or weeks, however, in some it was shortened by years. That was when the prophecies were born. Emries knew the powers Blaze, and he knew that he could use the limitless powers held in the emerald flames to revitalize his creations. However, if he were to attempt such a feat while Shau-ling lived, he knew that his brother would turn his creations against him. Such a fear would be proven true with Cedric Binosear, and again in this generation with Logan Ranthall. Once Shau-ling was eliminated, Emries could use the Blaze without fear and breathe new life into his creations. This would prove Emries' superiority over his brother, as well as prove his vision of the Cosmos to his father, the Creator. Perhaps Emries even had designs on unseating their father and taking the golden throne of the Heavens for himself.

Pushing himself up onto his knees, Shau-ling looked up into the violet eyes of his child Saurn. The phase smiled wider at the eye contact, and extended his hand to his fallen master. Shau-ling brushed away the offer, and forced himself to his feet. The pain rocketed through his body at that moment, the screaming searing torment of his muscles forcing him back down to his knees. Breaching the wall between worlds had taken far more of his energy than Shau-ling had anticipated, and had it not been worth the risk, he would not left himself so vulnerable. A generation prior he had been forced to fight the Flame, and before that he had fought Zarsi when the impudent creature thought he was powerful enough to unseat Shau-ling. However, this fight would be different. In his current condition, Shau-ling knew that his tie to the Blaze had been significantly weakened, and the power at his disposal was barely enough to match that of one of his children.

"My poor master," Saurn taunted, slowly circling. "How the mighty have fallen to the meek. For all your powers and all of your abilities, you made yourself vulnerable for two mortals."

Shau-ling winced. Saurn had been there for the creation of the portal and most likely knew why the portal was being created as well. Slowly, Shau-ling began to open himself up to the source of the Blaze that lay deep in the core of the world. While normally the power would have been sweet and fulfilling, now it was like pouring salt on a wound. Shau-ling knew that he needed the powers of the Blaze to sustain himself, drawing too deeply upon the fires of the Blaze was a pain that could not easily be quenched. Just as a man who drinks too much alcohol will become sick and possibly die, so too was true with the Blaze. That was why every use of the Blaze was met with a healthy dose of respect and fear, for even the phasia knew that the power which created them could also destroy them. While Shau-ling could never be consumed and destroyed by the Blaze, it did not mean that he could not be wounded by that eternal power.

"It's a bit of poetic irony isn't it," Saurn mused completing his circle of Shau-ling. "For so many generations you have been fighting and killing these pathetic mortals, and now you will lose your life after trying to help them."

Saurn let loose a long loud laugh and then fixed his eyes back on Shau-ling, the cold hard stare burning to his master's black heart.

"I shall not make the same mistake," Saurn chided, "and under my leadership, the Brotherhood of Phasia will crush any opposition that is levied against us and the plague known as man will be forever wiped from our world."

Saurn's blade rushed downward the next moment. It was a blow intended to strike his opponent down quickly and end the battle. However, Shau-ling had other ideas. Even in his weakened state, it took only a though to use the flows of Earth and harden the bones and skin of his clawed hand to the point where the steel of Saurn's blade would cause no damage. Shau-ling caught the sword in his left hand, and then mangled the polished steel, leaving it twisted and unusable in combat. It was a display of strength that was intended to remind Saurn that he was not challenging a simpleton. The petty trick would not be enough to dissuade Saurn from his chosen course of action, but perhaps it would by Shau-ling more time to recover.

"You dare bring a child's toy into a fight with a god?" Shau-ling taunted finally finding the strength to rise to his feet. "I thought that I made you of better stuff."

Saurn laughed again, but much of his confidence was beginning to fly. Kamen, then the Flame, made the mistake of challenging Shau-ling to personal combat in the last generation. But at the time, Shau-ling was at his peak of power. Saurn knew that he had more than a fighting chance, but as the battle wore on, he knew that Shau-ling would recover and then would crush Saurn like a bug. Saurn would have to use all of his abilities and strike quickly.

"Give me time old man," Saurn mocked, "you will see that you made me too well."

The blast of fire that erupted from Saurn's hands the next moment was not an attack that Shau-ling could have easily blocked, nor was there a way for him to dodge it. The ball of white-hot flames sped toward their target and connected to the very center of Shau-ling's chest. Shau-ling cried out in pain as the force of the blast propelled him across the room, leaving him sprawled out on the dais in front of his own throne. Reflexively, Shau-ling's hand reached for the contact point of the blast, and found his robes had been ruined by the searing heat. Also, the skin beneath had been charred black, and he could feel the crunch of the hardened flesh as he pawed at the scorched fabric. Saurn was quick to follow up his attack, sending small disks of super-heated steam launching at his opponent. This time Shau-ling was not caught unaware, and he was able to erect a shield of pure Chaos energy, sending the disks of steam rocketing off into the walls. Shau-ling kept the shield up as he forced his way to his feet and wiped the faint trickle of blood from the corner of his mouth. Feeling the force of the Blaze returning, Shau-ling released the shield of Chaos energy and then a full blast of wind hit Saurn, sending him toppling backwards, and with another thought, huge chunks of rock detached from the ceiling and fell toward the stunned phase. Saurn redirected the winds around him, and held the falling rocks at bay while he rolled out of the way and then released the wind letting the boulders crash to the floor. Shau-ling had expected Saurn to be direct and reckless. He needed to end the battle quickly before Shau-ling could recover, which limited the options he had available to him in the course of his assault. Defense against such assaults would be easier on Shau-ling, because he merely had to delay his opponent. As such, Shau-ling could allow some of the blows to connect, so long as they were not fatal.

A little more wary of his opponent, Saurn brushed himself off and then took two steps closer to Shau-ling and then struck, launching daggers of molten rock flying toward Shau-ling. Taking the natural defensive measure, Shau-ling pulled on the flows of the Blaze and a shield of ice formed around him. However, in his weakened state, the shield did not have the power that it would have normally had. After several of the molten blades hit, the shield shattered, and the remaining daggers ripped through Shau-ling's body. The pain was almost an afterthought, as the blood began to flow from the myriad of wounds. As he watched Shau-ling fall, Saurn sensed victory was at hand. Suddenly Shau-ling's hand shot upward and tendrils of black energy shot out wrapped around Saurn's throat and began to choke the phase. A short blade of fire appeared in Saurn's hand the next moment and then cut the tendrils allowing the breath to get to Saurn's straining lungs. Saurn's next attack was vicious as bolts of lightning streaked across the distance and struck Shau-ling. The fallen body convulsed and writhed on the ground. Saurn kept up the intensity of the attack, and when he finally released the strings of energy in his mind, Shau-ling's fallen body smoked and his breathing was ragged and labored. Smiling to himself, Saurn created a sword of pure fire and slowly walked over to where Shau-ling's broken form lay. Perched over his former master, Saurn held the point of the blade at Shau-ling's throat, and then lifted the sword high, ready to end the cycle for good.

The blade came streaking down from above, but suddenly a roaring noise filled the room, and something struck Saurn from behind. As a defensive reflex, Saurn released the string of fire and the blazing sword winked out of existence, and Saurn was thrown clear of Shau-ling's prone form. Saurn landed on his stomach, the breath forcefully expelled from his lungs. As he rolled onto his back and gasped loudly for breath, he could not see for a moment. Slowly the darkness lightened in his field of vision, and then when the sparkling lights appeared, Saurn knew that he had been hit harder than he could have imagined. There was a bitter taste in his mouth, and as he pawed at his lips, he realized that several of his teeth had broken on impact with the ground, and only the sharp jagged pieces remained. It took only a thought to mend the damage to his mouth, and by that time, his vision had totally returned, and the sight that welcomed him was one that he half expected in the pit of his heart.

Jeroch had always been Shau-ling's favorite, and it had been Jeroch that saved Shau-ling from Kamen in the previous generation. Jeroch was always the first to Shau-ling's side, and always his most staunch supporter in the Council. And while Saurn had a score to settle with Shau-ling, his true and most profound hatred was reserved for the phase dubbed the First of the

Shadows. Jeroch stood like an island in a hurricane, defiant of everything that stood against him. He would endure every storm that attempted to destroy him, and prove wrong every dissenter that wished to wrest him from his place at the top of the Council.

"Only a coward strikes like this, Saurn," Jeroch said.

Jeroch had been quick to Shau-ling's side, and he helped the broken man back to his feet. However, as Saurn looked closer, he realized that Jeroch was supporting most of Shau-ling's weight, and the so-called god had very little life left in him. However, it would only take a matter of time before the cleansing fires of the Blaze would rejuvenate his wounded body. Jeroch might be able to hold Saurn off long enough for Shau-ling to recover enough strength to crush Saurn. Keeping Saurn in his full view, Jeroch moved up the dais, and sat Shau-ling gently down on his throne. Relieved of the burden, Jeroch let the twin blades of Order and Chaos form in his hands, and then stepped forward slowly, a new fire of hatred kindling deep within him. If Jeroch had to sacrifice his own life to protect his lord and master, he would gladly do so, as long as with his last breath he could watch the life crushed out of his rebellious brother.

"How could you turn your back on Shau-ling, again?" Jeroch asked vehemently. "Didn't you learn your lesson in the last generation that treachery of this kind only serves to end your existence and make us weaker? If we would have worked together as master had always intended us to, then perhaps we could have turned the tide and kept the forces of the Light from invading the palace and prolonging this war for another generation. But it was your selfishness that has brought us to this, and it is your stupidity that will keep this sick game in motion for yet another lifetime."

Saurn smiled and let twin flame blades form in his hands.

"I'm not the fool in this little circle, Jeroch, you are. Don't you see that Shau-ling is the one who is making this war longer and more involved because of the rules that he and his brother Emries have put on this little game? Shau-ling has always told us that the death of innocents is forbidden. We can only kill those that fight against us, or stand against our quest. If not for that rule, we could kill every last human on this planet with volcanic eruptions, floods, hurricanes, and all other types of natural disasters that are well within our power to create. Then the pathetic *Coromor* and his followers would be reduced to nothing and we wouldn't have to fight these meaningless wars. Shau-ling is protecting the mortals as surely as Emries is. Why? Are they not the enemy just as must as their perverse patron is? Are they not the very source of the damnation that descends upon us? Better they should all fall than live one more day knowing that they will be coming for us."

"You're wrong," Jeroch countered, "and you have missed the entire point of this war. Shau-ling is not using his influence to protect the humans. He is using his influence to protect nature, the very thing that would be disrupted were we to use the methods that you are suggesting. The humans are like cattle, leverage that Emries thinks holds sway. Believe me, Saurn, I know more about the nature of this war than you ever will. Humans may have been the source of this war, but the war has outgrown them."

Saurn shook his head and smiled wider.

"I see you have been deluded by his ramblings after all these lifetimes Jeroch," Saurn taunted. "You have always rallied behind everything that Shau-ling has told you, even when part of you knew that it was wrong, or that there was a better way. However, because you were made with so many defects within you, you are unable to break away from the controls that have been bred into you. You know that what I say is true Jeroch, and I wish that you could join me brother in the new world that the remaining phasia will create. But I know you are not able to see the bright tomorrow that will be built for us, and so I must strike you down as I have your master."

"He made us, Saurn," Jeroch said holding his blades aloft, "doesn't that mean anything to you? Don't you understand that he sees more than you could ever possibly understand? Don't you see that there is nothing on this world that escapes his notice?"

"He made you, Jeroch," Saurn answered with all the venom that he could manage. "The Great Dark One made me."

Saurn sprang forward, both blades thrusting forward, the heat of their orange peaks rising and falling with each second. Jeroch braced for the attack, and when the four blades met, there was a bright light and for a moment, time stopped. Beads of sweat hung motionless on each brow, and the battle for leverage was a stalemate with muscles tensing, veins bulging, and each man's strength pushed to the very edges of its capacity. Then time sped forward again, as the four swords danced in the dim room, striking one another with appropriate flashes of color. Neither man held the advantage as blow after blow was met with the otherworldly forces of the other's blades. Finally the two children of the god Shau-ling brought their four blades together again, leaning all their might and power into the single test of will and strength. Moments passed, each one straining against the other before finally Saurn faltered and was sent hard to the floor. However, Jeroch was unable to follow up, all of his strength and balance dedicated to the test of strength. In an effort to keep his opponent off-balance, Saurn hurled one of his fiery blades at the helpless Shau-ling, causing Jeroch to divert his attention. Jeroch was easily able to knock the blade away, but not before Saurn was back to his feet with blades in hand. Mercilessly, Saurn struck at Jeroch, leaving two longs burn marks across the older phase's back. Jeroch faltered, but recovered in time to block the blows that surely would have ended his life. The attack had accomplished exactly what Saurn wanted, Jeroch was wounded, and now Saurn easily had the advantage.

The two leaned into each other again, but pain began to move its way through Jeroch's body, betraying him to the increasing pressure of the deep wounds. Finally, Saurn's relentless assault began to make its way through Jeroch's defenses, and slash after slash landed on Jeroch's skin, leaving long black trails of charred flesh behind. Saurn was almost sorry he was using blades of fire because he wanted to see his longtime nemesis bleed. It would only be a matter of time before the methodical attacks that Saurn was employing would rob Jeroch of his life, and then he could move onto finish what was left of Shau-ling. But Jeroch would not give up easily. The wounded phase charged, but the attack was wild and out of control. Saurn sidestepped the assault and tripped his opponent sending him to the floor again. Jeroch roared in pain and rage, recovering his feet quickly and turning to face Saurn. If Jeroch had been in full control of his senses, he would have seen the mistake that he was about to make. But in anger he never could have seen what would occur. Jeroch charged again, and Saurn was ready. Instead of sidestepping the blow, as Jeroch had expected, Saurn dropped to a knee and thrust one of his blades forward. Jeroch had no time to react and found himself impaled through the chest with the still burning blade of flame.

For a moment, there was nothing. Then, as Saurn stood and admired his handiwork, Jeroch let loose a scream of pain that would echo throughout the palace. Finally, when it was done, the wounded phase fell to the floor. Saurn watched carefully for a moment and then quickly withdrew his blade from the dying form and turned toward the throne. Shau-ling was barely holding himself upright, and the look in the serpentine eyes was one of utter defeat. In his condition, there was no way that Shau-ling could stand up to any member of the phasia, let alone Saurn. Saurn took several steps forward and then stopped. There was something in the room, an energy that he had not felt in a long time. It wasn't until he saw the flash of light from the far corner of the room and the man that followed the flashing blades that his memory sparked with a name.

"Aerith Seth," Saurn said coldly. "It's been a long time."

Aerith nodded and continued his long methodical walk to the dais. It took only a matter of moments before Saurn and Aerith Seth stood face to face before Shau-ling, but unlike the last time that they were in this position, Shau-ling was the prisoner whose life hung in the balance.

"Almost a hundred years if memory serves."

"I made you what you were, Aerith," Saurn said, instantly on the offensive, "don't you ever forget that."

Aerith pulled back the hood of his cloak and fixed his eyes on the evil phase.

"You're right about that, Saurn," Aerith said nodding, "in more ways than one. You got me out of the mines of Quea, which you put me in if I remember correctly, and brought all the tutors and trainers to exercise my mind and my body. Then you sent me to Bryn, and she trained my powers. Finally, you brought me here to Shau-ling and let me be killed so that I could become the *Chosen One*. In both life and death, you had a hand in everything that I would become, and now I'm here to return the favor. But never forget that I am just as much a child of Shau-ling as you are. And more than that, I'm better than you are."

Aerith stuck the points of his blades into the ground and quickly unfastened the cloak from around his neck and let it fall to the ground. Then Aerith recovered his blades and relaxed back into a defensive stance. One blade was held above and perpendicular to his body while the other was held in front of him, parallel, ready to parry any blow that was launched at him.

"You seem to fight well with your two swords, Saurn," Aerith taunted, "let a master show you how it's done."

In a moment, it would begin, and while Saurn knew that he had an incredible amount of control for a member of the phasia, he did not know what kind of chance he had against Aerith Seth, the first *Chosen One*. For several seconds the two stood looking at one another. While in Seth's eyes there was a quiet confidence from hundreds of duels, Saurn's eyes showed the hint of hesitation and doubt that would be his undoing if he let them come into play during the duel. Then suddenly Aerith Seth lashed out, his strike precise and deadly. Saurn was only barely able to get his sword up in time to block the quick forward thrust, but his attention quickly focused back to the duel and Saurn knew that one more lapse in concentration like that could cost him his life. Saurn's strike was not strong nor quick, and Aerith easily parried and counter the blow, forcing Saurn back on the defensive again. The man who was more than mortal continued the assault, and time and time again his blades came crashing down on the blazing swords held by the phase Saurn. Saurn slashed wide and Aerith stepped into the attack, slashing at Saurn's chest. Saurn was able to counter with is other blade, but it was Aerith's stroke with his off-hand that severed Saurn's right arm at the shoulder, sending him reeling backwards, blood spewing in all directions. Moments later the blood would stop flowing from the wound, but Saurn knew he did not have enough time to grow a new arm before Aerith would come again. Seth pressed his advantage, with downward slashes raining down upon the weakened and crippled phase. Aerith seemed to become more powerful with each and every stroke, and with a hard slash of his blade, Saurn fell to his knees only to find the point of Aerith's other blade buried deep into his heart. Death was coming soon for Saurn, but the first *Chosen One* sped it along by twisting the blade and driving it completely through the body of the man he once regarded as a father and trusted ally.

Aerith withdrew the blade quickly and let the lifeless body of Saurn fall to the ground as his tainted blood began to spread along the chamber floor. Unceremoniously, Aerith cleaned his blades on the back of Saurn's robes and then moved to where Jeroch lay motionless. Pressing an ear to the fallen man's chest, Aerith could hear the faintest breaths dragging in and out of the one remaining good lung. The other lung had been punctured by Saurn's strike and would not inflate to hold breath. Drawing on the powers that remained open to him, Aerith began to knit some of the more serious damage done to Jeroch, but knew that healing him completely was a job that would not leave enough of Aerith's precious power left to finish what he had begun. As Jeroch began to stir, Aerith moved up the dais and stood before Shau-ling. The wounded man looked much better than he had only a few moments ago, and Aerith watched as several of the gaping wounds began to pull themselves together and knit the broken flesh.

"I'm glad I didn't wait longer," Aerith said smiling.

"Yours is not a face I expected to see ever again," Shau-ling replied weakly, "but I am grateful for your assistance."

Aerith nodded and then turned back toward Jeroch.

"I can't do much else for him, but I'm sure you know why."

Shau-ling closed his eyes and looked deeper into the man that had been the start of the cycle that was supposed to end with Shau-ling's demise at Emries' hand. He could see the faint traces of power that remained and the flickering candle of the man's life essence.

"So, you have given away your powers," Shau-ling said nodding. "Good for you."

Aerith cocked his head and looked back at Shau-ling.

"I wish I could do the same," the god hissed back to the unspoken question.

Aerith turned and walked back down the dais.

"How much longer do you have?" Shau-ling asked rising.

"Long enough to find out the truth."

Shau-ling laughed.

"Are you sure you want to know?"

Aerith stopped and turned back to face the man who had once ordered the end of his life as a mortal.

"I have to know why."

"Very well," Shau-ling responded. "I know the question that you wished to ask of me, and all I can tell you is that you need not look farther than those who are closest to the boy. The hooks within him are not mine, but they are of me."

"Thank you Halicon," Aerith said bowing. "You're place is with the Creator, that much is certain, but as for your creations, few should be redeemed."

Shau-ling nodded again.

"Perhaps it is time I found who was worthy enough to stand and fight against my enemies and who should be destroyed."

Aerith turned again.

"Perhaps."

As Aerith began to fade out of view, Shau-ling sighed and spoke once more.

"Your father would be so proud of the man you've become, Aerith. It pains me that I did not fight for you when I had the chance, but in my failure, you have shown me it is time to become once again what I was. Perhaps it is also time I began to embrace those of human kind who fight for the right purpose, but for the wrong side."

A Father's Pryde

The legend of Pike Rhuiden's Enforcers had been making its way around the world quickly thanks to the bards who circulated through the major common rooms of the major taverns in the largest kingdoms. One bard would hear the story and then add his own dramatic flair to it as he retold the story. Day after day it grew in both power and status. For many, appearances by the great and powerful Lord Pike Rhuiden were a sign that the forces of the Light would be victorious in the coming war, and even a glimpse at the warriors that he had gathered under his wing was a blessing. In many of the more remote cities in the world, who had been far away from both wars, the Enforcers were more real than the People of the Dragon, or even the Lion's Mane. In fact, the way that many of the bards described the Enforcers, they were greater than the People of the Dragon in truth. Every comparison possible was drawn between the two groups, and it seemed to many who heard the tales that the comparisons were intentional. First there was the obvious pairing of Zak Parthan and Gideon Viruci. Both were thieves from Alimidar and both were fast and agile. However, what shaded the public bias to Zak's favor was always because many of Gideon's most wondrous feats had been hidden away from public knowledge. Not a single bard in the world told the tale of how Gideon Viruci had stood toe to toe with Aryx Terian and fought him to a stalemate. Also untold was the fight against the monstrous Snags in the ruined city of

Sarmeel. But the last and most important task forgotten was how Gideon Viruci had given his own life to save that of the Lady Dragon Elwyne Tamerlane. Many of these things were forgotten because those who survived never spoke of them. Logan and Elwyne Ranthall hid away from the attention that had befallen them as heroes, Midarin Rice seemed to speak only of the man she had loved, Gwydeon Sandar, and Pike Rhuiden's stories mostly recounted the battles against the phase Taron and the ordeals that led to his eventual revenge. Such was the reason that only Pike Rhuiden, Gwydeon Sandar, and Logan Ranthall were known as the heroes that they were, but even then only Pike had been elevated to the legendary status that Cedric Binosear had enjoyed for so long. In fact, Cedric's mysterious disappearance from the court of Marcwell, which helped to lead to Pike's ascendance, only added more fuel to the growing fires of legend. But for all the stories and all the wonder that surrounded the group known throughout the world as the Enforcers, they were still mortal.

And such would have been the opinion of anyone who had seen the battered group of travelers that emerged from the ruined town of Lakestone and slowly made their way toward the neighboring kingdom of Scalla. Two horses, who seemed on the edge of death, slowly pulled along a wagon flanked by a man and a woman. One walked with a faint limp, while the other twirled his axe in his hands nervously. On the seat of the carriage sat two other men, one wounded and bleeding, and the other guiding the slow-moving steeds. In the back of the carriage were two wounded people, a man and a woman. Another man was in the back hovering over the wounded woman. Anyone who looked on would have just seen a group of tattered and torn people. Unless they looked at the wounded man on the seat of the wagon, they never would have had a clue as to the identity of the tattered caravan. They would never guess that the great and powerful Enforcers had been defeated so soundly.

Pike Rhuiden sat silently and held the dressing to his side, trying to contain the blood that was trying spurt from the old wound. But there was more wounding Pike Rhuiden than the pains of his flesh. His heart had been wrenched by the death of Elizabeth and by the hateful words of Rachel, two women that he had grown to care about very deeply. The word love rolled through is mind but he shut it away quickly. That was an emotion that Pike knew he was not allowed to have, and it had gotten him into too much trouble in the past and would eventually be his undoing. Lust was a much safer emotion, but it too seemed to betray him. Pike quickly shook away those thoughts and looked back at Turok. He hovered over Celina as though his very presence were keeping her alive. When Turok looked up and met Pike's eyes, Pike could feel the hatred and rage in the stare as though Turok wished it were Pike laying prone in the back of the wagon rather than the woman he loved. Pike pulled his gaze away quickly and then forced his eyes back to the road. The Kingdom of Scalla grew closer with every minute that passed, and soon enough Pike would have to contend with his old ally Jerrard Mystic.

* * * * * * * * * * *

As the wagon pulled through the streets of the city of Scalla, it seemed that everyone was aware of who the people were inside it. Several men walked with the wagon, helping to guide the tired beasts through the streets toward the palace. Pike by this time had managed to get off the wagon, leaving Ren to finish the chore of steering the lethargic and exhausted animals. Zak was quick to move to his lord's side, pushing away the throng of people and despite his limp kept pace with Pike as he moved through the crowd. It took only a few moments before soldiers made their way down the road to help keep the crowd at bay, and Pike pulled one of them aside and sent him running back toward the palace with a message for Lord Jerrard.

Once inside the gates of the city proper, Celina was carried by Turok into one of the many houses, and put to bed as the healer's began their work. Despite laying prone in the back of the wagon for the whole trip from Lakestone, Galen was up and about as soon as the wagon stopped moving, the wound in his chest nearly fully healed. Pike knew there was something strange about the blind man that had saved their lives in Lakestone, but he could sense no evil behind the powers he had at his disposal. After tending to Celina, the healers began to make their rounds through the members of the Enforcers, applying balms and salves to the many wounds that had only started to cover over with dried blood. Many of the healers expressed dismay at the mud and stagnate water that was caked into many of the wounds, but as a measure to stop the bleeding, there was little else that could have been done. The only member of the

Enforcers that refused treatment was Rachel. One of the healers drew too close to her and very nearly found his head severed from his body. Pike tried to calm the man afterward, but he kept shouting about ungrateful women and stormed off. Off in the distance Pike could see another group of soldiers coming down the lane, and Pike was sure that would be Jerrard and his family. He was shocked to see Midarin and the man he had known as Aryx Terian with them. Pike pulled *Fury* instantly and Zak, Ren, and Valin fell in behind him. Jerrard took several steps forward and held his hand up.

"There is no need for that," Jerrard said strongly, "there is a lot to explain, but there will be no more blood shed here. I think you have had enough of that, and there are plenty of battles left to be fought."

Considering his ally's words, Pike lowered the blade of his axe, but did not let it be put to rest in the loop on his belt. Pike looked Aryx dead in the eyes.

"You're in pretty good shape for a dead man," Pike said coolly.

"The same could be said for you," Midarin said stepping forward.

Pike had been ignoring Midarin's presence, but now looked at her and forced a smile. Then he suddenly realized that there was no one else with Midarin.

"Where's Nathaniel?"

Midarin was hoping that the subject wouldn't come up. She didn't know how Pike would react to the news that she was about to tell him, but she took a deep breath and then started talking.

"Nathaniel, Gwillim, Lissa, and Sabrina are with Wolf Ranthall on their way to Barer to meet with Grawn and Bryn about some mysterious things that have been happening in your absence."

Pike stood still for a moment and opened his mouth as if to speak. Softly, he shut his mouth and took a long deep breath. Midarin could tell that he was trying to maintain his composure, and that the battle being fought deep within him was one of the most difficult he had ever fought.

Pike had long been known for his passion where the story of his revenge over Eldar's death was concerned, but very few people knew that it was not passion or love that drove him to that. Midarin had seen Pike in the few hours after Eldar had been killed, and the sight would be forever burned in her mind of the raging Pike burying his axe over and over again into stack of wood that was on the back of the *Monster of the Deep*, the vessel that delivered them from the ambush of the phase Taron and the forces of the Shadow. Pike's anger built through the days that followed, and even after he took his revenge on Taron, the man still seemed to have a chip on his shoulder. The rage and hatred would turn to sorrow after Shau-ling was defeated, and the restlessness for war sat heavy on the man's shoulders. Finally Pike returned *Fury* to the loop in his belt and spoke.

"I should have known something like this would have happened," Pike said shaking his head. "If I would have been there, then Nathaniel and the others would be right here with us when we launch an offensive on Lakestone and level it. But now they're off on some foolish crusade that will keep them away from where their talents could be most useful."

Pike then locked his eyes back on Midarin.

"You and I had an arrangement, Midarin," Pike said firmly. "The deal was that you were supposed to get Wolf Ranthall here with the rest of the Enforcers and then we could use all of the powers we have at our disposal and take the fight to Shau-ling. With the pieces of the Order of the Sword that you promised to the Raven's Wing and the People of the Dragon we could hunt down the phasia one by one. Then we would be sure that no obstacles stood in our way when we were ready for the final battle with Shau-ling. Now things will be more difficult."

Midarin was ready to defend her decisions, but Rachel cut her off.

"Your little plan to dispose of the phasia has done wonders so far, Pike," Rachel said hopping down from her perch on the back of the wagon and rounding on the larger man. "So far we've met two members of the phasia, and while both of them are still alive, Evan, Meredith, and Elizabeth are dead, and Celina would have been if it weren't for Galen."

Many reacted to the news of the dead, but Pike paid no heed to the reactions around him and answered Rachel's challenge.

"I did what I had to do for this war to be successful. Lakestone was a logical choice for Shau-ling and the rest of his flunkies to re-emerge in. There has to be something there that is valuable to him, and the fact that both Taron and the new phase Stryfe were there is proof of that. If we go back there now, we stand a good chance of catching them unaware and finding whatever it is that has been hiding there all this time."

Rachel growled.

"You damn fool. Don't you realize the only reason that Taron was there in the first place was to lure you in and get you out of the way? They baited you in, and you fell for it because of the hatred you have in your heart for Taron and all of his brothers in the phasia."

Grabbing Pike by the arm, Rachel continued.

"Do you think it's just a coincidence that Taron was the phase that came back first? Do you think that Shau-ling and the phasia couldn't have hidden their movements in Lakestone if they really wanted to?"

Pike pulled away from Rachel's grasp.

"Don't be such a stubborn fool and see what is happening around you before more of your friends end up dead."

Pike grabbed for the handle of *Fury*, but Zak grabbed his arm and held it firm. There was very little strength left in Pike's body after the fight in Lakestone, and as he looked in Zak's eyes, he felt the rage within him begin to subside. He could not believe that for a moment he was prepared to cut Rachel in half for her quick and angry words, but he knew deep down that she was right, deep in the part of himself that hadn't been corrupted by hate and pain. A moment later, the blind man Galen gently made his way toward Pike, his staff gently rapping at the stones of the walkway with every step.

"Forgive me for intruding," the man said softly, "but a point seems to be missed here, and perhaps it is this piece of the puzzle that will shed new light on whether or not the trap was one of design or merely one of coincidence."

The way the man spoke was something that very few within ear shot were ready for. There was wisdom in his voice and a timbre that Aryx for one found very familiar. But what Aryx was thinking wasn't possible. They were all extinct.

"Nightwing," Valin added quickly.

The blind man nodded.

"Why would Nightwing have been there with the offer from Shau-ling if Shau-ling had not known Lord Rhuiden was there? And the way that Taron reacted to it was strange as well, considering he did not know that he was to be your prize. Perhaps we are seeing the fact that there are plans within plans in motion within the ranks of the phasia, and that one hand is not necessarily washing the other."

Zak scratched his head with the hilt of one of his daggers.

"The man's got a point, boss," he said quickly, "in his own confusing way."

"Yes," Ren added. "Taron had intended to attack us all along, and that is why he enlisted the services of that devil Stryfe. Shau-ling wanted only to extend his offer and then give you the head of Taron as an assurance that his offer was sincere."

Pike shook his head and took a step backward.

"I can't believe what I am hearing. Do you all honestly believe that Nightwing was telling the truth and that Shau-ling wanted to talk about a truce?"

At this, Jerrard interjected himself into the conversation.

"A truce?"

"Yes," Ren answered. "Shau-ling offered to talk of a truce between the phasia controlled kingdoms and the kingdoms of Marcwell and Trelon, and a halt to all aggressions. The terms were to be discussed in a private meeting between Lord Pike and Shau-ling."

"It was a trick," Pike said finally. "He just wanted to get me alone in his throne room so he could gut me and get me out of the way. Shau-ling's afraid of me because of all the things that I know and the forces that I am lining up to oppose the Shadow. He thinks that if he can get me out of the way that my forces will disband and there will be no one left to fight."

Galen was the first to respond.

"A spoke in a wheel, while an important part of the whole is only a part. Even without the use of one spoke, the whole may be diminished, but still functions."

Midarin stifled a laugh, knowing that the blind man, whoever he was, had just challenged Pike's ego. No matter how dangerous, angry, vengeful, amorous, or sorrowful Pike was, there was one constant in the man's emotional state, and that was pride. Without the ego and boastful pride, Pike was just another man. But that was a secret that was more closely guarded than the identity of Pike's mistresses.

"You speak in riddles good sir," Aryx said finally. "Might I have the pleasure of your name and where you come from?"

Ren turned to face Aryx.

"I can personally vouch for the sincerity of this man in the fight against the forces of the Shadow. I have watched him combat two members of the phasia, defeating each in hand to hand combat with no powers other than his fists and his staff."

"And I fear," the blind man added, "that I lost my best staff in the process."

"Lost?" Midarin asked.

"Shattered actually," Rachel added. "Over Taron's back."

Many could not help but laugh as the image entered their minds.

"But to answer your question, Lord Aryx Terian," the blind man continued, "my name is Galen Pryde."

Aryx stopped for a moment. The name was very familiar, but he could not place it.

"And how did you know who I am?"

Galen smiled.

"I have heard your voice before Lord Terian, a long time ago. You and my uncle spent several days together before he met his end, and he was very good friends with Lord Arathorn Geoffry."

Suddenly Aryx remembered.

"Galanax Pryde was your uncle?"

Galen nodded.

"The very same. It was a pity that he did not return from the war as Lord Arathorn and yourself did; I should have liked to hear stories from a source that I knew I could trust. As it was, for a very long time I had to rely only on the bards, and they are very long on detail and very short on fact much of the time."

Aryx was too busy sorting out details in his mind to find humor in Galen's description.

"I think I have seen you here before," Jerrard said finally.

"You have dear," Erika added. "At one of our dinners for Lady Elwyne after Logan's death, I recall a blind man who looked much like Galen here being led by a young girl to pay his respects for Elwyne's loss."

Galen bowed.

"I am flattered that you remember me, my lady. The young girl is my daughter Kaylea. She is staying here in the city while I was on pilgrimage to Lakestone to pay my respects to the fallen of the first great war of the prophecies."

Aryx smiled.

"Many of your people lost their lives there, didn't they?"

Galen's head bowed slightly and he sighed.

"Many great warriors found their end serving the *Coromor*, and it is a pity that only a handful survived the great purge. Shau-ling hunted us for the years that followed Lord Cedric's triumph. When Lord Logan finally was able to begin his journey into darkness, only one of us was able to heed the call. Talos served him well, but also was consumed by the quest so that others could live to fight on."

Midarin's face lit up with understanding.

"You are a member of the Moridon?"

Galen nodded.

"So Talos wasn't the last," Pike commented suddenly taking interest.

"No," Galen responded. "He was not the last of the Moridon, but he was one of the last with the full gift of the use of Moridon magic. There are only two of us that remain now that have any knowledge of the mystical arts that the men and women of the Moridon once practiced, and that is myself and my daughter, though I must admit, those powers are not what they could be."

"It is good to know that their wisdom has not left this world forever," Jerrard responded quickly. "Perhaps in time, the teaching of the Moridon will spread to a new group of people so that the wisdom and grace that they lived with day after day can be felt again."

Suddenly Galen became very serious.

"I am afraid that such a thing has happened Lord Aryx," the blind man said quickly. "However, it is not the wonderful event that you have portrayed. The teachings have been perverted into a weapon for warfare rather than a tool for peace."

"The Torch," Midarin chimed in.

Galen seemed unprepared for the fact that someone else knew about the Creator's Torch Society. But he knew that there were portions of the story that no one could know who was not of the blood of the Moridon.

"That is correct, Queen Midarin," Galen responded. "The Creator's Torch Society has brought back the teachings of the Moridon. At first, their motives were pure, and they lived the life that had been laid out for them by those teachings. That life was one of study and fulfillment by the beauty that was to be found in nature. When the Moridon were alive, the streams and woods of the world held a music that few could hear, because no one took the time to listen. We were the link between humanity and nature because humanity had stopped seeing nature as anything but a means to an end. Man saw trees for the wood that would build their houses. Streams for the water that they could bathe in and use to grind their grain into flour. They saw the animals as food for their meals and sport for their entertainment. While the way of nature is for one species to feed on another to live, with humans, there was no respect for the land or the very thing that gave them life. Whole forests burned for no reason, animals and plants destroyed because of the battles that took place amongst them. The Moridon tried to bridge that gap, but eventually they lost their way and became wrapped up in the wars of man. They found new teachings, and learned to use the power of the world around them to start fires, cause storms, and make the ground quake beneath them. That was when Aralias Imstra came.

"Many of the Moridon thought that he was the messenger from the Creator himself, and so they followed him, becoming the Hand of the Light. The Hand fought every visage of the forces of Shau-ling and championed the cause of the *Coromor*. Before long, every member of the Moridon across the world had dedicated their lives to protecting the *Coromor* and ensuring that he would make it to the throne room of Shau-ling and continue the prophecies until Shau-ling was defeated once and for all. And so when Cedric Binosear launched his assault on Lakestone, most of his army was of the Moridon, and it is said that Exeter Lake ran red for months with the blood of the fallen Moridon. Many believed that this war was sanctioned when one of the Moridon was blessed with the power of the *Erieal* and drawn to the Lord Lion's side."

Aryx nodded slowly.

"I have never seen so much blood in my life then after the battle in those streets. Men and monster fell by the thousands, and it seemed as though nothing would ever wash away the smell of death or the stains of blood."

"And even though the Moridon had suffered losses that would have wiped out whole kingdoms," Galen continued, "the defense of the *Coromor* was still the only thought on our minds. We would kill and die at the *Coromor*'s command, and no threat from the forces of the Shadow would be strong enough to keep us from our task. But then when the phasia came again, they did not strike as they had with Lakestone. They came slower and more deviously. They took their time, fifteen years in fact, to hunt down and kill every one of us that they could find. Among those that survived the slaughter, it would be known as the Purge. They thought that Shau-ling killed those who were impure and not fit to serve the second *Coromor*. But when finally there were only three of us left, the hope was beginning to dwindle, and the thirst for phasia blood was beginning to wane."

Galen hesitated, the tale tasting bitter in his mouth.

"After Talos died, I felt as though I had woken from a long slumber. There was no more desire in me to fight, and I did not care that the *Coromor* would come again. All I wanted was to return to the peace that the Moridon once loved more than their lives. And so, my daughter and I began to travel."

A question formed in Midarin's mind, but before she could make it known, Galen answered it.

"I say that Kaylea is my daughter, but in reality she was a baby when her parents were killed in the Purge. I took her as my own and have raised her as my daughter ever since. Together we have wandered the land and visited the sites that we had only heard about in stories. We have been to the monument to the fallen in Frontier, and the grave of Eldar Merin in Kandor, Logan's Wood, the ruins of the *Inn of Good Faith*, and the *Wandering Maiden* in Illimar. Finally I made my pilgrimage back to where it all began for the Moridon in the southern fields near Rana and Rama, and it was there that I learned of the new group of men and women, the Creator's Torch Society.

"They spoke the words of the righteous Moridon, and their leader, a man named Dei, seemed as though he had been touched by the spirit of the Creator himself. But then his murder shook the group to it very foundation and I felt the change come over them, as it had over the Moridon all those years ago. They revoked their love of peace and harmony with nature and began to learn the teachings of Moridon magic and the calling of fire and wind. Before long they began to call themselves the new Hand of the Light was their leader Seraphina Masile acting as though she were Aralias Imstra incarnate. But for a long time, they were only words on the wind. However, before I made my way here, I learned that they had come under the command of a new leader. One who said he would lead them to the land in which the battles would be fought again, and that he would take them to their destiny against the forces of Shau-ling. But first he would have to strike down all of the old corrupted souls who stood on the path of the righteous. He would kill the man whom he called father so that he could sit on the throne of Marcwell and lead his people to their rightful place as the People of the Ram."

Pike stood silent knowing that his son Duncan was coming for him. Suddenly a horn blast hit the air and troops began to scurry in all directions. Jerrard pulled his polished black blade, a final gift from his departed father, from the scabbard on his hip and called to a soldier in one of the watch towers.

"What is it?"

"My lord," the soldier answered, "a force is approaching from the west. Their banners are white with a black device upon it."

"The Torch," Midarin and Aryx said at nearly the same time.

"So," Pike said finally, "Duncan is coming to claim his throne. Well, I intend to give the lad a coronation his followers will never forget."

CHAPTER 38

Epilogue

Shades of Gray

Creator's Calendar Year 1205; Dark Mirror

Words have power. Some words can hurt, and others can heal. The tender words of a lover late in the night can help soothe a troubled mind into the peace of sleep, while the angry words of that same lover can rip at the fabric of security and plague the mind through the silent hours. Logan Ranthall's declaration had several effects at the same time. Rael, Trece, and Caris felt a surge of power and pride deep within them, one that was decidedly unexpected, and whatever unconscious doubt they had about their new ally was washed away. On the other side of the conflict, the Dark Riders now found themselves against three full members of the Brotherhood of Phasia, and one man who could wield as much if not more power than any phase, even Jeroch. In the best of times, the *Chosen One* of the prophecies was not to be trifled with, and there were few on the side of the forces of the Light who had as much experience in fighting against the forces of the Shadow as Logan Ranthall. Gwydeon Sandar was perhaps more accomplished, but he did what he did with steel and guile. Logan had tasted power, the power that was denied a mortal like Gwydeon, and over the years necessity had honed Logan into a weapon. Now that weapon was poised to serve a new purpose.

Logan himself felt an effect from his words, and as he drew the powers of the Blaze into himself and prepared for combat, he could feel a pride and power that had not been in him since the early days of his war against Shau-ling. Everything was innocent then, but as he and his friends traveled father down the perverted road that Emries had laid out for them, they lost a bit of themselves. Now that he understood more about the nature of things, his skin crawled from the filth that he had endured under the thumb of a patron who saw him as nothing more than an insect. All the suffering and death that they had witnessed in Aradon, Illimar, Rana, Rama, Sador, Trelon, Taren, Marcwell, Frontier, Brea….it was all meaningless. So many of his friends had died, and for nothing. His brother, the woman he loved, friends that he had known since childhood; snuffed out not in heroic adherence to an ideal, but as monuments to greed and fanaticism. As the years passed after the war, the feeling of dread and incompleteness seemed to grow. Logan had allowed himself to wallow in self-pity and self-destructive anger until finally it was too much for him and he would either have to fall on his sword or take the fight to those who had caused him so much pain. But the more he lashed out at the forces of the Shadow trying to numb the pain of loss, the more inhuman he felt. Emries had trapped him into the cycle of killing, and Logan would fight over and over again until Shau-ling was dead or until he himself was struck down. Gwydeon, Midarin, and Gideon all were destined for the same fate. They were trapped just as surely as Logan was, but now Logan had broken the cycle because of his tainted blood, and because of the Elder's intervention. The scales had dropped away from his eyes long enough for him to be able to catch a glimpse of the truth. Gideon too had the possibility of breaking free of the trap since he also had phasia blood flowing through his veins. Gwydeon and Midarin on the other hand had no reason to leave the path that they were on. Pike seemed to be the only one who had a real chance to avoid the trap of pain. He had been away from the world for so long in his prison beneath the Island of Mist that he had the ability to look at the war with fresh eyes. Perhaps Emries would be wrong, and regardless of the side that Logan chose to fight on, his friends would be there standing beside him instead of against him.

The Flame took a step forward and waited. The wisdom of the living force of the Blaze rolled through its mind and filled it with doubt about the upcoming battle. When Kamen was the Flame, he could have stood toe to toe with three members of the phasia and won, but that would have been deep in the heart of Shau-ling's palace, in the Hall of Terrors near the core of the Blaze itself. Out here in the wild, the phasia had the advantage even against Kamen's great power. However, the Flame was no longer Kamen, it was but an echo of the great power that was one of the first children of Shau-ling. Though the Flame knew that this battle could not be won, however, Draven had ordered the strike against Rael and Trece, and the Flame was bound to his master's orders. Holocaust and Shadow began to move to either side of the massed group of phasia. In a moment it would begin, and if any member of the Dark Riders would survive, it would be by cunning rather than by sheer power.

Rael and Trece stood back to back, watching the floating skull and the sickening distorted movements of the walking shadow move to their flanks. Logan had squared off against the Flame, and Caris seemed to be waiting for the first blow to be struck before she determined where her powers would best serve the group. So many of the phasia fighting together against a common enemy was unusual, so their tactics were not practiced. Rael and Trece knew each other more intimately than should have been possible, but Logan and Caris would be a step slower to react to their tactics. The Dark Riders were designed to work together, to cover each other's weaknesses and to accentuate each other's strengths. Even if the Dark Riders could not match the raw power that their opponents brought to the battlefield, they could mask the deficit of power with tactics and teamwork. Rael took the hand of his sister and held it tightly, feeling her powers flow through him. From their birth, Rael and Trece had a connection that no other members of the phasia shared or could even comprehend. The two shared one power, and one focus. They knew what the other was thinking at all times, and they felt each other's thoughts. But it was more than that. If a person has a thought, it fills their mind, however, with Rael and Trece, there were two tracks of thought that constantly filled their minds. The first track was that of their own thoughts. The second track was the thoughts of their sibling. So, no matter where they were or how far they were apart, they were always together in thought. However, the same was not true for their powers. When Rael and Trece found themselves separated, there was an emptiness within them, like a piece was missing. Each also found that while apart they could not draw as deeply on the powers of the Blaze. Together though, they were as formidable as Jeroch or Draven in battle. Rael quickly released Trece's hand, but felt the connection of power continue throughout his body; his pulse quickening and the powers of the Blaze filling him to nearly overflowing. Logan too was bathed in the green glow of the Blaze, and Rael could see that he was filling the blade of the Dragon Sword with the dangerous and potent power.

The first bolt of power came from Holocaust. Both of the creature's hands raised suddenly, and sprays of fire sped at the assemblage of phasia. Rael and Trece dove to the ground, and Caris jumped backward, barely escaping the blast. Logan took the attack as his opportunity to strike and he charged forward at the towering Flame. One of the bolts of fire barely grazed Logan's shoulder, but he shrugged it off as though it hadn't happened. As soon as Rael hit the ground, he rolled and jumped back to his feet. Just then, something slammed into his back, sending him sprawling back to the ground. Suddenly his mind was filled with confusion and pain, a horribly distorted sound filling his ears and jumbling his senses. Shadow had picked his moment to attack, and had it not been for the blast of pure Order from Trece that sent Shadow jumping clear, Rael could have easily found himself watching the rest of the battle from the Other Side. Caris watched as Holocaust changed positions again and readied to launch another assault at Rael and Trece. Taking careful aim, Caris stamped her heel into the ground, sending a crack running through the ground toward the larger creature. Suddenly the crack opened wide, and Holocaust was unable to get out of the way. In a matter of seconds, the ground had swallowed him, sending the monster falling into a deep abyss. The next moment, Caris clenched her fist and the fissure closed, sealing Holocaust's fate.

"Too easy," she said under her breath and smoothing her dress.

* * * * * * * * * * * *

Logan was taking the fight to the Flame. Not intimidated by the power of his opponent, the Flame was launching assault after assault against the mortal. Beams of fire and pure Blaze energy erupted from the swirling mass that was the Flame's body. Logan ducked and dodged, leaping through every attack, trying to get close enough to strike a blow. Finally, the Flame was in range of the Blaze charged Dragon Sword. Logan swung with all his might, propelling himself past his huge opponent and burying the entire length of the blade into the massive girth. The blow carried Logan behind the Flame, and when Logan withdrew his blade from the body of his opponent, laughter filled the air.

"You fool," the Flame taunted. "I am forged with the power of the Blaze. Do you believe that your blade would be enough to harm me?"

An arm appeared from the swirling mass the next moment and struck Logan hard in the back. A burning sensation filled Logan, and reflexively he ripped the shirt over his head and sent the still burning fabric to the ground. Caris winced when she saw the long black mark on Logan's back, and as another strike flew from somewhere deep in the mass that was the Flame, Logan dove and rolled, coming up on his knee. With a thought, Logan began to channel the flows of Water into the Flame, trying to drop the temperature of the mass to the freezing point. Sensing the tactic, the Flame focused all of its power internally, and an eruption flared from inside of it. Caris looked on in horror as the Flame grew to twice its normal size.

* * * * * * * * * * * *

Rael and Trece kept pace with the quickly moving form of Shadow. It was moving with incredible speed, and fled deeper into the forest with each leap and bound. Suddenly, Shadow disappeared. Rael stopped dead in his tracks, and he could feel Trece's breath on his neck as the two waited for their prey to reappear. Pain hit Rael the next moment as a long wide gash opened in his forearm. Wincing in pain, Rael covered the wound with his hand. Trece saw the trails of Shadow's movements seconds later, her mind only beginning to interpret what she had seen. Again and again Shadow attacked, but his speed was such that neither member of the phasia could hope to dodge or counter the vicious assaults. Several wounds opened on Rael's chest, and Trece sported two long slashes, one on each of her cheeks. Rael turned and grabbed both of Trece's hands and began to channel all of his powers into her. Trece could feel the blood in her veins pump faster and it seemed that everything around her began to stop. Leaves that were being buffeted in the soft breeze now looked as though they were not moving at all. Even the wind stood still. Then suddenly Trece realized that Rael was using all of his powers to accelerate Trece to Shadow's level of speed. If he had miscalculated, it could have meant the death of both of them, but if the tactic proved successful, it would gain them one shot to even the odds. Off in the distance Trece saw something move, and it could have only been Shadow. There was no way that he could have realized what it was that Rael had done. Trece tried to stay as still as possible, not to alert Shadow that his advantage had been taken away.

Out of the corner of her eye, Trece saw the black clad form of Shadow running towards them. He was much easier to look at now that the after-images were no longer there. In his hands, he was wielding two long daggers, and they were both stained with blood. Just as he started to come into range, Trece let the powers of the Blaze fill her. She could see the sly smile on the face of Shadow, but the smile turned to a look of shock when suddenly Trece moved as fast as he did, bringing her hands up and loosing a stream of pure green flame. The blast of Blaze energy caught the shocked Dark Rider full in the chest. However, because of the incredible speed and force of the blast, it ripped right through the frail body and left a hole where the creature's chest had been. All that Rael saw in the next moment was Shadow appear out of thin air, nearly ripped in two. Trece stepped away from Rael's grasp the next moment and walked over quickly to examine the fallen form.

"Swift rain is little rain," she said looking back at her slightly older brother. The next moment an explosion echoed through the forest and the twin's eyes met, fear hitting their hearts. Together they ran back toward the clearing where they had left Logan and Caris facing off with the Flame.

* * * * * * * * * * * *

As the Flame grew in size, Logan back-peddled to keep from being consumed by the moving wall of Blaze power. He had made a mistake thinking that he could freeze the Flame, but the thought had been a good one at the time. What he had severely underestimated was the sheer volume of power at the Flame's disposal. Another hulking arm burst from within the cataclysmic mass of fire and hit Logan square in the chest, throwing him backwards. Logan's momentum was only barely stopped by a tree, and as he slumped to the ground, Logan felt the pain. Agony rocketed from his back, through his legs and arms, robbing all ability to move. The force of the impact had shattered the trunk of the tree, throwing shards of wood into the air like snow on a harsh winter morning. The top of the tree landed hundreds of feet away and the stump and roots had been dislodged from the firmly packed ground. Caris was about to run to Logan's aid when the ground under her feet began to rumble and shake.

Just then, the ground cracked opened like an egg shell and Holocaust returned to the battlefield. The beast's counterattack was launched moments later as a thick stream of liquid fire burst from Holocaust's hands and sped toward Caris. The green-clad phase dove out of the way, but found herself completely cut off from the prone form of Logan Ranthall. The Flame however was well within range to deal with the man who called himself Lord Phoenix. Sensing the end of the conflict was near, the Flame took hold of the man's leg, searing the flesh deeply and drawing screams of agony from the man even in his unconscious state. It took only a matter of seconds for the Flame to pull Logan toward it, and as Caris looked on in horror, the Flame engulfed Logan.

Rael and Trece returned to the scene of battle just in time to see the Flame's final attack on Logan, and as the last of the man disappeared in the whirling mass, the twin phasia began to send streams of Order and Chaos deep into the growing form. However, they had not seen Holocaust, and his stream of fire would have claimed both of them had it not been for the wall of rock summoned by Caris that thrust itself out of the ground at the last second. Despite being saved from the assault, Rael and Trece scattered, and changed the focus of their attention to Holocaust. Emerging from behind the wall of rock, Rael sent small bubbles of Chaos energy flooding the area that Holocaust had been in, flushing him out toward where Trece waited. When Holocaust was in position, Trece sent daggers of Order toward him. However, Holocaust was ready for an assault, and he turned to dodge the attack. Caris had other plans. The wall of rock that greeted Holocaust shocked him enough that he staggered back into Trece's attack. Daggers of Order ripped through the armor and Holocaust collapsed to the ground. The floating skull rolled away from the broken armor, the light going out of the eye sockets marking then end of the monstrous creature.

The three phasia turned their attention to the Flame the next moment, the churning mass of flame resonating with an incredible amount of power. Something was wrong. The Flame should have been lashing out at them and trying to destroy them with all of that incredible power. As Caris looked deep into her mind and found the power of the Blaze, she saw that there was no way the Flame could contain all the power that it was drawing upon. Something was feeding him power. As she looked deeper, she saw that Logan was using himself as a conduit to the powers of the Blaze.

Though his direct attempts to combat the creature had met with failure the impertinent mortal was nothing if not persistent.

"Rael, Trece," Caris called out, "pour every bit of the Blaze that you can manage into the Flame."

Rael looked hard at Caris.

"But you know that will make him stronger," he said strongly.

Caris nodded and flashed a wicked smile. As if catching the meaning, Rael opened himself to the full power of the Blaze and let the stream of green flame fly toward the fiery colossus. Caris's beam of energy joined Rael's the next moment, as did Trece's. For several seconds nothing happened. Then the hulking red giant began to change color. The Flame became darker and more menacing, its form shifting and bloating as it began to grow once again. Caris could feel the power filling her, but she was no longer channeling it. It felt as though someone or something else was simply using her as a means to get at the power. Caris felt the powers of the Blaze fill her as it never had before, with a strength and purity that bordered somewhere between bliss and agony. Floating in the sweet sensations, Caris almost did not feel the fear and worry that plagued the back of her mind. She knew that drawing this deeply could lead to death. Suddenly the flow was severed and her senses returned. Long ago Caris had set up defenses within her mind that would never allow her to draw upon the Blaze to the point where her body began to erode. However, as she looked deep into her mind, Caris realized that Rael and Trece were still pouring more and more power into the Flame. She could have cried out and warned them of the danger, but in the state of utter rapture that held them, they would never listen to her. Something else would have to jar them away. Caris let the Blaze fill her again, and reached out with her mind to the twin phasia.

Unlike most minds, Caris had a hard time finding a steady stream of thoughts that she could enter. Everything was a jumbled mass. It seemed as though there were four minds at work instead of two. Finding the challenge too daunting even for her powers, Caris concentrated on Trece first, knowing that the grudge that the redhead held against her would assist in pulling her away. However, upon entering Trece's mind, again Caris was confused by the conflicting tracks of thought and emotion. Suddenly she was met by the figures of both Rael and Trece. It was then that she guessed the truth. Rael and Trece shared a consciousness, so in talking to one, she was talking to both.

"You have to let go," Caris said into their minds.

"Why?" Both voices asked in unison. "This is what you wanted us to do."

"If you draw any deeper you'll die," Caris answered.

Trece's form stepped forward, but still both voices spoke.

"We are not drawing on the Blaze, it is being drawn through us."

Caris nodded.

"But it will still kill you. Shut yourselves off from it."

Suddenly Caris found herself expelled from their minds. Then, showing an amazing amount of control, the twins used their powers to break the other away from the control that had been exerted on them. Caris doubted that she would be able to get past their mental defenses now that they were no longer drawing so deeply on the Blaze. As Caris turned her attention back to the Flame, she realized that it was no longer paying attention to them, and was merely standing there, absorbing all the power that it could. Rael and Trece join Caris a moment later and as Trece looked up at the massive creature she spoke softly.

"How can it contain so much of the Blaze?"

Caris shook her head and looked deeply into the mass of fire before her. She saw the body of Logan Ranthall in the center of the mass, Dragon Sword still in hand. Something was different though. Logan's eyes were open, and he was once again conscious. As she looked deeper, she saw the truth. At the start, the Flame had been exerting all of its power and using Logan as a conduit to give it the energy that it needed to crush all of the opponents that stood before it. The Flame was intelligent enough to know that Logan's powers would be the perfect harness to hold the raging torrents of Blaze energy so that the Flame could draw on them without fear of harming itself. Caris had tried to overload the Flame with the power of three full members of the Brotherhood, and while that may have succeeded, it also caused something to change inside of Logan. He now was focusing all of his powers as the *Chosen One* of the prophecies to contain the incredible amount of power around him. It seemed that all of the power housed inside the body of the Flame was under his command, and he was slowly drawing it into himself.

"You fool!" Caris shouted into the pulsing flames. "You'll kill yourself!"

Logan was too far down the path that he had chosen to walk to turn back now. His long road as a mortal had come to an end, and in the cleansing fires of the Blaze he would be born again. Caris could only look on in horror as every bit of Blaze energy moved from the hulking mass of the Flame into the frail mortal body. But as she watched, Caris began to see the truth and potential of what Logan was trying to do. While the Blaze began to fill him and saturate every pore, duct, and cell, Logan concentrated on the powers that he had been blessed with by Aerith Seth. While any mortal or member of the phasia for that matter would have been burned to a cinder or ripped asunder by that amount of power, the black threads of Aerith Seth's mantle held Logan's body together and tried to contain that which only Shau-ling had been able to master. But the change that began to occur was unlike anything that Caris could have imagined. Logan Ranthall died. She listened to the tortured beating of the weakened pump, could feel the agony as it dragged the blood through the burning muscles and desperately tried to keep the whole alive. But no matter how much it tried, the effort was futile, and suddenly, it stopped. No breath filled the lungs, and no blood moved through the smallest veins.

The lifeless body floated in the fires of the Blaze, energy still pouring into the mortal's shell. Blood and tissue were bathed and bound by the life and death-giving powers that held him, and soon, a faint beat resounded in Logan's chest. Caris held her breath for a moment, waiting for another to follow, and it did. It was a familiar sound. There was a slow, cold, calculated rhythm. No matter the exertion, no matter the trial, no matter the emotion, the rhythm never changed. It was the first sound that a phase heard upon his birth, and it was the last sound that rang in his ears when he died in each lifetime. The smile on Caris' lips defied the thoughts in her mind. This mortal had done the one thing that only Shau-ling should have been capable of, but then with the amount of Blaze energy that was being used, Shau-ling could not have been ignorant. It took only a matter of moments before Logan began to move again, and when he had finally come back to his senses, the powers of the Blaze filled him again, healing the wounds from old injuries and giving him the sight that was a blessing to all phasia. He now knew what all phasia knew, and the hundreds of lifetimes that the Blaze had existed were now open to the mind of the man who had been mortal only a few moments ago.

Logan righted himself in the mass of fire and motion, and with a thought, sent waves of power rippling through the Flame. The massive creature convulsed and cried out in a primal roar that would echo for miles. Suddenly the colossal beast exploded into thousands of pieces. Caris had to shield her eyes from the explosion, but when she looked back, Logan was hovering there in mid-air, in nearly the same position he had been only moments earlier. Softly Logan lowered himself to the ground, and when his eyes met Caris' again, he smiled.

"You were saying something, sister?"

The statement was a simple one, but the words spoke volumes. Logan Ranthall was now a member of the phasia as much Caris or any of the others. The Blaze flowed through his veins as prominently as his own blood, and the longer he was out in the world, the more he would feel the need to go to the Council and replenish his strength from the source.

"I believe I called you a damn fool."

Logan smiled and laughed.

"It was something that had to be done, Caris. As long as I was somewhere between mortal and phase, there was no way that either side would be able to accept me, and there was no way that I could help win the war for Shau-ling and put an end to Emries. Now, even though they may resent me and wish me dead, the other phasia have to accept me as part of the Council, and the Jeresei and Shadowwalkers will take my orders."

"You are last-born now, Lord Phoenix," Caris answered. "Don't think acceptance comes that easily."

Rael added his voice to the conversation.

"And you are also part of the War for Ascension, and Draven will be looking to use you as a stepping stone on his road to Jeroch and leadership of the Council."

"The War for Ascension is the last of my worries Rael," Logan answered, "but I would be glad to take our friend Draven on and pay him back for our little duel in Trelon. Now though we have bigger fish to fry. I'm sure the entire Order of the Sword saw that explosion and Nathaniel definitely knows we're here, but we have no choice but to continue and take the fight to him."

"I'm with you Logan," Caris added.

"Good," Logan said taking her hand. "I'm going to need all the help I can get. But whatever you do, try to keep the killing down to a minimum. If we can get Nathaniel out of the way, I may be able to convince Midarin that I haven't lost my mind. We need all the allies that we can get, because I don't expect Emries to just roll over and die."

Trece looked around and suddenly realized that Holocaust was gone.

"Did anyone feel a portal?" she asked quickly.

"I wouldn't worry about that one," Rael said trying to calm his sister. "All it will do is go back to Draven and tell him what had happened here. It was bound to happen sooner or later, but I have a feeling that Draven has other matters that he has to worry about. There are many of us trying to kill him from both the phasia and the mortals, and if he gets his wish and crosses swords with Jeroch, I doubt we will have to worry about him after that."

Trece smiled.

"I still think we should have finished him when we had the chance."

Logan put his hand on Trece's shoulder.

"We'll get him soon enough. But right now we should focus on Nathaniel."

Trece nodded, drew her sword, and followed Logan, Caris, and her brother Rael into the palace of Sador. Their meeting with Nathaniel Sandar would most likely be a bloody one, but as she thought of the added power of Logan Ranthall in the ranks of the phasia, Trece could not help but feel that there was a new urgency to win the war for Shau-ling. The proof was there, as four members of the phasia were working together for a common goal. Somewhere Shau-ling would be smiling, as this was what he had wanted all along. Who would have thought that it would have taken a mortal to teach them how to make it happen?

Appendicies

Dramatis Personae

Cedric Binosear
The Lord Lion
First *Coromor* of the Prophecies
Twin Brother of Anabel Binosear
Son of Aerith Seth

Anabel Binosear
Sister of Cedric Binosear
Mother of Cairyn Binosear
Murdered by Aldridge Farran
Daughter of Aerith Seth

Arathorn Geoffry
Earth *Erieal* of the First Generation of
the Prophecies
Brother of Diana Geoffry Terian

Mailock
Member of the Moridon Tribe
Water *Erieal* of the First Generation
of the Prophecies

Aryx Terian
White Lightning
Fire *Erieal* of the First Generation of
the Prophecies
Husband of Diana Geoffry Terian
Former Host of Nightwing

Diana Terian Geoffry
Wind *Erieal* of the First Generation of
the Prophecies
Sister of Arathorn Geoffry
Wife of Aryx Terian
Mother of Lissa Terian

Arin Ranthall
First *Chosen One* of the Prophecies
Husband of Victoria Rhuiden
Father of Logan Ranthall
Father of Korrd Ranthall

Victoria Rhuiden
Sister of Tam Rhuiden
Wife of Arin Ranthall
Mother of Logan Ranthall

Logan Ranthall
The Lord Dragon
Second *Chosen One* of the Prophecies
Brother of Korrd Ranthall
First Cousin of Pike Rhuiden
Husband of Elwyne Tamerlane
Ranthall
Father of Wolf Ranthall

Elwyne Tamerlane Ranthall
Sister of David Tamerlane
Wife of Logan Ranthall
Mother of Wolf Ranthall

Korrd Ranthall
Second *Coromor* of the Prophecies
Brother of Logan Ranthall
Son of Arin Ranthall and Ellis
Chandara
Father of Gwillim Sandar

Pike Rhuiden
Water *Erieal* of the Second
Generation of the Prophecies
Son of Tam Rhuiden
Best Friend of Talon Aielin
First Cousin of Logan Ranthall
Eldar Merin's Former Husband
Lord of Kandor, Marcwell, and
Trelon
Husband of Cairyn Binosear
Father of Duncan Rhuiden and
Sabrina Binosear

Gwydeon Sandar
Son of Torris Sandar
Brother of Bella Sandar
Husband of Midarin Rice Sandar
Father of Nathaniel Sandar
Killed in the Battle of the Hall of
Terrors by Jeroch Yetre

Eldar Merin
Daughter of Alfred and Ariel Merin
Best Friend of Elwyne Tamerlane
Wife of Pike Rhuiden
Killed by Taron Steen at the Battle of
Taren

Emries
The First *Coromor*

Talon Aielin
Wind *Erieal* of the Second
Generation of the Prophecies
Best Friend of Pike Rhuiden
Killed during battle with Shau-ling

Arin Domae
Fire *Erieal* of the Second Generation
of the Prophecies
Former Soldier of the Army of Brea
Killed during Battle of the Hall of
Terrors

David Tamerlane
Brother of Elwyne Tamerlane
Killed in destruction of Aradon

Lane Toridon
Apprentice Magician
Killed by Taron Steen during battle of
Taren

Tam Rhuiden
Aradon City Council Member
Brother of Victoria Rhuiden
Father of Pike Rhuiden

Torris Sandar
Aradon City Council Member
Father of Gwydeon Sandar
Father of Bella Sandar

Gideon Viruci
Earth *Erieal* of the Second Generation
of the Prophecies
Killed in Battle with Shau-ling

Midarin Rice
Queen of the Kingdom of Brea
Wife of Gwydeon Sandar
Mother of Nathaniel Sandar
Mother of Liette Forer

Aerith Seth
General of the Hand of the Light
General of the Army of the Fox
The First *Chosen One*

Cairyn Binosear
Daughter of Anabel Binosear
Niece of Cedric Binosear
Queen of the Kingdoms of Kandor,
Trelon, and Marcwell
Wife of Pike Rhuiden
Mother of Duncan Rhuiden and
Sabrina Binosear

Leane Torne
General in the Army of Rama
Former Member of the Army of Brea

Jerrard Mystic
Lord of the Kingdom of Scalla
Son of Basille Mystic
Husband of Erika Belnosian

Erika Belnosian Mystic
Wife of Jerrard Mystic

Sabrina Binosear
Third *Chosen One* of the Prophecies
Sister of Duncan Rhuiden
Daughter of Pike Rhuiden and Cairyn
Binosear

Duncan Rhuiden
Heir to the Kingdom of Marcwell
Brother of Sabrina Binosear
Son of Pike Rhuiden and Cairyn
Binosear

Lissa Terian
Fire *Erieal* of the Third Generation of
the Prophecies
Daughter of Aryx and Diana Terian
Adopted Daughter of Pike Rhuiden
and Cairyn Binosear

Liette Forer
Daughter of Midarin Rice
Sister of Nathaniel Sandar

Nathaniel Sandar
The Lord Ram
Third *Coromor* of the Prophecies
Son of Gwydeon Sandar and Midarin
Rice
Brother of Liette Forer

Gwillim Sandar
Earth *Erieal* of the Third Generation
of the Prophecies
Son of Korrd Ranthall and Gabrielle
Crill
Adopted Son of Midarin Rice

Wolf Ranthall
Son of Logan Ranthall and Elwyne
Tamerlane Ranthall

Storm Mystic
Son of Jerrard and Erika Mystic
Water *Erieal* of the Third Generation
of the Prophecies

Taya Mystic
Daughter of Jerrard and Erika Mystic

Taya Viruci
Daughter of Gideon Viruci and Erika
Belnosian
Dark Mirror World

Turok Korven
Member of the Enforcers

Celina Veshaw
Member of the Enforcers

Ren Dalin
Member of the Enforcers

Zak Parthan
Member of the Enforcers

Valin Kren
Member of the Enforcers

Rachel Core
Member of the Enforcers

Elizabeth Merin
Member of the Enforcers

Meredith Heron
Member of the Enforcers

Evan Sinn
Member of the Enforcers
Former Lord of Kandor
Inheritor of Aerith Seth's power

Jared Vale
Son of Caris Vale and Cedric
Binosear

Shau-ling
Master of the Shadows
Father of the Phasia

Jeroch Yetre
The Lord Shadow
First Born of the Phasia
Father of Hawk Yetre

Bryn Aplee
The Lady Fox
Member of the Brotherhood of Phasia
Former Lover of Aerith Seth
Wife of Grawn Aplee
Mother of Gideon Viruci

Ellis Chandara
The Lady Leopard
Member of the Brotherhood of Phasia
Mother of Korrd Ranthall

Grawn Aplee
The Lord Shark
Member of the Brotherhood of Phasia
Husband of Bryn Aplee

Warron Ysamaran
The Lord Boar
Member of the Brotherhood of Phasia

Basille Mystic
The Lord Raven
Member of the Brotherhood of Phasia
Father of Jerrard Mystic

Farax Soar
The Lord Vulture
Member of the Brotherhood of Phasia

The Flame
Personal Guardian of Shau-ling
Keeper of the Hall of Terrors
Originally known as Kamen, Member
of the Brotherhood of Phasia

Zarsi Aeron
The Lord Cobra
Member of the Brotherhood of Phasia

Aldridge Farran
The Lord Hawk
Member of the Brotherhood of Phasia

Saurn Macco
The Lord Viper
Member of the Brotherhood of Phasia

Caris Vale
The Lady Wolf
Member of the Brotherhood of Phasia

Erdric Yarrow
The Lord Scorpion
Member of the Brotherhood of Phasia

Taron Steen
The Lord Jackal
Member of the Brotherhood of Phasia

Draven Batoe
The Lord Crow
Member of the Brotherhood of Phasia

Rane Larion
The Lady Falcon
Member of the Brotherhood of Phasia

Stryfe Cadre
The Lord Python
Member of the Brotherhood of Phasia

Grimm Salde
The Lord Bear
Member of the Brotherhood of Phasia

Cash Griffon
The Lady Lynx
Member of the Brotherhood of Phasia

Nightwing
Member of the Dark Riders
Shau-ling's Assassin

Shadow
Member of the Dark Riders

Wrath
Member of the Dark Riders

Holocaust
Member of the Dark Riders

Vengeance
Member of the Dark Riders

Hawk Yetre
Son of Jeroch Yetre and Caris Vale

About the Author

Brian Kershner is a life-long dreamer, writer, and problem-solver. He grew up absorbing anything and everything he could get his hands on, and as a child of the Star Wars era he constantly wanted to see the worlds beyond the little Indiana town he grew up in. There was no adventure too far, and no problem too big.

Emboldened by parents who always supported his curiosity and his thoughtfulness, Brian found himself bounding from Space Camp to Laser Summer Camp to Athletic Training Camp to Piano Lessons to Football Practice to Basketball Practice to Choir Practice and back again. Despite all of the roaming and traveling, his family remained close-knit and supportive.

Though he flirted with the idea of becoming a doctor, Brian's attentions always fell back to the computer world. He got his first computer when he was six, and not long after found his way into a word processing program and began crafting his own fantastic worlds and even more fantastic characters.

As he has grown and changed and experienced life, so too have his characters. He continues to write, craft, and create; whether it is websites for his customers, or characters and worlds for his audience.